DARK ASSASSIN

From his patrol boat Inspector William Monk, of the Thames River Police, watches helplessly as a man and woman fall to their deaths. Murder, suicide or accident? Monk knows he must solve the mystery to gain the respect of his men. Soon both he and Hester are involved in the story of the dead woman, Mary Havilland, and her quest to vindicate her father, James Havilland. An engineer for the Argyll Construction Company, Havilland had been found dead on his stable floor. Convinced of an impending disaster in the tunnels of London's new sewer system being built, he'd apparently shot himself. Mary had never accepted that. And now she was dead too. Was it chance or are there more sinister forces at work?

New York Times bestselling author Anne Perry lives in Portmahomack, Scotland. She also writes the Victorian mystery series featuring Thomas and Charlotte Pitt, which was adapted for television. *The Cater Street Hangman* was watched by millions of viewers when it was broadcast by ITV.

ANNE PERRY

DARK
ASSASSIN

Complete and Unabridged

CHARNWOOD
Leicester

First published in Great Britain in 2006 by
Headline Book Publishing
a division of Hodder Headline, London

First Charnwood Edition
published 2007
by arrangement with
Hodder Headline, London

The moral right of the author has been asserted

British Library CIP Data

Perry, Anne
    Dark assassin.—Large print ed.—
    A William Monk mystery.—Charnwood library series
    1. Monk, William (Fictitious character)—Fiction
    2. Monk, Hester (Fictitious character)—Fiction
    3. Police—England—London—Fiction 4. London
    (England)—Social conditions—19th century—Fiction
    5. Detective and mystery stories 6. Large type books
    I. Title
    823.9'14 [F]

    ISBN 978–1–84617–577–0

Published by
F. A. Thorpe (Publishing)
Anstey, Leicestershire

Set by Words & Graphics Ltd.
Anstey, Leicestershire
Printed and bound in Great Britain by
T. J. International Ltd., Padstow, Cornwall

This book is printed on acid-free paper

Dedicated to Timothy Webb
with belated thanks for your
friendship and help

1

Waterloo Bridge loomed in the distance as Monk settled himself a little more comfortably in the bow of the police boat patrolling the Thames for stolen cargoes, accidents, missing craft. There were four men: himself as senior officer, and three to take the four oars. Rowing randan, it was called. Monk sat rigid in his uniform coat. It was January and bitterly cold. The wind ruffled the water and cut the skin like the edge of a knife, but he did not want anyone to see him shivering.

It was five weeks since he had accepted the position leading this section of the River Police. It was a decision he already regretted profoundly, the more so with every freezing, sodden day as 1863 turned into 1864, and the winter settled ruthlessly over London and its teeming waterway.

The boat rocked in the wash of a string of barges going upriver on the incoming tide. Orme at the stern steadied the boat expertly. He was a man of average height, but deceptive suppleness and strength, and a kind of grace exhibited as he managed the oar. Perhaps he had learned in his years on the water how easy it was to capsize a boat with sudden movement.

They were pulling closer to the bridge. In the grey afternoon, before the lamps were lit, they could see the traffic crossing: dark shadows of hansoms, and four-wheelers. They were still too far away to hear the clip of horses' hoofs above the sound of the water. A man and a woman stood on the footpath close to the railing, facing each other as if in conversation. Monk thought idly that whatever they were saying must matter to them intensely that it held their attention in such a bleak, exposed place. The wind tugged at the woman's skirts. At that height, where there was no shelter, she must have been even colder than Monk was.

Orme guided the boat a little further out into the stream. They were going down-river again, back towards the station at Wapping where they were headquartered. Six weeks ago Durban had been commander and Monk had been a private agent of inquiry. He still could not think of it without a tightening of the throat, a loneliness and a guilt he could not imagine would ever leave him. Each time he saw a group of River Police, and one of them walked slowly with a smooth, ambling stride, a little rounded at the shoulder, he expected him to turn and he would see Durban's face. Then memory came back, and he knew it could not be.

The bridge was only two hundred feet away now. The couple were still there against the balustrade. The man held her by the shoulders as if he would take her in his arms. Perhaps they were lovers. Of course Monk could not hear their words — the wind tore them from their mouths — but their faces were alive with a passion that was clearer with every moment as the boat drew towards them. Monk wondered what it was: a quarrel, a last farewell, even both?

The police oarsmen were having to pull hard against the incoming tide.

Monk looked up again just in time to see the man struggling with the woman, holding her fiercely as she clung on to him. Her back was to the railing, bending too far. Instinctively he wanted to call out. A few inches more and she would fall!

Orme too was staring up at them now.

The man grasped at the woman and she pulled away. She seemed to lose her balance and he lunged after her. Clasped together, they teetered for a desperate moment on the edge, then she pitched backwards. He made a wild attempt to catch her. She flung out a hand and gripped him. But it was too late. They both plunged over the side and spun crazily, like a huge, broken-winged bird, until they hit the racing, filthy water and were carried on top of it, not even struggling, while it soaked into them, dragging them down.

Orme shouted and the oarsmen dug their blades in deep. They threw their backs against the weight of the river, heaving, hurtling them forward.

Monk, heart in his mouth, strained to keep the bodies in sight. They were only a hundred feet away, and yet he knew already that it was too late. The impact of hitting the water would stun them and drive the air out of their lungs. When at last they did gasp inward, it would be the raw sewage of icy water, choking, drowning. Still, senselessly he leaned forward over the bow, shouting, 'Faster, faster! There! No . . . there!'

The boat drew level, turning a little sideways. The oarsmen kept it steady against the current and the changing balance as Orme heaved the body of the young woman over the gunwale. Awkwardly, as gently as he could, he laid her inside. Monk could see the other body, but it was too far away to reach, and if he stretched he could tip the boat.

'Port!' he instructed, although the oarsmen were already moving to do it. He reached over carefully to the half-submerged body of the young man, whose coat was drifting out in the water, his boots dragging his legs downward. Awkwardly, straining his shoulders, Monk hauled him up over the gunwale and in, laying him on the bottom of the boat next to the young woman. He had seen many dead people before, but the sense of loss never diminished. Looking at his pale face, smeared with dirt from the river water and his hair plastered across his brow, Monk guessed him to be about thirty. He had a moustache, but was otherwise clean-shaven. His clothes were well cut and of excellent quality. The hat he had been wearing on the bridge was gone.

Orme was standing balancing easily, looking down at Monk and the young man.

'Nothing we can do for either of 'em, sir,' he said. 'Drown quick going orff the bridge like that. Pity,' he added softly. 'Looks no more'n twenty, she does. Nice face.'

Monk sat back on the bench. 'Anything to say who she was?' he asked.

Orme shook his head.

'If she had one o' them little bags ladies carry, it's gone, but there's a letter in 'er pocket addressed to Miss Mary Havilland o' Charles Street. It's postmarked already, like it's bin sent and received, so could be it's 'er.'

Monk leaned forward and systematically went through the pockets of the dead man, keeping his balance with less ease than Orme, as the boat began the journey downstream, back towards Wapping. There was no point in putting a man ashore to look for witnesses of the quarrel, if that was what it had been. They could not identify the traffic that had been on the bridge, and on the water they themselves had seen as much as anyone. Two people quarrelling — kissing — parting, who lost their balance and fell. There was nothing anyone could add.

Actually as far as Monk could remember there had been no one passing at exactly that moment. It was the hour when the dusk is not drawn in sufficiently for the lamps to be lit, but the light wanes and the greyness of the air seems to delude the eye. Things are half seen; the imagination fills in the rest, sometimes inaccurately.

He turned to the man's pockets and found a leather wallet with a little money and a case carrying cards. He was apparently Toby Argyll, of Walnut Tree Walk, Lambeth. That was also south of the river, not far from the girl's address on

Charles Street off Lambeth walk. Monk read it aloud for Orme.

The boat was moving slowly as only two men were rowing. Orme squatted on the boards near Argyll's body. On the shore the lamps were beginning to come on, yellow moons in the deepening haze. The wind had the breath of ice in it. It was time to trim their own riding lights, or they would be struck by barges, or the ferries going cross-current, carrying passengers from one bank to the other.

Monk lit the lantern and carefully moved back to the body of the woman. She lay on her back. Orme had folded her hands and smoothed the hair off her face. Her eyes were closed, her skin already grey-white, as if she had been longer dead than just a few minutes.

She had a wide mouth and high cheekbones under delicate arched brows. It was a very feminine face, strong and vulnerable, as if she had been filled with high passions in life.

'Poor creature,' Orme said softly. 'S'pose we'll never know what made her do it. Mebbe 'e were breaking orff an engagement, or something.' The expression in his face was all but masked by the deepening shadows, but Monk could hear the intense pity in his voice.

Monk suddenly realised he was wet up to the armpits from having lifted the body out of the water. He was shuddering with cold and it was hard to speak without his teeth chattering. He would have given all the money in his pocket for a hot mug of tea with a lacing of rum in it. He could not remember ever being this perishingly cold on shore.

Suicide was a crime, not only against the State but in the eyes of the Church as well. If that were the coroner's verdict she would be buried in unhallowed ground. And there was also the question of the young man's death. Perhaps there was no point in arguing it but Monk did so instinctively. 'Was he trying to stop her?'

The boat was moving slowly, against the tide. The water was choppy, slapping at the wooden sides and making it difficult for two oarsmen to keep her steady.

Orme hesitated for several moments before answering. 'I dunno, Mr Monk, an' that's the truth. Could've bin. Could've bin an accident both ways.' His voice dropped lower. 'Or could've bin 'e pushed 'er. It 'appened quick.'

'Do you have an opinion?' Monk could hardly get the words out clearly he was shaking so much.

'You'd be best on an oar, sir,' Orme said gravely. 'Get the blood movin', as it were.'

Monk accepted the suggestion. Senior officers might not be supposed to row like ordinary constables, but they were not much use frozen stiff or with pneumonia.

He moved to the centre and went to take one of the oars beside Orme. It was several strokes before he got into the rhythm, but then he began to feel better, and the boat certainly sped forward, cutting the water more cleanly. They rowed a long way without speaking again. They passed under Blackfriars Bridge towards the Southwark Bridge, which was visible in the distance only by its lights. The wind stole the breath almost before it reached the lungs.

Monk had accepted this position in the River Police partly as a debt of honour. Eight years ago he had woken up in hospital with no memory at all. Fact by fact he had assembled an identity, discovering things about himself, not all of which pleased him. At that time he was a policeman, heartily disliked by his immediate superior, Superintendent Runcorn. Their relationship had deteriorated until it became a debatable question whether Monk had resigned before or after Runcorn had dismissed him. Since the detection and solving of crime was the only profession he knew, and he required to earn his living, he had taken up the same work privately.

But circumstances had altered in the late autumn of last year. The need for money had compelled him to take the Louvain case, his first experience on the river, and because of it he had met Durban and involved him with the *Maude Idris* and its terrible cargo. Now Durban was dead, having, incredibly, recommended Monk to succeed him in his place at the Wapping station.

He could have had no idea how Monk had previously failed in commanding men. He was brilliant, ruthless, individual, but he had never worked easily with others, either in giving or taking orders. Runcorn would have told Durban that; would have told him that — clever or not, brave or not — Monk was not worth the trouble he would cost. Monk had been mellowed by time and circumstance, and above all, perhaps, by marriage to Hester Latterly, who had nursed in the Crimea with Florence Nightingale, and who was a good deal more forthright than most young women. She loved him with a fierce loyalty, and a startling passion, but also a very candid expression of her own opinions. Even so, Runcorn would have advised Superintendent Farnham to find someone else to take the place of a man like Durban, who had been wise, experienced and profoundly admired.

But Durban had wanted Monk, and Monk needed the work. During his independent years, Hester's friend Lady Callandra Daviot had had the money and the interest to involve herself in his cases, and support the Monks in the leaner months. Now Callandra had gone to live in Vienna, and the grim choice was either for Monk to obtain regular and reliable employment, or for Hester to return to private nursing, which would mean most often living in the houses of such patients as she could acquire. For Monk to see her as little as that was a choice of final desperation. So here he was sitting in the thwart of a boat, throwing his weight against the oar as they passed under London Bridge, heading south towards the Tower and Wapping Stairs. He was still bone-achingly cold, wet to the shoulders, and two dead bodies lay at his feet.

Finally they reached the steps up to the police station. Carefully, a little stiffly, Monk shipped his oar, stood up, and helped carry the limp, water-sodden bodies up the stairs, across the quay and into the shelter of the station house.

There at least it was warm. The black iron stove was burning, giving the whole room a pleasant, smoky smell, and there was hot tea, stewed almost black, waiting for them. None of the men really knew Monk yet and they were still grieving for Durban. They treated their new superior with civility; if he wanted anything more he would have to earn it. The river was a dangerous place, with its shifting tides and currents, occasional sunken obstacles, fast-moving traffic and sudden changes of weather. It demanded courage, skill and even more loyalty between men than did the same profession on the land. However, human decency dictated they offer Monk tea laced with rum, as they would to any man, probably even to a stray dog at this time of the year. Indeed, Humphrey, the station cat, a large white animal with a ginger tail, was provided with a basket by the stove and as much milk as he could drink. Mice were his own affair to catch for himself, which he did whenever he could be bothered, or nobody had fed him with other titbits.

'Thank you.' Monk drank the tea and felt some resemblance of life return to his body, warmth working slowly from the inside out-wards.

'Accident?' Sergeant Palmer asked, looking at the bodies now lying on the floor, faces decently covered with spare coats.

'Don't know yet,' Monk replied. 'Came off the Waterloo Bridge right in front of us, but can't be sure how it happened.'

Palmer frowned, puzzled. He had his doubts about Monk's competence anyway, and this indecision went towards confirming them.

Orme finished his tea. 'Went off together,' he said, looking at Palmer expressionlessly. 'Hard to tell if 'e were trying to save 'er, or could've pushed 'er. Know what killed 'em all right, poor souls. 'It the water 'ard, like they always do. But I dare say as we'll never know for certain why.'

Palmer waited for Monk to say something. The room was suddenly silent. The other two men from the boat, Jones and Butterworth, stood watching, turning from one to the other, to see what Monk would do. It was a test again. Would he match up to Durban?

'Get the surgeon to look at them, just in case there's something else,' Monk answered. 'Probably isn't, but we don't want to risk looking stupid.'

'Drownded,' Palmer said sourly, turning away. 'Come off one o' the bridges, yer always are. Anybody knows that. Water shocks yer an' so yer breathes it in. Kills yer. Quick's almost the only good thing to it.'

'And how stupid will we look if we say she's a suicide, and it turns out she was knifed, or strangled, but we didn't notice it?' Monk asked quietly. 'I just want to make sure. Or with child, and we didn't see that either? Look at the quality of her clothes. She's not a street woman. She has a decent address and she may have family. We owe them the truth.'

Palmer coloured unhappily. 'It won't make them feel no better if she's with child,' he observed without looking back at Monk.

'We don't look for the answers that make people feel better,' Monk told him. 'We have to

11

deal with the ones we find closest to the truth. We know who they are and where they lived. Orme and I are going to tell their families. You get the police surgeon to look at them.'

'Yes, sir,' Palmer said stiffly. 'You'll be going 'ome to put dry clothes on, no doubt?' He raised his eyebrows.

Monk had already learned that lesson. 'I've got a dry shirt and coat in the cupboard. They'll do fine.'

Orme turned away, but not before Monk had seen his smile.

★ ★ ★

Monk and Orme took a hansom from Wapping, westward along the High Street. The lights intermittently flickered from the river and the hard wind whipped the smell of salt and weed up the alleys between the waterfront houses. They went round the looming mass of the Tower of London then back down to the water again along Lower Thames Street. They finally crossed the river at the Southwark Bridge and passed through the more elegant residential areas until they came to the six-ways crossing at St George's Circus. From there it was not far to both Charles Street and Walnut Tree Walk.

Informing the families of the dead was the part of all investigations that every policeman hated and it was the duty of the senior man to fulfil it. It would be both cowardly and the worst discourtesy to the bereaved to delegate it.

Monk paid the driver and let him go. He had

no idea how long it would take him to break the news, or what he and Orme might find.

The house where Toby Argyll had lived was gracious, but obviously let in series of rooms as suited single men rather than families. A landlady in a dark dress and wearing an apron opened the door, immediately nervous on seeing two men unknown to her standing on the step. Orme had pleasant, ordinary features, but he wore a river policeman's uniform. Monk was taller, and had the grace of a man conscious of his own magnetism. There was power in his face, lean-boned with a broad, high-bridged nose, and unflinching eyes. It was a face of intelligence, even sensitivity, but few people found it comfortable.

'Good evening, ma'am,' he said gently. His voice was excellent, his diction beautiful. He had worked hard to lose the country Northumbrian accent that marked his origins. He had wanted passionately to be a gentleman. That desire was long past, but the music in his voice remained.

'Evenin', sir,' she replied warily.

'My name is Inspector Monk, and this is Sergeant Orme, of the Thames River Police. Is this the home of Mr Toby Argyll?'

She swallowed. 'Yes, sir, Never say there's bin an accident in one o' them tunnels!' Her hand flew to her mouth as if to stifle a cry. 'I can't 'elp yer, sir. Mr Argyll's not at 'ome.'

'No, ma'am, there hasn't been, so far as I know,' Monk replied. 'But I'm afraid there has been a tragedy. I'm extremely sorry. Does Mr Argyll live alone here?'

13

She stared at him, her round face paler now as she began to understand that they had come with the worst possible news.

'Would you like to go in and sit down?' Monk asked.

She nodded and backed away from him, allowing them to follow her along the passage to the kitchen. It was full of the aroma of dinner cooking, and Monk realised absently how long it was since he had eaten. She sank down on one of the hard-backed wooden chairs, putting her elbows on the table and her hands up to her face. There were pans steaming on the top of the huge black range, and the savoury odour of meat pie came from the oven beneath it. Copper warming pans glimmered on the wall in the gaslight, and strings of onions hung from the ceiling.

There was no point in delaying what she must already know was coming.

'I'm sorry to tell you that Mr Argyll fell off the Waterloo Bridge,' Monk told her. 'Mrs . . . ?'

She looked at him, face blanched, eyes wide. 'Porter,' she supplied. 'I looked after Mr Argyll since 'e first come 'ere. 'Ow could 'e 'ave fallen orff the bridge? It don't make no sense! There's railings! Yer don't fall orff! Are yer sayin' 'e was the worse for wear, an' went climbing, or summink daft?' She was shivering now, angry. 'I don't believe yer! 'E weren't like that! Very sober, 'ard-workin' young gentleman, 'e were! Yer in't got the right person. Yer made a mistake, that's wot yer done!' She lifted her chin and stared at him. 'Yer oughter be more careful, scarin' folks all wrong.'

'There's no reason to suppose he was drunk, Mrs Porter.' Monk did not prevaricate. 'The young man we found had cards saying he was Toby Argyll, of this address. He was about my height, or perhaps a little less, fair-haired, clean-shaven except for a moustache.' He stopped. He could see by her wide, fixed eyes and the pinched look of her mouth that he had described Argyll. 'I'm sorry,' he said again.

Her lips trembled. 'Wot 'appened? If 'e weren't drunk, 'ow'd 'e come ter fall in the river? Yer ain't makin' no sense!' It was still a challenge, clinging to the last shred of hope as if disbelieving could keep what she'd heard from being true.

'He was with a young lady,' Monk told her. 'They seemed to be having a rather heated discussion. They grasped hold of each other and swayed a little, then she fell back against the rail They struggled a little more — '

'Wot d'yer mean, 'they struggled'?' Mrs Porter demanded. 'Yer sayin' as they was fighting, or summat?'

This was worse than he had expected. What had they been doing? What had he seen, exactly? He tried to clear his mind of all the ideas since then, the attempts to understand and interpret, and recall exactly what had happened. The two figures had been on the bridge, the woman closer to the railing. Or was she? Yes, she was. The wind had been behind them and he had seen her billowing skirts poking between the uprights of the balustrade. She had waved her arms, and then put her hands on the man's shoulders. A

15

caress? Or pushing him away? He had moved his arm, back and up. Pulling away from her? Or raising it to strike? He had grasped hold of her. To save her, or to push her?

Mrs Porter was waiting, hugging herself, still shivering in the warm kitchen with its dinner-time smells.

'I don't know,' Monk said slowly. 'They were above us, outlined against the light, and almost two hundred feet away.'

She turned to Orme. 'Was you there too, sir?'

'Yes, ma'am,' Orme replied, standing upright in the middle of the scrubbed floor. 'An' Mr Monk's right. The more I think on it, the less certain I am as to what I saw, exact. It was in that sort of darkening time just before the lamps are lit. You think you can see, but you make mistakes.'

'Who were she?' she asked. 'The woman wot went over with 'im.'

'Was there someone you might expect it to be?' Monk parried. 'If they were quarrelling?'

She was clearly unhappy. 'Well . . . I don't like ter say . . . ' she trailed off.

'We know who it was, Mrs Porter,' Monk told her. 'We need to know what happened, so we don't allow anyone to be blamed for something they didn't do.'

'Yer can't 'urt 'em now,' she responded, the tears trickling unheeded down her cheeks. 'They're dead, poor souls.'

'But they'll have family who care,' he pointed out. 'And burial in hallowed ground, or not.'

She gasped and gave a convulsive shudder.

16

'Mrs Porter?'

'Were it Miss 'Avilland?' she asked hoarsely.

'What can you tell me about her?'

'It were 'er? Course, it would be. 'E din't never look at no one else, not ever since 'e met 'er.'

'He was in love with her?' Of course that could mean many things, from the true giving of the heart, unselfishly, through generosity, need, all the way to domination and obsession. And rejection could mean anything from resignation through misery to anger, or rage and the need for revenge, perhaps even destruction.

She hesitated.

'Mrs Porter?'

'Yes,' she said quickly. 'They was betrothed — at least 'e seemed to take it they was — then she broke it off. Not that it were formal, like. There weren't no announcement.'

'Do you know why?'

She was surprised.

'Me? Course I don't.'

'Was there another person?'

'Not for 'im, an' I don't think for 'er neither. Least that's wot I 'eard 'im say.' She gave a long sniff and gulped. 'This is terrible. I never 'eard o' such a thing, not wi' quality folk. Wot would they want ter go jumpin' orff bridges for? Mr Argyll'll be broke ter pieces when 'e 'ears, poor man.'

'Mr Argyll? His father?' Monk asked.

'No, 'is brother. Quite a bit older, 'e is. Least I should say so.' She sniffed again and fished in her apron pocket for a handkerchief. 'I only seen 'im five or six times, when 'e came 'ere fer Mr

17

Toby, like. Very wealthy gentleman, 'e is. Owns them big machines an' things wot's diggin' the new sewers Mr Bazalgette drew ter clean up London, so we don't get no more typhoid an' cholera an' the like. Took poor Prince Albert ter die of it, an' the poor Queen's 'eart broke before they do it. Wicked, I say!'

Monk could remember the 'Great Stink' of '58 very clearly, when the overflow of effluent had been so serious the entire city of London became like a vast open sewer.

The Thames had smelled so vile it had choked the throat, and caused nausea simply to come within a mile of it. The new sewer system was to be the most advanced in Europe. It would cost a fortune and provide work, and wealth, for thousands — tens of thousands if one considered all the navvies, brickmakers and railwaymen involved, the builders, carpenters and suppliers of one sort of another. Most of the sewers were to be built by the open 'cut-and-cover' method, but a few were deep enough to require tunnelling.

'So Mr Argyll was a wealthy young man?'

'Oh, yes.' Mrs Porter straightened up a little. 'This is a very nice class o' place, Mr Monk. Don't live 'ere cheap, yer know.'

'And Miss Havilland?' he asked.

'Oh, she were quality too, poor creature,' she responded immediately. 'A real lady, she were, even with 'er opinions. I never disagreed wi' airin' opinions, meself, for all as some might say it weren't proper for a young lady.'

Having married a woman with passionate

18

opinions about a number of things, Monk could not argue. In fact he suddenly saw Mary Havilland not as she was now — white-faced in death — but instead the slender, fierce and vulnerable figure of Hester, with her shoulders a little too thin, her slight angularity, brown hair and eyes of such passionate intelligence that he had never been able to forget them since the day they had met — and quarrelled.

He found his voice husky when he spoke again. 'Do you know why she broke off the relationship, Mrs Porter? Or was it perhaps a generous fiction Mr Argyll allowed, and it was actually he who ended it?'

'No, it were 'er,' she said without hesitation. ''E were upset an' 'e tried to change 'er mind.' She sniffed again. 'I never thought as it'd come to this.'

'We don't know what happened yet,' he said. 'But thank you for your assistance. Can you give us Mr Argyll's brother's address? We need to inform him of what has happened. I don't suppose you know who Miss Havilland's nearest relative would be? Her parents, I expect.'

'I wouldn't know that, sir. But I can give you Mr Argyll's address all right, no bother. Poor man's going to be beside 'isself. Very close, they was.'

*   *   *

Alan Argyll lived a short distance away, on Westminster Bridge Road, and it took Monk and Orme only ten minutes or so to walk to the

19

handsome house whose address Mrs Porter had given them. The curtains were drawn against the early winter night but the gaslamps in the street showed the elegant line of the windows and the stone steps up to a wide, carved doorway where the faint gleam of brass indicated the lion's-head knocker.

Orme looked at Monk, but said nothing. Breaking such news to family was immeasurably worse than to a landlady, however sympathetic. Monk nodded very slightly, but there was nothing to say. Orme worked on the river; he was used to death.

The door was answered by a short, portly butler, his white hair thinning across the top of his head. From his steady, unsurprised gaze, he clearly took them to be business acquaintances of his master.

'Mr Argyll is at dinner, sir,' he said to Monk. 'If you care to wait in the morning room I am sure he will see you in due course.'

'We are from the Thames River Police,' Monk told him, having given only his name at first. 'I am afraid we have bad news that cannot wait. It might be advisable to have a glass of brandy ready, in case it is needed. I'm sorry.'

The butler hesitated. 'Indeed, sir. May I ask what has happened? Is it one of the tunnels, sir? It's very sad, but such things seem to be unavoidable.'

Monk was aware that such mighty excavations as were at present in progress brought the occasional landslip or even cave-in of the sides, burying machines and sometimes injuring men.

There had been a spectacular disaster over the Fleet only days ago.

'Quite so,' he agreed. 'But this happened on the river, and I am afraid it is personal bad news for Mr Argyll. He needs to be informed as soon as possible.'

'Oh dear,' the butler said quietly. 'How very terrible. Yes, sir.' He took a deep breath and let it out silently. 'If you will come to the morning room, I shall bring Mr Argyll to you.'

The morning room was very sombre, in shades of browns and golds. The fire had been allowed to go out, but it was now well into the evening and presumably the room would not normally be used at this hour. Monk and Orme stood in the centre of the Aubusson carpet, waiting. Neither of them spoke. Monk noted the picture of Highland scenery over the mantelshelf and the small stuffed rodent in a glass case on the table by the wall. They were self-conscious suggestions that Argyll's wealth was old money, which brought to his mind that therefore it was probably not.

The door swung open and Alan Argyll stood in the entrance, pale-faced, his eyes dark in the lamplight. He was of more than average height, and lean, with a suggestion of physical as well as mental power. His features were well-proportioned, but there was a coldness in them as if he did not laugh easily.

It would have been ridiculous to say 'good evening'. Monk took a step forward. 'My name is William Monk, of the Thames River Police, sir. This is Sergeant Orme. I am deeply sorry to tell you that your brother, Mr Toby Argyll, fell off the Westminster Bridge earlier this evening, and although we reached him within a few minutes of it happening, he was already dead.'

Argyll stared at him, swaying a little as if he had been struck. 'You were there? Why in God's name didn't you . . . ?' He gasped, finding it difficult to catch his breath. He looked as if he were on the edge of collapse.

'We were in a boat on patrol on the river,' Monk answered. 'I'm sorry, sir; there was nothing anyone could have done. In such circumstances, a man drowns very quickly. I think he probably felt nothing at all. I know that is little comfort, but it may help in time.'

'He was twenty-nine!' Argyll shouted. He came further into the room and the light shone on his face. Monk could not help seeing the resemblance to his brother: the line of his mouth, the colour of his well-shaped eyes, the way his hair grew. 'How do you fall off a bridge?' he demanded. 'Was it a crime, and you're not telling me? Was he attacked?' Rage flared in his voice and his fists clenched.

'He wasn't alone,' Monk said quickly, before Argyll should lose control. Grief he was used to, even anger, but there was a thread of violence just under the surface in this man that was fast unravelling. 'A young woman named Mary Havilland was with him — '

Argyll's eyes flew wide open. 'Mary? Where is she? Is she all right? What happened? What are you not telling me, man? Don't just stand there like an idiot! This is my family you're talking

22

about . . . ' Again the fists were tight, skin on his knuckles stretched pale across the bone.

'I'm sorry, Miss Havilland went over with him,' Monk said grimly. 'They were holding on to each other.'

'What do you mean 'holding'?' Argyll demanded. 'What are you saying?'

'That they both went over, sir,' Monk repeated. 'They were standing together by the railing, having what appeared to be a heated discussion. We were too far away to hear. The next time we looked they were at the railing and the moment after they overbalanced and fell.'

'You saw a man and woman struggling and you looked away?' Argyll said incredulously, his voice high-pitched. 'What at, for God's sake? What else could possibly be — '

'We were on patrol,' Monk cut across him. 'We watch the whole river. We wouldn't even have seen that much had they not been so close to the rail. It appeared an ordinary conversation, perhaps a lover's quarrel, made up again. If we'd have continued watching it could have been intrusive.'

Argyll stood motionless, blinking. 'Yes,' he said at last. 'Yes, of course. I'm sorry. Toby . . . Toby was my only relative. At least . . . ' He ran his hand over his face almost as if to steady himself, somehow clear his vision. ' . . . my wife. You say Mary Havilland is dead also?'

'Yes. I'm sorry. I believe she was close to your brother.'

'Close!' Argyll's voice rose again dangerously, a note of hysteria in it. 'She was my sister-in-law.

23

Toby was betrothed to her — at least they were going to be married. She . . . she called it off. She was very disturbed . . . '

Monk was confused. 'She would have been your sister-in-law?'

'No! She *was*. Mary was my wife's sister,' Argyll said with a small, indrawn breath. 'My wife will be . . . devastated. We were hoping . . . ' He stopped again.

Monk needed to prompt him, painful as it must be for Argyll to answer further questions. This was an unguarded moment when he might reveal a truth that later he would, for decency or compassion's sake, have covered. Based on the landlady's words, Mary was a woman of spirit who had passionate opinions.

'Yes, sir? You were hoping . . . ?' he prompted.

'Oh.' Argyll sighed and looked away. He fumbled towards a chair and sat down heavily. He appeared to be in his mid-forties, considerably older than his brother. But that bore out what Mrs Porter had said.

Monk sat as well, to put himself on a level with Argyll. Orme remained standing discreetly, a couple of yards away.

Argyll looked at Monk. 'Mary's father took his own life almost two months ago,' he said quietly. 'It was very distressing. Actually both Mary and Jenny, my wife, were bitterly grieved. Their mother had died many years before, and this was a terrible blow. My wife bore it with great fortitude, but Mary seemed to lose her . . . her mental balance. She refused to accept that his death was indeed suicide, even though the police

24

investigated it, naturally, and that was their finding. We . . . we were hoping she was . . . '

'I'm sorry.' Monk found he meant it with savage honesty. He imagined Mary as she must have been when she was alive — the pale, river-wet face animated with emotion, anger, amazement, grief. 'That's a very hard thing for anyone to bear.' Like a physical blow he remembered that Hester's father had also taken his own life, and the pain of it was close and real in a way that no power of words alone could express. 'I'm truly sorry,' he said again.

Argyll looked at him with surprise, as if he had heard the emotion through the polite phrases. 'Yes. Yes, it is.' It was clear he had not expected Monk to allow his feelings to show. 'I . . . I don't know how poor Jenny will deal with this. It's . . . ' He failed to find the words for what he was struggling to say, perhaps even to himself.

'Would it be easier for Mrs Argyll if we were here, so that she could ask us any questions she wishes to?' Monk asked. 'Or would you prefer to tell her privately?'

Argyll hesitated. He seemed torn by a genuine indecision.

Monk waited. The clock on the mantel struck the quarter-hour; otherwise there was silence.

'Perhaps I should not deny her the chance to speak with you,' Argyll said at last. 'If you will excuse me, I shall inform her alone, and then see what she wishes.' He took Monk's acquiescence for granted and rose to his feet. He walked out of the room a little unsteadily, only saving himself from bumping into the door jamb at the last

25

moment, and leaving the door itself gaping open.

'Poor man,' Orme said softly. 'Wish we could tell 'im it were an accident.' He looked at Monk with a question in his eyes.

'So do I,' Monk agreed. It began to look as if Mary Havilland had at least temporarily lost her mental balance, but he did not want to say so, even to Orme.

The butler came in and stood like a black shadow just inside the door. 'Mrs Argyll asked me to see if there is anything I could bring for you gentlemen. Perhaps a glass of . . . ' he considered, ' . . . ale?' He was not going to offer them good sherry they would not appreciate, and certainly not the best brandy.

Monk realised how achingly hungry he was. Orme must be also. Perhaps that was at least in part why he was still cold.

'Thank you,' he accepted. 'We've come straight from the river. A sandwich and a glass of ale would be very gracious of you.'

The butler looked faintly uncomfortable, as if realising he should have thought of it himself. 'Immediately, sir,' he acknowledged. 'Would cold roast beef and a spot of mustard be right?'

'It would be perfect,' Monk answered.

Orme thanked him warmly as soon as the door was closed. ''Ope it comes before Mr Argyll gets back,' he added. 'Wouldn't be decent to eat it in front of 'im, specially if Mrs Argyll comes too. Don't reckon as she will, though. Most ladies take bad news 'ard.'

The sandwiches arrived and were consumed ravenously, just before Argyll returned. But

Orme was mistaken in his second guess: Jenny Argyll chose to see them. She came in ahead of her husband, a handsome woman with eyes and mouth startlingly like those of her dead sister, but darker hair and not the same high cheekbones. Now she too was bleached of colour and her eyelids were puffy from obvious weeping, but she was remarkably well composed, in the circumstances. She was wearing a dark red woollen dress with a wide skirt and her hair was elaborately coiffed in a style that must have taken her lady's maid at least half an hour to accomplish. She regarded Monk with civility, but no interest at all.

Argyll closed the door behind them and waited until his wife was seated.

Monk expressed his condolences again.

'Thank you,' Mrs Argyll said briefly. 'My husband says that Mary fell off Westminster Bridge. Toby was with her. Perhaps he tried to stop her, and failed. Poor Toby. I think he still loved her, in spite of everything.' The tears filled her eyes again but she ignored them and her face remained under control. It was impossible to tell what the effort cost her. She did not look at her husband, nor did she reach to touch him.

Monk should have accepted the answer implicit in her words, and yet in spite of all sense he refused to. When Hester's father had shot himself because of the unanswerable debt he had been cheated into, she had returned from the Crimea where she had been serving as a military nurse, and redoubled her efforts to strengthen her family and to fight all the wrongs she

27

encountered. It had been her fortitude and resolve that had strengthened Monk to struggle against the burden that had seemed impossible to him. She was acid-tongued — at least he had thought so — opinionated and unwise in her expression of it, hasty to judge and quick-tempered, but even he, who had found her so irritating, had never doubted her courage or her iron will.

Of course he had seen the passion, the laughter and the vulnerability in her since then. Was he imagining in Mary Havilland something she had never possessed? Whatever the cost to Mrs Argyll, he wanted to know.

'I understand that your father met his death recently,' he said gravely, 'and Miss Havilland found that very difficult to come to terms with.'

She looked at him wearily. 'She never did,' she answered. 'She couldn't accept that he took his own life. She wouldn't accept it, in spite of all the evidence. I'm afraid she became . . . obsessed.' She blinked. 'Mary was very . . . strong-willed, to put it at its kindest. She was close to Papa, and she couldn't believe that something could be so wrong and he would not confide in her. I'm afraid perhaps they were not as . . . as close as she imagined.'

'Could she have been distressed over the breaking of her betrothal to Mr Argyll?' Monk asked, trying to grasp on to some reason why a healthy young woman should do something so desperate as plunge over the bridge. And had she meant to take Argyll with her, or was he trying, even at the risk of his own life, to save her? Had

28

he still loved her so much? Or was it out of guilt because he had abandoned her, possibly for someone else? They really did need the surgeon to ascertain if she had been with child. That might explain a great deal. It was a hideous thought, but perhaps she had felt suicide the only answer — if he would not marry her — and she had determined to take him with her. He was, in a sense, the cause of her sin. But that would be true only if she were with child, and certain of it.

'No,' Mrs Argyll said flatly. 'She was the one who broke it. If anything, it was Toby who was distressed. She . . . she became very strange, Mr Monk. She seemed to take against us all. She became fixed upon the idea that a dreadful disaster was going to happen in the new sewer tunnels that my husband's company is constructing.' She looked very tired, as if revisiting an old and much-battled pain. 'My father had a morbid fear of enclosed spaces, and he was rather reactionary. He was afraid of the new machines that make the work far faster. I imagine you are aware of the urgency of building a new system for the city?'

'Yes, Mrs Argyll, I think we all are,' he answered. He did not like the picture that was emerging, and yet he could not deny it. It was only his own emotion that drove him to fight it, a completely irrational link in his mind between Mary Havilland and Hester. It was not even anything so definite as a thought, just words used to describe her by a landlady who barely knew her, and the protective grief over the suicide of a father.

'My father allowed it to become an obsession with him,' she went on. 'He spent his time gathering information, campaigning to have the company alter its methods. My husband did everything to help him see reason, and appreciate that deaths in construction are unavoidable from time to time. Men can be careless. Landslips happen; the London clay is dangerous by its nature. The Argyll Company has fewer accidents than most others. That is a fact he could have checked with ease, and he did. He could point to no major mishaps at all, but it did not calm his fears.'

'Reason does not calm irrational fears,' Argyll said quietly, his voice hoarse with his own emotion, unable to reach towards hers. Perhaps he feared that if he did they might both lose what control they had. 'Don't harrow yourself up any more,' he went on. 'There was nothing you could have done then, or now. His terrors finally overtook him. Who knows what another man sees in the dark hours of the night?'

'He took his life at night?' Monk asked.

It was Argyll who answered, his voice cold. 'Yes, but I would be obliged if you did not press the matter further. It was thoroughly investigated at the time. No one else was in the least at fault. How could anyone have realised that his madness had progressed so far? Now it appears that poor Mary was also far more unstable than we knew and her father's death had preyed upon her to the point where she herself could not exercise her human or Christian judgement any more.'

Jenny turned to look at him, frowning. 'Christian?' she challenged him. 'If anyone is so sunk in despair that they feel death is the only answer for them, can't we have a little . . . pity?' There was anger in her eyes.

'I'm sorry!' Argyll said quickly, but without looking at her. 'I did not mean to imply blasphemy against your father. We shall never know what demons drove him to such a resort. Even Mary I could forgive, if she had not taken Toby with her! That . . . that is . . . ' He was unable to continue. The tears spilled over his cheeks and he turned away, shadowing his face.

Jenny stood up, stiff and unsteady. 'Thank you for coming, Mr Monk. I think there is little of any use that we can tell you. Perhaps you would excuse us. Pendle will see you to the door.' She went to the bell rope and pulled it. The butler appeared almost immediately and Monk and Orme took their leave, after having given him a card, and requested that Mr Argyll should formally identify the bodies the following day, when he was a little more recovered.

'Poor devil,' Orme said with feeling when they were outside on the icy footpath again. Mist was veiling the streetlamps like gauze. A frail moon high above the rooftops, sickle-shaped, sailed between the stars. 'Both of 'em lost family in the one night. Funny 'ow an instant can change everything. D'you think she meant to?'

'Go over herself, or take him?' Monk asked, beginning to walk down towards the Westminster Bridge where they would be more likely to find a

31

hansom. He was still hoping it had been an accident.

'Not sure as I know,' Orme replied, keeping step with him. 'Didn't look to me as if she were trying to jump. Facing the wrong way, for a start. Jumpers usually face the water.'

Monk felt a rush of warmth even though the slick of moisture on the footpath was turning to ice under his feet. He was not going to let go of hope, not yet.

★ ★ ★

Monk reached home before nine o'clock. His return was far later than it would have been on a more usual day, but there was little that was routine in his new job. Even his best effort might not be enough; second-best certainly would not. Every day he learned more of the skills, the knowledge and the respect that Durban had had. He admired the qualities that had earned it, and they awed him. He felt continually a step behind Durban. No, that was absurd, he was yards behind him.

He knew people and crime; he knew how to smell fear; to probe lies; when to be confronting and when to be oblique. He did not know the patterns, the crimes and the escapes, the tricks that were unique to the river, and had never known how to inspire the love and loyalty of men under his command. Runcorn could testify to that! They admired his intelligence, his knowledge and his strength and they were frightened of his tongue, but they did not like him. There was none of the fierce honour and friendship he had sensed from the beginning between Durban and his men.

He had crossed the river by ferry — there were no bridges this far down — and he was on the south bank now, where he and Hester had moved after he had accepted the new job. They could hardly live in Grafton Street any more. It was miles from police headquarters in Wapping.

He walked up Paradise Street, the lamps misted moons, and he could smell the river and hear the occasional foghorn as the mist drifted across the water. There was ice on the thin puddles in the street. This setting was still strange to him, nothing familiar.

He put his key into the lock in the door and pushed it open.

'Hester!'

She appeared immediately, apron tied around her waist, her hair pinned hastily and crookedly. She was carrying a broom in her hand but she dropped it as soon as she saw him, and rushed forward. She drew in breath, perhaps to say that he was late, then changed her mind. She studied his face and read the emotion in it.

'What happened?' she asked.

He knew what she was afraid of. She had understood why he'd had to accept the job in Durban's place, both morally and financially. With Callandra gone to Vienna they could not afford the freedom or the uncertainty of taking on only private cases. Sometimes the rewards were excellent, but too often they were meagre. Some cases could not be solved, or if they were then the client had the means to reward him only modestly. They could never plan ahead, and there was no one to whom they could turn in a bad month, as they had before. Nor, it must be said honestly, at their ages should they need to. It was time to provide, not be provided for.

Hester could have gone outside the home and worked, and if necessity demanded, she would have. But one could not nurse except by being there all the time, and neither of them wanted her living away. After the horror of last year, for his peace of mind and heart he needed her at home.

'What is it? What's wrong?' she asked when he did not answer.

'A suicide off Waterloo Bridge,' he replied. 'In fact in a way, two. A young man and woman went off together, but we don't know if it was partly accidental or not.'

The relief flashed across her face, then instantly the pity. 'I'm sorry. Were you called to it?'

'No, we were actually there. Saw it happen.'

She smiled gently and touched his face with the back of her fingers, perhaps aware her hands were dusty. Had she been still occupied with housework this late in the evening to keep from worrying about him?

'That's horrible,' she said bleakly. 'They must have to be very desperate to jump into the river at this time of the year.'

'They'd die, whatever time it was,' he replied. 'The tide is very strong, and it's filthy.' To another woman he would have moderated his

34

answer, avoided the facts of death, but she had seen more people dying and dead than he had. Police work, no matter how grim at times, hardly compared with the battlefield, or the losses afterwards to gangrene and fever.

'Yes, I know that,' she answered him. 'But do you suppose they knew, before they jumped?'

Suddenly it was immediate and painfully, agonisingly real. Mary Havilland had been a woman like Hester, warm and full of emotions, capable of laughter and pain; now she was just an empty shell with the soul fled. Nobody any more. He put his hands on Hester's shoulders and pulled her towards him, holding her tightly, feeling her slender body yield almost as if she could soften the awkward bones and shape herself to him.

'I don't know if she meant to jump and he tried to stop her,' he whispered into her hair, 'Or if he pushed her over and she clung on to him, and took him with her, even if she meant to. I don't know how I'm going to find out, but I will.'

She held him for a few moments longer, silently, then she pulled back and looked at him. 'You're frozen,' she said practically. 'And I don't suppose you've eaten. The kitchen is still not really finished, but I have hot soup and fresh bread, and apple pie, if you'd like it.'

She was right: he was still cold from the long ride back from Waterloo Bridge Road to Wapping, and the even colder river crossing afterwards. The butler's sandwich seemed a long time ago. Monk accepted. Between mouthfuls he asked her about her day, and her progress of redecorating the house. Then he sat back, realising how warm he was in all the ways that mattered.

'Who was she?' Hester asked.

He did not want to think about it, but he knew she would not let it be. She had read the emotion in him. It was both comfortable and disturbing to be known so well. Years ago it would have terrified him. He would have felt intruded upon, even as if somehow his safety were threatened. He was amazed how quickly he had become accustomed to it. There was a greater sweetness than he had expected in not being alone, not having to explain yourself because you were understood, and found acceptable as you were.

But it also meant that he could not hide, even when he would rather. He could not evade the ugly or dangerous questions, the answers he would prefer not to know, because they both saw them, not just him.

'Who was she, William?' Hester repeated.

'Mary Havilland,' he replied. Was it worth avoiding the question as to why he cared? To do so would not bring him any peace, because implicitly it was a lie that would close a door between them, and even more than usually he did not want that. Had someone shut Mary out? Someone she loved, like her father? Refusing to tell her what had driven him to such despair?

'Her father took his own life a couple of months ago,' he said, watching Hester's face. He saw the shadow of grief in her eyes, and the tightening of her mouth. 'Her sister believes that she did not recover from it,' he added. 'I'm sorry.'

She looked away. 'It's over,' she said quietly. She was referring to her own father, not Havilland. 'Why did he do it?' she asked. 'Was it debt too?'

He ached for her, longing to be able to reach the wound that was too sore to heal. Perhaps it always would be.

'Apparently not,' he replied, answering the literal question. 'He worked for the Argyll Company and believed there was some danger of an accident in the tunnels. They're building some of the new sewers . . . '

'And not before time!' she said fervently. 'What sort of an accident?'

'I don't know.' He explained the family relationship briefly. 'Argyll says he had a terror of landslips, cave-ins and so on. He became obsessed, lost his senses a bit.'

'And is that true?' she pressed, still forcing herself to think only of the present case.

'I don't know.' He went on to tell her about Mary's engagement to Toby Argyll, that she had broken it off and no reason had been given except her distress over her father's death and that she refused to believe that he had caused it himself. She could not let the matter go.

'What was it then?' Hester asked. 'Accident? Or murder?' She was being severely practical, but he saw the stiffness in her, the deliberate control, and the effort.

'I don't know. But the police investigated it. It was Runcorn's patch.' He looked at her steadily with a bleak smile.

She understood why that added irony and pain to the case. More than he wished, she had seen his ambition for authority, the way he had fought with, crushed and infuriated Runcorn in the past. She might even have grasped some of the frail half-peace they had made during the case of the Funeral in Blue, when Monk had seen the sudden pity Runcorn had shown where he had least expected it. She did not know the flashes of memory and shame that Monk had had since then, the realisation of how he had used Runcorn in his own climb to success, before the accident that had taken his memory. There were things it was kind for forgetfulness to cleanse from the mind.

'But you're going to find out,' she said, watching him.

'Yes, I have to. She'll be buried in unhallowed ground if she meant to do it.'

'I know.' Tears filled Hester's eyes.

Instantly Monk wished he had not said it aloud. He could have kicked himself for such stupid honesty. He should have protected her, lied if necessary.

She saw that too. 'There's no such thing as unhallowed ground, really.' She swallowed. 'All the earth is hallowed, isn't it? It's just what people think. But some people care very much about being buried with their own, belonging, even in death. See what you can find. Her sister may need to know the truth, poor woman.'

2

The tide was high next morning and the river, with its smells of mud and salt, dead fish and rotting wood, seemed to be lapping right at the door as Monk walked across the dockside. The wind had fallen and the surface of the water barely rippled as it seeped higher around the pier stakes and up the stone steps that led to the quaysides and embankments. The rime of ice overnight had melted in places, but there were still patches as slippery as oiled glass.

'Morning, sir,' Orme said briskly as Monk came into the station. The stove had been burning all night and inside the room was warm.

'Good morning, Orme,' Monk replied, closing the door behind him. There were three other men there: Jones and Kelly busily sorting through papers of one kind or another, and Clacton standing by the stove, his clothes steaming gently.

Monk greeted them and received dutiful acknowledgement, but no more. He was still a stranger, a usurper of Durban's place. They all knew that it was in helping Monk that Durban had contracted the terrible disease that had brought about his death, and they blamed Monk for it. That Durban had gone both because he wished to, understanding the enormity of the danger, and because he considered it his duty, was irrelevant to their anger and the sense of unfairness that lay behind it. Monk had gone on the same task, and he was alive. They could not excuse that. They would have chosen Monk to die, every man of them.

Kelly, a softly spoken Irishman, small-boned and neat, handed him the reports of crime overnight. 'Nothing out o' the usual, sorr,' he said, meeting Monk's eyes then looking away. 'Barge ran aground at low tide, but they got it off.'

'Run aground intentionally?' Monk asked.

'Yes, sorr, I'd say so. No doubt the owners'll be reportin' some o' their cargo missin'.' Kelly gave a bleak smile.

'Dragging it up through the mud at low tide?' Monk questioned. 'If they worked as hard at something honest they'd probably make more.'

'Clever an' wise was never the same thing, sorr,' Kelly said drily, turning back to his work.

Monk took reports from Jones and Clacton as well, and spoke briefly to Butterworth as he came in. Kelly made tea, hot, and dark as mahogany. It would take Monk a long time to drink it with pleasure, but it would set him apart to refuse. Additionally, tea had the virtue of warming the inside and lifting the spirits, even when it was not laced with the frequently added rum.

When the last patrols had landed and reported, and the next was gone out, Monk told them of his decision.

'The two people off Waterloo Bridge yesterday,' he began.

'Suicides,' Clacton said with a pinched expression. 'Lovers' quarrel, I expect. Seems stupid for both of them to jump.' He was a slender, strong, young man of more than average height, who took himself very seriously and was prone to take offence where it was not intended. He could be alternately helpful or obstructive, depending upon his opinion, which he rarely changed, whatever the circumstances. Monk found him irritating and was aware of his own temper rising. He had caught the other men watching him to see how he would handle Clacton. It was another test.

'Yes, it does,' he agreed aloud. 'Which makes me wonder if that was what happened.'

'Thought you saw it?' Clacton challenged, moving his weight a little to stand more aggressively. 'Sir,' he added as an afterthought.

'From the river,' Monk replied. 'It could have been accidental during a quarrel, or she jumped and he tried to stop her. Or even that he pushed her.'

Clacton stared at him. 'Why would he do that? No one else said so!'

'I thought it could be,' Orme contradicted him. He was irritated by Clacton's attitude as well. His blunt, weathered face showed a quiet anger.

'If he was going to push her in, why wouldn't he wait half an hour until dark?' Clacton demanded, his expression tightening. He moved a little closer to the stove, blocking it from

41

Orme. 'Don't make sense. An' with a police boat right in front of 'im! No, she jumped and 'e tried to stop 'er, and lost 'is own balance. Clear as day.'

'Don't suppose 'e saw us,' Jones answered him. ''E'd a' bin lookin' at 'er, not at us on the water below.'

'Still make more sense to wait until dark,' Clacton retorted.

'Wot if she weren't goin' ter stand there on the bridge waitin' until it were dark?' Jones countered. 'Mebbe she weren't that obligin'.' He helped himself to more tea, deliberately taking the last of it.

'If 'e planned to push 'er over, 'e'd 'ave planned to get there at the right time!' Clacton said angrily, looking at the teapot, then moving to block the fire from Jones rather than from Orme.

'And o' course plans always go exactly right,' Jones added sarcastically. 'I seen that!'

There was a guffaw of laughter, probably occasioned by some failure of Clacton's in the past. Monk was still trying to learn not only the job itself but, at times even more importantly, the relationships between the men, their strengths and their weaknesses. Lives could depend on it. The river was a more dangerous place than the city. Even the worst slums, with their creaking, dripping tenement houses, blind alleys and occasional trapdoors, gave you ground to stand on and air to breathe. It had no tides to rise, to slime the steps, to carry things up or down stream. It was not full of currents to pull you under and drifting wreckage just beneath the surface to catch you.

'We don't know,' Monk said to all of them. 'Mary Havilland's father died recently, and according to her sister, Mary was convinced that he was murdered. I have to investigate that possibility. If he was, then perhaps she was murdered also. Or her death and Toby Argyll's may have been a quarrel which ended in a tragic accident, not suicide by either one of them.'

Kelly put down the final pieces of paper. 'And then we could have them buried properly. Their families'd want that.'

'Very much,' Monk agreed.

'But if she wasn't murdered, it's not our job.' Clacton looked at Kelly, then at Monk.

Monk felt his temper rising. One day he was going to have to deal with Clacton.

'It's my job now,' he replied, an edge to his voice that should have been a warning to Clacton, and anyone else listening. 'When I've done it, I'll give the results to whoever needs them, family, Church or magistrate. In the meantime, attend to the theft on Horseferry Stairs, and then see if you can trace the lost barge from Watson and Sons.'

He spoke briefly to Orme again, making sure everything was in order until he should return, and if Superintendent Farnham should ask where he was then Orme would give him an appropriate answer.

'Yes, sir,' Orme said unhesitatingly. 'Got to know if it was accident, suicide or murder. If the poor young woman's mind was turned by the death of 'er father, mebbe they won't blame 'er too much.'

With that thought in mind Monk took the long cab journey from Wapping to Mary Havilland's address in Charles Street, just off Lambeth Walk.

The house was not ostentatious, but it was handsome enough, and had an appearance of considerable comfort. There was a mews behind for the keeping of carriages and horses, so presumably the residents were accustomed to such luxuries. As he expected, the curtains were drawn and there was a wreath on the door. Someone had even laid sawdust in the street to muffle the sound of horses' hoofs.

The door was opened by a footman of probably no more than eighteen years old. His face was so white his freckles stood out, and his eyes were pink-rimmed. It took him a moment or two to collect his wits when he saw a stranger on the step. 'Yes, sir?'

Monk introduced himself and asked if he might speak to the butler. He already knew there was no other family resident. Jenny Argyll had said that Mary had been her only relative.

Inside, the house was in traditional mourning. The mirrors were covered, the clocks stopped, lilies in vases giving off a faint, hothouse perfume. Their very unnaturalness in January was a reminder that familiar life had ended.

The butler came to Monk in the stiff, very formal morning room. It was bitterly cold, no fire having been lit, and the glass fronts of the bookcases reflected the cold daylight that came under the half-drawn curtains like ice on a deep pond.

The butler, Cardman, was a tall, spare man with thick iron-grey hair and a bony face, which might have been quite handsome in his youth but was now too strong in the planes of his cheek and nose. His light blue eyes were intelligent and — unlike the footman — he had mastered his emotions so they barely showed.

'Yes, sir?' he said, closing the door behind him. 'How may I help you?'

Monk began by expressing his sympathy. Not only did it seem appropriate, even to a butler, but it was natural.

'Thank you, sir,' Cardman acknowledged. He seemed about to add something, then changed his mind.

'We are not certain what happened,' Monk began. 'For many reasons, we need to know a great deal more.'

A shadow of pain crossed Cardman's impassive face. 'Mr Argyll told us that Miss Havilland took her own life, sir. Is it necessary to intrude further into her unhappiness?'

His delicacy was admirable, but this was an inquiry that could either define guilt, or pronounce innocence, and — even to the dead — that was important. Monk could not afford to leave anything unprobed, or go about his questions in the least offensive way if it were also the least efficient.

'You were aware of her unhappiness?' he asked as gently as he could.

'Mr Havilland died less than two months ago,'

Cardman said stiffly. 'Grief does not heal so soon.'

It was a socially correct answer, giving away nothing and delivered with as much disapproval as a butler dared show.

Monk was brutal. 'Is your father still alive, Mr Cardman?'

Cardman's face tightened, the light of understanding flaming in his eyes, bright and angry. 'No, sir.'

Monk smiled. 'I'm sure you grieved for him, but you did not despair.' He thought briefly that part of the loss of his memory from the accident was complete obliteration of anything about his own father — or mother, for that matter. He knew his sister, Beth, but that only because she had tried to keep in touch. He wrote seldom. The shame of that bit into him without warning and he felt the heat in his face.

'No, sir,' Cardman said stiffly.

Monk sat down in one of the big leather armchairs and crossed his legs. 'Mr Cardman, I mean to find out whether this was suicide, or something else,' he said levelly. 'I have investigated deaths of many kinds, and I do not give up until I have what I seek. You will assist me, willingly or not. You can remain standing if you wish, but I prefer that you sit. I don't like staring up at you.'

Cardman obeyed. Monk noticed a rigidity in his movement, as if he were unused to sitting in the presence of a guest, and certainly not in this room. He had probably been a servant all his life, perhaps starting as a boot boy forty years ago, or more. Yet he could have spent time in the army. There was a ramrod stiffness to him, a sense of dignity as well as self-discipline.

'Were you surprised?' Monk asked suddenly.

Cardman's eyes widened. 'Surprised?'

'That Miss Havilland should throw herself off Waterloo Bridge?'

'Yes, sir. We all were.'

'What was she like? Retiring or opinionated? Intelligent or not?' Monk was determined to get a meaningful answer from the man, not the bland words of praise a servant would normally give his employer, or anyone would accord to the dead. 'Was she pretty? Did she flirt? Was she in love with Mr Argyll, or did she perhaps prefer someone else? Might she have felt trapped in a marriage to him?'

'Trapped?' Cardman was startled.

'Oh, come now,' Monk retorted. 'You know as well as I do that not all young women marry for love! They marry suitably, or as opportunity is offered them.' He knew this from Hester, and from some of the cases he had taken in his private capacity. The pressure and the humiliation of it barely touched the edges of his experience, but he had seen the marriage market at work, young women paraded like bloodstock for farmers to bid on.

Cardman was caught in an impossible situation. His expression registered his embarrassment, and his understanding. Perhaps grief, and the knowledge that he no longer had a mistress to serve, broke down his resistance.

'Yes, sir,' he admitted uncomfortably. 'I think

Miss Havilland did feel rather that she was taking the best offer that she had, and it would be the right thing to do in accepting Mr Toby.'

'And she broke the agreement after her father's death?' Monk had expected that answer, and yet it grieved him. The young woman with the passionate face that he had pulled from the river deserved better than that, and would have hungered for it more than some.

'Yes, sir.' Cardman's voice dropped and there was a huskiness that once again betrayed his emotion. 'She was very distressed by it indeed. We all were.'

'How did it happen?'

Cardman hesitated again, but he knew Monk would not allow him to go until he had told him. And perhaps there was something in him that wanted to share his bewilderment and his pain with at least one other person in front of whom he did not have to maintain his dignity or always appear to be master of any and every situation. He too was a leader in a tightly knit, hierarchical community with the most rigid rules on earth.

'Mr Havilland was a gentleman in the old sense of the term, sir,' he began. 'Not titled, you understand, and not with great wealth. It was a matter of honour to him. He was fair to everybody, and he never carried a grudge. If any man wronged him, and apologised, Mr Havilland forgot the thing entirely. He was a good friend, but he never put friendship above what he thought was right, and he respected a poor man as much as a rich one, if that man was good to his word.'

Monk was aware that Cardman was watching him, to see if he caught the unspoken thread bright between the words.

'I see,' Monk acknowledged. 'Much to be admired, but not one to take the way of many in society, or in business either.' He did not remember his days in merchant banking — they were gone with all the rest of his memory — but he had learned, piece by piece, much about the cost and the dishonour of some of his own acts, and those of people he had loved who had been ruined.

'No, sir, I'm afraid not,' Cardman agreed. 'He had many friends, but I think perhaps he had enemies as well. He was much worried before his death that the rebuilding of the sewers to Mr Bazalgette's plans was going ahead rather too hastily, and the use of the big machines was going to cause a bad accident. He became most concerned about it and spent all this time looking into matters, trying to prove he was right.'

'And did he prove it?' Monk asked.

'Not so far as I know, sir. It caused some unpleasantness with Mr Alan Argyll, and Mr Toby as well, but Mr Havilland wouldn't stop. He felt he was right.'

'That must have been very difficult for him, with both his daughters concerned with the Argyll brothers,' Monk observed.

'Indeed, sir. There was some unpleasantness. I'm afraid feelings ran rather high. Miss Mary sided with her father, and that was when matters between her and Mr Toby became strained.'

49

'And she broke off her arrangement?'

'No, sir, not then.' Cardman was obviously wretched speaking about it, and yet Monk could sense the weight of it inside the man, like a dam needing release before the pressure of it burst the walls.

'Mr Havilland was very concerned,' Monk prompted. 'You must have seen him frequently, even every day. Did he seem to you on the edge of losing his grip on self-control?'

'No, sir, not in the slightest!' Cardman said vehemently, his lean face alive with sudden, undisguised emotion. 'He was not in a mood anything like despair! He was elated, if anything. He believed he was on the brink of finding proof of what he feared. There had been no accident, you see; rather he felt it was to come! Something appalling, costing scores of lives, and he wanted above all things to prevent it.' Admiration shone in his eyes that was deeper than mere loyalty. He had believed in Havilland as one man believes in another when they have understood the same cause, in spirit even if not in fact.

'Have you always been in service, Cardman?' Monk said impulsively.

'I beg your pardon?' Cardman was taken by surprise.

Monk repeated the question.

'No, sir. I served for six years in the army. I don't see what that has to do with Mr Havilland's death.'

'Only your judgement of men under pressure.'

'Oh. I see.' Cardman was embarrassed and did not know how to accept what he realised was a compliment. He coloured faintly and looked away.

'Were you surprised that Mr Havilland took his life?' Monk asked.

'Yes, sir. Frankly I found it hard to believe, especially . . . ' Cardman took a moment to master himself. He sat perfectly still, his knuckles white, ' . . . especially in his own house, where Miss Mary was bound to know about it. A man can make such things look like an accident.' He breathed in and out slowly. 'It broke her heart. She was never the same afterwards.' There was anger in his face now. A man he admired had inexplicably let him down — more than that, he had let them all down, and most of all the daughter who also had trusted him.

'But you did believe it, none the less?' Monk asked. He felt like a surgeon cutting open a man still conscious and feeling every movement of the knife.

'I had no choice,' Cardman said quietly. 'The stable boy found him out there in the mews in the morning, a bullet through his brain and the gun by his hand. The police proved he'd bought it himself, from a pawnshop just a few days before.' There was obviously a great deal more he could have said — the feelings were naked in his eyes — but a lifetime's discretion governed him.

'Did he say why he bought a gun?'

Cardman's face was grim. 'No, sir.'

'Did he leave a note as to why he had done such a thing?' Monk asked.

'No, sir.'

'And he said nothing to you, or any of the other servants?'

'No, sir, simply that he wanted to wait up that night, and we should not concern ourselves but retire as usual.'

'And you detected nothing out of the ordinary in his manner? Even with the wisdom of knowing now what happened?'

'I have considered it, naturally, wondering if there was something I should have seen,' Cardman admitted, a faint colour on his pale skin. He had the air of a man who has lived through a nightmare. 'He seemed preoccupied, as if he were expecting something to happen, but in all honesty, I thought then that it was an irritation that plagued him, not a despair.'

'Irritation?' Monk pressed. 'Anger?'

Cardman frowned. 'I would not have put it as strongly as that, sir. Rather more as if an old friend had disappointed him, or something were wearisome and he found himself having to deal with it yet again. I formed the opinion it was a familiar problem rather than a new one. He certainly did not seem afraid, or . . . or desperate.'

'So you were totally shocked the next morning?'

'Yes, sir, totally.'

'And Miss Mary?'

Cardman's face pinched and his eyes were bright with tears he could not allow himself to shed. 'I've never seen anyone more deeply hurt, sir. Mrs Kitching, the housekeeper, feared Miss Mary might meet her own death, she was so

52

beside herself with grief. She refused to believe that he could have done it himself.'

'What did she think had happened?' Monk refused to picture Mary Havilland's face in his mind, or to remember Hester and the pain inside her that even now she could not look at; when it was too late to change anything, the guilt that if only she had been at home instead of in the Crimea, then somehow she could have prevented it, or at least saved her mother's slow death from shame and loneliness afterwards. The dishonour of debt and suicide had been too much for her mother to endure.

What in heaven's name had driven Havilland to do this to his daughter? At least with Hester's father it was the only way for him to answer the shame that had been placed upon him, through his own goodness of heart. He had been deceived, like so many others. He had considered death the only act left to an honourable man. What had Havilland feared or despaired of that had driven him to such an act?

'Why did she find it so hard to believe?' he said, more sharply than he had meant to.

Cardman started with surprise at the emotion in Monk's voice. 'There was no reason,' he said gravely. 'That is why Miss Mary believed he had been murdered. More and more she became convinced that either he had found something in the tunnelling works, or he was about to, and for that he had been killed.'

'What made her more convinced?' Monk said quickly. 'Did something happen, or was it simply her need to clear her father of suicide?'

'If I knew, sir, I'd tell you,' Cardman replied, looking very directly into Monk's eyes. There was a kind of desperation in him, as if he were clinging to a last thread of hope too delicate to name. 'Miss Mary read all through her father's papers, sat all day and up half the night. Over and over she searched them. Many's the time I'd go to his study and find her there at his desk, or fallen asleep in the big chair, one of his books open in her hands.'

'What kind of book?' Monk did not know what he was looking for but Cardman's emotion caught him also.

'Engineering,' Cardman said, as if Monk should have understood.

Monk was puzzled. 'Engineering, did you say?'

'Yes. Mr Havilland was a senior engineer and surveyor for Mr Argyll's company, until the day of his death. That's why they quarrelled. Mr Argyll's company has never had a bad accident — in fact they're better than most for safety — but Mr Havilland believed it would happen.'

'And he told Mr Argyll?'

Cardman shifted position slightly. 'Yes, of course. But Mr Argyll said it was just his feelings about being underground, closed in, as it were. He was embarrassed to admit to them. Argyll as much as called him a coward, albeit politely. Of course he never used that word.'

'Was that what Miss Havilland was doing also, enquiring into engineering, as regards the tunnels?'

'Yes, sir. I'm certain of it.'

'But she found nothing either?'

Cardman looked chagrined. 'No, sir, not so far as I am aware.'

'Did she continue to see Mr Toby Argyll?'

'She broke off their agreement, but of course she still saw him socially now and then. She could hardly help it, since he was Miss Jennifer's brother-in-law, and the Argyll brothers were very close.'

'Do you know Mrs Argyll's feelings on the subject?' Monk asked. 'She was surely caught in the middle in a most unfortunate way?'

Cardman's face tightened, his lips pressed together before he spoke.

'She was loyal to her husband, sir. She was convinced that her father's fears had unbalanced his judgement and she was annoyed with Miss Mary for pandering to him rather than encouraging him to abandon the matter.' There was a wealth of anger and distress in his voice

Monk was bitterly aware that the house in which Cardman lived was the centre of a double disgrace and there seemed no one left to care except himself, and the other servants for whom he was responsible. They no longer had employment, and would soon be out of a home as well. It caused him to wonder who would inherit the house. Presumably it would be Jenny Argyll, as the last surviving member of the family. Monk was sure Cardman did not relish the prospect. Perhaps she would sell it, and the servants would remain, at least until the new owners took possession.

'I see. Thank you very much for your honesty,' Monk said, rising to his feet. 'Just one more thing: who investigated Mr Havilland's death?'

'A Superintendent Runcorn,' Cardman replied. 'He was very civil about it, and seemed to be thorough. I cannot think of anything more that he could have done.' He stood also.

So Runcorn had done it himself! It was the worst answer he could have given. The past returned to Monk like a draught of cold air. How many times had he second-guessed Runcorn, gone over his work and corrected a flaw here and there, and altered the conclusion? It seemed as if he had always needed to prove himself the cleverer. Increasingly he disliked the man he had been then. The fact that he disliked Runcorn even more mitigated nothing.

'Mr Argyll did not doubt the correctness of the verdict?' he asked aloud, his voice rasping with emotion.

'No, sir, just Miss Mary.' Grief filled Cardman's face and he seemed unashamed of it, as if at least in front of Monk he felt no need to mask it any more. He swallowed hard.

'Sir, I would be most grateful if you could inform us when . . . when she is . . . if Mrs Argyll doesn't . . . ' He did not know how to finish.

'I will make certain you are told,' Monk said hoarsely. 'But . . . but you might consider whether the female staff wish to attend. Burials can be . . . very hard.'

'You are telling me it will be in unhallowed ground. I know, sir. If Miss Mary was strong enough to go to her father's burial, we can go to hers.'

Monk nodded, tears in his throat, for Mary

Havilland, for Hester's father, for uncounted people in despair.

Cardman saw him to the door in silent understanding.

Outside in the street Monk began to walk back down the hill towards Westminster Bridge. It would be the best place to catch a hansom, but he was in no hurry. He must face Runcorn in his own station and yet again challenge his judgement, but he was not ready to do it yet. Were it not for the thought of Mary Havilland buried in the grave of an outcast, her courage and loyalty to her father credited as no more than the dementia of a bereaved woman, he would have accepted the verdict and consider he had done all that duty required.

But he remembered her face, the white skin, the strong bones and gentle mouth. She was a fighter who had been beaten. He refused to accept that she had surrendered. At least he could not yet.

He wanted to prepare what he would say to Runcorn, weigh his words to rob them of criticism, perhaps even gain his support. The wind was cold blowing up off the river, whipping trousers around the ankles, and the damp in it stung the flesh and crept through the cracks between scarf and coat collar. The magnificent Gothic lines of the Houses of Parliament stood on the far bank. The clock in the tower that housed Big Ben said it was twenty minutes before eleven. He had been longer with Cardman than he had realised.

He hunched his shoulders and walked more

rapidly along the footpath. Hansoms passed him, but they were all occupied. Should he have asked Cardman outright if he believed Havilland had committed suicide? He thought the butler was a good judge of character, a strong man.

No. He was also loyal. Whatever he thought, he would not have told a stranger that both his master, and then his new mistress, had committed such an act of cowardice before the law of man and of God. His own judgement might have been wiser, and gentler, but he would not have left them open to the censure of the world.

Monk reached the middle of the bridge and saw an empty cab going the other way. He stepped out into the road and hailed it, giving the police station address.

The journey was too short. He was still not ready when he arrived, but then perhaps he never would be. He paid the driver and went up the station steps and inside. He was recognised immediately.

'Mornin', Mr Monk,' the desk sergeant said guardedly. 'What can we do for you, sir?'

Monk could not remember the man, but that meant nothing, except that he had not worked with him since the accident, nearly eight years ago now. Had he really known Hester so long? Why had it taken him years to find the courage within himself, and the honesty, to acknowledge his feelings for her? The answer was easy. He did not want to give anyone else the power to hurt him so much. And in closing the door on the possibility of pain of course he had closed it on the chance for joy as well.

'Good morning, Sergeant,' he replied, stopping in front of the desk. 'I would like to speak to Superintendent Runcorn, please. It concerns a case he handled recently.'

'Yes, sir,' the sergeant said with a hint of satisfaction at Monk's lack of authority in his voice. 'That will be on behalf of whom, sir?'

Monk forbore from smiling, although he wanted to. The man had not recognised his police coat. 'On behalf of the Thames River Police,' he replied, opening his jacket a little so his uniform showed beneath.

The sergeant's eyes widened and he let out his breath slowly. 'Yes, sir!' he said, turning on his heel and retreating, and Monk heard his footsteps as he went upstairs to break the news.

Five minutes later Monk was standing in Runcorn's office. It had a large, comfortable desk in it and the air was warm from the stove in the corner. There were books on the shelf opposite and a rather nice carving of a wooden bear on a plinth in the middle. It was all immaculately tidy as always — part of Runcorn's need to conform, and impress.

Runcorn himself had changed little. He was tall, barrel-chested, with large eyes a fraction too close together, above a long nose. His hair was still thick and liberally sprinkled with grey. He had put on a few pounds around the waist.

'So it's true!' he said, eyebrows raised, his voice too carefully expressionless. 'You're in the River Police! I told Watkins he was daft, but seems he wasn't.' His face stretched into a slow,

59

satisfied smile at his own power to give help, or withhold it. 'Well, what can I do for you, Inspector? It is 'Inspector', isn't it?' There was a wealth of meaning behind the words, the inflexion, the curve of his mouth. They had once been of equal rank, long ago. It was Monk's tongue that had cost him his seniority. He had been more elegant than Runcorn, cleverer, immeasurably more the gentleman, and he always would be. They both knew it. But Runcorn was patient, and prepared to play the game by the rules, bite back his insolence, curb his impatience, climb slowly. Now he had his reward in superior rank, and he could not keep from savouring it.

'Yes, it is,' Monk replied. He ached to be tart, but he could not afford it. What was a moment's stung pride compared with Mary Havilland's unsanctified burial?

'Down at Wapping? Live there too?' Runcorn pursued the subject of Monk's fall in the world. Wapping was a less elegant, less salubrious place than Grafton Street had been, or at least than it had sounded.

'Yes,' Monk agreed again.

'Well, well,' Runcorn mused. 'Would never have guessed you'd do that! Like it, do you?'

'Only been there a few weeks,' Monk told him.

Again Runcorn could not resist the temptation. 'Got tired of being on your own, then? Bit hard, I should imagine. Get some lean times.' He was still smiling. 'After all, most people can call the police, for nothing. Why should they pay someone? Knew you'd have to come back one day. What do you need my help with? Out of your depth already?' He oozed pleasure now.

Monk itched to retaliate. He had to remind himself again that he could not afford to. 'James Havilland,' he answered. 'About two months ago. Charles Street.'

Runcorn's face darkened a little, the pleasure draining out of it. 'I remember. Poor man shot himself in his own stables. What is it to do with the River Police? It's nowhere near the water.'

'Do you remember his daughter Mary?' Monk remained standing. Runcorn had not offered him a seat, but for Monk to be comfortable would seem inappropriate in this conversation, and with all the past that lay between them.

'Of course I do,' Runcorn said gravely. He looked unhappy, as if the presence of the dead had suddenly intruded into this quiet, tidy police room from which he ruled his little kingdom. 'Has . . . has she complained to you that her father was murdered?'

Monk was stunned, not by the question, but by the fact that he could see no outrage in Runcorn, no sense of territorial invasion that Monk, of all people, should trespass on his case.

'Who did she think was responsible?' he asked.

Runcorn was too quick for him. 'Did she?' he challenged him. 'Why did you say 'did'?'

'She fell off Waterloo Bridge yesterday evening,' Monk replied.

Runcorn was stunned. He stood motionless, the colour receding from his face. For an absurd moment he reminded Monk of the butler who also had grieved so much for Mary Havilland.

Yet Runcorn had hardly known her. 'Suicide?' he said hoarsely.

'I'm not sure,' Monk replied. 'It looked like it at first. She was standing near the railing talking to a man. They seemed to be arguing. He took hold of her, and a moment or two later they both were pressed hard against the railing, and then both overbalanced and fell.'

'A man?' Runcorn's eyes widened. 'Who? Argyll?'

'Why do you think it was Argyll?' Monk demanded.

Runcorn lost his temper, colour flooding up his cheeks. 'Don't play your damn-fool games with me, Monk!' he said harshly. 'You always were a heartless bastard! That young woman lost her father, and now she's dead too! It's my case, and I'll have you thrown out of the River Police, and every other damn force in London, if you try to use that to prove yourself fit to be an officer again. Do you hear me?'

Monk's temper flared also, then died again even more rapidly. He went on in a perfectly level voice. 'If you're fit to be a policeman of any rank at all, let alone superintendent, you'll care about the case, not guarding your little patch of authority,' he retorted. 'I don't know whether Mary Havilland jumped, fell or was pushed. I was watching when it happened, but too far away to see in the dark, and looking upwards from two hundred feet away.' He was not going to explain to Runcorn why he cared so much. He had no right to know about Hester's history. 'If I knew exactly what happened to Havilland it might help me.'

Runcorn grunted, took a deep breath and let it out slowly. His shoulders sagged a little. 'Oh. Well I suppose you do need that. Sit down.' He waved at a wooden chair piled with papers, and eased himself into his own leather-padded seat behind his desk.

Monk moved the papers on to the floor and obeyed.

Runcorn's face became sombre. He had dealt with death both accidental and murderous all his adult life, but this one apparently moved him, even in memory.

'Stable boy found him in the morning,' he began, looking down at his large hands rather than at Monk. 'Seems the boy lived out, a mile or so away, and used to walk to work every morning. Mews are small there and the room above the stable was kept for harnesses and the like. He could have slept in the straw, but seems he had an aunt with a lodging house in the area and he helped out there too, and got fed and looked after for it. He seemed like an honest lad, but we checked it all, and it was the truth. He was home all night, and Havilland's butler said they'd never had a day's bother with him.'

Monk nodded.

'Boy arrived about six,' Runcorn went on. 'Found his master on the floor of the room where they keep the hay and feed. Lying on his back, shot through the head. One clean bullet into the brain. Must've been standing near the middle of the room, and fell backwards. Blood exactly where you'd expect it to be. Gun fallen out of his hand but not more than a foot away.'

Monk felt a chill settle over him.

'Boy went in and told the butler — can't remember his name,' Runcorn went on. 'Carter, or something like that.'

'Cardman,' Monk supplied.

'That's right,' Runcorn agreed, blinking several times. 'He went out to look. Saw just what the boy had said, and sent the footman for the police. It was nearer eight o'clock by the time I got there. Didn't know Havilland personally, but I knew him by repute. A very decent man. Hard to believe he'd taken his own life.' He looked up at Monk suddenly. 'But one thing police work teaches you: you never know what goes on in somebody else's mind. Loves and hates that their own families don't ever dream about.'

Monk nodded. For once he had no quibble at all. He tried to imagine Runcorn and the scene: the small stable; the straw; the sound and smell of horses; leather harnesses; the gleam of lantern light on polished brasses; the dead man lying on the floor and the sickly smell of blood.

'Were the horses frightened?' he asked. 'Any injuries?'

Runcorn frowned. 'No. Bit nervous. They'd have smelled blood and they must have heard the shot, but nothing was disturbed as if there'd been a fight. No wounds, no wood kicked, no cuts, neither of 'em really spooked. And before you ask, there were no other marks on the body, no bruises, clothes as neat as you please. I'd lay my reputation no one struggled or fought with him before he was shot. And the way he was lying, either he shot himself, which everything pointed to, or whoever else did it stood within a couple of feet of him, because there was nowhere else to stand in a room that size.'

'And nothing was taken, nothing missing?' Monk asked without hope now. He had outwitted Runcorn many times in the past, but that was years ago. They had both learned in the time between: Monk to be a little gentler, and more honest in his reasons for cleverness; Runcorn to think a little harder before coming to conclusions, perhaps also to keep his attention on the case more, and less on his own vanity.

'Nothing to take in the stables,' Runcorn replied. 'Unless you count the odd horse brass, but stable boy said they were all there.'

'Coachman agree?' Monk put in.

'Seems a footman doubled as coachman,' Runcorn answered. 'He was handy, and with a butler and a junior footman who doubled as boot boy, that was all that was necessary.'

'And the house?' Monk pressed. 'Anyone intrude in the night? Or impossible to tell, if Havilland had left the door open? Had he?'

'Yes. Butler says he sat up late. Told them he wanted to work in his study, and sent them all to bed. But a thorough search was made and both Miss Havilland herself and the housekeeper said nothing at all was missing, or even moved. And there were plenty of nice things, easy to carry, if a burglar'd wanted. Easy to sell.'

'What time did he die?' Monk was not yet willing to give up, although it was beginning to look more and more as if Mary Havilland's belief in her father's murder was simply a desperate young woman's refusal to accept the truth that he had killed himself.

'Police surgeon reckoned between midnight and about three, close as he could tell. Pretty cold in the stables, late autumn. November the thirteenth to be exact. Frost was sharpish that night. I remember it was still white all round the edges of the leaves on the garden bushes we passed going in.' Runcorn was hunched up, as if the memory chilled him.

'No one heard a shot?'

'No.' Runcorn gave a tiny, bleak smile. 'Which was unusual. You'd think someone would've. Tried shooting the thing myself, and it was loud enough. Could hear it clear a hundred yards off on a still night like that. I followed that one all the way, but if anyone heard, they wouldn't admit to it.' There was long experience in his face, and fighting against it a very faint quickening of hope.

Monk realised with surprise that Runcorn wanted Mary Havilland to be right; he simply could not see the possibility.

'Muffled by something?' Monk asked.

Runcorn shook his head no more than an inch or two. 'Nothing there. Powder burns on his skin. If he'd wrapped a towel or a cloth around it to deaden the sound, that'd account for why nobody heard it, or maybe recognised it for a shot, but then the cloth would still be there, and it wasn't. Unless . . . somebody took it away!' He did not quite make it a question, but it was in his eyes.

'No sign of anyone else there?' Monk asked, seeking the same hope.

'Not a thing, and I looked myself.'

Monk believed him. Not only was Runcorn not easily a liar, there was evidently a painful hunger in him to believe better of Havilland than the circumstances justified. Even now, two months later, it was still there.

Monk asked the next, obvious question. 'Why? What was so wrong that he'd shoot himself in his own stables in the middle of the night?'

Runcorn pressed his lips together and hunched his shoulders a little more. 'I looked.' There was an edge of defence in his voice. 'As far as anyone knew, his health was excellent. He ate well, slept well enough, walked often. We checked into his affairs, he certainly was more than comfortably off. No unaccounted expenditure. He didn't gamble. And if anyone was blackmailing him, it wasn't for money. If he had a mistress we never found her. If he had bad habits we saw no sign of them either. He drank very little. Never been seen the worse for it. Wife died seven years ago. Had two daughters, Jenny, the elder, married to Alan Argyll, very successful businessman.'

Runcorn took a deep breath and let it out in a sigh. 'Havilland worked for his company as an engineer in the big rebuilding of the sewers. Well respected, well paid. Seemed to get on all right, until recently when Havilland took it into his head that the tunnels were dangerous and there was going to be an accident one day. We couldn't find any evidence for it. Argyll's safety record is good, better than most. And we all know the new sewers are necessary, and urgently. Nobody's forgotten the Big Stink, or is daft enough to imagine it won't happen again, if we don't do something about it.'

'And Mary?' Monk asked. He wanted to fault Runcorn, to find something he had forgotten, or done badly, but he couldn't.

Runcorn's face softened. 'The poor girl was beside herself with grief,' he said defensively, as if he felt he needed to protect her memory from Monk's intrusion.

Monk liked him the better for that.

'She couldn't believe he would do such a thing,' Runcorn went on. 'Said he was on a crusade, and people in crusades get killed sometimes, but they don't shoot themselves. She said he was on the edge of finding out something about the tunnels, and someone killed him to stop him doing that. Lots of money at stake. Fortunes to be made, and I suppose lost, in all this. And reputations.'

'What do you believe?' Monk asked.

'Asked a few questions about him,' Runcorn said unhappily. 'According to the men in the works, he'd got a bit eccentric. Scared stiff of tunnels and holes, so they said. Used to shake and go white as a ghost, break out in a sweat.' He lifted one shoulder very slightly. 'Happens to some people. Others it's heights or spiders, or snakes. Whatever. Usually think of women being frightened of that sort of thing, but it doesn't have to be. Worked a case once with a woman who fainted at the sight of a mouse. Can't think why, but such fear doesn't have to have a reason. Knew another one terrified of birds, even a harmless little canary.' He stopped. All the lines of his face were downwards, making him look older, tireder than before. 'He did seem obsessed with the dread of an accident, and as far as I could see, there was no reason for it.'

'What did Mrs Argyll think of her father in this?' Monk asked, remembering Jenny Argyll's stiff back and carefully controlled face.

'Blamed herself for not seeing how far his madness had gone,' Runcorn answered, weariness and confusion in his eyes. 'Said she would have had him better looked after if she'd known. Not that there was a thing she could've done, as her husband told her. As long as he breaks no laws — and Havilland didn't — a man's entitled to go as daft as he likes.'

'And Mary?'

Runcorn sighed. 'That's the thing. Poor girl refused to accept it. Determined her father was right and wouldn't let it rest. Started reading all his books, asking questions. Broke off her engagement to Toby Argyll and devoted herself to clearing her father's name. Wanted him buried in consecrated ground if it took her her life's work to do it.' His voice sank even lower. 'Now it looks as if the poor soul'll lie beside him. Do you know when they're going to do that, because — ' He stopped abruptly and cleared his throat, then glared defensively at Monk as if challenging him to mock.

Monk had no desire to. In his mind's eye he

69

could see again and again the figure of Mary tipping over the rail, clinging on to Toby Argyll, and the two of them plunging down into the icy river. He still did not know what had happened, nothing was clear and he ended up not remembering but imagining, because he wanted her not to have done it herself.

And he remembered the strong bones and the gentle mouth of the white face they pulled out of the river, and that Mrs Porter had said she was a woman of opinions and the courage to declare them.

'No, not yet. But I'll tell you when I do. Have to tell the butler, Cardman, as well.'

Runcorn nodded, then looked away, his eyes too bright.

'You said you found where he bought the gun.' Monk changed the subject.

Runcorn did not look at him. 'Pawnshop half a mile away. Owner described him close enough. He was wearing a good coat, dark wool, and a scarf. Nothing odd in that, especially on a November night.'

'Not very specific. Could have been anyone.'

'Could have, except it was the same gun. Had one or two marks and scratches on it. He was certain enough.'

'But why would Havilland have killed himself?' Monk persisted.

Runcorn shook his head. 'Argyll told me he was becoming an embarrassment to the company. He was reluctant to say so, but he was going to have to dismiss him. Havilland was upsetting the men, causing trouble. Argyll felt very badly about it, but he had no choice.

70

Couldn't let everyone suffer because of one man's obsession. Said he hadn't told his wife, and certainly Mary didn't know, but had intimated as much to Havilland himself. He begged us not to tell them, for their own sakes, especially Mary. It wouldn't alter his suicide, and it would reduce him in their eyes. In fact it would make suicide seem more rational. Maybe he did tell her after all.' There was no relief in his face, no sense of resolution.

Monk remembered again the sudden softness he had seen in Runcorn's face at the graveside of another dead woman. He had believed Runcorn despised her, and his misjudgement was a condemnation of his own hastiness.

'Poor man,' he said briefly. 'If he told her at last, and she went off the bridge, taking Toby Argyll with her, he's going to feel a guilt for the rest of his life.'

'What else could he do?' Runcorn said reasonably, his face still puckered in distaste.

'If Havilland was murdered, who did Mary think was responsible?'

'Her brother-in-law,' Runcorn replied unhesitatingly. 'But he wasn't. We checked up and he was out all evening at a function, and went home with his wife a little after midnight. She'll swear for him, and so will the servants. Footman waited up, so did the lady's maid. No way he could have been there. Same for his brother, before you ask.'

'He lives close by. No servants to swear for him,' Monk pointed out.

'He was out of London that night,' Runcorn

responded. 'Wasn't within a hundred miles. Checked on that too.'

'I see.' There was nothing left to argue. He stood up with a strange hollowness inside him. 'Thank you.'

Runcorn rose as well. 'Are you giving up?' It sounded like a challenge. There was a note in it close to despair.

'No!' Monk denied, without knowing what he meant. It was as much a defiance of Runcorn as any sense of purpose in himself. He had no idea where else to look for evidence. Inevitability closed in on him.

'Tell me,' Runcorn said, frowning, 'if you find anything. And . . . '

'Yes, I will,' Monk promised. He thanked him, and left before their meeting could grow any more awkward. There was nothing else for them to say to each other and the brief truce was best unbroken by trying.

★　★　★

Monk returned to Wapping and spent the afternoon in the general duties that were part of his new job. He disliked the routine, especially writing reports and, even more, reading other people's, but he could not afford to do less than his best. Any error or omission could be the one that spelled failure. He must succeed. He had no other skills than for his work and most certainly no other friends like Callandra Daviot who could or should help financially.

At five o'clock it was totally dark. Worse than

that, there was a heavy fog rolling in from the east, shrouding the river so closely he knew he would not find a boatman to attempt rowing him across. Already the streetlamps were dimming, blurred yellow ghosts fading altogether within twenty yards so the night was impenetrable. The mournful baying of the fog horns on the river broke the silence and there was little else to be heard but the steady drip of water and the slurp of the tide on the steps and against the embankment.

Monk left at half-past five to begin the long walk up towards London Bridge where, if he were very fortunate, he might find a hansom to take him over, and as far as Southwark Park and home.

He buttoned his coat, pulled his collar up and set out.

He had gone about a quarter of a mile when he was aware of someone behind him. He stopped just beyond one of the mist-shrouded lamps and waited.

An urchin came into the pale circle of light. He looked about nine years old, as much as one could see of his face through the grime. He was wearing a long jacket and odd boots, but at least he was not barefoot on the icy stone.

'Hello, Scuff,' Monk said with pleasure. The mudlark had been of help to him in the *Maude Idris* case, and he had seen him a dozen times since then, albeit briefly. Twice they had shared a meat pie. This was the first time he had seen the boots. 'New find?' he asked, admiring them.

'Found one, bought the other,' Scuff replied,

catching up with him.

Monk started to walk again. It was too cold to stand still. 'How are you?' he said conversationally.

Scuff shrugged. 'I got boots. You all right?' The second was said with a shadow of anxiety. Scuff thought Monk was an innocent, a liability to himself, and he made no secret of it.

'Not bad, thank you,' Monk replied. 'Do you want a pie, if we can find anyone open?'

'Yer won't,' Scuff said candidly. 'It's gonna be an 'ard winter. You wanna watch yerself. It's gonna get bad.'

'It's pretty bad every winter,' Monk replied. He could not afford to dwell too long on the misery of those who worked and slept outside, because he was helpless to do anything about it. What was a hot pie now and then to one small boy?

'This in't the same,' Scuff replied, keeping step with Monk by skipping an extra one now and then. 'Them big tunnels wot they're diggin' is upsettin' folk down there. Toshers in't 'appy.'

Toshers were the men who made their living by hunting for and picking up the small objects of value that found their way into the sewers, including a remarkable amount of jewellery. They usually hunted together, for fear of the armies of rats who could strip a man down to the bone in a short while if he were unlucky enough to lose his footing and injure himself, even if he did not drown. And there was always the possibility of a build-up of methane gas given off by the sewer contents, and, of course, a wave of water if the rain were torrential enough.

'Why are the toshers unhappy?' Monk asked. 'There'll always be sewers, just better ones.'

'Change,' Scuff said simply, and with exaggerated patience. 'Everybody's got their stretch, their beat, if yer like, seein' as yer a policeman, o' sorts.'

'I'm a perfectly regular policeman!' Monk defended himself.

Scuff treated that assertion with the silence it deserved. In his opinion Monk was a dangerous novice who had taken Durban's position out of a misguided idea of loyalty. He was totally unsuited for the work and was much in need of the guidance or occasional protection of someone who knew what they were doing, such as Scuff himself. He had been born on the river, and at nine years old — or possibly ten, he wasn't sure — he knew an enormous amount, and was not too proud to learn more every day. But it was a heavy responsibility to look after a grown man who thought he knew so much more than he did.

'Is there going to be a fight over the new stretches?' Monk asked.

'Course there is,' Scuff replied, sniffing. 'An' lots o' folk gotta move their places. 'Ow'd yer like it if some bleedin' great machine came an' crashed yer 'ole street down wi'out a word, eh?'

Scuff was referring to the entire communities on the edge between honest poverty, close to destitution, and the semi-criminal underworld, who lived nearly all their lives in the sewers, tunnels, and excavations beneath London. To drive a new tunnel through the old was like putting a hot poker into a wasps' nest. That had been Orme's analogy.

'I know,' Monk replied. 'Mr Orme has already warned me. I'm not doing this alone, you know.' He looked from left to right through the thickening fog to see if he could see the lights of any kind of pedlars of food, or even a hot drink. The cold was like a tightening vice around them, crushing the heat out of their bodies. How did an urchin like Scuff — so thin he was merely skin and bone — survive? The baleful cry of the fog horns was growing more frequent on the water, and it was impossible to place the sound in the distortion of the mist.

''Ot chestnut seller that way,' Scuff said hopefully, sniffing again.

'Tonight?' Monk doubted it. It would be a bad night for barrows; no one would be able to see them in this.

'Charlie,' Scuff said, as if that were explanation enough.

'Do you think so?'

'Course.'

'I can't see anything. Which way?'

'Don' need ter. I know where 'e'll be. Yer like chestnuts?' There was a definite lift in Scuff's voice now.

'Hot, I'd eat anything. Yes, I do.'

Scuff hesitated, as if considering whether to strike a bargain, then his charity got the better of his business sense. Monk needed all the help he

could get. 'I'll take yer,' he offered magnani-
mously.

'Thank you,' Monk accepted. 'Perhaps you
would join me?'

'I don' mind if I do,' Scuff agreed.

3

The Portpool Lane clinic was a large establishment, not with the open wards that made nursing easy, but with lots of separate bedrooms. However, it had the greatest advantage any establishment could have that was devoted to the treatment of the penniless, and it was rent-free. It had once been a highly disreputable brothel run by one Squeaky Robinson, a man of many financial and organisational skills. He had in the past made one serious technical error, and it was that upon which Hester, with the help of Sir Oliver Rathbone, had capitalised. It was then that the brothel had been closed down, its extortion business ended and the building turned into a clinic for the treatment of any street woman who was either injured or ill.

Some of its former occupants had remained to work at the more tedious but far safer occupations of cleaning and laundering sheets. Squeaky Robinson himself lived on the premises, and under vociferous and constant complaint, kept the books and managed the continuing finances. He never allowed Hester to forget that he was there under duress and because he had been tricked, even though she was as aware as he that actually he had, against his better judgement, developed a fierce pride in the whole enterprise.

After the terrible period during which Claudine Burroughs had come and experienced such a change in her life, Margaret Ballinger had also finally accepted Oliver Rathbone's proposal of marriage. Both women were working at the clinic and fully intended to continue, leaving Hester with far less responsibility for its welfare, either in the raising of funds to pay for the food, fuel and medicines, or in the day-to-day chores.

The same bitter morning that Monk began investigating the death of James Havilland, Hester was checking the account books in the office at the clinic for the last time.

After the appalling weeks last autumn, when she had so nearly died, Monk had demanded that she gave up working here. She hated to lose it. It meant far more to her than simply a necessary refuge for street women who were ill or injured. It was more than a charitable work. It filled a need in her to heal, to do what she could to lessen some of the pain that she had seen and could never entirely forget.

But Monk had been so afraid for her that she had lost every argument with him about her remaining. She saw the fear in his face and felt it in his touch. She had no choice but to yield. She could not explain to him why looking after the house, cooking, cleaning and caring for him was not enough for her. She could make it fill her time, but not her need to struggle against difficulty, to reach out to people no one else cared for. She could work to exhaustion, sometimes succeed in healing, sometimes fail, but she was using every gift and strength she possessed. There was an ease of heart in that.

She could not say that to him. He would feel rejected, and she could not bear that. So she dragged out the last duties in the clinic, putting off the moment of having to leave.

She would greatly have preferred to perform this task in the familiar kitchen where the stove kept the whole room warm, and the lamps gave a pleasant yellow glow on old pans polished with use, and odd china of varying colours and designs. Strings of onions hung from the bare beams along with bunches of dried herbs, and at least one airing rack was festooned with laundered bandages ready for use on the next disaster.

But the ledgers, bills and receipts as well as the money itself were all in the office, so she sat at the table, feet cold and hands stiff, adding up figures and trying to make the results hopeful.

There was a brisk knock on the door and as soon as she answered it, Claudine came in. She was a tall woman, narrow-shouldered and broad at the hips. Her face had been handsome in her youth, but years of unhappiness had taken the bloom from her skin and marked her features with an expression of discontent. A couple of months of dedicated purpose, and the startling realisation that she was actually both useful and liked, had only just begun to change that. She still wore her oldest clothes, which were of good quality but out of fashion now. The newer ones were left at home to be worn on her increasingly rarer forays into Society. Her husband was annoyed and puzzled by her preference for 'good work' over the pursuit of pleasure, but she no longer believed he had earned the right to inflict further happiness upon her, and very seldom spoke of him. If she had any friends of her own aside from those at the clinic, she did not refer to them either, except in so far as they might be persuaded to donate to the cause.

'Good morning, Claudine,' Hester said, trying to sound cheerful. 'How are you?'

Claudine did not take pleasantries for granted. 'Good morning,' she replied, still not sure whether to address Hester by her Christian name or not. 'I'm very well, thank you. But I fear we can expect a good deal of bronchitis in this weather, and pneumonia as well. Got a stab wound in last night. Stupid girl hasn't got the wits she was born with, working out of a place like Fleet Row.'

'Can we save her?' Hester asked anxiously, unintentionally including herself in the cause.

'Oh, yes.' Claudine was somewhat smug about her newly acquired medical knowledge, even if it came from observation rather than experience. 'What I came about was new sheets. We can manage for a little longer, but you'll have to ask Margaret about more funds soon. We'll need at least a dozen, and that'll barely do.'

'Can it wait another few weeks?' Hester regarded the column of figures in front of her. She ought to tell Claudine that she was going, but she could not bring herself to do it yet.

'Three, perhaps,' Claudine replied. 'I can

bring a pair from home, but I don't have twelve.'

'Thank you.' Hester meant it. For Claudine to provide anything out of her own home for the use of street women was a seven-league step from the wounding distaste she had felt only three months earlier. The charity work she had been used to was of the discreet, untroublesome kind where ladies of like disposition organised fêtes and garden parties to raise money for respectable causes, such as fever hospitals, mission work and the deserving poor. Some profound disruption to her personal life had driven Claudine to this total departure. She had not confided in anybody what it had been, and Hester would never ask.

'Breakfast will be ready in half an hour,' Claudine responded. 'You should eat.' And without waiting for a reply, she went out, closing the door behind her.

Hester smiled and returned to her figures.

The next person to come in was Margaret Ballinger, her face pink from the cold, but with nothing of the hunched defence against the weather that one might expect. There was a confidence about her, an unconscious grace as of one who is inwardly happy, all external circumstances being merely peripheral.

'Breakfast's ready,' she said cheerfully. She knew Hester was going, but she refused to think of it. 'And Sutton's here to see you. He does look a little . . . concerned.'

Hester was surprised. Sutton was the rat-catcher who had helped them all last autumn, even at the risk of his life. Nothing she could do for him would be too much. He had only to ask. She stood up immediately. 'Is he all right?'

'He's not hurt . . . ' Margaret began.

'And Snoot?' Hester was referring to the rat-catcher's eager little terrier.

Margaret smiled. 'In excellent health,' she assured Hester. 'Whatever concerns Sutton, it is not Snoot.'

Hester felt immeasurably relieved. She knew how Sutton loved the animal. He was possibly all the family he had, certainly all he spoke of.

Downstairs in the kitchen there was porridge on the large, cast-iron stove, which was kept burning almost all the time, cleaned and blacked when anyone had an hour to spare. Two kettles were boiling and the door to the toasting fire was closed again after an entire loaf of bread sliced and browned on the fork was now sitting crisping in two wooden racks. There was butter, marmalade and blackcurrant jam on the table. They were obviously quite well in funds at the moment.

Sutton, a lean man not much more than Hester's height, sat on one of the few unsplintered kitchen chairs. He stood up the moment he saw her. The brown and white Jack Russell terrier at his feet wagged his tail furiously, but he was too tightly disciplined to dart forward.

Sutton's thin face lit up with pleasure, and what looked as if it might have been relief. 'Mornin', Miss 'Ester. 'Ow are yer?'

'I'm very well, Mr Sutton,' she replied. 'How are you? I'm sure you could manage some breakfast, couldn't you? I'm having some.'

'That'd be very civil of yer,' he accepted, watching, then sitting down as soon as she had.

Margaret had already eaten at home; she never ate their rations unless she was there for too long to abstain. She collected most of the clinic's funds through her social acquaintances, and she was far too sensitive to the difficulty of that to waste a farthing or consume herself what could be used for the sick. She would make an excellent mistress of the clinic in Hester's place.

Sutton had porridge and then toast and marmalade. Hester had just the toast, and blackcurrant jam. They were both on their second cup of tea when Claudine excused herself and they were left alone. Much against her own better judgement, Claudine had given Snoot porridge and milk as well, and he was now happily asleep in front of the hearth.

'She'll spoil 'im rotten, that woman,' Sutton said, as Claudine closed the door. 'Wot good'll 'e be fer rattin' if 'e's 'anded 'is breakfast on a plate?'

Hester did not bother to answer. It was part of the slow retreat by which Claudine was going to allow Sutton to understand that she granted him a reluctant respect. She was a lady, and he caught rats. She would not bring herself to treat him as an equal, which would have made both of them uncomfortable, but she would be more than civil to the dog. That was different, and they both understood it perfectly.

'What is it?' Hester asked, before they should

be interrupted again by some business of the day.

He did not prevaricate. They had come to know each other well during the crisis of the autumn. He looked at her earnestly, his brow furrowed. 'I dunno as there's anything yer can do, but I gotta try all I can. We all knows about the Great Stink an 'ow the river smells summink evil, an' they're doin' summink about it, at last. An' that's all as it should be.' He shook his head. 'But most folks 'oo live above ground in't got no idea wot goes on underneath.'

'No,' she agreed with only a faint gnawing of concern. 'Should we?'

'If yer gonna go diggin' around in it wi' picks and shovels an' great machines, then yeah, yer should.' There was a sudden passion in his voice, and a fear she had not heard before. He had been so strong in the autumn. This was something new, and over which he clearly felt he had no control.

'What sort of thing is there?' she asked. 'You mean graveyards, and plague pits, that sort of thing?'

'There are, but wot I were thinkin' of is rivers. There's springs and streams all over the place. London's mostly on clay, yer see.' His face was tense, eyes keen. 'I learned 'em from me pa. 'E were a tosher. One o' the best. Knew every river under the city from Battersea ter Greenwich, 'e did, an' most o' the wells too. Yer any idea 'ow many wells there is, Miss 'Ester?'

'There must be . . . ' she tried to think and

realised she had no idea, ' . . . hundreds, I suppose.'

'I don't mean where we get water up,' he explained. 'I mean them wot's closed over and goes away secret, like.'

'Are there?' She did not know why it troubled him, still less why he should have come to her about it.

He understood and grimaced at his own foolishness. 'Thing is, Miss 'Ester, there's 'undreds o' navvies workin' on all this diggin'. 'As bin for years, wot with one tunnel an' another for sewers, roads, trains an' the like. It's 'ard work an' it's dangerous, an' there's always bin accidents. Part o' life. But it's got worse since all this new diggin's bin goin' on, an' everyone's after a bit o' the profit. An' it's all in a terrible 'urry 'cos o' the typhoid, an' the Big Stink, an' all, an' Mr Bazalgette's new drawings — it's gettin' more dangerous. People are usin' bigger and bigger machines, an' goin' faster all the time 'cos o' the 'urry, an' they in't takin' the time ter learn proper where all them streams and springs is.' His face was tight with fear. 'Get it wrong an' clay slips somethin' 'orrible. We've 'ad one or two cave-ins, but I reckon as there'll be a lot more, an' worse, if folks don't take a bit more care, an' a bit more time.'

She looked at his drawn, tired face and knew that there was more behind his words than he was able to tell her.

'What is it you think I could do, Mr Sutton?' she asked. 'I don't know how to help injured workmen. I don't have the skill. And I certainly

86

don't have the ear of any person with the influence to make the construction companies take more care.'

His shoulders slumped a little, looking narrower under his plain, dark jacket. She judged him to be in his fifties, but hard work — much of it dangerous and unpleasant — plus many years of poverty may have taken more of a toll on his strength than she had allowed. He might be younger than that. She remembered how he had helped them all here, but most especially her, tenderly and fearlessly. 'What would you like me to do?' she asked.

He smiled, realising she had given in. She hoped profoundly that he did not know why.

'If anyone'd said ter me a year ago as a lady oo'd bin ter the Crimea would take ol' Squeaky Robinson's place an' turn it inter an 'ospital fer tarts off the street,' he answered, 'an' then get other ladies ter cook an' clean in it, I'd 'a throwed a bucket o' water at 'em till they sober'd up. But if anyone can do somethin' ter get them builders ter be'ave a bit safer, it's you.' He finished his tea and stood up. 'If you can come wi' me, I can show you the machines wot I'm talkin' about.'

She was startled.

'It'll be quite safe,' he assured her. 'We'll go ter one o' them that's open, but yer can think wot it'd be like underneath. Some tunnels is dug down then covered over. Cut-and-cover, they call 'em. But some is deep down, like a rat 'ole, under the ground all the way.' He shivered very slightly. 'It's them that scares me. The engineers might be clever with all kinds o' machines an'

87

ideas, but they don't know 'alf o' wot's down there, secret for 'undreds o' years, twistin' an' seepin'.'

Hester felt a chill at the thought, a coldness in the pit of her stomach. The daylight was coming in brighter now through the windows into the scullery. There was a sound of footsteps across the cobbled yard where deliveries were made, and where during the worst times last autumn the men had patrolled with dogs.

She stood up. 'How close will they let me come?'

'Borrer a shawl from one o' yer patients an' keep yer eyes down, an' yer can come right up close, wi' me.'

'I'll go and speak to Miss Ballinger.'

But it was Claudine she met just outside the kitchen door. She began to explain that she was going to be away for a few hours. The books would have to wait. She was happy enough to stretch out the task as long as she could.

'I heard,' Claudine said gravely, her face puckered into lines of concern. She was unaware of it, but her anger was so fierce that her sense of social class had temporarily ceased to register. 'It's monstrous. If people are being injured by hasty work, we must do what we can to fight it.' Unconsciously she had included herself in the battle. 'We can manage perfectly well here. There's nothing to do but the laundry and the cleaning, and if we can't manage that then we need to learn. Just be careful!' This last warning was given with a frown of admonition as if Claudine were somehow responsible for Hester's safety.

Hester smiled. 'I will,' she promised, aware that Claudine had become fonder of her than perhaps she herself knew. 'Sutton will look after me.'

Claudine grunted. She was not going to admit to trusting Sutton; that would be a step too far.

★ ★ ★

In spite of there being little wind, it was fiercely cold outside. The narrow streets seemed still to hold the ice of the night. Footsteps sounded loud on the stones and the brittle crack of puddles was sharp in the close air. This was the time of year when people who slept huddled in doorways could be found frozen to death at first light.

Hester walked beside Sutton, Snoot trotting at their heels, until they came to the Farringdon Road and the first omnibus stop. The horses were rough-coated for winter and steamed gently as they stood while passengers climbed off and on. Hester and Sutton went up the winding steps to the upper level, since they were going to the end of the line. Snoot sat on Sutton's knee, and she envied him the warmth of the little dog's body.

They talked most of the way because she asked him about the rivers under London. He was enthusiastic to tell her, his face lighting up as he described the hidden streams like Walbrook, Tyburn, Counter's Creek, Stamford Brook, Effra, and most of all the Fleet, whose waters once ran red from the tanneries. He talked of springs such as St Chad's, St Agnes', St

Bride's and St Pancras Wells, and Holywell. All had been reputed as sacred at one time or another, and some became spas, like Hampstead Wells and Sadler's Wells. He knew the underground courses and bridges, some of which were believed to date back to Roman times.

'Walbrook's as far up as yer could get a boat when the Romans was 'ere,' he said with triumph.

He was so busy telling her tales of earlier travels, including the danger of highwaymen, such as the infamous Dick Turpin, that they nearly missed their stop.

They alighted into a busy street, workmen crowding around a pedlar selling sandwiches and hot pies. They were obliged to slip out over the gutter on to the cobbles to pass them, and were nearly run down by a cartload of vegetables pulled by a horse whose breath was steam in the air.

At the corner half a dozen men huddled around a brazier, talking and laughing, tin mugs of tea in their hands.

'Not sure as I like so much change,' Sutton said dubiously. 'Still, can't be 'elped.'

Hester did not argue. They had only a few yards further to go before she saw the vast crater of the new tunnel. It would carry not only the sewer, but beside it the gas pipes for the houses that had such luxuries. Skeletons of woodwork for cranes and derricks poked above it like fingers at the sky. There was a faint noise from far within of grinding and crushing, scraping, slithering and the occasional shouts and the rattle of wheels.

Hester stood on the freezing earth and felt the freshening wind from the tide on the river, with its smell of salt and sewage. She turned to her left and saw the roofs of houses in the near distance, and closer, the broken walls where they had been flattened to make way for the new works. To the right it was the same: streets cut in half as if they had been chopped by a giant axe. She looked at Sutton and saw the pity in his face, and the fury he was trying to suppress. To build the new they had broken so much of the old.

'Keep close and don't meet no one's eyes,' he said quietly. 'We'll just walk through, like we got business. There's them as knows me.' And he led the way, making a path through the rubble and keeping wide of the groups of men. Every now and again he put out his hand to steady her, and she was grateful for it because the rubble was crumbling and icy. Snoot trotted along at their heels.

There was a thick fence around the actual pit in which the men worked, possibly to keep out the idle and to prevent the careless from falling in.

'Got ter go round the end there.' Sutton pointed and then led her through a shifting, slithering wasteland of debris. The line of pipes was easy enough to trace with the eye by the wreckage that lay in its path. Twice they were stopped and questioned as to who they were, and if they had any business there, but Sutton answered for them both.

Hester kept silent and followed him patiently. At last — her feet sore and her boots and skirt splattered — she reached the point below which the men were actually working by flares at the face of the tunnel. The earth was excavated deeper than she had expected. She was close to the edge of the drop and a feeling of vertigo overcame her for a moment as she stared down almost a hundred feet to the brickworks at the bottom of the abyss. She could quite clearly see the floor of what would be the new sewer, and the arching brick sides already laid and cemented. There was scaffolding over it, holding the walls apart all the way up. Here and there other pipes crossed it. Fifty yards away, well on the other side, a steam engine hissed and thumped, driving the chains that held heavy buckets and scoops to draw up and empty the waste rubble and broken brick.

She turned and met Sutton's eyes. He pointed down to where she could see men below, foreshortened to funny little movements of hands and shoulders. They walked, pushing barrows. Others swung pikes or heaved on shovels of soil and rock.

'Look.' Sutton directed her eyes towards the walls on the far side. The earth itself was held firm by planks of heavy wood and there were crossbeams every few yards both the height and the length of the entire work that she could see. Then she followed Sutton's gaze and saw the water seeping through, just a dribble here and there, a bulge in the wood where the boards had been strained, and were coming away.

On the bank opposite stokers were keeping the great steam engine going. She could hear the wheeze and thump of its pistons and smell the steam, the oil.

She was aware of Sutton watching her. She tried to imagine what it would be like to work down that cleft in the earth, seeing nothing but a slit of sky above you, and knowing you couldn't get out.

'Where's the way up?' she asked almost involuntarily.

''Alf a mile away,' he answered quietly. 'All right ter walk ter, if yer in no 'urry. Nasty if yer need ter move quickish — like if them sides springs a leak.'

'A leak? You mean a stream . . . or something? You don't mean just rain?' The picture of that bulging wall giving way filled her mind — a jet of water gushing out, not just dribbling as it was now. Would it fill the bottom? Enough to drown them? Of course it would! Who could swim in a crevasse like that, with freezing water coming down on top of you?

'That's a sewer,' Sutton said quietly, standing close to her. 'The sewers o' London takes everything, all the waste from all the 'ouses an' middens in the 'ole city, and from the sinks an' gutters and overflows everyw'ere. If yer a tosher or a ganger, yer know the tides an' all the rivers an' springs, and keep an eye ter the rain, 'cos if yer don't, yer'll not last long. An' o' course there's the rats. Never go underground alone.

93

Slip and fall, an' the rats'll 'ave yer. Strip a man ter the bone if yer unlucky an' fetch up where they can reach yer. 'Undreds o' thousands o' them down there, there are.'

Snoot had pricked up his ears at the word 'rats'. Hester said nothing.

'An' there's the gas,' Sutton added.

'Is that what that pipe is?' she asked, gesturing to the one that crossed the deep gash in the earth about fifteen feet down, going diagonally on a quite different track from the cutting.

Sutton smiled. 'No, Miss 'Ester, that's gas fer lights an' things in there. I'm talking about the sort o' gas that collects up under the ground 'cos o' wot sewers is for carryin'. Gives off methane, it does, an' if the air or water don't carry it away it's enough ter suffocate a man. Or if some fool lights a spark, with a tinder or a steel boot on stone, then whoomph!' He jerked his hands apart violently, fingers spread to indicate an explosion. 'Or there's the choke-damp wot yer gets in coal mines an' the like. That'll kill yer too.'

Again she said nothing, trying to imagine what it would be like to have no skill except one that obliged you to labour in such conditions. And yet she had known navvies before, in the Crimea, and a braver, harder-working group of men she had never seen. They had built a railway for the soldiers across wild, almost uncharted terrain, in the depth of winter, in a time most others had considered totally outside any possibility. And an excellent railway it was too. But that had been above ground.

The great steam engine was still pounding away, shaking the earth with its strength, hauling as men and beasts never could. Foot by foot the sewers were formed that would make London clean, safe from the epidemics of typhoid and cholera that had carried away so many in appalling deaths.

'It's that damn great thing wot worries me,' Sutton said, staring at the steam engine. 'There's other ones like that, even bigger, wot I can't show yer, 'cos o' where they are. Everyone's in an 'urry an' they in't taking care like they should. A wheel gets away from yer, chain breaks loose on one o' them things, an' before yer knows it, a man's arm's ripped out, or a beam o' wood's broke wot's 'oldin' up 'alf the roof o' somethin'.'

'They're in a hurry because of the threat of typhoid and cholera such as we had in the Great Stink,' she said quietly.

'I know. But 'cos they're tryin' ter beat each other an' get the next order too,' he added. 'An' no one says nothin' 'cos they don't want ter lose their jobs, or 'ave other folks think they're scared.'

'And are they scared?'

'Course they are.' He looked at her ruefully. 'Yer must be froze. I'll take yer to see someone not a mile from 'ere oo'll give us a decent cup o' tea. Come on.' And without waiting for her to accept, or possibly not, he turned and began walking back from the crevasse the way they had come through the rubble and piles of timber, much of it rotted. As always the little dog was beside him, jumping over the stones, his tail wagging.

Hester followed after the rat-catcher, having to hurry to catch up. She did not resent his pace; she knew it came from the emotion driving him, the fear that a tragedy might occur before he could do anything to stop even the smallest part of it.

They did not talk in the half-hour it took them to weave their way through the narrow streets and alleys, but it was a companionable silence. He was very careful to keep step with her and now and then to warn her of a particularly rough or slippery stretch of road, or of the steepness of the step up to an occasional pavement.

She wondered if this was where he had grown up. During the brief space they had known each other, there had been no time to speak of such things, even had either of them wished to. Before today she had not known that his father was a tosher. But hunting the sewers for accidentally flushed treasures and keeping down the worst of the vast rat population that emerged from that underworld were closely allied trades, though rat-catching was the superior. The tosher would have been proud of his son. He should have been even prouder of his courage and humanity.

The streets were busy. A coal cart trundled over the cobbles. A costermonger was selling fruit and vegetables on the corner where they crossed. A pedlar of buttons brought to Hester's mind the need to replenish her sewing basket, but not now. She hurried to keep up with Sutton's swift pace. Women passed them carrying pails of water, bundles of clothes or groceries. They skirted around half a dozen children playing games — tossing knucklebones or skipping a rope. For an instant she ached to be able to do something for them — food, boots, anything. She dismissed it from her mind with force. Cats and dogs and even a couple of pigs foraged around hopefully. It was still appallingly cold.

The door where Sutton finally stopped was narrow with peeling paint and no windows or letter box. In some places that would indicate that it was a façade placed to hide the fact that there was a railway behind it rather than a house, but here it was that no letters were expected. None of the other doors had knockers either.

Sutton banged with the flat of his hand and stood back.

A few minutes later the door was opened by a girl of about ten. Her hair was tied with a bright length of cloth and her face was clean, but she had no shoes on. Her dress was obviously cut down from a longer one, and left with room to fit her at least another couple of years.

''Allo, Essie. Yer mam in?' Sutton asked.

She smiled at him shyly and nodded, turning to lead the way to the kitchen.

Hester and Sutton followed, driven as much by the promise of warmth as anything else.

Essie led them along a narrow passage, which was cold and smelled of damp and old cooking, and into the one room in the house that had heat. It was just a small black stove with a hob large enough for one cauldron and a kettle. Her mother, a raw-boned woman who must have been about forty, but looked far older, was scraping the eyes and the dirt from a pile of potatoes. There were onions beside her, still to be prepared.

In the corner of the room nearest the stove sat a large man with an old coat on his knees. The way the folds of it fell, it was apparent that most of his right leg was missing. Hester was startled to see from his face that he was probably no more than forty either, if that.

Sutton ordered Snoot to sit, then he turned to the woman.

'Mrs Collard,' he said warmly, 'this is Mrs Monk, 'oo nursed some of the men in the Crimea, an' keeps a clinic for the poor in Portpool Lane.' He did not add specifically what kind of 'poor'. 'And this is Andrew Collard.' He turned to the man. ''E used ter work in the tunnels.'

'How do you do, Mrs Collard, Mr Collard?' Hester said formally. She had long ago decided to speak to all people in the same way rather than distinguish between one social class and another by adopting what she felt would be their own pattern of introduction. There was no need to wonder why Andrew Collard did not work in the tunnels any more.

Collard nodded, answering with words almost indistinguishable. He was embarrassed — that was easy to see — and perhaps ashamed because he could not stand to welcome a lady into his own home, meagre as it was.

Hester had no idea how to make him at ease.

She ought to have been able to call on her experience with injured and mutilated soldiers. She had seen enough of them, and enough of those wasted by disease, racked with fever or unable even to control their body's functions. But this was different. She was not a nurse here, and these people had no idea why she had come. For an instant she was furious with Sutton for the imposition upon them, and upon her. She did not dare meet his eyes, or he would see it in her. She might then even lash out at him in words, and be bitterly sorry afterwards. She owed him more than that, whatever she felt.

As if aware of the rage and misery in the silence, Sutton spoke. 'We just bin and looked at the diggin',' he said to Andrew Collard. 'Freezin' at the moment, and not much rain, but it's drippin' quite a bit, all the same. 'Ow long d'yer reckon it'll take some o' that wood ter rot?'

Mrs Collard glanced from one to the other of them, then told Essie to go outside and play.

'They're movin' too fast for it ter matter,' Collard answered. 'In't the wood rottin' as is the trouble, it's them bleedin' great machines shakin' everythin' ter bits. Does it even more if they in't tied down like they should be. Only Gawd 'Isself knows what's shiftin' around underneath them bleedin' great things.'

'Tied down?' Hester asked quickly. 'Aren't they dug somehow to the earth?'

'Staked,' he said. 'But they shake loose if yer don't do 'em real 'ard an' careful, miss. Them machines is stronger than all the 'orses yer ever seen. Stakes look tight ter begin wi', but arter an

99

hour or two they in't. Yer need ter move the 'ole engine a dozen yards or so ter fresh ground an' start over. But that takes time. Means that — '

'I understand,' she said quickly. 'They're losing loads going up and down when they take up the bolts and move the machine, then stake it and start it up again. And the more firmly they bolt it, the longer it takes to move it.'

'Yeah, that's right.' Collard looked slightly taken aback that she had grasped the point so quickly.

'Don't all companies work the same way?' she asked.

'Most,' he agreed. 'Some's more careful, some's less. Couldn't all get engines the same. But more'n that, the earth in't the same from one place ter 'nother. If yer ever dug it yerself you know Chelsea in't the same as Lambeth, an' Rother'ithe in't the same as the Isle o' Dogs.' He was looking at her now, his eyes narrow and tired with pain. 'There's all sorts: clay, rock, shale, sand. An' o' course there's rivers an' springs, but Sutton knows that. More'n them, there's old workings o' all sorts: drains, gutters, cellars, tunnels and plague pits. Goes back ter Roman times, some of 'em. Yer can't do it quick.' He stared into the middle distance. Hester could only imagine what it was like for him sitting helpless in a chair while the world narrowed and closed in on him. He saw disaster ahead and was unable to do anything to prevent it. He was telling her because she had asked, and she had come with Sutton, but he did not believe she cared, or could help either.

His wife lost patience. 'Why don't yer tell 'em straight?' she demanded, ignoring the boiling kettle except for a swift moment to remove it from the heat. If she had intended to make tea it was forgotten now. 'Were a cave-in wot took my 'usband's leg,' she said to Hester. 'One o' them big beams fell on 'im. Only way ter get 'im out before the 'ole lot caved in were ter take 'is leg orff. If they go on usin' them great machines shakin' everything ter bits up on top like that, sooner or later the sides is gonna cave in on top o' the men wot's diggin' an' 'aulin' down the bottom. Or when we get rains like we 'ave in Feb'uary, one o' them sewers bursts, an' 'oo's gonna get the men out before it floods, eh?' she demanded, her voice high and harsh. 'I know a score o' women like me, oo's husbands 'a' lorst arms an' legs ter them bleedin' tunnels. An' widders as well. Too many o' them damn railways is built on blood and bones!'

'There've always been accidents,' Hester said reluctantly. 'Is any contractor especially bad?'

Collard shook his head angrily, his face dark. 'Not as I know. Course there's accidents, no one's gurnin' about that! Yer do 'ard work, yer take 'ard chances. The wife's just belly-achin' 'cos it in't easy fer 'er. In't no better bein' a coal miner or seaman, or lots of other things.' He smiled mirthlessly. 'Don't s'pose it's always rum and cakes bein' a soldier, is it?' He waited for her answer.

'No,' she agreed. 'What is it then that you are concerned about?'

The smile vanished.

101

'I'm more'n concerned, miss, I'm downright scared. They got 'ole lengths o' new sewer built, an' o' course there's still most o' the old bein' used. Get a couple o' slides, mud, cave-ins, an' yer got men cut orff down there. If yer don' get drownded, it could be worse — burned.'

'Burned?'

'Gas. There's 'ouse'old gas pipes in them sewers as well. Get a shift in the clay an' one o' them cracks, an' first spark you'll 'ave not only the gas from the sewage, but back up inter every 'ouse as 'as gaslight. See wot I mean?'

'Yes.' Hester saw only too well. It could be a second Great Fire of London, if he was right. 'Surely they've thought of that too?' They had to have. No one was irresponsible enough not to foresee such a catastrophe. A few navvies drowned or suffocated she could believe. There had been a cave-in when the crown of the arch of the Fleet Sewer had broken. The scaffolding beams had been flung like matchwood into the air, falling, crashing as the whole structure subsided and the bottom of the excavation moved like a river, rolling and crushing and burying.

Sutton was watching her too. 'Yer 'memberin' the Fleet?' he asked.

She was startled. Of course he had told her about the Fleet River running under London in the tales his father had told him. Now she knew why. He had described the whole network of shifting, sliding, seeping, running waters.

'Doesn't everybody know this?' she said incredulously. 'It's — '

It was Lu Collard who answered. 'Course they do, miss. But 'oo's gonna say it, eh? Lose yer job? Then 'oo feeds yer kids?'

Collard shifted uncomfortably in his imprisoning chair. His face was more wasted with pain than Hester had appreciated before. He was probably in his mid-thirties. He had been a good-looking man when he was whole.

'Aw, Andy, she can see it!' his wife said wearily. 'In't no use pretending! That's wot them bastards count on! Everyone so buttoned up wi' pride nob'dy's gonna say they're scared o' bein' the next one 'urt — '

'Be quiet, woman!' Collard snapped. 'Yer don't know nothin'. Their men in't — '

'Course they is!' she turned on him. 'They in't stupid! They know it's gonna 'appen one day, an' Gawd knows 'ow many'll get killed. They don't say nothin' 'cos they'd sooner get crushed or drownded termorrer than starve terday! An' let their kids starve. Shut yer eyes, an' wot yer don't see don't 'urt yer!'

'Yer gotta live!' he said, looking away from her.

Sutton was watching Hester, his thin face anxious.

'Of course you have,' Hester answered. 'And the new sewers have got to be built. We can't allow the Great Stink to happen again, or have typhoid and cholera in the streets as we had before. But no one wants another disaster like the Fleet Sewer, only worse. There's too much money involved for anyone to do it willingly. There needs to be a law involved, one that can be enforced.'

103

'They won't never do that,' Collard said bitterly. 'Only men wot's got money can vote, and Parliament makes the laws.'

Hester looked at him gently. 'Sewers run under the houses of men with money more than they do under yours or mine. I think we might find a way of reminding them of that,' she answered. 'At least we can try.'

Collard sat perfectly still, then very slowly he turned to look at Sutton, to try to read in his face if Hester could possibly mean what she said.

'Exactly,' Sutton said very clearly, then turned to Mrs Collard. ''Ow about a cup o' tea, then, Lu? It's colder'n a witch's . . . ' he stopped, suddenly remembering Hester's presence, ' . . . 'eart,' he finished.

Collard hid a smile.

Lu glared at him, then smiled suddenly at Hester, showing surprisingly good teeth. 'Yeah. O' course,' she replied.

★   ★   ★

That evening Hester spent a couple of hours cleaning and tidying up after the plasterer, who was now finished. Not only were the walls perfectly smooth ready for papering, there was also elegant moulding all around the edge of the wall and ceiling and a beautiful rose for the pendant lamp. But all the time her hands were busy with brooms, dustpans, scrubbing brushes and cloths, she was thinking about her promise to Andy Collard, and more importantly to Sutton. As Collard had observed, Parliament made the laws. That was the only place worth beginning. She must find out who was the Member most appropriate to approach.

When Monk came home she proudly showed him how the house decorating was going, and asked after the success of his day. She said nothing about Sutton, or her interest in the building of the new sewers. It was not difficult to conceal it, nor did she feel deceitful. She was deeply concerned over the apparent suicide of the young woman Mary Havilland who had so recently lost her father in a way Hester could understand far more than she cared to remember. She had thought her own loss had been dealt with in her mind and the wound of it healed over. Now it was like a bone broken long ago, but that aches again with the cold weather, a pain deep inside, wakening unexpectedly, too covered over with scars to reach again, and yet sometimes hurting as sharply as when it had been new.

She wanted to hide it from Monk. She could see in the shadow in his eyes, the line of his lips, that he was aware of the memory in her, and that he was pursuing the Havilland case at least in part because in Mary he thought of Hester. Inside he was reacting to the old injustice as well as the new.

She wanted to smile at him and tell him that it did not hurt any more. But she would not lie to him. And it was going to hurt more in the loneliness of the house with only chores to keep her busy, no challenge, nothing to fight. She reached out to touch him, to be close to him and say nothing. Words were unnecessary. Sometimes explanations intruded into understanding that was better in silence.

★   ★   ★

In the morning Hester visited a gentleman she had once nursed through a serious illness. She was delighted to see that he was in much improved health, although he tired more quickly than earlier. She had gone principally for the purpose of learning from him which Member of Parliament to seek regarding the method and regulations of the new construction of sewers.

She came away with the conviction that it was unquestionably Morgan Applegate. She even obtained a warm letter of introduction so that she might call upon him immediately.

Since she was already dressed in the best clothes she had, and incidentally the warmest, she bought herself a little luncheon from a street pedlar — something she had become used to lately. By early afternoon she was at the front door of the home of Morgan Applegate, MP.

The door was opened by a short, extremely plump butler who took her letter of introduction. He showed her into a very fine morning room with a roaring fire, which gleamed red and gold on the polished furniture, and in the copper globes that decorated the very handsome fender.

It was a full quarter-hour before Morgan Applegate himself appeared. He was a most agreeable-looking man of average height and aquiline face, which yet managed to look mild, in spite of a very obvious intelligence. His fairish hair was receding and he was clean-shaven.

He greeted Hester courteously, invited her to sit, then asked what he might do to be of assistance to her.

She told him of her visit to the excavations the previous day, without mentioning Sutton's name or occupation.

He stopped her in mid-sentence. 'I am aware of this problem, Mrs Monk.'

Her heart sank. Perhaps she had been naïve, expecting him to take issue in what was a highly emotive subject. The fear of typhoid was everywhere, and the Queen was in the grip of a desperate, almost uncontrollable grief since Prince Albert's death from the disease. If Applegate were a man of any ambition he would not risk his career by stating an opinion that must be bound to anger and offend many.

'Mr Applegate,' Hester said earnestly, 'I do understand the very immediate need for new and adequate sewers. I nursed men dying of typhoid in the Crimea, and it is something I could never forget, or take lightly. But if you had seen the dangers — '

'Mrs Monk,' he interrupted her again, leaning forward a little in the chair he had taken opposite her, 'I am aware of the matter because it was drawn to my attention by someone else, even more disturbed by the possibility of disaster than you are. She gave her whole time and attention to it, and I fear perhaps even her sanity.' His face was very grave and there was an acute consciousness of pain in his eyes. 'My wife was very fond of her, and I held her in high regard myself.'

'Held?' Hester said with a chill. 'What happened to her?'

Now there was no mistaking his distress. 'Of that I am not certain. I was informed only of the merest details, and since they are unclear, I prefer not to repeat them. It is no slight upon you, Mrs Monk, it is a respect for the dead. She was a young woman of great courage, a kind of high daring. In spite of personal loss and forfeit of much chance of happiness, she placed honour first, and it seems to have exacted from her a terrible price. Please do not press me to say more.'

But it was impossible for Hester to leave it. She was the equal of anyone on earth for compassion, and had the fire and courage to make it of practical use, but she had never excelled in tact. She was too fierce and too impatient. 'If she placed honour first then all the more important, and urgent, that we should follow her!' she said intently. 'How can you wish to say nothing of her? Are you not proud of her? Do we not all owe her something?'

Now he seemed embarrassed, and very clearly uncertain how to answer. 'Mrs Monk, there are some tragedies that . . . that should remain . . . unexplained. I can think of no better word. Please . . . '

She saw the great crevasse in the ground in her mind's eye again, and her stomach turned at the thought of its collapse. She imagined how it would be for the men at the bottom, possibly even seeing it begin to bulge and give way, knowing what would happen and unable to do anything but watch. They would see the water explode through, carrying earth and timber with it to crash down on top of them, bruising, breaking, burying in the filth and darkness. She could not keep silent.

'Mr Applegate, there is no time for the niceties of feeling! If she saw what I did today and understood what could happen to these men — almost certainly will do one day, sooner or later — would this woman really wish you to respect her delicacy now she is dead? Think of their lives, who still have a chance if we act, if we achieve what she began? Is not the greatest compliment, the greatest service to her, that we take up her cause?'

He was looking at her with profound indecision in his eyes. He was a kind man, torn by conflicting principles of overwhelming power.

Hester realised she was leaning forward as if physically to touch him. Reluctantly she sat back, not in apology, but because it might be a bad strategy, and certainly bad manners.

Without explanation Applegate stood up. 'Excuse me,' he said huskily, and he left the room.

Hester was crushed. She had liked the man instinctively, and it seemed she had driven him to the point where he had found her so oppressive he had actually retreated from her presence, as if not knowing how else to deal with her. Was she really so insensitive? Was she dragging out the memory of a woman he had perhaps loved, and treating it with unbearable disrespect? How ugly! And how stupid.

She did not know what to do next.

Then the door opened and a woman came in. She was tall, perhaps even an inch or so taller than Hester, and equally slender. She had a most unusual face. It was handsome in its own way, but far more than for the beauty, it was remarkable for the humour in it, a great readiness for the enjoyment of life. She was dressed in warm, grey-brown wool made fashionable by touches of black, and flattering by white at the neck.

She was immediately followed by Applegate himself, who introduced her to Hester as his wife, Rose, then by way of explanation, added, 'We were both fond of Mary, but my wife the more so. Before I break confidence I felt I should consult her opinion.'

'How do you do, Mrs Monk?' Rose Applegate said warmly. 'Nice of you to consult me,' she glanced at her husband, 'but quite unnecessary.' She invited Hester to resume her seat, since she had naturally stood up when Mrs Applegate came in. Rose sat opposite, leaving her husband to sit where he would. 'Mary died a couple of days ago, and we are all very distressed about it, and angry. I don't believe for an instant her death was as simple as they say. She wouldn't do it, she just wouldn't.'

'My dear . . . ' Applegate began.

She did not exactly say 'hush' to him, but almost. It was apparent that he was devoted to her and she was sufficiently confident in that not to defer to him when she felt passionately.

Suddenly Hester had a flash of understanding. 'Mary Havilland!' she said quickly. 'Are you speaking of Mary Havilland?' It would make perfect sense with the little Monk had told her of the death on the river.

Morgan Applegate and Rose looked at each other, then at Hester. Rose was now pale, her hazel eyes troubled. 'The news has spread so widely already?' she asked softly.

Applegate reached over to put his hand on her arm. It was an extraordinarily protective gesture, as gentle as if he touched some wound.

'No,' Hester answered, lowering her own voice, aware now that she was dealing with real and present pain. 'I know of it only because my husband is in the River Police and was the one who actually saw it happen.'

Rose gave an involuntary gasp and Applegate's hand tightened slightly on her arm. Hester could see in their eyes that they wanted to ask more, and dared not, afraid of the finality of the answer.

'He isn't sure what happened,' Hester told them. 'It wasn't possible to see from that distance, and, of course, they were looking upward.'

She knew why Monk was so reluctant to believe it, but she could not tell these people of her own loss. She had thought the pain of it was all healed over, safe, as long as it was not touched. She had not tried to remember her father's face for a long time, perhaps not since she had learned to believe that Monk loved her enough to let go of his fears of the teeming unknowns within himself and acknowledge it, take the risks. There was no such thing as safety, except in caring about nothing enough for it to give you pain — or joy. But now sudden memories came back, a word, a tone of voice, a gesture, and she was in the past when her father was alive. It had been before the Crimean War, the bereavement of so many with its violence abroad and its duplicity at home, and afterwards, the makers and manipulators of loss.

'He is trying to find out,' she added. 'In case it wasn't as simple as that.'

Rose blinked. 'You mean . . . it might not be taken as suicide?' There was a flare of hope in her eyes. 'She would never have killed herself! I'd stake anything on that!'

'Rose . . . ' Applegate began.

She shook him off impatiently without taking her eyes from Hester's. 'If you had known Mary I wouldn't have to tell you that. She had far too much courage to give up. She simply wouldn't! She was too . . . too angry to let them get away with it!'

Hester saw Applegate wince, but was beginning to appreciate already that he had no control over his wife's enthusiasm, and almost certainly no desire to have. If she were outspoken, that was part of her nature, and of what he loved in her.

'Angry with whom?' Hester asked. 'Circumstances or people? The Big Stink was appalling. We can't allow it to happen again. And the typhoid was even worse. Some of the soldiers died of typhoid in the Crimea. I wouldn't wish it on Satan himself.'

'Oh, I know we must build the new sewers,' Rose agreed. 'But Mary was sure that some of the machines were being used without regard to safety. People are so determined to be faster than their competitors that they are ignoring the rules, and sooner or later the men are going to pay the price. You know about the collapse of the Fleet Sewer? Of course you do. It was in all the newspapers. That will be nothing to what could happen if — '

'Rose, you don't know that!' Applegate interrupted her at last. 'Mary believed it, and she may have been right, but she — '

'She's still right!' Rose corrected him.

'But she had no proof!' he finished.

'Exactly!' Rose said as if that sealed her point. She stared at Hester. 'She knew there was proof and she intended to get it. She was certain she could. Does that sound to you like someone who would take their own life?' Unconsciously she leaned forward towards Hester, just as Hester had done towards Applegate, impelled by her fervour. 'She loved her father, Mrs Monk. They understood each other in a way few people do who are of different generations. She had a strong, clear mind and immense courage. I don't know why people think women can't be like that! It's our skirts that stop us from running, not our legs!'

'Rose!' Applegate expostulated.

'You are not shocked, are you?' Rose asked

113

Hester with a flicker of anxiety.

Hester wanted to laugh, but it might hurt their feelings, as if she did not take death seriously. She did! Infinitely seriously. But she knew that in the drowning, suffocating horror of war or epidemic disease that laughter, however black, was sometimes the only thing that held on to sanity and survival. But one could not say so in a London house where one was a guest.

'No, no,' she assured Rose. 'In fact I would like to remember it to say again. There will be countless times when it will be appropriate. Would you like attribution, or prefer I forgot who said it first?'

Rose blinked, but it was with pleasure as well as self-consciousness. 'I think it might be better for my husband's position if you forgot,' she replied reluctantly. 'The House of Commons is extremely robust in its opinions, but then there are no ladies speaking, and that makes all the difference.' Her mouth pulled in an expression of wry distaste.

Hester understood. She had been freer to say what she thought on the fringes of the battlefield, and had found the return to England painfully restrictive. She went back again to the subject of Mary Havilland.

'Did you know her family?' she asked.

Rose shrugged. 'Slightly. I liked Mary very much, and it was difficult to do that and be more than civil to the rest of them.'

'They were at odds?'

'Oh, yes. You see Jenny — that is her elder sister, Jenny Argyll — is completely devoted to her husband and children, as she has to be.' An expression crossed her face that was a mixture of irritation and surrender.

'Has to be?' Hester asked quickly.

'What choice has she?' Rose said reasonably. Her smile was suddenly very sweet. 'I have no children to depend upon me, and a husband whom I would trust to the ends of the earth. But few women are as fortunate as I am, and Jenny Argyll is certainly not among them.' She shrugged again. 'I believe Alan Argyll is reasonable enough, but if he has faults, she may naturally prefer not to be more aware of them than she is obliged to be. She will not appreciate her sister finding them for her, since she cannot afford to address them! When you are helpless, ignorance is a great comfort.'

'And Mary . . . did that?' Hester asked. 'Either they were very grave indeed, or she was very insensitive.' A darker picture was forming at the back of her mind.

'I don't know,' Rose admitted. 'Of course when we love someone we can be so afraid for them we don't always exercise the best sense when warning them of what we perceive to be a danger. But I know nothing of that. I do know that Mary broke off her own betrothal to Toby Argyll, Alan's younger brother. She was candid about it to me.'

'Candid?' Hester pressed, uncertain what Rose meant. 'You mean she told you why she broke it off?' She imagined a young woman of passionate ideals in love, and then discovering something that disillusioned her beyond bearing. The grief

115

must have been terrible. Could it really have been more than she could live with?

'Was it something she learned of him?' she asked. She would rather not have known, but it could not be avoided now. 'Was that what — '

'Oh, no!' Rose said quickly. 'You mean did she learn that Toby had some part in her father's death? And she couldn't bear it? Is that what you are thinking?'

'Yes,' Hester admitted. 'It might be enough to break one's spirit, even someone very strong.'

'Not Mary.' Rose had no doubt in her voice at all. She was sitting upright in the chair now, back straight. 'She wasn't in love with Toby, not really in love, not enough for her world to be plunged in darkness without him! She liked him well enough. She thought his was probably the best offer as she would get. After all, how many of us really fall headlong in love with someone we can marry?' She smiled as she said it, her hands were utterly relaxed in her lap and Hester knew that she was not including herself when she spoke. 'Most women make an acceptable bargain,' Rose continued, 'and Mary was realist enough to do that. But believe me, she was not plunged into despair to break it.' She lowered her voice confidentially. 'In fact I think that part of it was no small relief to her. She could refuse him with an easy conscience. No one would expect her to marry so soon after her father's death, poor soul.'

'My dear, you should not repeat that,' Applegate warned.

'I shan't,' she promised, disregarding the fact

116

that she just had. In her mind, telling Hester was a matter of honour, a debt to Mary she had no intention of neglecting. 'She did not take her own life, Mrs Monk. If you knew how passionately she believed that her father had not done so either, that he never would because it was not only a sin against the Church, but to him, far worse than that, it was a sin against himself. It was cowardice, a betrayal of his own integrity and his duty to honour. And if it was true for him, then it must be true for her. I don't know what happened, but I will do anything and everything I can to help you to find out. Any information I can find, any door I can open, you have but to tell me. Perhaps we can still effect the reform she was working on, and save at least some of the lives of men who would be killed if there were further accidents in the construction.'

'Thank you,' Hester accepted warmly. 'I will call on you the moment I have a clearer idea of what to do.' She turned to Applegate. 'What information was Mary Havilland going to bring you? What do you need to know before you can act?'

'Proof that the safety rules are not being kept,' he replied. 'And I am afraid that will be very hard to find. Engineers will say that they have surveyed the ground, and the old rivers and streams as well as is possible. Men who work with the machines are used to danger and know that a degree of it is part of life. Just as men who go to sea, or down the mines live with danger and loss, without complaining, so do navvies. They would consider it cowardly to

117

refuse or to show self-pity, and would despise any man who did. And more than that, they know they would lose their jobs, because for every man who says he will not, there are a dozen others to take his place. His family will starve, and he knows that, and so do they.'

'And lose arms or legs, or be crushed to death?' Rose demanded. 'Surely . . . ' she stopped, looking to Hester for support.

Hester remained silent. What Applegate said was true. There were tens of thousands like Andy Collard: proud, angry, stubborn, desperate. He was one of the ones who was already hurt, that's all.

She stood up. 'Thank you, Mr Applegate. I will do all I can to find the proof Mary Havilland was looking for. As soon as I have something I shall return.'

'Or if we can help,' Rose added. 'Thank you for coming, Mrs Monk.'

*   *   *

'No!' Monk said firmly when Hester told him that evening. 'I'll pursue it until I find what happened to both Mary Havilland and her father.'

'There's going to be a disaster if nothing is done, William,' she argued urgently. 'Do you expect me to sit by and let that happen?' She made no reference to giving up Portpool Lane, but it hung unsaid between them.

They were standing in the kitchen, the dishes cleared away and the kettle pouring steam into the air as she intended to make the tea, and had allowed her enthusiasm to distract her.

'Hester, Mary Havilland may have been murdered to prevent her doing precisely that!' he said angrily. 'For the love of heaven, isn't that what you've just been telling me?'

'Of course I can see it!' she retorted. 'Are you going to stop your investigation?'

'Am I . . . ? No, of course not! What's that got to do with it? Take that damn kettle off before it explodes! Or a disaster in the sewers won't be the only accident to happen.'

She yanked the kettle off the hob and then ignored it. 'It has everything to do with it!' She raised her voice to equal his. 'You can risk your life every day, but when I want to do something I believe in, suddenly I'm not allowed to, if you have decided it might be dangerous? I'm only going to ask questions!'

'That is completely different. You are a woman. I know how to protect myself,' he said, as if it were a fact beyond dispute. 'You don't.'

She drew in a deep breath. 'You pomp-ous . . . ' she began, then stopped, afraid she would say too much and let all her frustration and loss pour out. She would never be able to retract it because he would know it was true. She forced herself to smile at him instead. 'Thank you for being afraid for me. It's really very kind of you, but quite unnecessary. I shall be discreet.'

For a moment she thought he was going to lose his temper entirely. Instead he started to laugh, and then laughed harder and harder until he was gasping for breath.

'It is not all that funny!' she said waspishly, swinging around to face the kettle.

'Yes, it is,' he replied, wiping his eyes with the back of his hand. 'You've never been discreet a day in your life.' He took her by the shoulders, quite gently but with thorough strength that she could not escape. 'And you are not going to pursue Mary Havilland's path finding proof that any of the construction machines are being used dangerously!'

She said nothing, but when she picked up the kettle she realised it had boiled nearly dry. She would have to let it cool a bit, then refill it and begin again.

'William,' she said gently, 'I'm afraid the tea will have to wait a little. I'll bring it through to you when it's ready, if you like?' If he wanted to think that was any kind of admission of defeat, or of obedience, this was not the time to point out to him that it was nothing of the sort.

'Thank you,' he accepted. 'That will be a good idea.' And he turned and went back into the sitting room.

'Really!' she said under her breath, but glad their exchange was over for the moment, and she could be alone to gain control of her feelings again.

4

Monk smiled in the stern of the ferry next morning as it made its way across the choppy waters. Waves were slapping the sides of the small boat, damp, raw wind finding its way between coat collar and scarf, stinging the skin, freezing the cheeks and arms. The boatman needed not only his strength but his skill to keep from 'catching crabs' with the oar blades and drenching them both.

At least the wind had driven the fog away and the long strings of barges were going down-river on the tide, carrying goods from the Pool of London to every place on earth.

He had spoken to Hester last night as if he were afraid for her safety, and he was. He did not want to prevent her from doing what she believed was right, but when she became involved in a cause she lost all sense of proportion. More than once it had endangered her, and last autumn it had nearly cost her her life. He could not and would not allow that to happen again. He felt sick and cold even at the thought of it. Was that little obedience asking for the earth?

He looked at the dark choppy water, turgid and filthy. Perhaps if he could remember all his youth, his other experiences of women, of love, he would be more realistic. But he remembered nothing, and he wanted Hester as she was: naïve, rash, stubborn, vulnerable, passionate, opinionated, loyal and sometimes foolish, always honest — too honest — and never mean of spirit and never, ever a coward. But he wanted her alive, and if she did not have the sense to protect herself, then he must do it for her.

He would find out what had happened to Mary Havilland, and to her father, because Hester would despise him if he did not.

How had she felt seven years ago over her own father's suicide? He had only just met her then and they had scraped each other raw to begin with. She had found him cold and arrogant. Perhaps he had been, but he had also been bewildered by the unknown world around him because of his total loss of memory, and his increasing awareness that he was disliked, and then, worst of all, the nightmare terror of his own guilt in Joscelyn Gray's death. It was her strength and courage that had saved him from it and kept hope alive in spite of the mounting evidence against him.

Had she felt guilty that she was not in England and at home when her parents both so desperately needed her? Was that at least in part why she was determined now to fight for Mary Havilland and, through her, for her father?

He had not even thought of that before.

They were at the Wapping shore. He paid the ferryman, climbed the steps up into the harsher wind and strode over to the police station door.

122

It was warm inside but several minutes elapsed before the heat thawed through his numb flesh. His hands tingled as the blood circulated again and he was aware of the men putting on heavy overcoats and then caps as they went out to begin the next patrol.

He spoke to them briefly, listening to the report of the night's events: a couple of robberies, and several fights, one ending in a knifing. The victim had died, but they had the man who had done it, and apparently it was the culmination of a long feud.

'Anyone else involved?' he asked.

Clacton gave him a sideways look eloquent of contempt, and Monk realised his mistake. He was treating Clacton as an equal, as he would Orme. Clacton was spoiling for a fight, inching round and round to find a weakness to jab. Monk held his temper with an effort. A man who loses his temper at a subordinate's rudeness isn't fit to command. No one must manipulate him. Nor must he be seen to need Orme's help. He was alone. Orme wanted him to succeed. Clacton wanted him to fail. For none of them would he ever take Durban's place. He did not mind that. He must make his own place, and none of them could admire Durban more than he did, who understood what he had done better than they, and who carried a far greater burden of guilt for it.

He would not correct himself and rephrase the question. He must retrieve the situation another way. He turned to Butterworth. 'Mr Clacton seems unwilling to reveal their names. Friends of his, perhaps. Or informants. Perhaps you can be more enlightening?'

Clacton moved his mouth to protest, and then looked at Monk's face and decided better of it.

'Yes, sir!' Butterworth said, barely concealing his smile. 'No one else injured, sir, far as we know. No witnesses admitting, but we know 'oo they worked for. It was more likely personal. Been grumblin' on for a couple o' months since a scrap down-river a bit. Drink an' bad temper, most like.'

'Do you expect any revenge?' Monk asked.

'No, sir, but we'll keep an eye.'

'Good. Anything else?'

He dealt with the few other details and the men went out, Butterworth with a grin, Clacton a scowl, the other two non-committal.

Monk found Orme in one of the small offices. Orme looked up from the ledger he was writing as Monk closed the door.

'Mornin' sir,' he said, regarding Monk solemnly. 'Got the doctor's reports on Miss 'Avilland and Mr Argyll. Nothing we didn't know about, 'ceptin' for sure she couldn't've bin with child. She was just like she should've bin. No man 'ad touched 'er.' There was a deep sadness in his eyes. 'They're gonna bury 'er this mornin'. 'Er sister didn't even ask the Church to 'elp, let alone give 'er a place. I s'pose she knows it don't do no good for 'er pa, poor soul.'

Monk sat down at the other side of the small wooden table. He felt suddenly sick. It was no use raging against the blindness, the arrogance to judge or the lack of human pity that Mary had

124

been ruled unfit for a decent burial. None of it would do any good. No man's act or failure would affect God's judgement of Mary, or anyone else. It was the brutality towards the emotion of those who had loved her he hated, and his anger would only hurt them more.

'Thank you,' he said quietly. 'Where?'

'On the land outside St Mary's Church on Princes Road. It's just opposite the Lambeth Work'ouse.' He added nothing but his voice was thick and he lowered his eyes.

'Thank you,' Monk repeated.

'Eleven o'clock,' Orme added. 'You'll 'ave time ter see Mr Farnham an' then go.'

'No I won't — not if I tell the butler, and Superintendent Runcorn.'

Orme looked at him gravely.

'Please tell Mr Farnham I'll see him when I get back.'

'Yes, sir. Would that be Superintendent Runcorn o' the Metropolitan Police?'

'Yes. He was the one who investigated James Havilland's death.' Monk told Orme what Runcorn had said, and his clear sadness over Mary's death as well, including his reluctance to believe it was suicide.

'But there weren't no doubt 'er father killed 'isself,' Orme said quietly. His round blue eyes held no hope that Monk could be wrong, but he did not hide his disappointment.

'Couldn't find any,' Monk admitted. 'Except that she didn't believe it. She was certain that he was a fighter and would never have given up.'

Orme's mouth tightened. 'Well, she wouldn't

125

easy think 'er own pa were the kind ter shoot 'isself, would she!' It was not a question. 'Mebbe she 'eld out as long as she could, and when something turned it for 'er so she couldn't kid 'erself any longer; that was what broke 'er?' He stared down at the table. 'Poor creature,' he said very gently. 'Poor little soul.'

Was that it? Monk wondered. Was he being loyal to Mary, whom he had never known, imagining her to be something like Hester because of superficial circumstances? Or only disloyal to Durban, who had died because of him, and blindly, idiotically, had entrusted Monk to take his place? Durban must have told Farnham something extraordinary that he could have accepted the recommendation! Monk's reputation as a solver of crimes was superb, and he had earned it. But as a leader of others it was dreadful. That too was justified. He inspired fear more than obedience, admiration for his ability more than loyalty to his character, resentment more than friendship. That was what his discoveries about his own past in the Metropolitan Police had forced him to accept.

But he had promised Hester, and if he did not follow it all the way, then she would. She would not say anything, but she would be disappointed in him.

'Did you think she jumped, at the time?' he asked Orme.

Orme blinked. 'Funny way ter go over, backwards, like. But she was strugglin' wi' young Argyll. You mean was 'e tryin' to stop 'er, or ter make sure as she went? Why? 'Cos she turned

126

'im down? That's a bit . . . ' he spread his hands, not able to find the right word.

'No,' Monk said. 'Because she was looking for the proof of danger that she thought her father was on the brink of finding.'

'Why'd they do that? Seems daft. Nob'dy wants a cave-in,' Orme pointed out. 'Costs a fortune to repair. An' Argyll stands out as a man 'oo likes his pennies, every one of 'em.'

'You think so?'

'Yes, Mr Monk, I do. I done a bit of askin' about 'im. Just 'cos o' that poor girl. Does very well fer 'isself, Mr Argyll, but all proper and careful. No big accidents, just the usual little ones they all 'ave. If there's bin none o' those I'd 'ave reckoned they was coverin' summink. But they do work awful fast an' take some o' the big money 'cos of it. I can't see 'em takin' kindly ter any questionin' of 'is methods.'

'But you found nothing ugly?'

'No. An' I looked.' He did not need to explain why. 'Yer gonna go on a bit longer, sir?'

'A bit.' Monk forced himself to trust him, hoping he was not going to regret it later. Orme might even prefer not to know. Keeping the distance between them might be more comfortable. Monk disregarded it. 'My wife was approached by someone concerned about the chances of a really bad cave-in.' Orme did not need to know about Hester's involvement with the clinic at Portpool Lane, or that the friend was a rat-catcher. 'He took her to see one of the big tunnels, very deep. The man knew all the underground rivers and wells and he's afraid

127

the tunnellers are going too fast.'

Orme was watching him with anxiety now, his attention total.

'She promised to help if she could,' Monk went on. 'She found the Member of Parliament chiefly concerned, and went to see him.' He ignored Orme's amazement. 'It seems Mary Havilland had been there already, and had impressed both him and his wife most favourably. They are very distressed indeed about her death, which they knew of already, and are keen to do all they can to assist in reform, if anyone can find proof that there is a real danger.'

'Well, well.' Orme sat back in his chair. 'So she was really doing something.' His face filled with a sudden pity so sharp he became conscious of it, blinked and turned away, as if needing to shelter himself from Monk's eyes.

Monk found the emotion in himself deeper than he wanted. It might have been simpler if Orme had argued. Then he would have been angry, and anger was always easier than letting the pain take over, at least to begin with. But Orme was too honest for that. Monk liked him the better for it, and resented being forced to. He was not ready yet for such a burden of loyalty.

'I'm going to pursue it at least another day or two,' he said tersely, 'see if I can find out exactly what Havilland was looking at, and what he found. I need to know if it was real, or just his own fear of being closed in.'

Orme nodded. 'Mr Farnham isn't going to like it,' he warned. ''E likes ter be tellin' us what ter do, an' there's plenty o' theft, same as always. All this diggin' o' new sewers an' tunnels is makin' folks restive. So many navvies around's makin' it 'arder ter move stolen goods too. The Fat Man's one o' the biggest fencers o' the good stuff — jewellery, gold, ivory, silks an' the like. 'E's un'appy with so much comin' an' goin'.'

'I know.'

'Jus' sayin',' Orme replied.

'Thank you. Theft is important, but murder, if it is murder, is more so.'

Orme gave a little downward smile. ''E won't say it's murder. An' it's the people who're stole from who run the river. That's where the money is.'

'You're a wise man,' Monk conceded. 'Remind mc of that again in a day or two. Meantime, it's dead women like Mary Havilland to whom we owe justice as well.'

Monk took a hansom to the burial and picked up both Runcorn and Cardman. They rode in silence to the church. They were early, but it seemed appropriate to stand on the short strip of withered grass and wait, three men united in anger and grief for a woman one had known all her life, one only the last two months of it, and the third not at all.

They stood stiff in the icy wind, each in his thoughts, oblivious of the traffic or the bulk of the workhouse black against a leaden sky.

The gravediggers had done their job; the earth gaped open. The small cortège was led by the minister, whose unsmiling countenance was like the face of doom, followed by Jenny

Argyll in unrelieved black and so heavily veiled her face was invisible. Monk knew her only because it could be no one else with Alan Argyll, although she took no notice of him at all, nor he of her. They looked as isolated as if the other were not there.

Was Argyll thinking only of his dead brother? The bitterness in his face suggested it.

There was no service, nothing said of the hope of resurrection. The burial was without mercy. The wind whipped the mourners' coat-tails and the ice on it stung the bare skin of cheeks, making them red, contrasting with white lips and hollow eyes.

Monk looked once each at Runcorn and Cardman, then did not intrude further on their emotions. Perhaps it was the reminder of death, and exclusion, the total rejection from all mankind even in this last extremity, but both men stood motionless, bleached with pain.

Monk turned to the minister and wondered what manner of God he believed in, whether he did this willingly or under protest because he had a wife and children to feed. He was overwhelmingly grateful his own faith was not hostage to financial need, his own or anyone else's. He should pity the man his bondage, and yet there was no questions in his face, and all Monk could feel from him was anger.

The burial was over almost before Monk realised it. Without a word, the cortège departed. In silence Runcorn, Cardman and Monk left, in the opposite direction, not because it was where they needed to go, but because going the same way as the cortége was not acceptable in any sense.

They found a hansom and returned as they had come, briefly equals — even friends.

*   *   *

'Suicide,' Monk's superior said brusquely when Monk went into his office early in the afternoon. 'For God's sake, man! She jumped right in front of you, and took with her the poor devil who was trying to save her! Don't make it even worse for the family by drawing it out!' Farnham was a big man, broad-shouldered and heavy-bellied. His long-nosed face could break into a sudden smile, and there were those who spoke of certain acts of kindness, but Monk felt uneasy in his presence, as if never certain he would be true to the best in himself. Farnham had sought authority and won it, and now he wore it with intense pleasure.

Arguments of belief or intuition would only be mocked. Anything Monk put forward would be seen as enlightened self-interest for the River Police. 'It probably is suicide, sir,' he agreed aloud. 'But I think we should make certain.'

Farnham's eyebrows rose. He had trusted Durban and had known where he was with him, or at least he had assumed he did. He resented the fact that now he had to learn the strengths and weaknesses of a new man. He was sufficiently aware of what had really happened to hold Monk accountable for Durban's death, however much it had followed Durban's own sense of duty; his courage, and hideous

131

misfortune none of them had noticed until it was too late. But Monk had survived, and Farnham blamed him for that.

'Not much is ever sure in police work, Monk,' he said sourly. 'Thought you would have known that!' The criticism was implicit.

Monk swallowed his impatience. 'I'm not thinking about what happened on the bridge, sir, but of what she was investigating to do with the sewer tunnels and their construction.'

'Not our concern!' Farnham snapped. 'That's the Metropolitan Police.' The distaste with which he said that was exactly what Monk had expected; had already seen in him in the few weeks he had been here. It was part of what Farnham disliked in Monk himself, and the fact that he had been dismissed from the Metropolitan Police was, conversely, a point in his favour.

'Yes, sir,' Monk agreed, with difficulty. 'But if there is something, and it causes a real disaster and we knew about it, or at least had a chance to find out, do you think they'll see it that way?'

Farnham's eyes narrowed. 'You can have a couple of days,' he warned. 'If you find something worth pursuing then give it to them, on paper, and keep a record of it here! Understood?'

'Yes, sir.' Monk thanked him and left before he could change his mind, or add any further restrictions.

He began by learning as much as he could about the vast network of new and old sewers, and how they interconnected. It was an immense complex, intended to take the ocean of waste from London's three million people eastwards away from the city and its present egress into the river, and instead process it through large purification works closer to the sea. Then the surplus water could be released, comparatively clean, and the solid waste otherwise disposed of. The Great Stink would never happen again. It was a brilliant feat of engineering, costing a king's ransom of money, but for the capital of the Empire and the seat of government for quarter of the world, it was absolutely necessary.

It took more time to find the exact place of the Argyll brothers' company in the scheme, and Monk was surprised how large it was. It must have cost a considerable effort and influence to obtain it, and no doubt would not be easily forfeited. They had three sites close to each other. Two were cut-and-cover, like the deep crevasse that Hester had described, but one was too deep for that method. They were actually tunnelling, burrowing like rabbits under the ground, scraping out the earth and rock and carrying it back to the entrance to get rid of it. The necessity for this was created not only by the depth, but by the fact that other rivers and gas lines crossed above it in several places, and could have collapsed had they been exposed by the more open method.

He searched, but could find no adequate map that charted all London's old wells, springs and submerged rivers, old gutters, drains and waterways that had altered over the course of the centuries. Clay slipped. Some earth absorbed water, some rejected it. Some old drains, dating back to the Roman occupation, had survived. Some had been broken or caved in, and the land had subsided, diverting them deeper or sideways. The earth was a living thing, changing with time and usage. No wonder Sutton, whose father had been a tosher and knew all the waterways large and small, was now frightened by the vast steam engines that shook the ground, and the knowledge that men were digging, shovelling and moving, disturbing what was settled.

Monk was very circumspect about mentioning Havilland's name, but he would not learn anything further of use if he did not. It gave him a wry, half-sour pleasure that inquiry was far easier now than in his independent days because he could use the power of the River Police to ask for what he wanted. He was cramped by rules, hemmed in and robbed of freedom by the necessity of answering both upward to Farnham, and in a sense downward to Orme and the other men. He could not lead if he could not inspire men to follow him. The mere holding of office could force obedience for a while, but it could not earn respect or the loyalty that mattered. He would not replace Durban anywhere except in the records on paper.

He made detailed enquiries of clerks at the construction offices regarding old maps, earlier excavations, waterways, the nature of soil, graveyards and plague pits, anything that might affect new tunnelling. He was told of James Havilland's investigations.

'And Miss Mary Havilland?' he insisted.

'Just like I said,' the clerk replied.

'She asked just the same questions as Mr Havilland?' Monk said with sharp interest. 'Did she explain her involvement? Weren't you curious that a young woman should know anything about such matters, or care?'

'Yes, I was,' the clerk agreed. 'That's 'ow come I remember. She told me as 'e were 'er father, an' 'e were dead, so she were doin' what she could ter finish 'is work. 'E worked fer one o' the big firms, the Argyll Company.'

'She told you that?'

'No. I know that meself. Not that I knew 'im, like, but I seed 'im on works once or twice. Didn't look well. Sort o' pale an' sweatin'. Mind, I seen men like that when they 'as ter go down deep. Scared o' bein' closed in. An' o' the rats an' the water.' He shuddered. 'Don't like 'em much meself.'

Monk pressed it a little further, noting down the details, then he thanked the clerk and left.

The rest of the day yielded nothing new. Mary Havilland had followed in the footsteps of her father in half a dozen places. Obviously Havilland had believed that the steam engines were dangerous, but had he learned anything that proved it?

Monk turned the question over in his mind as he walked back along the dockside towards the station. It was dark and there was a fine rain. The smell of the tide was harsh, but he was becoming used to it. Even the constant slurping of the water against the embankment and on the steps down to the ferryboats and barges assumed a kind of familiar rhythm. The fog horns were

135

booming again and the rain blinded his vision. Lights loomed on him out of the darkness before there was time to change course.

He wondered about Scuff. Where was he on a night like this? Had he eaten? He had shelter, Monk knew that, but had he any warmth? Then he remembered that the chief booty of mudlarks was coal. Very often the lightermen would deliberately knock pieces off their barges into the shallow water for the small boys to get. Perhaps he had a fire. The riverside was full of children scraping survival the best way they could — like the rest of the city. It was irrational to worry about one.

He forced his mind back to the case.

Had Havilland found anything that someone would kill him to hide? It seemed unlikely. Argyll had had no serious accidents. But Havilland had been an engineer himself, and he knew exactly what the huge machines were capable of, what safeguards were taken, and that Argyll, of all people, would not want injuries or time lost. A bad incident might kill scores of men, but it would ruin the company.

But *had* he really learned something so dangerous he had been murdered to hide it? And then Mary had followed in his footsteps and found it also, and in turn been murdered?

Or was Havilland simply a man who had lost his mental balance, become obsessed and imagined danger where there was none? Were the diverted streams and the threat of slippage an excuse rather than a reason, to close that tunnel and avoid ever going down there again? Was it even possible he had some kind of a grudge against Argyll personally? Mary, devoted to him, had believed his view, and then when she had finally been forced by the evidence to face the truth had she been unable to bear it? Only for her it was worse! First her father's error, his suicide, her own broken betrothal to Toby Argyll, then an estrangement from her sister, the shame of her false accusations, and nothing to look forward to in the future, not even financial security.

Had Toby told her some truth so bitter it had broken her at last? Could she even have lashed out at him, because of it?

Hester would be hurt to know that. Monk winced and shuddered in the cold as he thought of having to tell her, perhaps tomorrow or the day after.

The next day he decided to go directly to the deepest tunnel, again using his authority to oblige the engineers to allow him in.

The site was a vast hive of labour, men wheeling, digging, hacking, shoring up at the entrance where load after load of earth, clay, stones and shale came out in wagons and was hauled up the forty-foot cliff face to the level above. The tunnel itself was like the entrance to a mine, high enough for a man to walk in. But it would be far less when the brickwork was laid. It would become a hollow tube with occasional holes for storm drains to empty. Iron-ringed ladders would lead up to the street and daylight, so sewer men could go down and clear any blockages and the piled-up waste, which would impede the flow.

A huge steam engine pounded, shuddering the ground, drawing the chain that pulled up the loads of debris and carried them away to a pile where they were emptied. It hissed and belched steam, and the noise of it necessitated the men shouting to each other within twenty or thirty yards of it. Stokers shovelled more coal into the furnace, then returned to hauling and tipping.

Monk showed his police identification. Grudgingly the site managers gave him access to the bottom down a steep cutting, but no one went with him. He found himself slipping and losing his balance several times, only just avoiding falling into the wet clay beneath him. Several times he banged against the loosely timbered sides.

Once at the bottom he could walk more easily on the boards laid on the rubble and clay. The swill of dirty water seeped from the sides and gathered in puddles, trickling very slightly downward towards the tunnel mouth. He looked upward quickly. How deep was he? He felt a flutter of panic. The walls towered up to a narrow strip of sky and the movement of cloud across it made him reel.

He was sharply aware of the smell all around him — wet, earthy, mouldy, as if nothing were ever dry, and the wind never cleansed it.

He faced the dark hole ahead of him with a reluctance that startled him. He had never before felt such a crowding sense of being enclosed. He had to force himself to keep walking and try to dull his imagination.

The shadow closed over him. The winter daylight did not penetrate far. Beyond a few yards the tunnel was lit by covered gaslight. A naked flame could ignite the fumes in the air. He had heard of mine explosions and men buried for ever in collapsed shafts. Could that possibly happen here? No, of course not! This was one straight tunnel, which was going to be bricked around, held with steel. Sewers did not collapse.

The noise of hammering and shovelling was ahead of him. He kept on walking, the water slopping underneath the boards. Where were the nearest rivers? Did anybody even know for certain? How much did rivers secretly change course because of subsidence, the great engines above the ground shaking the earth, compressing it down, or rattling it loose? He was sweating and his heart was pounding in his chest.

He was still walking at exactly the same speed along the boards. The steadiness of his pace gave him an illusion of being in control, at least of himself. The water was dripping. It seemed to be everywhere, a sheen on the walls in the gaslight. A rat appeared from nowhere, making him start. It ran along beside him for a dozen yards, then the shadows swallowed it up.

Ahead there were brighter lights, shouts and the noise of pick blades striking with a sharp clang against rock, and a dull thud at clay. He saw it, a machine like a huge drum, almost the size of the tunnel itself, the power of it thrumming as if it were the heartbeat of the earth.

There were at least twenty men labouring at

one task or another and not one of them looked up or took the slightest notice of Monk. The air was stale and cold and had a strange taste to it.

A man trundled past him with a barrow-load of debris. Another rat shot out of the shadows, and then back in again. The sides of the tunnel beyond the last of the boards gleamed wet, and here and there were dribbles of water running down to the sodden earth.

If the diggers broke into a small underground stream it would gush in here like an open tap, except there would be no way of turning it off. He must not allow himself to think of that, or he might panic. He could feel the sweat on his body now.

He strode forward and deliberately drew the attention of the best-dressed man present, one of only two wearing jackets, and presumably who supervised rather than performed the labour themselves.

The man was broad-shouldered and already spreading a little at the waist, although he looked no more than in his middle-forties. His features were regular, even handsome, except that his mouth was a trifle large. His hair was dark with a heavy wave and he had a thick, dark moustache. He turned blue eyes to Monk.

'Yes?' he said with surprise. He spoke loudly to be heard above the din of the machine and the crushing and grinding of earth and falling stones.

'Monk, River Police,' Monk replied. 'I need to talk to the man in charge here.'

'That's me! Aston Sixsmith,' the man told

140

him. 'What is it, Mr Monk?'

Monk waved his arm to indicate that they should go back towards the entrance away from the noise, and he had to concentrate deliberately in order not to turn immediately and walk ahead. He began to feel far more sympathy for Havilland than he had even an hour ago. He could understand any man who felt oppressed by these walls, the darkness, and above all the close, stale air on his face and clogging his lungs.

Sixsmith walked in front of him and stopped a hundred feet away from the digging. 'Well, Mr Monk, what can I do for you?' He looked curious. 'You said River Police? We haven't any trouble here, and I haven't taken on any new men in the last month or so. Are you looking for someone? I'd try the Thames Tunnel, if I were you. There's a whole world down there. Some people live pretty well all their lives under the ground. This time of the year it's drier than up above. But I imagine you know that.'

'Yes, I do,' Monk replied, although the world of the Thames Tunnel was one he had not yet had time to explore. The river itself kept him constantly alert, always learning, finding the vast gaps in his knowledge and little, stupid mistakes out of ignorance. His face was hot with the memory of the times Orme had rescued him, albeit always discreetly. He could not go on like that. 'I'm not looking for a man.' He faced Sixsmith squarely, meeting the clear blue eyes. 'I believe you used to work with James Havilland?'

Sixsmith's expression darkened with a sudden sadness. His face was more mobile, more easily marked with emotion than Monk had expected. He looked not unlike the navvies himself and blended with them easily, but his voice both in tone and diction placed him as far different, a man of more gentleness and considerable education, whether formally acquired or not.

'Yes. Poor man,' he replied. 'In the end the tunnels got to him.' His eyes searched Monk's, and Monk had the distinct feeling that his own fear was sensed if not seen.

'What can you tell me about him?' Monk asked. 'Was he a good engineer?'

'Excellent, if a little old-fashioned,' Sixsmith answered. 'He wanted new ideas tested more thoroughly than I think was necessary. But he was a sound man, and I know no one who didn't both like and respect him. I certainly did!'

'You said the tunnels got to him,' Monk continued. 'What did you mean?' He was glad they started to move towards the entrance again, even if it was to a crevasse rather than the level ground.

Sixsmith sighed and moved his hands in a slight gesture of regret. Despite the dirt on them, both the power and the grace were visible. 'Some men can't stand the closed-in places,' he explained. 'You've got to have a special kind of nerve to work underground. He hadn't. Oh, he tried his best, but you could see him losing control.' He sighed and pulled his wide mouth tight. 'I tried to persuade him to stay up the top, but he wouldn't listen. Pride, I suppose.'

'Was there anything in particular he was afraid of?' Monk asked as innocently as he could.

Sixsmith looked at him carefully. His gaze was very direct and it was impossible to miss the intelligence in his eyes. 'I suppose there's no point in trying to conceal it now,' he said resignedly. 'The poor man's dead, and the world knows his weaknesses. Yes, he was afraid of a stream bursting through and sending the whole side caving in. If that happened of course men would be buried alive or drowned. He became obsessed with the idea of lost underground rivers just waiting to find a way in, almost like an evil presence.' He looked at Monk defensively. 'It's not insane, Mr Monk, not entirely. It's just the exaggeration of something real, fear taken beyond reason, so to speak. Tunnel engineering is a dangerous business. Men died in building the Thames Tunnel, you know? Crushed, gassed, all sorts of things. It's a hard profession and it's not for everyone.'

'But you liked him personally?' Monk was shivering in spite of his heavy coat. He clenched his teeth, trying to hide it.

'Yes, I did,' Sixsmith said without hesitation. 'He was a good man.' He pushed his hands in his pockets. He walked easily, casually even.

'Did you know Miss Mary Havilland?' Monk pursued.

A shadow of exasperation crossed Sixsmith's expressive face. 'Yes, I did. Not well. She took her father's death very hard. I'm afraid she was a bit less well . . . well-balanced than he was, or her sister, Mrs Argyll. Very emotional.'

Monk found himself resenting Sixsmith, which was unreasonable. He had never known Mary

Havilland in life and Sixsmith had. He must remember that her likenesses to Hester were superficial — matters of circumstance, not nature. And yet her face had looked so gentle and so sane. Emotional certainly, but they were the passions of a strong woman, not the fancies and indulgences of a weak one.

It was difficult for him to speak of her death to this man who saw her so differently. He hesitated, looking for the words he wanted, even, for an instant, forgetting how far ahead the light still lay.

Sixsmith was there before him. 'Is that why you are here? You said River Police. She died in the river, didn't she?' He pursed his lips. 'I'm deeply sorry about that. And young Toby too. What a terrible tragedy.' He was looking at Monk intently now. 'Are you assuming that she killed herself because of her father? You are almost certainly right. She couldn't accept the truth. Fought against it all the way, poor soul.' He gave a slight shrug of his powerful shoulders. 'Maybe I would, if it had been my father. It's hard to face something like that about your own family.'

Monk swung to face him, but there was nothing but a crumpled pity in Sixsmith's face.

'Everyone was very sorry for her,' Sixsmith went on. 'Turned a deaf ear to her questions and accusations, hoped she'd grow out of it, but it doesn't seem to have helped. Perhaps she finally saw the truth, and it was too much for her. She idolised him. Not wise. We are all human. Perhaps no man could live up to what she believed of him. I don't know what else to say to help.'

Monk looked into his powerful, sad face and felt the weight of his conviction, and his pity for it. 'Thank you. I'll come back if there seems anything further.' He held out his hand.

Sixsmith grasped it with a sudden smile so warm it entirely changed him. They could have been friends met again after a long separation. 'Do come back,' he said, letting Monk's hand go. 'Any help I can be.'

★ ★ ★

In spite of what Sixsmith had said, Monk still went to check one more time on Havilland's suicide. Even as he rode in a hansom along the Embankment he was aware that Farnham would have expected him to attend to the urgent crime on the river, which was his job, but he knew Orme would deal with all the regular accidents and crimes. He realised ruefully that he did much of the time anyway. He was teaching Monk more than he was learning from him.

Mary Havilland and Toby Argyll had died in the river. Had she really believed that he and his brother were responsible for her father's death? If so, then perhaps she had taken Toby over the edge with her intentionally, as, in the heat of shock at his loss, Alan Argyll had implied. If that were so, then it was murder.

Did Monk need to know if that was true? Or was the damnation of suicide as much burden and punishment as she needed to bear? While the balance of her mind was turned? Any judgement against her now was beyond human reach.

He had only seen her face when she was dead. It had seemed strong, even beautiful to him. But how much difference is made by the spirit within? Would she have seemed ugly, even mad, if he had seen her alive?

He would spend one more day seeking to lay at rest the doubts that swirled around in his mind. Then he would have to tell Hester the truth, however sad or brutal it was.

Last time at the Havilland house he had spoken only to Cardman, who was intensely loyal. Perhaps if he spoke to a different servant, who had been there less time and would very shortly be seeking another place anyway, he would hear a different story.

It was a grey day with sleet on the wind. Monk was glad to reach the house again and be permitted into the kitchen where he was offered a fresh, hot cup of tea and some Madeira cake. The reason for such hospitality was quickly revealed.

'You're police, the law?' the cook asked him, offering a second piece of cake.

He accepted. It was excellent and he told her so. 'Yes,' he agreed, with his mouth full and an upward lift in his voice to encourage her to continue.

'Can yer tell us what's going to happen to us, Mr Monk? Mr Argyll's too upset over the death of 'is brother to take up any business matters, an' Mrs Argyll must be broke to pieces about poor

Miss Mary. It's just that we don't know our position, like. Me and Mr Cardman'll stay as long as we're needed. But we 'ave ter tell some o' the maids an' the footmen, like. It in't always that easy ter find a good place, an' coming from a tragedy like this don't 'elp.'

He looked at her plump, anxious face. Her fair hair was greying, pulled back into a loose knot. She was trying hard not to sound callous, but one suicide in the house was damaging, two could make domestic re-employment far harder than held any justice. The fear was in her eyes.

'I don't know, Mrs Plimpton, but I will find out, and see that you are informed as soon as possible. We are not sure yet how Miss Havilland came to fall into the river . . . ' He stopped, seeing the wordless emotion in her face. It would take great delicacy to draw from her what she really believed. She might not even have put it into words herself. 'Or Mr Toby Argyll,' he added, watching her.

He saw the flicker of anger — a flash — then she hid it again. She was a woman whose position in life had never allowed her to leave her feelings uncontrolled. He read the dislike of Toby that she dared not tell him.

'Thank you, sir,' she replied.

He needed more. 'I imagine you knew Miss Havilland a long time?'

'Since she was born,' Mrs Plimpton replied, her voice thick with grief.

Monk tried a different approach. 'Was she extremely fond of Mr Argyll?'

'No,' she said abruptly, then realised she had

been too forthright. 'I mean . . . I mean o' course she liked 'im, but it were she as broke it off, not 'im.' She gulped. 'Mr Monk, she would never 'ave taken 'er own life! If yer'd 'ave known 'er yer wouldn't even think on it. She were that determined to prove as poor Mr 'Avilland were killed, not took 'isself, an' she were on the edge o' doin' it! That excited, she were . . . ' She stopped, sniffing and turning away.

'If she didn't take her own life, Mrs Plimpton, what do you think happened?' he asked. He said it gently, letting her know he took her opinion seriously.

She looked back. Her eyes were red-rimmed and puffy, her nose pink. Perhaps it was the sympathy in his voice, or the fact that he was sitting at her kitchen table, eating her cake, which gave a kind of stature in their situation.

'I think she found out 'oo sent that letter to 'er father an' lured 'im into the stable ter be shot,' she said defiantly. 'The master'd never 'ave shot 'isself, any more'n she'd go jumpin' off bridges.' She took a deep breath. 'An' don't you go sittin' there eatin' my cake an tellin' me as they would.'

He was startled. No one else had spoken of a letter.

'What letter, Mrs Plimpton?' he said quietly, controlling the urgency in his voice with an effort.

'Letter as come ter 'im the night 'e died,' she answered.

'Mr Cardman didn't mention it.'

''Cos 'e didn't know,' she replied reasonably,

148

automatically refilling Monk's cup from the big brown teapot. 'It came ter the back door an' Lettie took it to 'im. 'E read it and then burned it, apparently. But it was right after that that 'e told Mr Cardman as 'e'd decided ter sit up, an' no one was ter bother waitin' fer 'im. 'E'd lock up 'isself. It were somebody as was goin' ter meet 'im, I'd set me life on it!' She drew in her breath in a little gasp, as if realising suddenly that she was right: Havilland had done just that, and lost his life.

'You are quite sure?'

'Course I am!' She was shaking now but her eyes did not waver.

'May I speak to Lettie?' Monk asked.

'Yer think I'm making it up!' she accused him, her face pinched, her breathing heavy.

'No, I don't,' he assured her. 'If you were, there would be no point in my speaking to Lettie, would there? I want to see what she remembers of it: paper, ink, handwriting. I'd like to know if she saw Mr Havilland open it, and how he reacted. Was he surprised, afraid, alarmed, or excited, even pleased? Was he expecting it or not?'

'Oh . . . yes. Well!' She could not bring herself to apologise, but she pushed the cake plate across to him on the table. 'Well, I'll send for Lettie.' She walked to the door and called the kitchen maid to fetch the housemaid.

Lettie appeared and answered his questions. She was about fifteen and stood in front of him twisting her fingers in her apron. The letter had been brought by a youth, and she had never

149

seen him before or since. She could not read, and had no idea about the paper or the writing, but she remembered quite clearly that Mr Havilland was both surprised and disturbed by the letter. After reading it he had put it straight into the fire and then told her to send Cardman to him. He had written no reply.

'Have you any idea who the letter was from?' he asked.

'No, sir, I ain't.'

'What did Mr Havilland say, as clearly as you can remember?'

'Ter send Mr Cardman straight away, sir.'

'That's all?'

'Yes, sir.'

'Have you ever seen the handwriting before?'

'I dunno, sir. I didn't never look.'

Monk thanked her and Mrs Plimpton. He left the house through the scullery door and the tradesmen's yard, past the coal and coke sheds and up the area steps into the bitter wind slicing down the street. Who had written to Havilland that disturbed him so much? Was it to arrange a meeting in the stables that evening, or something completely different? Certainly Havilland had dismissed the servants immediately after receiving it, and apparently changed his plans to retire as normal. It would even explain his presence in the stables. But who would he meet in such a place on a winter night, rather than in his house where it was warm and dry, but presumably less private?

Why would he need such extraordinary privacy? Was his own study not sufficiently discreet, with the servants in bed, and presumably Mary also? Had he taken the gun in order to protect himself, expecting attack? Why? From whom? Perhaps Mary Havilland was right. If she were, then certainly she had also been killed deliberately, and it could only be by Toby Argyll.

It was now impossible for Monk to turn his back on the chance that Havilland had found some real danger in the tunnels and been murdered to silence him before he could ruin their business by making it public.

But the visitor had then taken the gun from him, and shot him with it. A man younger and stronger, more ruthless, and with the element of surprise? Havilland was frightened, but he had come essentially to talk. The other man had come intending to kill.

Alan Argyll?

And was that what Mary had learned, and why Toby Argyll had killed her too?

Monk bent forward into the wind, feeling the ice in it sting his face. He began to walk a little faster.

5

When Monk arrived home that evening Hester could see that he was in some mental turmoil. He was shivering from the river crossing and he concentrated on warming at least his hands and feet before he even attempted to say anything beyond a greeting. He ate the bowl of soup she brought him and gradually he stopped shaking.

She wondered yet again if they would have been wiser to have found a house on the northern bank of the Thames, even if the area were less to their liking.

When she had gone to Portpool Lane she had taken the omnibus westwards and over whichever of the bridges was appropriate, but since they were directly opposite Wapping, it made sense for Monk to cross by ferry, and be at the police station in fifteen minutes or so. Sometimes the patrol boat picked him up directly from the steps.

But the cold was intense, and on a night like this of drifting sleet she wished profoundly he did not have to be on the open water.

She sat opposite him, looking at the red glow of the fire on his face, the soup bowl in his hands, and wondered if it had been a good idea for him to join a regular force again. She had offered to apply for a regular nursing job at one of the big hospitals, even though 'nursing' in those circumstances was actually almost nothing to do with the care of patients. One was rather more like a domestic servant in circumstances where a usual household maid would refuse to go.

She had tried it before their marriage; then she had been full of zeal to reform the practice of hospital nursing after her experience in the Crimea. She had failed spectacularly, very nearly incurring legal action against herself for insubordination, and worse. But still she would have swallowed her pride and applied again, if it would have helped. Monk had refused outright to allow her.

Now she looked at him sitting relaxing at last in the chair opposite her, and worried that he was finding the obedience to authority harder than he had expected, and the restriction and demands of leadership too cramping to both his nature and his abilities. She was trying to think of the words to ask him when he spoke.

'Sixsmith, who's in charge of the practical side of the tunnelling, is certain that Havilland committed suicide when he couldn't cope with the pressure of working underground,' he said, watching her face.

She felt herself tighten, ready to argue, but kept her temper, waiting for what else he would say.

He smiled very slightly, just an easing of the tiredness in him. 'I went back to the Havilland house and spoke to the cook, and one of the maids,' he went on. 'They said Havilland received a note that night, hand delivered to the back door. As soon as he read it he burned it, and then told the butler to go to bed and he would lock up himself.'

'He was going to meet someone in the stable!' she said instantly, sitting upright and staring at him. 'Who?'

He looked rueful. 'They had no idea. The envelope had only his name on it. The cook saw it briefly, and the maid who carried it doesn't read.'

'Well, who could it be?' she said eagerly. At last there was something to grasp hold of. She felt a surge of hope, which was absurd. It should not matter to her so much. She had never known Mary Havilland. She might not have liked her in the least if she had. She was remembering her own grief, the feeling of having been bruised all over, stunned by confusion, when she had first stood on the dockside at Scutari and read the letter from her brother, telling her of her father's suicide, and then her mother's death from what was termed 'a broken heart'. She could not help imagining Mary Havilland feeling the same searing pain.

Except that Hester had believed it, and Mary had not. Had she been wrong, making it harder for herself, and for her sister, by refusing to accept the inevitable? 'Who could it be?' she repeated.

Monk was watching her, his eyes soft with knowledge of her pain.

'I don't know, except that since he immediately made arrangements to meet the person, it

154

must have been either someone he knew, or at the least someone he was not surprised to hear from. Nor did he seem to need to answer it, so whoever it was knew he would come.'

'You must find out!' she said unhesitatingly.

It was unreasonable, and she knew it as she spoke, but he did not argue. Was that for her? Or was the anger at loss still raw inside him too, the sense of incompleteness, or worse, the challenge that he must be perfect at his new job, equal his own vision of what Durban would have done?

'William . . . ' she started.

'I know.' He smiled.

'Do you?' she asked doubtfully.

His eyes were gentle, amused. 'Yes.'

*   *   *

However, in the morning Hester set out on her own path towards learning what she hoped would be both more about Mary Havilland and something to further the cause in which she had promised to help Sutton.

First she called at the clinic in Portpool Lane and completed the books and ledgers and passed them to Margaret.

'That's complete and up to date,' she said, suddenly finding it difficult to hide her emotion. She was going to miss the work, the struggles and victories, and most of all the people. The sense of loss was even worse than she had expected.

Margaret was looking at her, aware for the first time that there was something new and harsh

155

still unsaid. 'What is it, Hester?' Her voice was so gentle it brought Hester to the edge of tears.

How much could she say it was Monk, and not she, who was forcing this decision?

'I have agreed to stay at home for a while,' she began. 'William's new job is . . . different.' She swallowed hard. 'You're managing very well now. Claudine is excellent, and Bessie. I could never raise money as you do.'

Margaret looked stunned. 'A while? How long a while?' She bit her lip. 'You mean always, don't you?'

'I think so.'

Margaret stepped forward and put her arms around Hester, hugging her tightly. She did not say anything. It was as if she understood. Perhaps, knowing Monk and remembering last year, she did.

Hester did not want to say goodbye to Bessie and the other girls, especially to Claudine, but it would be cowardly not to. She would promise to call in occasionally, and she would keep her word. Monk could not object to that.

She left into the cold, sharp morning, not as confident or light of foot as she had come. That was foolish, even vain. She must shake herself out of it.

She arrived at the Applegates' house still a little early for the most civil calls, especially to someone she barely knew. However, she had been in the morning room only a matter of minutes when Rose Applegate came sweeping in. She was dressed extremely elegantly, as if she were expecting important company. Hester's

156

heart sank. Perhaps Rose's original enthusiasm was more an intention of kindness than a real desire to become involved. Hester had misread it because she wanted to. Certainly Rose's gown, with its gorgeous lace high neck and tiny velvet bows on the skirt was up-to-the-minute fashion. By comparison she herself was dowdy. She was acutely aware of the social gulf between them. It seemed at that moment an uncrossable abyss.

'Good morning, Mrs Monk,' Rose greeted her, her curious face alight with pleasure. 'Has there been news? Is there something we can do?' Then she looked a trifle self-conscious. 'I'm sorry, that is most discourteous of me. How are you?'

It was not customary to offer refreshment of any kind at this hour, and it seemed Rose observed the proprieties exactly. The room was formal; the maid had been immaculate in starched cap and apron. The hall was already polished and swept. Hester had smelled the pleasant, damp aroma of wet tea leaves scattered and taken up to collect the dust, and of lavender and beeswax to shine the wood.

'Good morning, Mrs Applegate,' she replied. 'No, I'm afraid there is little fresh so far.' She had nothing to lose by telling the truth. It was probably all lost anyway! 'My husband learned a little more about Mr Havilland's anxieties, but if Mr Havilland found out anything precise, we do not know what it was. According to Mr Sixsmith, who is in charge, he had something of an obsession about enclosed spaces and finally became quite irrational about it. Mr Sixsmith said that was what finally unhinged his reason and brought about his death.'

Rose was clearly startled. 'Good heavens!' She sat down rather suddenly, disregarding the crumpling of her skirt, and motioned for Hester to sit also. 'That sounds so terribly reasonable, doesn't it? But it's not true!'

Hester recounted what Monk had told her the previous evening — at least regarding the cook's opinion of Mary, though not yet about the letter.

'That is the Mary I know,' Rose agreed quickly. She leaned forward. 'She was not a sentimental sort of person, Mrs Monk. She was very practical and quite able to stand up to a truth she did not wish to hear, if it was indeed the truth. I don't know where to begin, but if you have any idea at all, please let us do something to establish her innocence.'

'Innocence . . . '

'Of having killed herself!' Rose said quickly, the emotion now clear in her face, her eyes very bright as though on the brink of tears. 'And if the account is true, God forgive me, innocent of having taken Toby Argyll with her. That is a terrible thing to think of anyone, and I refuse to let it be said by default, because it would be easier for us all to pretend it was over.'

Hester was suddenly heartened. 'What are the alternatives?' she asked. 'What did happen? How can we demonstrate it so it cannot be denied?'

'Oh dear!' Rose sat bolt upright. 'I see what you mean. If it was not suicide, then it was an accident, or it was murder. That is a very dreadful thought.'

'It seems to me to be inescapable,' Hester pointed out.

The door opened and Morgan Applegate came in. His eyes went immediately to his wife, then to Hester. He was polite, pleased to see her, to judge from the expression in his face. However, there was something faintly protective in the way he went to Rose and remained standing by her chair as if, without even giving it a thought, he would make certain Hester did not somehow distress or disturb her.

'How are you, Mrs Monk?' he said agreeably. 'Has there been progress so soon?'

Rose swung around to look at him. 'In essence there has, Morgan,' she replied. 'We came face to face with irrefutable logic, and we must go forward. Actually, Mr Monk allowed the possibility of accident, but I do not. Two such accidents — it is absurd. Either Mr Havilland and Mary both took their own lives, or Toby Argyll tried to kill her, and fell in himself.'

'Rose . . . ' he started to say, his face now heavy with concern.

'Oh, it's inescapable,' she brushed aside his interruption, turning again to Hester. 'The question is, if so, was he also responsible for the death of James Havilland?'

Applegate spoke gently, but his voice was quite firm. 'If Toby Argyll was responsible, then he has already paid the ultimate price.'

Rose looked at him patiently. 'You have missed the point, Morgan. I am not concerned with trying to have someone pay! I wish to clear Mary of the sin of suicide, and of Toby's death also, if

159

any might suppose she pulled him over, meaning to. And I want to vindicate her father as well, which is what she wanted above all things.'

'But — ' he started.

'And possibly even more important,' she went on as if he had not spoken, 'I want to show that they were both right in their fear of some terrible accident, so that we can still prevent it. So, you see, we are anything but finished! Is that not so, Mrs Monk?' She turned her steady, bright gaze on Hester.

'Rose!' Applegate said exasperatedly. 'You are placing Mrs Monk in an impossible position! Please, you must not embarrass her . . . '

'I am not embarrassed,' Hester lied quickly. 'But if I were, it could hardly matter! We are speaking of other people's deaths, and of the possible deaths and mutilation of scores of men, even hundreds if there were to be a major cave-in, or a flood.'

'You see?' Rose said with finality. 'We must do everything we can, and we shall begin by learning whatever it was that Mary already knew.'

Applegate looked at Hester with some desperation. 'You seem to have an understanding of logic, Mrs Monk. Either you are right, or you are mistaken in this. If you are mistaken, there is no point in pursuing it, and you may damage the reputations of good men who have already suffered deeply in the loss of those they loved. I speak in particular of Alan Argyll.' He spread his hands. 'But if you are right, then he has been the cause of Havilland's death, and now of Mary's and his own brother's, albeit he did not intend the latter. Surely you must see that in that case he is a most dangerous man, and will not hesitate to harm you, if he has the chance? And please do not be rash enough to suppose you can outwit him!' He turned to his wife, touching her shoulder. 'And for you, my dear, I am afraid I forbid you to endanger yourself in this way.' He smiled — a sweet, gentle gesture that lit his face so his emotions were unmistakable. 'Or any other way.'

Rose's eyebrows shot up. 'Good gracious! What on earth do you imagine I am going to do? Go down a sewer and accuse some engineer of carelessness? Or perhaps visit Mr Argyll in his mourning and tell him I think he is a murderer? Really, Morgan, credit me with a little sense! Mrs Monk is primarily concerned with the safety of navvies, which is a very right and proper thing for a Member of Parliament's wife to care about also, especially the Member who is most involved with this work.' She rose to her feet and stood facing him, very patiently. 'I shall be sociable and charitable. Mrs Monk does great work for the poor and has served with Miss Nightingale, nursing soldiers. Who more appropriate to take with me when considering the injured?'

He looked bewildered. She had robbed him of argument, and yet he was obviously unhappy. Hester wondered why he was still quite clearly afraid for her.

'I promise you we shall not behave inappropriately,' she said to him, wishing to make him feel

161

less apprehensive, but also knowing that without Rose's knowledge of Alan Argyll, and of what Mary had already discussed, she had little chance of success.

There was something Applegate wished to say, and yet obviously felt restrained. He looked at Rose again. 'Please be careful . . . '

'Of course I shall be careful!' she said with the very slightest edge of irritation. 'I am merely going to visit some of the men who have been injured in the past, and to whom Mary might have spoken.' She looked at Hester. 'What could we take them that would be useful and not condescending?'

'Honesty,' Hester replied. She took a deep breath. 'And perhaps a less fashionable gown?'

'Oh!' Rose blushed, glancing down at her beautiful dress. 'Yes, of course. This is quite inappropriate, isn't it? Will you excuse me for fifteen minutes? I'm sure I can find something better. Morgan, please don't spend the time trying to persuade Mrs Monk that I am not suitable for this task. It would be humiliating for me. I like her, and I wish to impress her as competent.' She gave him a dazzling smile and kissed his cheek. 'Thank you, my dear.'

Hester mastered her expression with difficulty, reaching very quickly for a handkerchief and coughing into it to hide her smile.

Morgan Applegate blinked also, but he did not say anything.

When Rose returned in a less showy dress Hester suggested that although it would take a little longer and definitely be a great deal less

162

uncomfortable, it would be wiser if they were to travel by public omnibus rather than in Rose's carriage. The day was viciously cold with intermittent sleet and snow piling in dirty drifts at the edges of gutters and walls, and causing the drains to overflow so everything was wet underfoot.

'Of course,' Rose agreed, her face reflecting momentary distaste. 'I shall appreciate my carriage more next time, I suppose.' Then she realised that Hester almost certainly did not have a carriage. 'I'm sorry!' she said, the tide of colour washing up her cheeks.

Hester laughed. 'I had a carriage before I went to the Crimea,' she told her. 'Before the war my family had very comfortable means.'

'You lost it in the war?' They were walking briskly down the street towards the omnibus stop.

'My father did,' Hester replied as they passed two women going in the opposite direction. 'He was cheated out of it by a man who made a fortune doing that. He was an ex-army officer invalided out. A hero, so people trusted him.'

There was a quick sympathy in Rose's face, but she did not interrupt.

'My father took his own life,' Hester found it difficult to say, even now, so many years after. 'But there was no question about it. He felt it was the only honourable way to act . . . in the circumstances. My mother died shortly afterwards.'

'Oh!' Rose stopped still in the street, ignoring the spray of icy water from a passing carriage.

'How unbearable for you!'

'One has to bear it,' Hester replied, taking Rose's arm and moving her away from the edge of the kerb. 'Doing something helps a great deal. The days pass, and it gets better. Do you think that was what Mary Havilland was doing?'

They started to walk again.

'No, no, I don't think so,' Rose said gravely. 'She was too . . . too excited. She grieved terribly for her father, of course, but she really believed she was going to prove his innocence — I mean of — Oh!' It was a wail of horror at herself. She was aghast at her own clumsiness in piling one pain on top of another.

Hester was forced to smile. There was a ridiculous humour to it, in spite of the tragedy. 'I never thought my father acted dishonourably,' she said truthfully. 'In his mind he was paying the price for his error.'

'What happened to the soldier who . . . ?'

'He was murdered,' Hester answered. 'Very violently, by someone else he had . . . robbed. What was Mary like? Please tell me the truth, not what kindness dictates because she is dead.'

Rose thought for a long time, in fact until they reached the omnibus stop and stood side-by-side waiting.

'I liked her,' she began. 'Which means that my opinion is probably not accurate. She was brave in her opinions, and in fighting for what she cared about. But she was afraid of certain kinds of failure.'

'I think we all are,' Hester agreed. 'There are things we can afford to lose, and things we know

164

we can't, and stay whole at heart.'

Rose looked at her, then lowered her glance. 'I think Mary was afraid of being alone, but also of marrying someone she did not love. And she did not love Toby. I am not certain if in the end she even liked him. She preferred the safety of being a good daughter. She did that superbly.'

'And she thought there was no risk in it,' Hester added.

'Exactly.' Rose met her eyes again. 'But she never thought of her own danger in defending her father. I think her courage may have cost her her life.'

'You think Toby meant her to go over the bridge?'

'I know the Argylls only socially. We've met maybe a dozen times in the last few months, but anyone could see they were very close. Toby was clever, and ambitious. Alan was proud of him.'

'But Alan was a success already?'

'Oh, yes! Very much. He is very wealthy. And well thought of, so my husband says.' She frowned. 'Actually his company's record of safety is excellent, better than that of many other companies. If Mary found anything untoward then she must have either discovered it by chance, or have been extraordinarily clever.'

The omnibus arrived and they climbed upstairs, awkwardly, struggling to hold wet skirts out of the way. They did not continue talking until they had found seats and the horses moved off again.

'Then our search won't be easy,' Hester observed. 'I cannot help assuming that Mary was

165

unusually intelligent, and of a very practical turn of mind.'

'Yes, absolutely,' Rose agreed. 'In fact she was a little unfeminine in her grasp of logic, mathematics and such things as engineering. At least — she was told so, and I think she believed it.'

'Did she care?'

'Yes. She was a little self-conscious,' Rose admitted. 'She was defensive about it, so I suppose that means she did. But that is the thing: the week or so before she died she was more fully herself than ever before! She had realised that she had her father's gift for engineering and was happy with it.' Her face was very earnest. 'Mrs Monk, she really was not going to kill herself!'

'Even if she had discovered her father to be mistaken?' Hester hated having to say it, but it would not only be dishonest but destructive of all they hoped to do, for themselves and for others, to conceal it now.

'I believe so,' Rose said without hesitation.

The omnibus reached the end of the line. They dismounted and walked briskly round the corner to the stop for the next one, which would take them as far as the hospital where most injured men would have been taken after the collapse of the Fleet Sewer. On this journey they discussed tactics, and decided that Rose should begin the conversation as the wife of a Member of Parliament, but when it came to medical details, then she would ask questions as Hester prompted her.

It was a long time since Hester had been inside such an institution, but it was exactly as she remembered. In the long hallway she smelled again the forced cleanliness masking the odours of sickness, blood, coal dust and alcohol. Almost immediately she saw junior doctors, excited, self-conscious, walking with that mixture of arrogance and terror that betrayed they were on the verge of actually practising surgery, cutting into human flesh to heal, or kill.

She found herself smiling at her own innocence in the past, imagining she could change everything except for a few individual people.

It took them half an hour to gain access to the appropriate person. Rose was magnificent. Standing a little behind her, Hester could see her hands knotted with tension, and she already knew her well enough to be very aware of how much she cared, however much she might lie with candid and superb ease, at least on the surface.

'How kind of you, Dr Lamb,' she said charmingly when they were in the chief surveyor's office. 'My husband wished me to learn a few facts, so that he will not be caught out if asked questions in the House.'

Lamb was a middle-aged man with a quiff of sandy-grey hair and rimless eyeglasses, and not quite as tall as Rose, so he was obliged to look up at her. 'Of course, Miss . . . Mrs Applegate. What is it the Honourable Gentleman wishes to know?'

'It's really fairly simple,' Rose replied, still

standing in front of his desk, thus obliging him to remain on his feet also. 'It is a matter of the nature and frequency of serious injuries to men involved in the work on the new sewer system.'

'Absolutely vital!' Lamb said earnestly. 'The state of public hygiene in the city of London is a disgrace to the Empire! Anyone would think we were the edge of the world, not the centre of it!'

Rose drew in her breath, then let it out again. 'You are quite right,' she agreed diplomatically. 'It is so very important that we must be absolutely certain that we are correct in all we say. To mislead the House is an unpardonable sin, you know?'

'Yes, yes,' Dr Lamb nodded, pushing his eyeglasses up to the bridge of his nose again. 'What is it you wish from me, Mrs Applegate? I am sure figures are already known, from the companies concerned.'

Rose and Hester had already decided on the answer to that. 'Naturally, but they have a powerful interest in the number of injuries being as low as possible. But there is the world of difference between an engineer's estimate of an injury, and a surgeon's.'

'Of course. Please be seated, Mrs Applegate. And Miss . . . Mrs . . . ?' He waved at Hester without looking at her.

'We would like specifics,' Rose continued, sitting upright with a ramrod-stiff back, and smiling at him. 'Descriptions of actual injuries, and the names of the men concerned, so that it is apparent that we have investigated the matter more than superficially.'

Lamb looked uncomfortable.

Rose waited with an air of expectancy, eyes wide, her mouth in a half-smile ready to beam upon him if he should do as she wished. 'As full a list as possible,' she added. 'So we do not seem to be singling out any particular company. That would not do.'

Reluctantly Lamb reached into his waistcoat pocket and took out a small key. He rose and opened a filing cabinet and from one of the drawers he took out a folder of papers. He returned to the desk and read from them, selectively. 'I cannot see what use this will be in the House of Commons,' he said finally.

He had described accidents and injuries in the blandest terms, using laymen's words, making them seem slighter than they were. Rose might not know that he was being evasive, but Hester did. She spoke for the first time.

"There was an Albert Vincent. His right leg was crushed when a load overturned on him, breaking his femur, I think you said in two places.'

'That is correct,' he agreed, frowning at her, puzzled as to why she had spoken at all. He had assumed her to be there merely as chaperone, or perhaps a maid of some sort.

'You did not mention the treatment given him. Was that because he died?'

'Died?' He looked appalled. 'Why ever should you think that, Mrs . . . ?'

'Mrs Monk,' she supplied. 'Because from the description it could have torn the femoral artery, which would have meant he bled to death in a matter of minutes. If there had been anyone there on the scene to amputate the limb and rescue him, surely it would have been mentioned?'

He was clearly flustered. 'The details are not there, young lady, and I hardly think it is something about which you would have any knowledge, even if you can read a little and bandy words around as if you understood them.'

'Oh, she does!' Rose said with a sweet smile. 'Mrs Monk was in the Crimea with Miss Nightingale. She is acquainted with battlefield surgery, in the most distressing circumstances.'

'You didn't say so!' he accused, the colour now hot in his face. 'That is, if I may be candid, most deceiving of you!'

'Is it?' Rose said ingenuously. 'I'm so sorry. I had imagined you would say exactly the same whoever you spoke to. Had she been of a delicate disposition and likely to faint, I would not have brought her, of course. But that is quite different. I cannot imagine what you would have said differently had you known Mrs Monk is very practised in such tragic and terrible things.'

He glared at her, but could apparently think of nothing to escape from the pit he had unwittingly dug for himself.

'Thank you,' Rose said again, keeping her smile fixed. 'I shall just make a few notes so that we cannot find ourselves mistaken. It would be dreadful to quote figures that are not true. And embarrassing.' She looked straight at him and his face was tight-lipped, but he did not argue.

Outside on the steps with the wind tugging at

170

their skirts, victory seemed already fading. Rose turned to Hester. 'Now what do we do?'

'We have addresses,' Hester replied. 'We find a cup of tea, or better, chocolate, if we can. Then we go and see some of these people and find out which of them, if any, Mary Havilland asked also.'

Fortified by a cup each of thick, rich cocoa and a ham sandwich bought from a pedlar, then, a hundred yards further on, hot chestnuts, they set out to the nearest of the addresses. The early afternoon turned colder. The sleet changed into intermittent snow, but still the street was too wet for it to lie except on the windowsills and lower eaves. Of course the roofs were white except for around the chimneys where the heat melted the snow and sent it in dribbles down the slates. Cab horses looked miserable. Pedlars shivered. The wind flurried, scattering newspapers, and grey smoke hung in the air like shadows of the night to come.

At the first house the woman refused to allow them in. At the second there was no answer. At the third, the woman was busy with three children, the oldest of whom looked barely five.

Hester glanced at Rose and saw the pity in her eyes. However, Rose masked it before the woman could recognise its nature.

'I in't got time ter talk to yer,' the woman said bitterly. 'Wot d'yer think I am? I got washin' ter do wot in't never gonna dry in this weather, an' summink ter find fer tea. Wot's a Member o' Parliament ter me? I in't got no vote, nor's any o' me family. We in't never 'ad an 'ouse wot's ours,

171

let alone big enough ter let us vote. Anyway, me man's crippled.' She started to push the door closed, pushing the small girl behind her and moving her skirts awkwardly.

'We don't want your vote,' Hester said quickly. 'We just want to talk to you. I'll help. I'm good at laundry.'

The woman looked her up and down with disbelief growing into anger at being mocked. 'I 'ear yer, missis. Ladies 'oo talk like you, all proper, don' know a scrubbin' brush from an 'air brush.' She pushed the door again.

Hester pushed it back. 'I'm a nurse and I keep a clinic for street women in Portpool Lane.' She remembered too late that it was no longer true. 'I'll wager you a good dinner I've done more dirty washing than you have!' she added.

The woman's hand went slack with surprise, allowing the door to swing open, and Rose took full advantage of it.

Inside, the house was bare and cold with the sort of poverty that teeters on the edge of starvation. Hester heard Rose draw in her breath, then very carefully let it out silently and tried to compose her face as if she saw such things every day.

It was like the Collards again, only worse. This man was sickly pale, his eyes hollow and defeated. He had been crushed from the waist but his legs were still there, deformed and — from the way he lay and the pinching around his mouth — a constant agony.

Patiently and with trembling gentleness Rose tried to elicit facts from him, and he refused. No

172

one was to blame. It was an accident. Could have happened to anyone. No, there was nothing wrong with the machines. What was the matter with them that they could not understand that? He had told the others the same.

Hester half listened as she started on the laundry with lye soap and water that was almost cold. The physical misery of it did nothing to assuage her sense of guilt. Even as she did it she knew that was ridiculous. Her hour or two of discomfort would be pointless. But the biting cold on her skin pleased her, and the drag on her shoulders when she heaved the wet sheets out and tried to wring them by hand. At the clinic at least they had a mangle.

It was the fourth house after that before they learned anything further. Mary Havilland had been there also.

'You are certain?' Hester said to the handsome, weary woman busy sewing shirts. All the time she was talking to them her fingers never stopped. She barely needed to look at what she was doing.

'Course I am. Don't forget summink like a young lady — an' she were a lady — comin' an' askin' about sewers an' drains an' water wot runs under the ground. Knowed about it too, she did — engines too. Knew one from another.'

Rose stiffened, glancing at Hester then back at the woman.

'She knew about underground streams?' Hester asked, trying to keep the urgency out of her voice.

'Summink,' the woman replied. 'Queer,

173

though.' She shook her head. 'She wanted ter know more. I said me pa'd bin a tosher, afore 'e got took, an' she wanted ter know if I still knew any toshers now. Or gangers. I tol' 'er me bruvver were a tosher, but I in't seen 'im in years. She asked me 'is name. Now wot'd a nice young lady like that wanna find a tosher for?'

'To learn more about hidden streams?' Rose suggested.

The woman's eyes opened wide. 'Wo' for? Yer don' think one o' them's gonna break through, do yer?'

'Did she say that?'

'No! Course she din't! D'yer think I'd be sittin' 'ere wi' a needle in me 'and if she 'ad? Me sister's husband's down there diggin'.' She made no reference to her own husband, one-armed, who was out somewhere in the streets trying to earn a living running errands for people. 'Is this wot you're on about? Wot 'appened to 'er anyway? Why are yer 'ere?'

Hester debated only for an instant. 'She fell off Westminster Bridge and drowned. We are concerned it may not have been an accident. We need to know what she learned.'

'Nothin' from 'ere that'd get 'er topped, I swear that on me muvver's grave!'

They stayed another ten minutes, but the woman could add nothing.

Outside it was dark and the snow was beginning to lie, even though it was only shortly after six.

'Do you suppose she went looking for toshers?' Rose said unhappily. 'What for? To tell

174

her where the underground streams were? Surely Argyll would have done all that? He can't want a disaster. It would ruin him most of all.'

'I don't know,' Hester admitted, beginning to walk towards the omnibus stop. Moving was better than standing still. 'It doesn't make any sense, and she must have known that. But she learned something. What could it be, other than that they are somehow using the machines dangerously, in order to be the fastest, and therefore get the best contracts? Are Argyll's machines different from other people's? We need to find out. Could they be more dangerous?'

Rose stopped, shuddering with cold. 'It seems they work faster — maybe they are? What can we do? These men won't tell us anything — they daren't!' There was anguish in her cry.

'I don't know,' Hester answered. 'All we can do is find out what happened to Mary . . . maybe. If she found proof of some sort — I mean something that would have shut down the works until the machines were made safe, even if it were slower — who would she have told?'

'Morgan,' Rose said straight away. 'She didn't. She never came back.'

They started walking again; it was too cold to stand.

'Perhaps she wasn't certain,' Hester suggested. 'If her knowledge were only almost complete, she was perhaps lacking one point?'

They reached the bus stop and stood side by side, moving their weight from one foot to the other to prevent themselves from freezing.

'Toby?' Hester pressed. 'She might have told him?'

'She didn't trust him,' Rose shook her head. 'He and Alan were very close.'

'Toby worked in the company?'

'Yes. She said he was very ambitious, and at least as clever as Alan — with engineering, at any rate. Perhaps not as good at handling men and as quick in business.'

Half an idea flashed into Hester's mind, and then dissolved before she grasped hold of it. 'So he would understand the machines?'

'Oh, yes, so others said.' Rose's eyes widened. 'You mean she might have been . . . been deliberately playing him . . . drawing information from him to get her final proof?'

'Mightn't she?' Hester asked. 'Would she have the courage to do that?'

Rose did not hesitate. 'Yes . . . by heaven, she would! And he was playing her, to see how much she knew! And it was too much! He had to kill her, because in the end his loyalty was to his brother.'

'And to his own ambition,' Hester retorted. She saw lights along the road and prayed it was the omnibus at last. Her teeth were chattering with the cold.

'How will we ever know?' Rose said desperately. 'I absolutely refuse to let them get away with it, whatever it costs!'

The omnibus stopped and they climbed on, being obliged to stand, jammed between tired workmen and women with bags of shopping, or mending, followed by exhausted children with

176

loud voices and sticky hands.

At the changeover to the second omnibus Rose gave a wry, blisteringly honest smile, as she climbed onto the next platform and inside. 'I shall never be rude to a coachman again!' she whispered fiercely. 'I shall never insult the cook, outrage the maids or argue with the butler, no matter what any of them do. And above all, I shall never let the fire go out, if I have to carry the coal in myself!'

Hester swallowed a laugh that was a little on the edge of hysteria.

'What are we going to do?' Rose demanded.

Hester's mind raced, struggling between the practical and the safe. Safety won, at least for Rose. 'You are going to see what chances there are of passing some kind of law to help the injured. Mary might have thought of that. It was probably why she approached Mr Applegate in the first place. I am going to see if I can find the toshers Mary spoke to and see what they told her. If anyone knows where the old sunken rivers are, or if anything's changed course, it'll be them. If I can find out exactly what she knew, it will be a big step forward.'

'Be careful!' Rose warned anxiously.

'I will,' Hester assured her.

But she did not tell Monk anything other than that she had visited some of those injured in past cave-ins, and other machine accidents, and certainly nothing of her plans. She sent a letter to Sutton, as brief as possible, telling him of her need to learn more from the toshers who knew the old system best. Only after she had sent it did she realise that she had no idea whether Sutton could read or not! He did all his business in cash. Perhaps even the best houses did not wish a bill or a receipt from a rat-catcher.

She waited all day for an answer, busying herself with chores, cleaning up after the plasterer.

Sutton came just after dark, at about half-past four.

'Yer sure?' he asked carefully, studying her face in the kitchen gaslight. He sipped a steaming cup of tea, and had accepted a piece of fruitcake. He was scrupulously fair, giving Snoot a tiny portion, just so he felt included. It probably amounted to no more than a couple of raisins. Snoot took them delicately and licked his lips, waiting hopefully for more.

'That's yer lot!' Sutton told him, shaking his head, then turned back to Hester.

'Well, if yer sure yer really want ter know wot's 'appened, someone as'll tell yer the truth, we'd best go under the Thames Tunnel an' find some o' the folks wot's not still 'opin' fer work, or got loyalties to them as is.' He looked her up and down anxiously. 'But yer can't come like that. If I take yer with me, yer gotta look like yer belong. If I bring yer the clothes, can yer come as me lad wot I'm teachin'?'

She was taken aback for a moment, amusement replaced by the sudden jar of reality. 'Yes,' she said soberly. 'Of course I can. I'll tie my hair back and put a cap on.' It was an unreasonably displeasing thought that with a change of attire she could be taken for rat-catcher's apprentice. And yet had she been

178

more buxomly built, with a rounder, more womanly face, then she would not have been able to go at all.

Then she thought of the faces of the women she had seen yesterday, worn out and old long before their time, colour and softness taken from them, and such self-regard seemed not only ridiculous but disgusting. 'I'll be ready,' she said firmly. 'What time shall we begin?'

'I'll come 'ere,' Sutton said, still uncertain of himself. 'At breakfast. We'll start early. Not as it makes much difference under the . . . ground.'

She knew he had been going to say 'river', and stopped himself at the last moment in case the thought should be too much for her, especially since they had been talking of cave-ins, floods, gas, and such things.

'I'll be here,' she said with a smile, catching his eye and seeing the answering humour in it, and a flicker of admiration, which pleased her quite unreasonably.

He nodded, and rose to his feet.

★ ★ ★

The clothes Sutton brought were laundered, but shabby and badly patched. However, Hester found them more comfortable than she had expected. It was an oddly naked feeling to have no skirts. Even on the battlefield she had been used to the nuisance of skirts around her legs, making striding out difficult, especially in wind or rain. Trousers were marvellous, even if she did feel totally indecent.

Scraping her hair back into a knot and clipping it tight so it appeared short was not difficult, but it was certainly unflattering. But there was no help for it. A flat cap on her head covered most of it anyway, even down over her ears. Sutton had been thoughtful enough to provide a thick, woollen muffler, which made her feel less naked, and a lot warmer. The coat, which came almost to her knees, was the last item, apart from a pair of hard, worn men's boots.

She left the room where she had changed and walked self-consciously, awkwardly because the boots were too big, along the passage towards the stairs down.

'Yer done wonders,' Sutton said approvingly. 'Come on, Snoot! We got business.'

She explained to him as they walked what she and Rose Applegate had learned, and the further thoughts it had put in her mind.

'That's funny,' he said, considering it carefully. 'Were she lookin' fer streams an' the like, or trying ter find out wot 'er pa knew? If 'e knew summink ter kill 'im for? But why for? Streams in't no secret, least ways if they cross one an' it makes a cave-in, the 'ole world's gonna know!'

'It doesn't make any sense,' she agreed, walking more quickly than she was accustomed to keep up with him. 'There's something major in this that we don't know. Either that, or somebody is very stupid.'

He flashed her a dazzling smile with no belief in it of a word she was saying.

She did not reply. She held no hope either that it was so simple.

They travelled by omnibus again, back the way Hester had come, until they reached the northern entrance to the tunnel at Wapping. Hester was startled to see that the building in which it was situated was large and very handsome, so much so that she felt as if she were entering the hall of some concert chamber. She glanced sideways at Sutton, who bent and picked up Snoot, then solemnly carried him down the long, circular steps to the level below where the tunnel itself opened on to something rather like a hallway. With a dawning of amazement Hester realised that no vehicle could get out into the open air. The only way up or down was the great stair.

Sutton put Snoot down and the little dog trotted obediently at his heels across the paved floor to the tunnel entrance. Because of the many windows there was plenty of light in this part, but she realised that as soon as they were any distance inside, there would be only such light as was afforded by gas jets.

'Stay close to me,' Sutton warned. 'There's lots o' folk down 'ere, an' most is 'armless enough, but the livin' is 'ard and people fight for a scrap o' food or a yard o' space, so don't do nothin' but look.'

She kept pace with him obediently. The light became dimmer as they progressed. The air took on a hazy quality, and she was acutely aware of the damp on her skin and the changed smell. The ceiling was far higher than she had expected and after a few yards it was lost from sight, giving a sensation of being closed in that was felt rather than seen. She knew that only a little further on above it was the teeming, filthy water of the Thames. She refused to think of the weight of it or wonder how the arch resisted the weight of earth and then the river bottom, not to mention the currents and the tides.

How deep were they? It smelled stale and it was bitterly cold. But then one would hardly heat the tunnels with fires. There was no possible ventilation here. To create any sort of outlet to the open air would undermine the safety of the tunnels. If it fell in they would be entombed here for ever!

What a ridiculous thought! If you were dead they buried you anyway! What difference would it make? Or perhaps death was not a ceasing to exist, but an endless journey through hell, and Dante was right, it was a pit like this, full of strange, half-heard noises, whispers without words, not human any more.

All senses were distorted. Damp clung in the nose and on the skin. There were gas jets on the walls, and in the dusk-like light Hester could see people moving like shadows, most of them women. They seemed to be buying and selling, by touch as much as sight in the flickering gloom as if it were one nightmare arcade of stalls, a sort of hell's market. Sound was heavy and unnatural, a susurration of feet and skirts and snatches of voices.

'Don't stare!' Sutton warned her under his breath. 'Yer 'ere ter catch rats, not sight-seein', Miss 'Ester.'

'I'm sorry,' she apologised. 'Who are they all?

Do they come down here every day?'

'Most of 'em don't never go up,' he answered. 'We might 'ave 'alf a mile ter go.'

'Who are we looking for?'

They were keeping to the middle of the way, but as her eyes became accustomed to the gloom she was more aware of alcoves to the side. Those hollows must be where people might eat and sleep, and — from the rank odour that now filled the air — conduct other aspects of their lives. It was a whole subterranean world, always damp and yet without natural water. She tried to ignore the scurrying of inhuman feet, the rattle of claws or the pinpoint of red eyes in the shadows.

'People 'oo live in one tunnel often know things about other tunnels,' Sutton answered her question. 'Everything 'ere 'as to be fetched from somewhere else. I'll find yer a tosher 'oo knows the 'idden rivers as well as the ones on the maps, an' mebbe someone 'oo knows a navvy or two 'oo's bin 'urt an' isn't so quick ter defend 'is old bosses. Jus' leave the askin' ter me, right?'

'Right,' she said, keeping her voice low as if the shadows could remember her. They continued deeper under the river and the silence was broken only by voices so low that they seemed wordless amid the scraping and the hiss of the gas jets. Every now and then there was the clang of metal on metal or the duller thud of wood as someone worked. It was an eerie world where daylight was unknown.

Sutton pressed on, stopping now and then to greet someone by name, ask a question, make a

183

wry, bitter joke. Hester hated it. There was no wind, no plants, no animals except rats, and of course the occasional dog. Snoot trembled with excitement at the scent of so much prey, looking up at Sutton and waiting for the word that never came.

They had already spoken to five people and were nearly half a mile under the river when Sutton found the man he most wanted. In the yellow glare of the gas his face looked cast of metal. It was scarred down one side, his ear torn and his hair tufted where the scalp had been ripped away. He was lean, and his hands were gnarled and huge-knuckled with rheumatism.

''Allo, Sutton!' he said with surprise. 'Not enough rats for yer in the Palace, then?' He grinned, showing strong teeth.

''Allo, Blackie,' Sutton replied. 'I done such a good job they're all gorn. 'Ow are yer?'

'Stiff,' Blackie replied with a shrug. 'Can't get after 'em fast enough no more. Got 'elp, 'ave yer?' He looked at Hester curiously.

'Not much use yet,' Sutton shrugged. 'But 'e'll do. In't built fer navvyin'.'

Blackie looked at Hester thoughtfully and she stared back at him, refusing to lower her eyes. Blackie laughed. It was a wheezy, cheerful sound. ''Ope 'e's clever then. 'E in't good fer much else, eh?'

Hester wanted to respond, but she remembered just in time that she could not mimic the accent she would have if she were really learning to be a rat-catcher, nor could her voice sound

184

like that of a boy of the height she was.

'Navvyin' in't so clever,' Sutton shook his head. 'Too chancy these days. Railways are one thing, tunnels is another.'

'Yer damn right!' Blackie agreed.

Sutton looked at him closely. 'Yer reckon one of 'em's goin' ter cave in, Blackie?'

'That's wot they're sayin'.' Blackie curled his lip, making his lopsided face look less than human in the yellow light. 'Word is them stupid sods is gonna keep on cuttin' till they cross a river an' drown 'alf the poor devils wot are diggin' there like a lot o' bleedin' moles.'

Hester drew in her breath to ask him to be more specific, then gasped as Sutton kicked her sharply. She shut her mouth and bit her lip with pain to stop crying out.

''Oo's works?' Sutton asked casually. 'I don't wanna get caught in it.'

'Go down, do yer?' Blackie squinted at him.

'Bin known ter,' Sutton acknowledged it. 'Think it'll be Bracknell and 'is lot?'

'Mebbe. More like Patersons.'

'Argyll?'

Blackie gave him a keen look. 'You 'eard summink, 'ave yer?'

'Whispers? They true?'

'They move faster'n most, but Sixsmith's a canny bastard. Very careful, 'e is. But the engines wot 'e uses are big, and stronger than most. I reckon they done summink to 'em, made 'em better. Could slice through an old sewer wall and bring a cave-in quick as spit.'

Hester was aching to ask for details, but her

185

leg was still smarting from where Sutton had kicked her.

'So I 'eard,' Sutton agreed. 'But I thought it were just daft talk o' some girl. 'Er pa were scared o' the dark, or summink. Lost 'is nerve an' shot 'isself, they said. Mind, she never believed it. Said someone else done 'im in.'

Blackie's eyes narrowed and he leaned forward sharply. 'I'd keep yer face shut about that, if I was you, Sutton,' he said very quietly. 'Stick ter rattin', eh? It's nice an' safe, an' yer know wot yer doin'. Don' go down no 'oles in the ground, an' don' go askin' no questions. O' course they 'ave safety rules, an' o' course they don't use 'em. Fastest one through gets the next contract, easy as that. Better buried alive fer maybe than starved or froze fer sure.' He dropped his voice still further. 'I owe yer, Sutton, an' I owed yer pa, so I'll tell yer for nothin': stick ter rattin'. It's clean an' yer don't upset no one but the rats. There's things about tunnels as yer don't want ter know, an' people in 'em yer sure as 'ell's burnin' yer don' want as should know you! One feller special, so keep yer nose ter yerself — got it?'

Sutton nodded. 'Mebbe yer right,' he conceded. 'Don't you go down no 'oles in the ground neither, Blackie. If they bump inter a river accidental, it in't gonna care that yer a tosher an' 'ave worked these ways all yer life. It'll come down there like a train, faster than a man can run, an' pushin' everythin' in front o' it.'

'I don' go there no more,' Blackie said with a twist of his mouth. 'I know which ones is safe an'

186

which in't. But yer listen ter me, Sutton! Water, gas, fire an' rats in't all there is ter watch fer! There's money in this, so there's men as'd commit murder. Keep out of it, see? Go, an' take that lad there wi' the eyes out of 'ere. I dunno wot yer come fer, but there's nothin' 'ere fer you.'

'I reckon not,' Sutton agreed. Taking Hester by the arm, holding her hard, he turned and started back the way they had come. They had gone a hundred yards before Hester dared speak.

'Mary can't have come down here, surely?' she asked a little shakily.

'Mebbe, mebbe not, but they know about 'er,' Sutton replied. 'She must 'ave asked a lot o' questions — the right ones, by the sound o' it.'

'But they wouldn't tell her anything,' she protested. 'What harm could she do then that they killed her?'

'I dunno,' he admitted unhappily. 'But if anyone killed 'er, it must 'a bin Toby Argyll. Thing is — 'oo told 'im ter?'

'I need to know!' she insisted. 'Otherwise how do we prove that she didn't kill herself?'

'I 'ave ter know too,' he agreed, 'or 'ow do we stop 'em from goin' on faster and faster till they bring the 'ole bleedin' roof in an' maybe bury an 'undred men alive? Or, worse'n that, set the gas alight an' start another Great Fire o' London.'

She said nothing. She did not know the answer, but it troubled her. If Mary had been right, could she possibly have been the only one to see the danger? Surely her questions alone would have been sufficient to alarm other

187

people? Was that what Alan Argyll had been concerned about — not the actual situation but the fears and suspicion Mary was stirring up? Was there ever cause to think they could have started a panic?

'They don't seem afraid,' she said aloud. 'They don't really think it'll happen, do they?'

Sutton looked at her. 'Afraid o' what?' he said gently. 'Think about it too 'ard, an' yer'll be afraid o' the 'ole o' life. Bein' 'urt, bein' 'ungry, bein' cold, bein' alone. Or yer mean bein' drownded or buried alive? Don't think too far ahead. Just do terday.'

'Is that what Argyll counts on? Poor Mary.'

'Dunno,' he confessed. 'But it don't make sense like it is.'

She did not argue, and they walked in companionable silence to the bus stop.

6

Monk was standing in the kitchen when he heard Hester come in at the front door. He spun round and strode into the hall. He was about to ask her where she had been so late, then he saw how she was dressed, and how cold she was, and that her face was pinched and weary. Her hair was straggling as if she had tied it in a knot rather than bothered dressing it at all, and her sleeves and trousers were wet.

'Where in hell have you been?' he said abruptly, alarm making his voice sharper than he had meant. He was very close to her, almost touching her. 'What's happened?'

She did not even try to prevaricate. 'I've been in the tunnels, with Sutton. I'm perfectly safe, but there's something terribly wrong there,' she said, looking directly at him. 'It isn't as easy as I thought. The engines are very big, and they're shaking the ground, but everybody knows that. It's nothing to do with what Havilland or Mary discovered. They all know it's dangerous; it's part of the job.' Her eyes were searching his face now, looking for help, explanations to make sense of it. 'They all know about the fact that there are streams underground, and wells, and that the clay slips. Hundreds of people live down there! But Mary was going from one person to another asking questions. What could she have been looking for, and why did it matter?'

Monk forced himself to be gentle. He stood back and made room for her to walk past him into the warmth of the kitchen. She had been gone all day; but he had cleaned out the stove and relit it. He was not in the least domestic by nature, but he could do that much. With Hester's absences in the clinic caring for the desperately ill and dying, he had been obliged to learn. To complain about such a thing could be contemptible. Caring for himself was something he did not even think about when he had been so terrified that he would lose her permanently to the horror there had been only a few months ago.

He took her coat from her and hung it up on the peg where it could dry. She made no attempt to be evasive, which in itself alarmed him. She must be very badly frightened. He could see it in her eyes in the brightness of the kitchen gaslight. 'Where exactly have you been?' he asked. 'Where did you learn all this?'

'The Thames Tunnel,' she answered. 'Not alone!' she added hastily, and repeated, 'I was perfectly safe.' Involuntarily she shuddered, her whole body in a spasm of memory uncontrollable. She pushed a shaking hand through her hair. 'William, there are people who live down there, all the time! Like . . . rats. They never come up to the wind or the light.'

'I know. But it's probably no more a root of crime than the waterside slums or the docks, places like Jacob's Island.' He put his arms round her and held her close. 'You're not setting up any clinic for them!'

She laughed in spite of herself, and ended up coughing. 'I hadn't even thought of it. But now that — '

'Hester!'

She smiled at him, a bright, warm smile full of laughter.

He breathed out slowly, forcing himself to be calmer. He put more water in the kettle and slid it on to the hob. There was fresh bread and butter and cheese, and a slice of decent cake in the pantry.

'William.'

He stopped and faced her, waiting. Her face was very grave, tense with the power of her feelings.

'Mary went to all sorts of places and asked questions about rivers and clay, and how many people had been hurt, but she asked about engines as well. And apparently she knew something about them. I mean she knew one sort from another. She took terrible risks. Either she didn't realise, or . . . ' she stopped. Her eyes suddenly filled with tears. She was so tired her skin was white and in spite of his holding her, she had not stopped shivering. Nothing he could do would take away the fear inside her. She could not take comfort like a child. She would have to face her fear or her pain before she could let herself go.

'Do you think she was foolish enough to be unaware of the dangers?' he asked.

'No,' Hester said in a soft, unhappy voice, but she did not pull away from him. 'I think she cared about the truth so passionately that she preferred to take the risk rather than run away. I think she was afraid of a real disaster, worse than the Fleet.'

'Because it's in a tunnel?'

'Fire,' she told him. 'Gas pipes go up into houses above ground as well.'

He understood. The possibilities were terrifying. 'And they know?'

She nodded, and moved back a step at last as the shivering eased. 'It looks like it. She just couldn't prove it yet. Or maybe she could. Do you think that's why she was killed?'

'It could be,' he said gently. 'And it also might be why her father was killed, so don't imagine they would give a moment's thought as to whether or not they should kill you, if they see you as a threat! So — '

'I know that!' she cut across him. 'I have no intention of going back there again, I promise.'

He looked at her closely, steadily, and saw the fear in her eyes. She would keep her word, he did not need to ask her for a promise. 'Not only your life,' he said, his voice softer. 'Others too.'

'I know.' She was tightly clenched, but a warmth deeper than that of the room had reached her at last. 'What are you going to do?'

'Make the tea,' he said ruefully. 'Then I'm going to think how I can prove who had the opportunity to kill James Havilland. We'll never prove that Toby meant to kill Mary, and since he went over as well, the matter of justice has been rather well settled.'

'Do you think she held on to him and took him with her on purpose?' she asked.

'Yes,' he said. 'I think she could have done that.'

'It isn't enough, though, is it?'

'No. It doesn't make sense that Argyll would take a risk like that. It would ruin him. There's something else that we don't know. We haven't got all of it.'

She put her arms around him again, holding him more tightly.

* * *

In the morning the situation seemed less clear-cut. If it were Toby Argyll, young and ambitious, who was behind it all, then he was beyond anyone's reach now, and blackening his name would be seen as pointlessly cruel. Alan Argyll would do everything possible to prevent that, and Monk would earn for the River Police a bitter enemy. His proof would have to be absolute. No one would care about rescuing the reputation of James Havilland, and even less about Mary's. Naturally Farnham would see no purpose in it at all.

Monk's accountability to Farnham was one of the prices to pay for the authority his uniform gave him, and a regular and very reasonable income. He did not fear financial insecurity this winter as he had last.

Thinking of ways to skirt around Farnham's

prejudices was a small enough price to pay!

He needed to know a lot more about both Toby and Alan Argyll. It was difficult to form an opinion of someone who was dead, especially if they had died young and tragically. No one liked to speak of them except in hushed and careful tones, as if death removed all weaknesses from them, not to mention actual sins.

Perhaps a good place to begin would be with those who had cared for the other dead people, James and Mary Havilland. This time he would see the housekeeper, Mrs Kitching. He might even ask Cardman again, and persuade him to be rather less stiffly discreet.

⋆   ⋆   ⋆

Cardman greeted Monk with courtesy warmed by memory that he had listened and believed him, but his emotion was too raw beneath his disciplined manner to afford him the luxury of revealing it. He stood in the morning room to answer Monk's questions, and if his mask slipped, it was only to show a swift anger that Mary Havilland was regarded by the Church as a sinner who, by the finality of death, had forfeited her chance of repentance.

Monk felt helpless to reach out to the man's hard, isolated grief. Cardman was intensely private; perhaps it was his only armour. Monk had no wish to breach it. He could remember his own isolation too vividly, the pride and the fear of other human beings that had kept it in place. Unlike Monk, Cardman had found no woman

194

like Hester to crash through it, ruining it and piling up the richer treasures at the same time.

Perhaps also he was honouring his own duty to care for the rest of the staff until such time as they were released and could seek new positions with written recommendations from someone of Argyll's power. There was no one of the Havilland family to help.

Monk asked if he might see the housekeeper, and was conducted along the corridor and, after a brief enquiry, shown into her room.

'Good morning, Mrs Kitching,' he began.

'Hmph,' she said, back straight as a ruler in the chair opposite him in her small, neat sitting room with its polished surfaces and samplers on the walls. She looked him up and down, noting his police uniform jacket — a sartorial burden he bore with difficulty — and then his white shirt collars and beautiful leather boots. 'Police officer, is it? More of the officer, and less of the police, maybe? And what is it you're wanting now? I'll not say ill of Miss Havilland, so you can save your time. I'll go to my own grave saying she was a good woman, and I'll tell the Good Lord so to his face.'

'I want to know why she died, and who was the cause of it, Mrs Kitching,' Monk replied. 'I'd like to know a little more about the other people concerned in her life. For example, did you know Mr Toby Argyll? I imagine he called here to see her quite often, especially after her father's death?'

'And before,' she said quickly.

'Were they very close to each other?'

'Depends what you mean.' It was not a prevarication — she wished to be exact. Her eyes were more direct than those of any servant he could ever remember questioning before.

A thought flashed across his mind. 'Will you be looking for another position after this, Mrs Kitching?'

'I've no need to. I've saved a bit. I'm going to live with my brother and his wife, in Dorking. I'm just staying here till matters are settled.' She did not add that he need not threaten her, because she was impervious to it, but it was in her face.

He smiled. She was exactly the witness he was looking for. 'What I mean, Mrs Kitching, is, was he in love with her, and she with him?'

She gave a little sigh. 'She certainly wasn't in love with him, but she started out liking him well enough. He was very personable, and he had wit and intelligence.'

'And he?'

'Oh, she was handsome, Miss Mary.' She blinked and took a deep breath. It was very clearly difficult for her to govern her distress. She glared at him, as if waking her grief were his fault. ''Cos that's what most gentlemen like, until they know you a little better.'

'And then?' He kept his expression perfectly bland. Thinking of Mary's dead face streaked with Thames dirt was enough to remove all vestige of humour.

'And then they'd rather you didn't have too many opinions of your own,' she said tartly, the tears standing out in her eyes. The thought

196

flashed to him that perhaps she was thinking not only of Mary Havilland, but perhaps some grief of her own now long in the past, but still tender, still haunting her with loss. Many cooks and housekeepers were given the honorary title of 'Mrs', even if they had never married. It was a mark of adulthood rather than marriage, just as when a man moves from being master to mister. It was a distinction that had not occurred to him before. But then women were not legal entities in the same way that men were.

Again he found his sympathy for Mary was clouding his judgement. He was imagining her as someone with courage, honour and wit, someone he would have liked. But it might not have been so at all. To begin with, he had loathed Hester! No, that was not true. He had been fascinated by her, attracted to her, but afraid of his own weakness. He had been certain that he wanted someone far more comfortable: a soft woman who did not challenge him, did not force him to live up to the best in himself, sometimes even beyond what he believed was in him. Hester's gentleness was deeper than mere agreeableness; it was a passion, a tenderness of honesty, not of indifferences, or the lack of the courage or interest to argue. Never, ever was it the lack of an opinion of her own.

Before her, he had fallen in love with quiet, discreet women who never argued, and then realised he was desperately, soul-achingly lonely. Nothing within them touched anything deeper than his skin.

What had happened to Toby Argyll? Had he

had the courage to love Mary? Or had he found her too challenging, too thwarting of his vanity?

'You say he did not like her opinions, Mrs Kitching, but was he in love with her?'

For the first time in their interview she was uncertain. It was sharp in her face.

He smiled bleakly. 'I frequently disagree with my wife, and I have seldom prevailed over her. If she changes her mind at all, it is reasons, not people, which change it. Yet she would be loyal to me and love me through anything, good or bad. I know this because she has done so, without ever telling me I was right, if she thought otherwise.'

She stared at him, shaking her head. 'Then you wouldn't have liked Mr Toby,' she said with conviction. 'He expected obedience. He had the money, you see, and ambitions. And he was clever.'

'Cleverer than his brother?' Monk said quickly.

'I don't know. But I've a fancy he was beginning to think so.' She suddenly realised how bold she was being in so speaking her mind, and a flash of alarm crossed her face, and then disappeared again. She was tasting a new and previously unimagined freedom.

In spite of the gravity of their discussion, Monk found himself smiling at her. Cardman would have been horrified. She was perhaps a year or two older than he. Monk wondered what the relationship had been between them. Superficial? Or had their station in life prevented what would have been a testing but rewarding love?

He thrust the notion from his mind. 'Mr Alan Argyll was different?' he asked. 'And is Mrs Argyll at all like her sister?'

Mrs Kitching's face hardened. 'Mr Alan's a very clever man, a lot cleverer than Mr Toby realised,' she answered without hesitation. 'Mr Toby might have thought he'd get the upper hand in time, but he wouldn't. Miss Mary told me that. Not that I didn't think so myself, just seeing them in the withdrawing room. Miss Jenny's a realist, never was a dreamer like Miss Mary. Easier to get along with. Never asks for the impossible or fights battles she can't win. Been a good wife to Mr Alan. I suppose Mr Toby thought Miss Mary'd be the same. Well, he thought wrong!' She said that last with considerable satisfaction. Then she remembered that Mary was dead. The tears washed down her cheeks and this time she was unable to control them.

Monk was embarrassed, and angry with himself for being so. Why should he? It was an honest grief; there was nothing in it to apologise for.

He thanked her with deep sincerity, and then excused himself.

★   ★   ★

By midday he was back across the city at the construction works again. This time he found Aston Sixsmith above ground and able to speak more easily. There was no point in asking him about Mary. He would be unlikely to know

199

anything of use, but he might know something of the relationship between the two brothers. Monk knew he would have to be far more circumspect here. Sixsmith would be loyal out of the need to guard his job, even if not from personal regard.

'Was Mr Toby Argyll aware of Havilland's fear of tunnels?' he asked. They were standing on the bare clay at least a couple of hundred yards from the nearest machine and the noise of it seemed distant in the brief winter sun.

Sixsmith pulled his wide mouth tight. 'I'm afraid we all were. If you were watching the man you couldn't miss it. And to be honest, Mr Monk, it's part of your job to look for the man that'll crack because he's a danger to everyone else, especially if he's in charge of anything. I'm sorry.' His highly expressive face was touched with sadness. 'I liked Havilland, but liking's got nothing to do with safety. If he'd gone barmy or started telling the men that there was a river going to break through the walls, or chokedamp in the air, or a cave-in coming, he'd have started a panic. God knows what could have happened.' He looked at Monk questioningly to see if he understood.

Monk understood completely. A man of Havilland's seniority and experience losing his nerve would be enough to start the kind of hysteria that could bring about the very disaster he was afraid of. At the very least it would disrupt work, perhaps for days, and consequently the next project would be sure to go to a rival.

'Did you suspect it could be deliberate?' he asked.

Sixsmith was momentarily puzzled. 'Deliberate weakness? He'd make himself unemployable
anywhere else, which would be stupid. Why
would any man do that? And he and both the
Argyll brothers were friends. Family, in fact.'

'I meant sabotage, for a suitable reward,'
Monk explained, but it sounded ugly as he said
it, and he saw the revulsion in Sixsmith's face.

'From another company?' Sixsmith's lips
curled. 'If you'd known Havilland you wouldn't
even ask. He might have hid his weaknesses, and
he might even have been something of a coward,
but he was absolutely honest. He'd never have
sold out. I'd lay my own life on that. And believe
me, Mr Monk, when you work with a man on
things like that — ' he jabbed his thumb
downwards towards the tunnels beneath them
— 'you get to know who to trust, and who not
to. Get it wrong and you don't always live to talk
about it.'

'So both of the Argyll brothers must have
known of Havilland's fears, and that he was
possibly a danger?'

Sixsmith's face tightened and he pushed his
hands into the pockets of his jacket. 'I'm afraid
so.'

'And was Mary a danger also?'

Sixsmith considered for a moment before
answering. He looked uncomfortable. 'Not
really. She had very little idea what she was
talking about. Can't you . . . can't you call it an
accident — Mary's death, I mean?'

Monk noticed that he had not mentioned
Toby's death. 'Both of them?' he asked. 'Mary

and Toby Argyll too?'

A flash of understanding lit Sixsmith's eyes. 'Would have to be, wouldn't it?'

'Well, if hers wasn't suicide, then his wasn't either,' Monk said reasonably. 'The only alternative would be murder. Could he have meant to push her over? She went over backwards, hanging on to him.'

Sixsmith breathed out slowly. 'Trying to save herself, or trying to pull him in with her, you mean?' His face brightened. 'Changed her mind, and trying to save herself! There you are. Unfortunately she was too late. Already lost her balance, and his too. Tragedy. Simple.'

'You didn't say — 'but Toby would never hurt her',' Monk observed.

Sixsmith looked at him very steadily, and now his expression was unreadable. 'Didn't I? No, I suppose I didn't. Got to get back to work now, Mr Monk. Can't afford delays. Costs money. Good day.' He walked away easily with a long, swinging stride.

Monk stood still for a moment or two, thinking, aware of the cold again, and the noise of engines and men shouting. The next thing he needed to ascertain was the exact time James Havilland had died, or as near as the police surgeon could tell him.

★ ★ ★

'What the devil for?' the surgeon demanded when Monk found him in his consulting rooms. He was a lean man with a harassed air as if

202

constantly put upon and always trying to catch up with himself. 'You come to me two months afterwards and ask me what time the poor man shot himself?' He glared at Monk. 'Haven't you anything better to do? Go and catch some thieves! My neighbour's house was broken into last week. What about that?'

'Metropolitan Police,' Monk replied, not without pleasure. 'I'm Thames River Police.'

'Well, poor Havilland died of a gun shot,' the surgeon snapped. 'Not a drop of water anywhere near him, even tap water, never mind the damn river!' He glared at Monk with triumph. 'None of your business, sir!'

Monk kept his temper with difficulty, and only because he wanted the information. 'His daughter believed he was murdered — '

'I know that,' the surgeon interrupted him. 'The grief unhinged her. A great shame, but we don't have a cure for grief, unless the priest has. Not my field.'

'Her death was very definitely from drowning in the river,' Monk went on. 'I saw her go in myself, and that could have been murder.' He saw the doctor's startled look with satisfaction. 'Unfortunately the young man who may or may not have pushed her overbalanced and went in himself,' he continued. 'Both were dead when we pulled them out. I need to investigate her accusation, even if only to lay it at rest, for both families' sakes.'

'Oh. Well, why the devil didn't you say so, man?' The surgeon turned away and began to look through a stack of papers in a drawer behind him. 'Fool!' he muttered under his breath.

Monk waited.

Finally the man pulled out a couple of sheets with triumph and waved them in the air. 'There you are. Very cold night. Lay on the stable floor. Warmer than outside, colder than the house. Should say he died no later than two in the morning, no earlier than ten. But as I remember the household staff say they heard him up at eleven, so that gives you something.'

'Anything medical to prove he shot himself?' Monk asked.

'Like what, for God's sake? That's police work. Gun was on the floor where it would have fallen. If you're asking was he shot at point-blank range, yes he was. Doesn't prove he did it himself. Or that he didn't.'

'Any sign of a struggle — bruises, scratches, a man defending himself? Or didn't you think to look?'

'Of course I looked!' the surgeon snapped. 'And no, there wasn't! There was no struggle. Either he shot himself, or whoever else shot him took him by surprise. Now go and bury the dead decently, and leave me to get on with something that matters. Good day, sir.'

'Thank you,' Monk said sarcastically. 'It's as well you deal with the dead. Your manner wouldn't do for the living. Good day, sir.' And before the doctor could respond, he turned on his heel and marched out.

It was already approaching four o'clock and the winter dusk was closing in. Funny how the weather always became worse as the days began to lengthen after Christmas. It was snowing lightly in the street and within an hour or two the snow would start to lie. Monk began to walk, hands in his pockets, shoulders hunched.

So there had definitely been no fight. There was no evidence of a break-in and nothing had been stolen. Someone had sent Havilland a note, almost certainly requesting a meeting in the stable. Either that person had taken Havilland by surprise and shot him, making it look like suicide, or Havilland had shot himself, presumably after his visitor left.

If it were the former, then the person had gone to some considerable trouble to make Havilland's death look like suicide rather than a burglary interrupted, or a quarrel. Why? Surely it would have been simple enough to make it seem as if Havilland had seen a light and heard a sound, and disturbed a thief. That would not have implicated anyone. So why the appearance of suicide?

The answer was glaringly obvious: to shame him, to discredit anything he might have been saying during the last few weeks of his life. If that were the case, then it had to be Alan or Toby Argyll, or both. Mary had known it, had possibly been on the verge of finding proof, and had paid for it with her life as well.

Without realising it, Monk had been walking towards the police station, as if he had already made up his mind to go back. Why could it not have been anyone in charge of the case but Runcorn? Any other police superintendent would have been easier. At least he assumed it would. He might have made many enemies. He was absolutely certain he had no friends he could call upon. If there were any debts of kindness to be collected from the past, he had forgotten them, along with everything else. The crimes he had solved as a private agent had not endeared him to the police.

He was still walking because it was too cold to stand still. Could he go forward with this case without Runcorn? There was too much envy, shame and wounded pride between them. Every word would be flavoured by memories, given twists and layers of meaning it would not have with others. They would move in a crowd of ghosts.

The alternative was not to tell him but to look into Havilland's death alone — which would be a form of deceit, a declaration of mistrust. Monk did not believe they could work together, put old wounds and vanities aside and seek the truth, even for the victim's sake, or for justice's sake.

And what would Orme make of that? Exactly what anyone else would: that Monk was unfit to command men; his own vanity came before duty or truth.

That was not so! From this instant on, it would not be so! He increased his speed and five minutes later he was outside the police station. Ten minutes after that he sat in Runcorn's office telling him what he had found out, and what he feared.

Runcorn sat silently, his face furrowed with thought.

'I'm going ahead with it,' Monk said, then instantly wished he had not. In one sentence he had excluded Runcorn, and made a challenge of it. He saw Runcorn's body stiffen, his shoulders hunch a little. He must retrieve the mistake, whatever it cost, and quickly. 'I think you will too,' he said, swallowing hard. 'Now you know about the letter. We'll do more if we do it together.' That sounded like an offer, and he meant it as one.

Runcorn stared at him. 'Metropolitan Police and River Police?' His blue-grey eyes were filled with amazement, memory, something that could almost have been hope.

Monk felt the old guilt back like a wave. They had been friends once, watched each other's back in times of danger with an unquestioning trust. It was he who had broken the friendship, not Runcorn. Runcorn had repaid that original hurt a score of times. He had been slow, stubborn, bigoted, too quick to judge, too slow to forgive. But it was still Monk who had broken the bond first. Runcorn was only retaliating, hurt because he was the duller, the clumsier, the less articulate, and knew it every bit as well as Monk did. Runcorn must wonder if this were another chance, or just another trick.

'Actually I meant you and I,' Monk replied. 'At least to begin with. Nobody's going to like it if we prove Havilland was murdered, because it has to be one of the Argylls behind it, or both.'

Runcorn's face set hard. 'If they murdered a man to hide what he knew, then I don't care who likes it or who doesn't, I won't stop till I get him,' he said grimly. 'And I won't let that girl stay buried as a suicide if Toby Argyll killed her, whatever for. Right, Monk. Where shall we start? No! You don't tell me — I'll tell you. It was my investigation and I'm in charge.' He rose to his feet, a big, angry man, stung deep with pain. 'We'll start again along the street where Havilland lived. I know neither of those two brothers did it himself, because they were both well accounted for. I got that far, on Mary's word. Toby was in Wales, a hundred miles away, and Alan was at a party the other side of the city with a hundred witnesses. His wife's word I wouldn't believe, but twenty Members of Parliament I have to. But whoever shot Havilland must have been there. Maybe someone saw him, heard him, noticed something. Come on!'

Monk followed eagerly. There was an element of recapturing the past in walking the dark, bitter streets beside Runcorn. It was colder again and the wind had fallen. Ice slicked the stones and the snow was starting to lie. In the ghostly half-light between the lamps they could see only the outlines of each other. They could have been young men again, voices familiar to each other: Monk's precise diction Runcorn admired so much, hearing the beauty of words as well as the meaning, Runcorn's a good tone but more careless of sound, less precise of grammar.

They moved from one place to another, finding off-duty hansom drivers huddled around a brazier, or local police on the beat. They separated to ask the questions and waste less time, but still learned nothing. Big, lazy flakes of snow now drifted out of the sky into the lamplight and settled feather-light on the ground. Monk began to wonder more honestly what time had given Runcorn in the years since they had started out as equals. Monk himself had been badly hurt, lost his profession, been to the edge of an abyss of fear, of a self-knowledge unendurable even now. At the last moment it was Hester who had helped him prove to everyone — above all to himself — that he was not the man he dreaded he might be.

He had little enough materially. His reputation was dubious. He was still clumsy when it came to command. He had much to regret, to be ashamed of. But he had won far more than he had lost. He had solved many cases, fought for the truth and mostly he had won.

Far above any of that he had personal happiness, an ease of heart that made him smile in repose, look forward to going home at the end of the day, certain of kindness, of trust and of hope.

What did Runcorn have? What gave him pleasure when he closed the office doors and became merely a man? Monk had no idea.

They stopped at a public house and drank a pint of ale each and ate a pork pie with thick crumbly pastry, then set out again. For all their failure, the silence became companionable. They left black foot-prints on the white of the pavement. The reflection of the pale street made the lamps look yellow, like eerie moons on stalks. Their breath was visible, like smoke. Carriages passed them in the street, hoofs

209

muffled by snow. It was midnight.

'Been to the theatre, most likely,' Runcorn remarked as another carriage passed them, looming out of the darkness, and then was swallowed again between the lamps, reappearing outlined against the falling snow.

'One of them may have witnessed something!' Monk said eagerly. He did not mention the unlikelihood of partygoers returning late from an evening's entertainment remembering seeing an unusual event or a person unknown to them, two months earlier. It was all they had, and both of them knew that sometimes luck favours the persistent. They increased their step.

'Mews,' Runcorn said.

'What?'

'Mews,' he repeated. 'We need the coachmen. People will have gone inside and be in no mood to help us at this hour. Coachmen'll still be up. Got to unharness, cool the horses, rub them down, put everything away. It'll be another hour before they can go to bed.'

Of course. Monk should have thought of it himself. In trying to wrench his mind into the habits of river boats, he had forgotten the obvious.

'Right,' he agreed, turning to follow Runcorn, who was still hesitating. The rank he had attained over the years had not taken from him the inner conviction that somehow Monk was the leader. His brain knew better, but his instinct was slower.

He had to force himself to do it, but deliberately Monk walked half a step behind. He needed Runcorn to be present — wholeheartedly — whole mindedly — not still trying to assert his own worth as if threatened by Monk's ambition, the elegance of his quicker tongue. It was not out of guilt, he told himself, it was certainly not mercy, it was practical sense.

They were sheltered for a few yards along the alley; then as they turned into the mews itself the snow caught them again. All the stable lights were on, the doors open. Three men were busy along the length of the mews, working hard backing vehicles into coach houses, soothing animals. And unharnessing them, trying to get finished as fast as possible and get out of the biting cold to warm up before going to bed.

'Names and addresses,' Runcorn said, unnecessarily. 'We'll not get much more than that out of the poor devils at this hour.'

Monk smiled to himself. The 'poor devils' were going to get home into the warmth a long time before he was.

'Evening,' Runcorn began cheerfully as they approached the first man, who was busy unfastening a harness on a handsome bay horse.

'Evening,' he replied guardedly. The horse threw its head up and the man caught the rein, steadying it. 'Quiet now! 'S all right! I know yer want ter go ter bed. So do I, boy. Steady now! What is it, sir? Yer lorst?'

Runcorn introduced himself. 'Nothing wrong,' he said mildly. 'Just wonder if you've been to the theatre, or something like that, and if you have, if you go quite often. You might have seen something helpful to us. We'll come back at a better time to look into it.'

The man hesitated. In the carriage lights his face was marked with weariness and the snow was dusting his hat and shoulders. 'Prince o' Wales Theatre,' he answered guardedly.

'Go often?' Runcorn asked.

'Couple o' times a week, if there's something good on.'

'Excellent. Which number house do you belong to, and what's your master's name?'

'Not tonight,' the man shook his head.

'Course not,' Runcorn agreed. 'Tomorrow, maybe, at a decent hour. What's his name?'

Monk gave a half-salute and moved on to the next coachman, who was clearly visible in the lights about four houses along.

In half an hour they collected a reasonable list. They agreed to resume the following evening, a little earlier this time.

Monk indulged himself and took a hansom all the way home. He arrived at just after one o'clock, tired, frozen, but with a sense that perhaps he was on the brink of achieving something real, not merely another question.

*   *   *

His mood was considerably deflated when he arrived at the station in Wapping a little late the next morning.

'Mr Farnham wants to see you, sir,' Clacton said with a smile composed far more of satisfaction than friendliness. The smile broadened. ''E's bin waiting a while!'

Monk could think of no reply except one that would not play straight into Clacton's hands. But the resolve hardened inside him to deal with Clacton decisively as soon as he could create the opportunity. This time he simply thanked him and went to report to Farnham.

'Cold getting to you, Monk?' Farnham said unsympathetically before Monk had closed the office door.

'Sir?' The room was warm and comfortable, smelling slightly of woodsmoke, and there was a cup of tea steaming on the desk next to a pile of papers.

'Fancy your bed more than a brisk river crossing?' Farnham elaborated. 'Didn't see that that's what the job would need? On the water, Monk! That's where the work is!' He did not add that Durban would have been here long before this hour, but it was implicit in his expression.

'Yes, sir. It was a cold night,' Monk agreed, biting his temper with great difficulty. Private work might leave him frighteningly short of money, but it afforded him the luxury of not putting up silently with remarks like that. He had to remind himself with cruel bluntness what it would cost him to retaliate now. 'It was a harsh night,' he added. 'It was snowing quite hard when I got home at half-past one.'

Farnham looked irritated. 'Chasing that suicide again? Do I have to remind you that river crime is up, which is our business — your business, Monk? There aren't many passenger boats on the water this time of year, but the few there are are experiencing more thefts than

213

usual, and we aren't doing anything about it! Some people are suggesting that is because we don't care to.' His face was hard and there were blotches of colour in his cheeks.

Monk realised Farnham was losing control of his anger again, because the emotion inside him was too powerful to govern. It was fear, the possibility of disgrace to the police he loved and which was his source, not only of income and power, but of his belief in himself. It had been his decision to allow Monk to replace Durban, perhaps to honour Durban, and against his own judgement. He needed to please the men, and to retain their loyalty, but if Monk proved inadequate to the job it would be Farnham who would take the blame.

'I'm sorry to hear that, sir,' Monk said dutifully, standing very straight. 'It is totally wrong. We care very much, and we must prove it.'

'Yes, you damned well must!' Farnham agreed vehemently. 'Nobody cares about a suicide. Tragic, but they happen. Girl was apparently of unsound mind ever since her father took his life.' He grimaced. 'Seems to run in the family. Leave it alone. Let the dead be buried in as much peace as possible. It's hard enough for the family left, without you nosing around asking pointless questions and keeping it in the forefront of everybody's minds.'

He started to pace up and down. He had apparently forgotten his tea. 'People are saying that the River Police are corrupt!' The pink deepened in his cheeks. 'That has never

214

happened before since I've been in the force! They even said we're taking a rake-off ourselves!' He stopped mid-stride and glared at Monk, his eyes bright and hot. 'I won't have my force destroyed by that slander. I lost my best man in Durban. He was wise, brave and loyal, and above all he was honest. He knew this river like his own back yard, and he knew its people, good and bad.' He jabbed his finger at Monk. 'No one would have said such a monstrous thing about us if he were alive. I don't expect you to take his place. You wouldn't know where to begin! But you'll clear up this mess and prove we don't look the other way at crime, any crime! And we take nothing out of it but our pay, which is hard-earned and by the best bunch of men who ever wore Her Majesty's uniform! Do you understand me?'

'Yes, sir, I do.'

'Good. Then get out and begin to do what you are hired for. Good day.'

'Good morning, sir.'

Monk went back to the outer room and his own desk where the reports were of the monetary theft. None of the men commented, but he felt Clacton's eyes on him. The patrol had already gone out before Monk had arrived. He read the account of the night's events, the usual minor thefts, disturbances, and accidents. There was only one major incident, but it had narrowly avoided becoming a disaster, largely due to the rapid action of the River Police on duty.

Monk made a note to himself to congratulate

the men concerned, and to do it as publicly as possible.

Farnham was not exaggerating. The thefts reported on the passenger boats going up and down the river had increased alarmingly. He had read the old reports from the same time last year, in Durban's neat, strong hand, and the crime had more than doubled since then. The escalation had come since Monk had taken over.

Was that coincidence? Or had the thieves taken advantage of a new and slacker regime, a commander who was ignorant of a great deal of their names and habits, their connections with each other, their methods and tricks? A commander who also did not know his own men and whose men in turn had little confidence in him?

Then a darker and even uglier thought forced itself into his mind. Were Durban's figures a good deal less than accurate? Was it possible that for his own reasons he had altered them, either to hide the true degree of crime, or — a thought that was even more painful — because the accuser was right and the police were pocketing some of the takings themselves?

No. He refused to think that. Durban would not have stolen. Monk had known him. He was a man whose honour shone through his acts, never spoken, never needing to be.

But that was simplistic. People were not single-layered. There were many loyalties that could bind one, often pulling in different directions. What if he had hidden things to protect one of his own men? Perhaps one to whom he owed his life from some dangerous incident on the river that had gone wrong. It happened. One could collect debts without ever intending to, and all debts had to be honoured. That was the safety, and the danger of working with other men. They watched your back, defended your vulnerabilities, and you defended theirs, whatever the cost. It was the only way you could survive and work on the river with its violence, its hazards and its ever-shifting population.

Monk had known Durban only briefly. Mainly for one terrible incident where Durban had shown himself to be a giant among men. Monk had not only admired him but liked him as a friend and companion. But he knew now that he had no idea what other friends he had, or enemies, what debts, paid and unpaid.

He realised with surprise that he intended to protect Durban — from Farnham, from whoever it was that accused the River Police of corruption, even from Orme, if necessary. It was not a matter of paying his own debt, it was simply out of friendship.

How to build such a defence was a great deal more difficult. He sat looking through the figures of recent crime again, reading and rereading them, trying to see a pattern in order to understand what had changed. Half an hour later he was forced to accept that he did not know any more than when he had begun.

He could not afford the luxury of pride and would have to ask one of his men. He sent for Orme. It was a risk confiding in him. If he did not understand what Monk was trying to do he might feel confused and defensive, fearing that Monk was seeking to undermine Durban and establish himself on the ruin of another man's reputation.

If he already knew of the corruption and even were a party to it, then Monk would have left himself vulnerable in a way that might prove his ultimate defeat. With Orme against him he could not succeed in any part of his job.

'Yes, sir?' Orme stood in front of him, his jacket buttoned straight, his clean collar fastened a little tightly around his neck. He looked anxious.

'Close the door and sit down,' Monk invited him, indicating the wooden chair at the far side of his desk. 'Mr Farnham says that thefts have gone up alarmingly on the passenger boats,' he said when Orme had obeyed. 'Looking at the figures in all the reports, he's right. They're much higher than this time last year. Is that coincidence, or is there something I have neglected to do?'

Orme stared at him, confused by his candour. Perhaps in the work they had done together he had already realised that Monk was a proud man and had difficulty in relying on anyone else.

All Monk's instincts were to retreat, but he could not afford to. He had everything to gain from winning Orme's trust, and everything to lose without it. He forced himself to speak gently. 'Mr Farnham says that there are people suggesting we are corrupt. We have to clear this up and prove them wrong — or liars, if that's what they are.'

Orme paled, his body stiff. His eyes met Monk's in a long, puzzled, unhappy gaze.

'The River Police have had a name for honesty for over half a century,' Monk went on, his own voice quiet and angry. 'I won't have it changed now! How do we stop this, Mr Orme?'

Orme snapped to attention. Suddenly he realised Monk was asking his help, not somehow challenging him, and far less blaming him.

'There's a lot for us to do, sir,' he said carefully, as if testing Monk's intent.

'There is,' Monk agreed. 'There are the usual fights and robberies in the docks and along the barges and moored ships, the accidents, the dangerous wrecks or cargoes, the thefts, fights, sinkings, and fires.'

'And murders,' Orme added, watching Monk's eyes.

'And murders,' Monk agreed, questioning Orme in turn by the slight inflexion of his voice.

'Do you reckon as she meant to go over, Mr Monk?'

So he was thinking of Mary again, as if he too were haunted by her courage, her loneliness, the unsolved questions.

'No, I don't.' He was being more honest than he had intended, but there was no help for it now but to go on. If he could not rely on Orme he was lost anyway. 'I think she knew of something in the tunnelling more dangerous than just the engines, or even the speed with which they're cutting. Her father knew it as well.

219

I don't know what it is yet, but I think they killed him over it.'

'Argyll?' Orme said with surprise.

'Not directly, no. I think he probably paid someone to do it, and she found that out too.'

Orme's face was grim with the anger a normally gentle man feels when he is outraged. There was something frightening in it, unselfish and implacable. 'I think as you should keep followin' that until you find out who it was, sir,' he said levelly. 'It's wrong ter let that go by. If we don't see it right for a woman like that, what use are we?'

'And the thefts from the passenger boats? Our reputation matters too,' Monk pointed out. 'It's part of our ability to do the job. If people don't trust us we're crippled.'

'We got to do what's right, and trust it'll be seen as right,' Orme said stubbornly. 'I can't find out who killed 'er, I haven't got the skill fer that. Never done it with people of that class. Give me a river fight, dockers, thieves, lightermen, sailors even, and I can sort it out. But not ladies like that. You done that for years, Mr Monk. You know murders what are quiet. I know a punch in the face, you know a knife in the back. We'll get it all, between us.'

'What about a hand in the pocket, a slit in the purse and your money gone?' Monk asked.

Orme's mouth tightened. 'I'll take care o' that. And o' people with big mouths and small minds. I know a lot of people who've got secrets I could help, or tell in the right place. You can't help getting enemies in this job, but if you're careful, an' keep your promises, you get friends as well.'

'I don't know where the enemies are yet,' Monk admitted.

Orme smiled mirthlessly. 'Not yet, but I do. There's a few I can use, an' I will. Believe me, sir, them boat thieves'll wish they 'adn't started. You find who killed that poor girl. I'll be be'ind you, an' I'll watch yer back against Mr Farnham.'

'Thank you,' Monk said simply and whole-heartedly.

7

That evening Monk and Runcorn were in Charles Street again. They were about to begin the task of knocking on the doors of those who had been to the theatre the night before, and might possibly have returned at about that same hour the night when James Havilland had died. The day's rain had turned last night's snow to slush, but now it was freezing again and the pavements were slippery underfoot. The pall over the city from so many domestic fires and factory chimneys blocked out the stars. The streetlamps glowed yellowish white with a halo of mist around each one and the cold of the night caught in the throat. The noise of hoofs was sharp and loud, and carriage wheels crunched on the frozen slush.

Monk and Runcorn walked as swiftly as it was safe to do without losing one's footing. They kept their heads down out of the wind, their hats low, coat collars turned up.

Runcorn glanced at Monk as if about to speak, then seemed to change his mind. Monk smiled, partly to himself. He knew that Runcorn was thinking — just as he was himself — that they were almost certainly wasting their time. But having come this far, they might just as well try every house whose front door, servants' entrance or mews might possibly have allowed one of the occupants to see someone come or go to Havilland's mews that night.

Monk had earlier checked with the library of past newspapers exactly which theatres had been open and the hours when the curtains had come down.

'Better get on with it,' Runcorn said grimly, approaching the first door and climbing the steps.

That attempt was abortive, as was the second. The third took a little longer, but also yielded nothing. The man who came to speak to them was polite, but quickly made it apparent that he did not wish to become involved in anything that had happened in the street, or anyone else's home. They left feeling more despondent than if he had simply denied being out.

Runcorn pulled his coat collar up higher and glanced at Monk, but he did not say anything. They were now four doors away from Havilland's house, and on the opposite side of the street. Monk continued the investigation from habit, in the perverse refusal to surrender rather than any hope of achieving anything.

He and Runcorn walked up to the step side by side, but it was Runcorn who knocked on the door.

The footman who answered was young and somewhat flustered. He had very clearly not been expecting a caller at this hour of the night. 'Yes, gentlemen?' he said with some alarm.

'Nothing wrong,' Runcorn soothed him. 'Is

your master at home?'

'Yes!' the young man blinked. He should have been more circumspect, even at this hour, and he realised it the moment the words were out of his mouth. The colour washed over his face. 'At least . . . ' He did not know how to finish it without obviously lying.

'That would be Mr Barclay, and Mrs Ewart?' The lift of puzzlement was barely discernible in Runcorn's voice.

'Yes, sir.' The footman's face was pink. He was plainly embarrassed and trying very hard to find a way out of his predicament. He was still struggling when a man in his middle thirties came across the hall behind him and into the vestibule. He was tall and rather elegant, and dressed in evening clothes as if he had only lately returned from some formal event.

'What is it, Alfred?' he asked with a frown. 'Who are these gentlemen?'

'I don't know, sir. I was — '

'John Barclay,' the man said brusquely. 'Who are you and how may we be of assistance? Are you lost?'

'Superintendent Runcorn, Mr Barclay,' Runcorn introduced himself. 'And Inspector Monk, of the Thames River Police. Sorry to disturb you so late, sir, but since you've been out at this hour, we wondered if you might do so quite often.'

Barclay's eyebrows rose. 'Certainly. What of it? It's hardly your concern. And what on earth can it have to do with the River Police? I haven't been anywhere near the river. Except across the bridge, of course. Did something happen? I saw nothing.'

'Not tonight, sir,' Runcorn was shivering so his words were a trifle blurred.

Monk sneezed.

'I haven't seen anything to interest the police at any time,' Barclay said a little impatiently. 'I'm sorry, I can't help you.' He glanced at Monk. 'For heaven's sake, man, go home and get a hot toddy, or something. It's nearly one in the morning!'

Something in his attitude irritated Runcorn. Monk saw it in the tightening of the muscles of his jaw and a slight alteration to the angle of his head. 'Were you acquainted with Mr James Havilland, four doors up, across the road, sir?' he asked.

Barclay stiffened. 'I was, but not more than to be civil to. We had little in common.'

'But you knew him?' Runcorn was determined either to keep Barclay on the step, or to be invited inside. The night was bitter and the wind was coming from the northeast, and blowing right into the house.

'I've told you, Inspector, or whatever your rank is — ' Barclay began.

'Superintendent, sir,' Runcorn corrected him.

'Yes, Superintendent. I knew him as one knows neighbours! One is civil, but one does not mix with them socially if they are not of the same . . . interests. Do I have to spell it out for you more closely than that?'

There was a light tap of heels across the parquet floor of the hall behind him and the door opened, showing a woman of about his own age. She too was slender, with brown hair and blue eyes, and winged brows that gave her face a highly individual look.

'It's nothing, Melisande,' he said hastily. 'Go back into the warmth. It's a filthy night.'

'Then don't keep the gentlemen on the step, John,' she said reasonably. She looked beyond him at Runcorn, and then at Monk. 'Please come in and speak in comfort. Perhaps you would like something hot to drink? As my brother says, it's a rotten night. Your feet must be frozen at least. I know mine are.'

'For heaven's sake, Mel, they're police!' Barclay hissed in what might have been intended as an aside, but was perfectly audible probably as far as the street.

'Oh dear! Has something happened?' She came closer. Monk could see in the vestibule light that her face was lovely, but there was a patience and even a sadness in it that suggested that life was not as easy for her, or as rich as superficial judgement might assume.

'Nothing that needs to concern you, my dear,' Barclay said pointedly. 'They are merely looking for witnesses.'

She did not move away. 'It must be urgent to bring you out at this time of night.' She looked to Runcorn, who was standing more in the light than Monk was. 'What is it you need to know, Mr . . . ?'

'Runcorn, ma'am,' he replied, suddenly a trifle self-conscious. There was something in the elegance of her gown, the flawless curve of her

226

throat, which made him more than normally aware of her, not only professionally but personally. Monk knew it, but he did not know how.

She smiled. 'What is it that we might have seen, Mr Runcorn?'

Runcorn coughed as if his throat were tight. 'There's not much chance, ma'am, but we're pursuing everything we can. It's about Mr James Havilland.'

'I'm afraid I didn't know him well — ' she began.

'You didn't know him at all,' Barclay cut across her, then turned to Runcorn again. 'We really have no idea what happened or why, except that the poor man shot himself. Frankly I can't imagine why you're wasting your time still delving into it. Is there not enough crime to keep you busy? If you don't know where it is, I can certainly tell you!'

'John!' his sister remonstrated, then looked at Runcorn as if in apology. 'What is it you think we may have seen?'

There was a sudden gentleness in Runcorn's face. Monk was beginning to realise how much he had changed in the last two years. Some kind of confidence within him had enabled him to look outwards with less need to defend himself, more awareness of the hurt of others.

'Anyone else in the street, or coming out of the mews,' he answered her, 'apart from your own immediate friends and servants — any stranger at all, or person you wouldn't expect to see. Actually anyone else at all, because they might

227

have seen something and be able to help.'

'Help what?' Barclay asked scathingly. 'Let the dead rest in peace! At least grant them that much decency. His poor daughter took her own life as well. I presume you know that?'

Monk spoke for the first time, with an edge to his voice. 'I was there, on patrol on the river. She went over the bridge. I am not certain that she intended to.'

Barclay looked surprised. 'No one else seems to have any doubt. But even if she fell by accident, that has nothing to do with us. It was miles from here, and we can't help you. I'm sorry. Good night.' He stepped back.

Melisande's gown was light and she was obviously cold, but she refused to step out of his way. She looked at Monk. 'Is there some chance she did not take her life?' Her face was soft, her eyes lit with hope. 'I didn't know her very well, but I would so much like to think that she was not so filled with despair that she would do such a thing, and of course also that she could have a proper burial. The other is so . . . brutal.'

'Yes, there is a chance, ma'am,' Monk replied. 'That is part of what we are still investigating.'

'And if we saw anyone in the street the night of her father's death, that might help?'

'Yes.'

Runcorn was staring at her with a steady, unwavering gentleness. Had he seen the sadness in her too, the vulnerability?

As if aware of it she turned and answered as though it were Runcorn who had elaborated rather than Monk. 'We were at the theatre that night,' she told him. 'I can't remember what we saw, and it doesn't matter now. It went right out of my head when I heard the next day what had happened. But we did return about half-past midnight, and we saw a man coming out of the mews opposite.'

'He wasn't coming out,' Barclay contradicted her with a wince. 'He was on the footpath, staggering around. He had clearly been over-indulging. I've no idea who he was so I couldn't tell you where to find him. But even if I could he would be useless to you. He couldn't even see where he was going, let alone be a credible witness to anything.' His brow furrowed, his expression sharper. 'But even if he'd seen Havilland put the gun to his head and pull the trigger, how would that help anyone? You know what happened. Let it be mercifully forgotten. It's no one's fault, and nothing whatever to do with us.'

Monk was freezing. His body and Runcorn's were to some extent sheltering Barclay and his sister, but even so he felt a heat of resentment rise up inside him. 'It is possible, sir, that he did not kill himself!' he said sharply.

'Don't be absurd!' Barclay was angry now, rattled. 'Are you suggesting there's some maniac going around shooting people in their own homes, in the middle of the night? Here?' He put his arm out as if to protect his sister.

She moved fractionally away from him, just out of his reach, her eyes still on Runcorn.

It was Runcorn who answered, not to contradict Barclay so much as to reassure

Melisande. 'No, sir. If it was someone else then it was deliberately planned and arranged, and it was to do with his work. There is no need at all for anyone else to be alarmed. If we are right then the man concerned is miles away from here and the last thing he'd be likely to do is draw attention to himself by coming back.'

Melisande smiled. 'Thank you,' she said quietly. 'And he did come out of the mews. He staggered around a little as if he were drunk, and he said he was.'

'He said he was?' Runcorn was startled. 'What did he say exactly?'

'He had a stain on his jacket.' She touched her shoulder, about the place where she would have pinned a corsage. 'About here. Quite a large stain, three or four inches across, dark, as if it were wet. He saw me looking at it, only briefly. I suppose that was rude, but it was such an odd place to have a stain so large. He said he had tripped and fallen in the mews. He . . . ' she made a slight gesture as if brushing herself down, ' . . . he said he didn't know what he fell in, and would prefer not to think of it. Then he apologised and went on down the road.' She glanced at her brother. 'If he fell in the mews then he should have smelled of horse manure,' she said seriously.

Barclay's eyes showed not only his disgust but also his impatience. 'I dare say he did, Mel!' he said sharply. 'Dirt and horse dung.' He made a guttural sound in his throat. 'I'm perished standing out here. There really isn't anything more to say. Good night, officers.'

230

Melisande refused to move, disregarding his growing anger. 'But he didn't!' she insisted. 'He didn't smell at all. He was very close to me. He passed only a foot away, and he didn't smell of anything except . . . sweat, and something a little sickly, and . . . something else quite strong, but I didn't recognise it.' Again she was looking at Runcorn.

Monk felt a tingle of excitement, the first scent of meaning. He glanced at Runcorn and had to bite his lip to keep silent.

Runcorn let out his breath slowly. 'What kind of smell, ma'am?' He was achingly careful not to suggest anything to her. 'Can you describe it?'

'Really!' Barclay lost his temper. 'What's the matter with you, man? Asking a lady to describe the precise stink of a drunkard! I don't know what kind of person you are used to . . . '

The colour washed up Melisande's checks. Her brother's rudeness clearly embarrassed her far more than the nature of the question.

Runcorn blushed also — for her, not for himself. Monk could see that in the anger and confusion in his eyes. He longed to help her, and he had no idea how to. Something in her manner, her particular kind of loneliness, had found his sympathy and he was utterly and wholly in her defence.

Could Monk help, without robbing Runcorn of the chance? Which was better: to rescue her, or to leave it that if Runcorn could not then it was not possible? She had been raised to obey, to acquiesce. He thought of Hester with an inward smile he did not dare show.

Runcorn stared at Barclay with cold dislike. 'It matters, sir,' he said. His voice was shaking a little, but that could have been attributed to the cold. He and Monk were shuddering now, their feet almost numb. 'This man may have seen a murder. I don't willingly distress anybody, but it sometimes happens that those who can help the most are also those who are sensitive to the . . . unpleasant details.'

'Please, John, don't try to protect me from doing my duty. That would not be a service to me.' Melisande looked at Runcorn, gratitude in her smile. 'It was rather an acrid, smoky kind of smell. Not very pleasant, but not sour or dirty.'

'Probably picked up someone's old cigar end.' Barclay wrinkled his nose.

'No, it wasn't,' she replied. 'I know tobacco smoke. It definitely wasn't that, but it was rather smoky.' She paled suddenly. 'Oh! You mean it was gun smoke?'

'It might have been,' Runcorn agreed.

'You can't base a charge of murder on that!' Barclay protested.

'I don't.' Runcorn could not conceal his dislike. He looked at Barclay coldly. 'There are other reasons for believing that Mr Havilland might not have shot himself.' He turned back to Melisande and his eyes softened. 'Do you recall anything of this man's appearance, ma'am? Of what height was he? A big man or a small man? Anything about his face?'

She took a moment to bring it back to her mind. 'He was very lean,' she replied. 'His face was thin, what I could see of it. He had a scarf — ' she made a gesture around her throat and chin — 'and a hat on. I think he was very dark . . . '

'It was the middle of a winter night!' Barclay said, with an obvious effort to be reasonable in spite of everyone's else's unreason. 'He was of very average height and build and he had a dirty old coat on, and his collar turned up, as anyone would out on such a night. That's all!'

'If his coat was dark, how did you see the wet stain on it?' Runcorn asked.

'All right then, it wasn't dark!' Barclay snapped. 'It was a light coat, but it was still dirty. Now we've told you everything we can and you have kept my sister standing here in the cold for more than long enough. Good night!'

Melisande drew in her breath, perhaps to point out that it was he who had chosen to remain on the step. She had tried to invite them inside. But she might have remembered it was Barclay she was dependent upon, not Runcorn or Monk.

'Good night,' she said with a swift, apologetic glance, then turned to go inside.

The door closed, leaving the policemen in a sudden darkness. They were so numb from the icy wind that their first few steps were almost stumbling.

Runcorn walked in silence for nearly a hundred yards, still lost in his own thoughts.

'Better see if anyone else saw him,' Monk said at last. 'Might be a groom from one of the houses.'

Runcorn gave him a sideways look. 'Might be,'

he agreed drily. 'I'm betting it was an assassin, hired by one of the Argyll brothers to get rid of Havilland. But we've got to rule out everything else, so tomorrow we'd best ask all around. I can put my men on that. I suppose you've got river things to attend to?'

Monk smiled. The sudden appreciation of his position was an oblique way of thanking him for not showing off in front of Melisande Ewart. 'Yes. Spate of robberies, actually. Thank you.'

Runcorn stared at him for a moment, as if to make sure there was no mockery in his eyes. Then he nodded and began walking again.

★ ★ ★

Monk was late to Wapping again in the morning. He had not meant to be, but he had fallen asleep after Hester had wakened him, and even her noisy riddling of the ashes from the stove had not roused him.

It was nearly ten o'clock when he climbed the steps from the ferry. They were slicked over with ice and dangerously slippery. He reached the top and saw Orme coming out of the station door. Had he been waiting for him? Why? Another warning that Farnham was after him? He felt cold inside.

Orme came towards him quickly, his coat collar up, wind tugging at his hair.

'Morning, sir,' he said quietly. 'Like to walk that way a bit?' He inclined his head to indicate the stretch southwards.

'Good morning, Orme. What is it?' Monk took

the hint and turned to keep in step.

'Did a good bit of looking around yesterday, Mr Monk. Asked a few questions, collected a favour or two,' Orme answered in a low voice. He led Monk away from the station and within a few moments, out of sight of it. 'It's right enough there's bin a lot more thievin' in the last month or two — neat like, all tidy. Passenger standin' talkin'. Piece goes, watch or bracelet or whatever it is. Like as not it isn't noticed for a little while, then o' course it's too late. Could be anywhere. There's always someone beside you as couldn't 'ave done it, an' they always say as they saw nothing.'

'Several people working together,' Monk judged. 'One to distract, one to take it, a passer, another to block the way with offers of help, and maybe a fifth to take it and disappear.'

'Yer right. An' from what I 'eard, I'm pretty certain at least one of 'em was a kid, ten or eleven, each time.'

'Not the same child?'

'No, just that sort of age. People take 'em for beggars, mudlarks, just strays 'anging around for a bit of food, likely, or to keep warm. Better in a boat than on the dockside in the wind.'

Monk thought of Scuff. He would probably rather work than steal, but what was there for a child to do on the river in midwinter? The thought of hot food, a dry place out of the wind, a blanket, would be enough to tempt anyone. He was brave, imaginative, quick, the ideal target for a kidsman, one of those who took in unwanted children and made thieves of them. It was a far from ideal life, but in return they ate and were

235

clothed, and to some extent protected. The thought of Scuff ending like that sickened him. There was no leniency in the courts for children. A thief was a thief.

'Any idea who?' He found the words difficult to say.

Orme must have heard the emotion in his voice. He looked at him quickly, then away again. 'Some. Only the arms and legs of the gang, so to speak. Need to catch the 'ead to be any use. Won't be 'easy.'

'We'll have to plan,' Monk replied. 'See if there's any pattern in the reports of theft. Any of the goods turn up? Who'd take that kind of stuff? Opulent receivers?' They took the valuable things and knew where and how to dispose of them. Durban would not have had to ask — he would have known their names, their places of business and storage, the goods in which they specialised.

'Yes, sir.' Orme did not add anything.

Monk realised, as if he had suddenly come to a yawning hole in the earth in front of him, how much Orme missed Durban, and how far short Monk still was of filling that space. Perhaps he could never earn that loyalty or give the men cause to accept him as they had Durban, but he could earn their respect for his skill, and in time know that they could trust him.

For now it was Orme they trusted, Orme they would be loyal to and obey. Monk would get no more than lip service, and less than that from Clacton. That was a problem that still had to be addressed, and they would all be waiting to see how Monk handled it. Sooner or later Clacton himself would provoke a confrontation, and Monk's authority would hang on whether he won, and how.

He tried to think of other plans he had used in the past to catch rings of thieves, but since the accident that had taken his memory he had worked largely on murder cases. Petty thieving belonged to a past before that — in the early years, when he and Runcorn had worked together, he thought wryly, not against each other. He had had flashes of going into the rookeries, those vast slums, which were part underground tunnels, part sagging tenements. There were passages, trapdoors, sudden drops and blind ends, a hundred ways to get caught, and your throat cut. No one would know, or see you again. Your corpse would possibly go out on the tide, or if it finished in the sewer, most of it would be eaten by rats.

That world was violent and ugly. The poverty in it was so absolute that only the strongest and the luckiest survived. Police seldom went there at all, but if they did then they took with them someone they trusted not only in loyalty but in skill, speed and nerve as well, and above all courage. He and Runcorn had trusted each other like that once.

In the rotting tenements of the waterlogged patch on the south bank known as Jacob's Island, there could be a hundred men hidden in the wrecks of buildings sinking slowly into the mud. The same was true of the teeming slums of the docks, the ever-shifting tides of the Pool of London, with its great ships, its cargoes here one day and gone the next. The opium dens of Limehouse or the wrecks on the long stretches towards the sea might conceal anything. He would need to trust Orme with his life, as Orme would have to trust him. Such trust would not come quickly, or without testing.

'I'll work on a plan,' he said aloud at last. 'If you've got one, tell me.'

'Yes, sir. I was thinking . . . '

'Go on,' Monk prompted.

'I'd like to catch the Fat Man,' Orme said thoughtfully. 'Owe him a lot, that one, over the years.'

'I assume you mean a lot of harm, not a lot of good?'

'Oh, yes, sir, a lot of harm indeed.' There was an edge of emotion in Orme's voice that was extraordinarily sharp, as if from an accumulation of pain.

Monk was overwhelmed by how much he did not know about these men. Orme seemed not to resent him. In fact he had deliberately steered him away from the station just now so that Farnham would not see him come in late. And he had covered for him yesterday so he could pursue the Havilland case.

An icy thought washed past Monk's mind that Orme was deliberately allowing him to do those things in order to betray him to Farnham — giving him enough rope to hang himself. Why had Orme himself not got Durban's job? He was extremely able and the men trusted him and admired him. He was far better qualified for it than Monk! Why had Durban suggested Monk?

Was that a betrayal too?

He was floundering. His ignorance was like a vast, black tide carrying him towards destruction.

'I was thinking, sir.' Orme was still talking. 'I know that if we get rid of the Fat Man, who's the best opulent receiver on the river, then someone else'll take 'is place. I reckon that someone'll be Toes. An' Toes is someone we can keep better under control. 'E's greedy, but that's all. At least for now. The Fat Man is different. 'E 'as streaks of cruelty we need to get rid of. 'E isn't above getting people cut up slow if they really cross 'im. Clever with a knife, he is. Knows 'ow to 'urt without killing.'

Monk looked at Orme's grave, pinched face and read the pain in it again.

'Very well, let's get rid of him,' he agreed.

Orme looked at him steadily. 'Yes, Mr Monk. An' no private scores settled. No favours and no revenge, that's what Mr Durban used to say.' He turned away quickly, his breath catching in his throat, and Monk knew that the ghost of Durban was always going to be there.

So he would use it. He would spend the day going through all Durban's records until he had worked out what Durban would have done to trap the kidsmen, and trace the goods to the Fat Man, legitimately. No favours, no revenge. He also wanted to know why Orme had not been made commander. Or perhaps he would be better off in ignorance, but he had to find out. It might matter one day; his life might even depend upon it.

Most of the cases that he studied were routine crimes exactly like those he had dealt with since he came. The only unusual thing in Durban's notes was that they were briefer than Monk would have expected, and more personal. His handwriting was strong, but occasionally untidy, as if written hastily or when he was tired. There were flashes of humour, and discreet asides that suggested to Monk that Durban had not been especially fond of Clacton either. The difference was that he had known how to keep him under control, largely because the other men would not tolerate his disloyalty.

Monk smiled. At least he had found that solution, if he could work out how to use it.

He read carefully the reports of thefts from passenger boats. They seemed to vary, but in no particular pattern that he could detect. There were various other crimes, some very serious. One Durban had written on for many pages, and had apparently been disturbed by considerable emotion. The writing was sprawling and many of the letters only half formed. There was a kind of jaggedness to it.

Monk read it because the urgency in it held him. It had nothing to do with theft or with passenger boats at all. It concerned the murder of a prosperous man in his early forties. His body had been found in the river, apparently shot to death some time the night before, and dumped into the water. He was identified as Roger Thorwood, of Chelsea, a barber of considerable wealth and influence. He was mourned by his wife, Beatrice, and three surviving children.

Durban had put a great deal of time and energy into the investigation and followed every lead. His hope and frustration were clearly marked in his notes. But after nearly three months he had learned nothing of value and been obliged to abandon his concentration on it and turn his entire attention to other duties. The death of Roger Thorwood remained a mystery. Durban's last entry on the subject was scribbled, and in places almost illegible.

I have spoken to Mrs Thorwood for the last time. There is nothing more I can do. All trails are closed. They lead either nowhere, or into a hopeless morass. I never thought I would say of any murder that it is better left, but I do of this. And it is wrong to expect Orme to carry the responsibility here any longer. It is not even as if one day he might be justly rewarded for his work or his loyalty. He owes that not to me, but because that is his nature, but none the less I am profoundly grateful to him. There is no more to say.

Monk stared at the page. It was oddly difficult to turn over and continue with the murders, robberies, fights and accidents that occurred later. There was something painfully unfinished about it, not only the mystery of Roger Thorwood's death but Durban's obvious involvement in its solution, or lack of it. He had cared about it personally. His anger and disappointment were there, and something else less obvious, and which he was too guarded to name. Guarding someone else, or himself?

There was also his oblique reference to Orme never receiving appropriate recompense for his work. It seemed he had covered for Durban as well as for Monk. It raised the question again as to why he had not received the promotion his skill had earned him. It seemed that Durban knew the reason. Monk realised that perhaps he ought to, in order to make a better judgement of Orme. But he was glad there was no time to search now.

What he needed was a plan to catch the thieves on the passenger boats. More importantly, he wanted to trace them back to the opulent receiver who was organising them, and probably the kidsman as well.

It was two o'clock in the afternoon when Orme returned. Together, without mentioning Durban at all, they carefully constructed a series of actions that would be dangerous, require perfect judgement of timing, but should succeed in catching not only the actual thieves, but also put an end to the receivers behind them.

Orme looked nervous, but he did not hesitate, nor did he argue with Monk's intention to be present.

'And Clacton,' Monk added.

Orme looked at him quickly.

Monk smiled, but he did not explain himself.

Orme's mouth tightened, and he nodded.

★　★　★

Monk met Runcorn by the hot-chestnut stand just off the Westminster Bridge Road. It was four in the afternoon and already dark. A heavy cloud hung like a pall over the city. There was the smell of chimney smoke in the air, and the wind held the sting of snow to come. Down-river on the incoming tide was a drift of fog, and standing within sight of the dark, flat water Monk could hear the boom of fog horns drifting up. Although there were several of them, it was an eerie sound of utter desolation. Now it echoed vaguely. When the fog came in it would be swallowed, cut off half finished, like a cry strangled in the throat.

'Found the cabby,' Runcorn said, blowing on a hot chestnut before putting it into his mouth. 'Took the man Mr Barclay and Mrs Ewart saw in the mews as far as Piccadilly. Remembers him quite well because he did an odd thing. He got out of that cab, crossed the Circus, which was pretty quiet at that time in the morning, all the theatres on the Haymarket and Shaftesbury Avenue being out long since. Then he got straight into another cab and disappeared east along Coventry Street, towards Leicester Square.' He looked up from his chestnut, watching for Monk's reaction. 'Why would a man change cabs when there's nothing wrong with the one he's in?'

'Because he wants to disappear,' Monk replied. 'I expect he changed again, maybe twice, before he got where he wanted to be.'

'Exactly,' Runcorn agreed, taking another

243

chestnut and smiling. 'He wasn't drunk, he wasn't a beggar, he certainly wasn't anyone's groom.'

'He could have been . . . ' Monk started.

Runcorn's eyebrows rose. 'With the price of a cab fare from Westminster Bridge Road to the East End?'

Monk could have bitten his tongue. He looked away from Runcorn. 'No, of course not. Whoever he was, he had money.'

'Exactly!' Runcorn repeated. 'I think Mrs Ewart saw the man who shot James Havilland. She gave us quite a good description of him, and the cab driver added a bit. Seems he has black hair, above his collar, and at least at that time he was clean-shaven. He had the impression of a hollow sort of face and long nose, thin between the eyes.'

'A very observant cab driver,' Monk remarked a little sceptically. 'You sure he wasn't just trying to get on the good side of the police?'

'No, that's accurate,' Runcorn replied, looking down and concentrating on the few pieces of chestnut he had left in his hand. 'It ties in with what Mrs Ewart remembered of him. What we have to do is find out who hired him. It'll be the same person that wrote to Havilland to get him out of the house and into the stables in the middle of the night. It was all very carefully done. Nothing was taken. Man never even went into the house, by all we can see. No trace of him.'

Monk did not argue. It had been arranged to the last detail with precision and some skill, and obviously with a personal knowledge of Havilland. He had not hesitated to go out to the stables, nor had he requested Cardman or one of the footmen to go with him, or to wait up. He had not been afraid of whoever he expected to meet. And whoever it was had not taken advantage of his opportunity to rob the house. Either he had panicked — which did not seem to be the case — or he was compensated for what he did in some other way. Monk said as much to Runcorn.

'Money,' Runcorn replied bitterly. 'Someone paid him to kill Havilland.'

'That sort of arrangement's usually handed over in two halves,' Monk pointed out. 'First before the deed, second after. We might be able to trace the money. It's a risk to commit murder in an area like this. It can't have come cheap.'

'I know. Could have been saving up for a while . . . '

'Maybe, but I think it was urgent,' Monk argued. 'Something precipitated it. Havilland found something down those tunnels and had to be silenced quickly.'

'Who sent that letter? That's what I want to know. That's who's guilty, who really betrayed him.' Runcorn looked at Monk, searching his face for agreement. 'That's who he was expecting to meet!'

Neither of them said it aloud, but Monk knew Runcorn was thinking of Alan Argyll, just as he was himself. Alan was married to one of Havilland's daughters, and Toby was betrothed to the other. Havilland might disagree with

245

them, distrust their engineering skills or business practices, but he would not fear personal violence from them.

'Why midnight? And why the stables?' he asked.

Runcorn's eyebrows rose. 'Could hardly shoot him much earlier! And obviously he wouldn't want to do it in the house!'

'I mean what reason would Argyll give for meeting in the stables at midnight? And why did Havilland agree?'

Runcorn took the point immediately. 'We need to find that letter! We have to know at the very least who sent it.'

Monk took one of the chestnuts and ate it. It was sweet and hot. 'The maid said Havilland burned it.'

'Maybe he didn't burn the envelope.' Runcorn was still hopeful.

Monk ate the last chestnut. 'Come on.' He turned and started to walk.

★   ★   ★

Cardman was surprised to see them again but invited them in.

He was immaculately dressed, but the hall had a bare look. The black crepe had been taken down and the wreaths, but the clock was still stopped and there was no heating at all. 'What can I do for you, gentlemen?'

It was Monk who spoke first this time. 'You may be aware that Mrs Plimpton and the maid Lettie mentioned to me a letter Mr Havilland received the night he was killed, and which took him to the stables. I know the maid said that Mr Havilland destroyed the note, but it is extremely important that we learn everything about it that we can — even from the envelope, if it still exists?'

Cardman's eyes widened. He had heard the one word that had mattered to him. His voice trembled a little. 'You said he was killed, sir. Did you mean that someone else was responsible after all? Miss Mary was right?' He was pale but there were two spots of colour in his cheeks, as if hope had suddenly woken the life inside him again.

'Yes, Mr Cardman, it looks very like it,' Monk replied.

Cardman's face tightened. 'And if you can't find it, sir, does that mean you won't be able to prove who did it?'

'Somebody lured him to the stable,' Monk told him gravely. 'We are certain it was someone else who actually killed him. Whether we can catch the second person I don't know, but it's the first we want most.'

'Yes, sir.' The colour had gone from Cardman's face now. Perhaps he was at last realising that it had to be someone who knew Havilland and whom he trusted, and all the evidence suggested the Argylls. 'I'm afraid we've long ago disposed of all the rubbish in the study. There are only Mr Havilland's papers there now and, of course, household bills and receipts. Miss Mary took care of everything like that. No one has been here yet to . . . to see to . . . ' He trailed off, swamped by the small realities of loss again.

'I'm sure Mr Argyll will appoint someone,' Monk said. Then the moment the words were spoken he realised the appalling urgency of searching his study just in case there was anything among his papers at all. But surely Mary would have looked? But would she have recognised the envelope for what it had contained?

'Which is the study?' Runcorn asked.

Cardman showed them. 'Would you like a pot of tea, sir?' he offered. 'I'm afraid the room is extremely cold.'

They both accepted, speaking together.

Two hours later they knew a great deal about both Havilland's domestic arrangements, and how efficiently Mary had continued with them. Everything had been precisely and carefully dealt with. The bills had been checked and paid on time. There were also no unnecessary papers kept, no unanswered letters, no notes made on envelopes or scraps of paper.

'Perhaps it was always going to be a waste of time,' Runcorn said wearily. 'Damn!' He swore with sudden fury. 'I'd stake my life it was Argyll! How the hell do we catch him? Come on, Monk! You're so damn clever you could tie an eel in knots. How do we get the bastard?'

Monk's mind was racing. He too was certain it was Alan Argyll, either with or without Toby's help. But he was equally certain that they had not yet learned the true reason. Havilland had discovered something far more immediately dangerous than the damage done by unguarded engines, or even the risk of breaching one of the small, uncharted streams that might have changed course. Whatever had prompted his death, it had been something he had stumbled across suddenly, not a long-held belief proved right.

'There'd have been a lot of blood on his clothes,' he began, thinking aloud.

Runcorn did not see the point. The irritation flickered across his face. 'So there would. What does it matter now?'

'Probably too much to clean off. Anyway, who'd want the clothes a man was wearing when he committed suicide?'

'No one — oh! You mean they're still somewhere! There might be something in the pockets!' Runcorn stood up as if suddenly regaining energy. He walked towards the door, then remembered that there was a bell in the room for summoning servants. Avoiding Monk's eyes, he turned back, reached for it and pulled.

Cardman answered, and five minutes later they were in James Havilland's dressing room. The clothes he had been wearing at his death were piled neatly on one of the shelves in the tallboy. It was obvious that Mary had never had the stomach to come into the room since that night, and had not permitted the servants to either. Perhaps she would have done so after she had proved that he was not a suicide. Everything seemed to be waiting.

Monk unfolded the clothes slowly. The trousers were marked only by dust and a few pieces of hay. The jacket was quite heavy — a natural enough choice for a man going out to the stables in the middle of a winter night, possibly to wait a little while until someone arrived.

The question rose again — why had Havilland agreed to meet someone he knew in the stables? If he wished to be private, it was easy enough to send the servants to bed and open the front door for the guest himself. Monk had a crowding sense that there was some major fact that had escaped him completely.

Runcorn was waiting, watching him.

He unrolled the jacket and laid it on the dresser. There was blood, thick and dark, on the left lapel and over the shoulder. It was completely dried now and stiff. A few spots had fallen on the sleeve but not a great deal. After all, it had been a shot to the head and Havilland would probably have died instantly.

'Look,' Runcorn instructed.

Without hope of finding anything, Monk pushed his hands into the inside pocket and his fingers closed on paper. He pulled it out. It was folded up, but unmarked. An envelope. On the back were scrawled some notes, 'Tyburn', and some figures, and then 'no name' and some more figures in the same grouping. He turned it over. On the front was his name, 'Mr James Havilland'. There was no address. It had been hand-delivered. He looked up at Runcorn.

Runcorn's eyes were bright. 'That's it!' he said, excitement making his voice tremble. 'That's the envelope from the note he got!' He held out his hand.

Monk passed it to him.

'Woman's writing,' Runcorn said after only a

250

second or two, disappointment so keen he could not mask it. He looked up at Monk, pain and confusion naked. 'Was it an assignation after all? Who the devil shot him? A husband? Was the man in the two cabs nothing to do with it?'

Monk was unhappy too, but for an entirely different reason. 'Jenny Argyll . . . ' he said. 'If it were she who wrote, he would go out there to meet her. Don't forget Mary was in the house. Maybe he wanted to speak with Jenny without Mary knowing? Or Jenny with him?'

Runcorn looked around for the bell straight away this time, and Cardman answered a few moments later.

Runcorn held out the envelope. 'Do you know whose handwriting that is?' he asked.

Cardman looked stiff and miserable, his eyes haunted, but he did not hesitate. 'Yes, sir, that is Miss Jennifer's handwriting — Mrs Argyll, that is.'

'Thank you,' Monk acknowledged. Then he realised what Cardman might think. Possibly Runcorn would disapprove, but he intended to tell Cardman anyway. 'There was a man seen leaving the mews at about the time Mr Havilland was shot. He passed two people returning from the theatre who say he smelled of gun smoke. We traced his movements. He took a cab as far as Piccadilly, then changed cabs and went east. It seems very possible it was he who actually killed Mr Havilland.'

Cardman's voice was hoarse, barely a whisper. 'Thank you, sir.' He blinked, gratitude showing in his eyes, and tears.

251

Jenny Argyll greeted them far more coolly. At this time in the day her husband was either at his office or at one of the sites.

'The matter is closed,' she said bluntly. She had received them in the withdrawing room because the morning-room fire was not lit. After such a double bereavement the Argylls were still not receiving callers. Everything was draped in black. There were wreaths on the doors leading into the hall, the mirrors were covered and the clocks stopped. Presumably in this house the state of mourning was more for Toby Argyll than for Mary, although Jenny might well grieve privately for her sister. Monk had not forgotten Argyll's rage on hearing the news of their deaths, and his instant blame of Mary. If Toby had killed her, had it been at his brother's command?

This time Runcorn allowed Monk to take the lead.

'I am afraid the matter is not closed, Mrs Argyll,' Monk said firmly. She was wearing black. It was completely unrelieved, and it drained from her what little colour she might have had. He judged that she would normally be an attractive woman, but she had not the strength he had seen in Mary's face, or the passion, even when it had been lifeless and wet from the river. There had been something in the bones, the curve of her mouth, which had been unique.

'I cannot help you,' she said flatly. She was standing, staring away from them out of the window in the flat, winter light. 'And I cannot

252

see what good turning our pain over and over can do. Please allow us to grieve in peace — and alone.'

'We are not at the moment concerned with the deaths of Miss Havilland and Mr Argyll,' Monk replied. 'It is the events on the night your father died that we are looking into.'

'You have already looked into it,' she said. Her voice was quiet, but the hurt and the anger were plain in her face. Her shoulders were stiff, straining the shiny black fabric. 'There is nothing more to say. It is our family's tragedy. For pity's sake, leave us alone! Haven't we suffered enough?'

Monk hated having to continue. He was aware of the same distress in Runcorn standing a couple of yards away from him. But he could not let it go. One person, perhaps two, were branded as suicides. However, what was far more urgent than that, there might be some appalling tragedy about to happen in the tunnels, and it lay within possibility that he could prevent it. What was one woman's fear or disillusion compared with that? Or even the ripping apart of her beliefs in her family? Guilt or innocence hardly ever touched only one person.

'You wrote a letter to your father and had it hand-delivered the night of his death, Mrs Argyll.' He saw her start and draw in her breath with a little gasp. 'Please don't embarrass us all by denying it,' he continued. 'It was seen, and your father kept the envelope. I have it.'

She was ashen and she turned to face him angrily. 'Then what do you want from me?' Her

253

voice was so stifled in her throat that it was barely audible. Her eyes burned hot with hatred of them for the shame they were inflicting on her.

'I want to know what was in the letter, Mrs Argyll. You arranged for your father to go to the stables in the middle of the night, alone. He did so, and was killed.'

'He killed himself!' she burst out, her tone rising dangerously. 'For the love of heaven, why can't you leave it alone? He was mad! He had delusions! He was terrified of closed spaces, and at last he couldn't face it any more. What else do you need to know? Do you hate us so much that you gain some kind of pleasure from seeing us suffer? Do you have to open the wounds again, and again, and again?' She was almost out of control, her voice shrill now and louder.

'Sit down, Mrs — ' Monk started.

'I will not sit down!' she snapped back. 'Do not patronise me in my own home, you . . . ' She gasped in a breath again, lost for a word she might dare use.

There was nothing for Monk to do but tell her the truth, before she became hysterical and either fainted or left the room and refused to see them again. He had little enough authority to be here. Farnham would not back him up.

'A man was seen leaving the mews just after your father was shot, Mrs Argyll. He smelled of gun smoke. He was a stranger in the area and left immediately, travelling in several cabs back to the East End. Do you know who that man was?'

She stared at him incredulously. 'Of course I don't! What are you saying — that he shot my father?'

'I believe so.'

She put her hands up to her mouth and sank rather too quickly into the chair, as if she lost her power to remain standing. She stared at Monk as if he had risen out of the carpet in a cloud of sulphur.

'I'm sorry,' he said, and meant it more than he had thought he could. 'What did you say in your letter to your father, that sent him out into the stable at midnight, Mrs Argyll?'

'I . . . I . . .'

He waited.

She mastered herself with intense difficulty. The struggle was naked and painful in her face. 'I asked him to meet my husband to allow a proper discussion of the tunnels they were building, without Mary knowing and interrupting. She was very excitable.'

'At midnight?' Monk said with surprise. 'Why not in the offices in the morning?'

'Because Papa was concerned there was going to be an accident, and he would not come into the offices to discuss it any more,' she said immediately. 'He was going to speak to the authorities. They would have had to close down the works until they had investigated, and of course discovered that it was completely untrue. But they could not afford to take my husband's word for it when men's lives are at risk. My father was . . . mad, Mr Monk! He had lost all sense of proportion. He was terrified, and it disturbed his judgement about everything else. It . . . it happens sometimes. The danger underground, the darkness . . . it plays on the mind.'

'So you arranged this meeting, urgently?'

'Yes.'

'But your husband didn't go!' he pointed out. 'He was at a party until long after midnight. You told the police that you attended it with him. Was that not true?'

'Yes, it was true. I . . . I thought my father must have refused to meet Alan. He was . . . stubborn.' Her gaze did not waver from his.

'Is that what Mr Argyll said?' he asked.

She hesitated, but only for a moment. 'Yes.'

'I see.' He did see. He had never supposed that Alan Argyll intended to shoot Havilland himself. He had paid the assassin with the black hair and the narrow-bridged nose to do that. 'Thank you, Mrs Argyll.'

'Do you suppose he paid the money himself, or had someone else do it whom he trusted?' Monk asked when they were outside, matching his step to Runcorn's on the icy pavement.

'Toby?'

'Probably, but not necessarily. Who would even know where to find an assassin for money?'

Runcorn thought for a while, walking in silence.

'Who else would he trust?' he said at last.

'Can you trace the money?' Monk asked him.

'Unless he'd been saving it up, penny by penny over the years, certainly I can. But I agree it was done on the spur. Havilland found something and Argyll couldn't wait. He had to

256

have got the money out of the bank, or wherever he kept it, and paid the assassin within a day or two of the actual murder. It's my case, Monk. I've got the men to put on it, and the authority to look at bank accounts or whatever it takes. I'll find out where Argyll was every minute of the week before Havilland was shot. And after. Unless he's a fool, he won't have paid all of the fee until the deed was done.'

'What do you want me to do?' The words were not easy for Monk to say, but Runcorn's plan made every sense. He could deploy his men to search, to question, to force out answers that Monk could not. He needed to return to Wapping and start earning some of the loyalty he was going to need from his own men. Havilland's death was nothing to do with them.

Runcorn smiled. 'Go back to your river,' he replied. 'I'll send you a message.'

★　★　★

After two days the letter came, written in Runcorn's careful, over-perfect hand. It was brought by a messenger and given to Monk personally.

Dear Monk,

Traced the money. Came from Alan Argyll's bank, but he gave it to Sixsmith for expenses. Argyll can account for all his time, both before and after the event. Clever devil. No second sum paid. Could be lots of reasons for that

— but if Sixsmith cheated him then he's a fool!

I am sure Argyll is the man behind it, but it was Sixsmith who actually handed it over, whatever he believed he was paying for. Followed his movements, found where he did it. I have no choice but to arrest him straight away. I am not happy. We have the servant, not the master, but I have to charge him. We still have work to do.

Runcorn

Monk thanked the messenger and scribbled a note of acknowledgement back.

Dear Runcorn,

I understand, but we damned well do have work to do! Everything I can do, I will. Count on me.
Monk

He gave it to the messenger. Then when the door was closed he swore with a pent-up fury that shocked him.

Argyll had cheated them. They had followed the trail, and ended by being forced to arrest a man they knew was innocent, while Argyll watched them, and laughed. Damn him!

8

It was three days before Monk had time to consider the Havilland case again. There was a large fire in one of the warehouses in the Pool of London and the arsonists had attempted to escape by water. It was brought to a successful conclusion, but by the end of the second day Monk and his men were exhausted, filthy and cold to the bone.

At half-past eight, with the wind howling outside and the wood stove smelling of smoke, Monk was sitting in his office and finishing the last of his report when there was a knock on the door. He answered it and Clacton came in, closing the door behind him. He came over to stand in front of the desk, looking casual and more elegant than perhaps he was aware. He regarded Monk with a very slight smile, as if they were equals.

'What is it?' Monk asked.

'Worked pretty 'ard the last couple o' days,' Clacton observed.

'We all did,' Monk replied. If Clacton was expecting any leave he would be disappointed.

'Yeah,' Clacton agreed. 'You most of all . . . sir.'

Monk was uncomfortable. He saw the gleam

of anticipation in Clacton's eyes. 'You didn't come in here to tell me that.'

'Oh, but I did, sir,' Clacton answered him. 'I know 'ow 'ard it must 'a bin for you, wot with your own business on the side, an' all. Can't 'ave 'ad much time for that.'

'What the hell are you talking about?' Monk demanded.

Clacton blinked and smiled. 'Yer bit o' private work. For Mr Argyll, is it? Finding out 'oo killed 'is pa-in-law, and get 'em off the 'ook? Worth a bit, I shouldn't wonder.' He left the added suggestion hanging in the air.

Monk's mind raced. He had envisioned all kinds of attack from Clacton, even to the remote possibility of physical violence. He had not foreseen this insinuation. How should he deal with it? Laughter, anger, honesty? What would Clacton's next move be?

'Didn't think I knew, did yer?' Clacton said with satisfaction. 'Look down on the rest of us like we're beneath you. Not as clever as the great Mr Monk! 'Oo don't know a damn thing when it comes ter the river. Come to 'ave Orme 'old yer 'and or yer'd fall in! Well, the rest of 'em might be stupid, but I'm not. I know wot yer doin', an' if yer don't want Farnham ter know as well, yer'd be wise ter let me 'ave a bit o' the price.'

There was no time to weigh the consequences.

'I doubt Mr Argyll will pay me for anything I've found out so far,' Monk said drily. 'It looks like he's responsible for Havilland's death.'

'Yeah?' Clacton's fair eyebrows rose. 'But it's Sixsmith they've arrested. Now why would that be, d'yer think? A bit of shiftin' around of evidence, mebbe?'

Monk was cold and tired, and his bones ached, but now he was assailed by fear also. He recognised both cunning and hatred in the young man in front of him. There was no loyalty to Durban, or anyone else, just pure self-interest. He had no time to care why. Clacton was dangerous.

'Do you think you can find this supposed evidence?' he asked bluntly.

Clacton's eyes were bright and narrow. 'You bettin' I can't?'

'I'll be happy if you can,' Monk replied. 'It's Argyll I want!'

For the first time Clacton was thrown off balance. 'That's stupid! 'Oo'll pay yer?'

'Her Majesty,' Monk replied. 'There's a conspiracy behind Havilland's death. Thousands of pounds in the construction business, and a lot of power to be gained. Go and tell Mr Farnham what you think, by all means. But you'd be better to go and get on with your job, and be glad you still have one.'

Clacton was confused. Now he was the one needing to weigh his chances and it angered him. The tables had turned and he had barely even seen it happen.

'I still know yer crooked!' he said between his teeth. 'An' I'll catch yer one day!'

'No,' Monk told him. 'You won't. You'll fall over yourself. Now get out!'

Slowly, as if still unsure whether he had another weapon left, Clacton turned and walked

261

out, leaving the door open behind him. Monk could see that as soon as he was in the main room his swagger returned.

Monk's tea was cold, but he did not want to go and get more. His hand was shaking a little, and the breath caught in his throat. Clacton's accusation had been worse than he had anticipated.

*　*　*

The following morning he went to Sir Oliver Rathbone's office. Monk was prepared to wait as long as necessary to see him, but it proved to be no more than an hour. Rathbone came in as elegantly dressed as always, today with a grey wool suit and a heavy overcoat against the biting east wind. He looked surprised to see Monk, but pleased. Since he had realised how much he loved Margaret Ballinger his rivalry with Monk had softened considerably. It was as if he had reached a kind of inner safety at last, and was now open to a gentler range of emotions.

'Monk! How are you?' He regarded him closely and sincerely. Rathbone was very different from Monk, a man of excellent education, comfortable with himself. His elegance was entirely natural.

Monk smiled. In the beginning Rathbone had discomfited him. Time and experience had shown him the humanity beneath the veneer, and he no longer felt so. 'I need your help in a case.'

'Of course — why else would you be here in

the middle of the morning?' Rathbone made no attempt to conceal his amusement, or his interest. If Monk were out of his depth legally then it offered an interesting problem, which was exactly what he craved. 'Sit down and tell me.'

Monk obeyed. Very briefly he described Mary Havilland's fall from the bridge with Toby Argyll, then his discovery of James Havilland's earlier death and the course of the investigation that had led to the arrest of Aston Sixsmith.

'Surely you don't want me to defend Sixsmith?' Rathbone said incredulously.

'No ... at least not to act as defence for him,' Monk replied. He was beginning to wonder if what he was intending to ask was impossible. Again, fury at Argyll washed over him, and a sense of helplessness in the face of the skill with which he had manipulated both Sixsmith and the police into the position he wanted them. Monk could picture his angry, slightly arrogant face marred by grief as if he had seen him only moments ago. 'I want you to prosecute Sixsmith, but in such a way that we get the man behind him,' he answered Rathbone. 'I don't think Sixsmith had any idea what the money was for. Argyll told him what to do and he did it, either blindly or out of loyalty to the Argylls, believing it was for some legitimate purpose.'

Rathbone's fair eyebrows rose. 'Such as what, for example?'

'Tunnelling is a hard trade. I don't say he wouldn't cut corners, or pay bribes to some of the more violent elements of those who know the sewers and the underground rivers and wells. I don't know.'

Rathbone thought for a moment or two. Clearly his interest was caught. He looked at Monk. 'You believe the elder Argyll brother used Sixsmith to pay an assassin to kill Havilland, because Havilland was a threat to him. Who found this assassin, if not Sixsmith?'

Monk felt uncomfortable, as if he were on the witness stand. It would be impossible to escape with inaccurate or incomplete answers. 'Alan Argyll himself, or perhaps Toby,' he answered. 'Alan has taken great care to account for all his own time before and after Havilland's death, but Toby was several years younger and spent more time on the sites and knew some of the tougher navvies.'

'According to whom?' Rathbone said quickly.

Monk smiled, but without pleasure. 'According to Sixsmith. But it can be easily verified.'

'You'll need to do it,' Rathbone warned. 'The money came from Argyll, you say?'

'Yes.'

'Proof? If he says it was for wages, or a new machine, and that Sixsmith misappropriated it, can you prove he's lying?'

Monk felt his muscles tighten defensively. 'No, not beyond doubt.'

'Reasonable doubt?'

'I don't know what doubt is reasonable. I'm certain myself.'

'Not exactly relevant,' Rathbone said drily. 'Why would Argyll want Havilland dead so much that he would be prepared to use Sixsmith to hire an assassin?'

'Knowledge that the tunnels were dangerous and work should be stopped,' Monk replied.

'Isn't all such work dangerous? The Fleet Sewer collapse was appalling.'

'That's cut-and-cover,' Monk told him. 'Imagine that underground, possibly collapsing at both ends, with water — or worse, gas.'

'Is gas worse? I would have thought water would be pretty dreadful.'

'The gas would be methane. That's flammable. It would need only one spark and the whole thing would be ablaze. If it came up through the sewers it could start another Great Fire of London.'

Rathbone paled. 'Yes, I have the idea, Monk. Why do you think that is anything more than a madman's nightmare? Surely Argyll wouldn't want that any more than Havilland, or anyone else? If it were a real danger he'd stop work himself. What was he afraid of — that Havilland would frighten the work force and they'd strike? Why not just bar him from the site? Isn't murder excessive, not to mention dangerous, and expensive?'

'If it wasn't the navvies Havilland was going to, but the authorities, that would be different. Argyll couldn't stop that so easily. And even a totally unfounded fear could close the excavations for enough time to delay the work seriously, and cost a great deal of money. To a ruthless man, one perhaps running rather close to the edge of profit and loss, or with an overlarge investment, that could be a motive for murder.'

Rathbone frowned. 'But motive is not enough, Monk, which you know as well as I. Why not suppose it was Sixsmith, exactly as it appears to be?'

'Because it was Argyll's wife who sent the letter to her father asking him to be in the stable after midnight,' Monk answered decisively. 'At Argyll's request.'

'And if Argyll says he did not ask her to write it?' Rathbone asked. 'You cannot force her to incriminate him. It would be profoundly against her interest.'

'Others will swear it is her handwriting.'

'You have the letter? You didn't say so . . . '

'I don't! I have the envelope.'

'The envelope! For God's sake, Monk! Anything could have been in it! Did anyone see the letter? Is the envelope postmarked?'

Monk felt the argument slipping out of his grasp. He knew Rathbone was being perfectly reasonable, doing what he had to. And for him to expose the weaknesses in the case now when they were in private was infinitely better than later in public. Still, his temper rose and he wanted to lash out. But to lose control was childish, and it helped Argyll. That last realisation was enough to crush his rage at source.

'The envelope was hand-delivered,' he replied levelly. 'But it is beyond reasonable doubt that it was the one he received that evening because he made notes on it in his own hand, and it was in the pocket of the jacket he was wearing. That's where we found it.'

'Could have belonged to another letter sent at an earlier time?' Rathbone followed it all the way.

'There were notes on it relating to events that happened that evening,' Monk said with satisfaction.

'Good. So Mrs Argyll sent him a note. If they ask her to swear it was an invitation to dinner in a week's time, and she is willing to, what have we?'

'A woman prepared to lie to two police officers, under oath.'

'To save her husband, her home, her source of income and position in society, and thus also her children.' Rathbone puckered his mouth into a tight, bleak smile. 'Not an unusual phenomenon, Monk. And not one you would find it easy, or popular, to destroy. You would not win the jury's favour with that.'

'I want their belief, not their favour!' Monk snapped.

'Juries are driven by emotion as well as reason,' Rathbone pointed out. 'You're playing a dangerous game. I can see about charging Sixsmith as an accessory, possibly an unknowing one as far as murder is concerned, and hope to draw out enough to implicate Argyll, but you'd have to come up with a lot more than you have so far.' His face pinched a little. 'It happens sometimes. You can catch everyone but the real culprit. It looks as if Argyll's protected himself pretty well. To reach him you'll have to destroy this man Sixsmith, who may be completely innocent of anything except a fairly usual business bribe. You'll also destroy Argyll's wife,

267

who is doing what any woman would to protect her children, perhaps even to protect her belief in her husband as a decent man. And she may need that to survive with any kind of sanity. Not to mention the children themselves.'

Monk hesitated. Was it worth it? Do you destroy the slightly tarnished, those culpable only of ordinary human weakness, in order to reach the truly guilty? For what — vengeance? Or to protect future victims?

'You don't have a choice now,' Rathbone said quietly. 'At least not as far as Sixsmith is concerned. I'll prosecute, by all means, and uncover everything I can. Meanwhile you work on finding out more about this mysterious assassin. Show who contacted him, if he ever took the second payment, if he knows who employed him. Above all, you need to show what Havilland was going to do that was sufficient to make Argyll want to kill him. So far all you have is an engineer who lost his nerve and became a nuisance. Sane men don't commit murder for that. Give me chapter and verse of what Argyll would lose, and connect it to him, not just to Sixsmith.'

'If he wasn't going to close down the excavation, then why would Sixsmith want him killed either?' Monk challenged him. 'The motive is the same.'

'Exactly,' Rathbone agreed.

'It's Argyll's company, not Sixsmith's!' Monk argued. 'Sixsmith can get another job anywhere else. He's a damn good engineer with a fine reputation.'

'He wouldn't have if there were a collapse,'

Rathbone said drily.

Monk stood up. 'I'll find it! How long have I?'

'Till it comes to trial? Three weeks.'

'Then I'd better start.' He moved towards the door.

'Monk!'

He turned back. 'Yes?'

'If you're right and it is Argyll, be careful. He's a very powerful man and you work in a dangerous job.'

Monk stared at Rathbone with sudden surprise. There was a gentleness in his face he had not expected to see. 'I will,' he promised. 'I have good men around me.'

★   ★   ★

Monk began by going back to speak with Runcorn. He was probably as aware as Rathbone of the thinness of the case; nevertheless Monk outlined it in legal terms while Runcorn sat behind his desk and watched him grimly.

'Need to know more about this man in the mews,' he said when Monk had finished. 'Might get a better description of him if we ask the cabby again, push him a bit more.' He coloured very faintly. 'And we'll have to ask Mrs Ewart to see if she can say anything more.'

She was surprised to see them again, but it was apparent that she was not displeased. She was wearing a woollen dress of a dark, rich wine colour, which lent warmth to her face, and she looked less tense than the previous time. Monk wondered if that were in any part caused by the fact that her brother was not at home at this hour of the day.

She received them in the withdrawing room, where there was a bright fire sending its heat into the air. The room was not what Monk would have expected. There was a pretentiousness about it that took away something of the comfort. The pictures on the walls were big and heavily framed, the sort of thing one chooses in order to impress rather than because one likes them. There was an impersonal feel to them, as there was to the carved ivory ornaments on the mantelpiece and the few leather-bound books in a case against the wall. The volumes sat together, uniform in size and colour, immaculate, as though no one had ever read them. Then Monk remembered that she was a widow and this was Barclay's house, not hers. He wondered for a moment what her own choice would have been.

She was looking at Runcorn. Her face in the morning light was less tired than the first time they had seen her, but still held the same sadness at the edge of her smile, and behind the intelligence in her eyes.

'I'm sorry to bother you again, ma'am,' Runcorn apologised, looking back at her steadily. 'But we've looked into the matter further, and it seems very much as if the man you saw could have shot Mr Havilland. There's a man arrested for hiring him coming to trial soon, but if we don't find a good deal more information, he might get off.'

'Of course,' she said quickly. 'You must catch the man who did it, for every reason. What else can I do to help? I have no idea where he went, except towards the main road. I imagine he would find a hansom and leave the area as fast as he could.'

'Oh, he did, ma'am. We traced him as far as Piccadilly, and the east after that,' Runcorn agreed. Not once did he glance at Monk. 'It's just that the cabby didn't look at him except for an instant, and he isn't all that good at description. If you could remember anything else at all about him it could help.'

She thought for several moments, withdrawing into herself. She gave a little shiver as if thinking not only of the cold of that night, but now also of what had taken place less than a hundred yards from where she had stood. Runcorn's admiration of her was clear in his eyes, but it was the vulnerability in her, the sadness that held him. Monk knew that because he had seen a flash of it before, and knew Runcorn better than he realised. There was a softness in Runcorn he had never before allowed, a capacity for pity he was only now daring to acknowledge.

Or was it Monk who had only just developed the generosity of spirit to see it?

Mrs Ewart was answering the question as carefully and with as much detail as she could. 'He had a long face,' she began. 'A narrow bridge to his nose but his eyes were not small, and they were heavy-lidded.' Suddenly she opened her own eyes very wide, as if startled. 'They were light! His skin was dark and his hair, which was above his collar, was black — at least it looked black in the streetlights. And his brows

271

too. But his eyes were light — blue, or grey. Blue, I think. And . . . his teeth . . . ' Then she shivered, and there was a look of apology in her face as if what she was going to say were foolish. 'And his eyeteeth were unusually pointed. He smiled when he explained the . . . the stain. I . . . ' she gulped. 'I suppose that was poor Mr Havilland's blood? I saw his teeth when he smiled.' She looked at Runcorn, waiting for his reaction, although it was inconceivable that it should matter to her. Yet Monk could not help but believe that it did. Had she seen that gentleness in him? Or was it just that she needed someone to understand the horror she felt?

Monk was astounded and embarrassed to find himself defensive of Runcorn, aching for that sudden, hopeless dream in him that he had allowed to awaken. He felt an extraordinary mixture of anger, impatience and hurt, a confusion he would have denied as a possibility even a year ago.

Runcorn was thanking her, but still probing. Was he prolonging the interview on purpose? What about the man's clothes, he was asking. Had he worn gloves? No. Had she noticed his hands? Strong and thin. Boots? She had no idea. Anything else? If she thought of anything, send for him. He gave her his card.

They thanked her and left. Monk had barely spoken a word. Even outside in the bright air, wind ice-edged off the river, Runcorn kept his face forward, refusing to meet Monk's eyes. There was no purpose in forcing communication where none was needed. Later they could discuss what each would do next. They walked side by side, heads down a little, collars high against the cold.

* * *

The only place Monk could begin was with the nature and opportunities of the man who had paid the assassin.

Was it Alan Argyll who had found him, or Toby? Or perhaps Sixsmith had actually contacted him first, for the task he had claimed?

That was an obvious place to start. Monk could speak to toshers who combed the sewers for lost valuables, to gangers who led the men who cleared the worst build-up of detritus and silt that blocked the narrower channels. They were all displaced. It would take a while before their services were needed, and there was no trade in which to earn their way in the meantime.

He was walking from the Wapping station towards one of the cut-and-cover excavations when Scuff caught up with him. The boy still had his new odd boots on and the coat that came to his shins, but now he also had a cloth cap with a brim that sat uncomfortably on his ears. The hat needed something inside the band to make it a little smaller. Monk wondered how he could tell Scuff this without hurting his feelings.

'Good morning,' Monk said conversationally.

Scuff looked at him. 'Yer doin' all right?'

Monk smiled. 'Improving, thank you.' He knew the enquiry was nothing to do with his health; it was his competence in the job that Scuff was concerned about. 'Mr Orme is a good man.'

Scuff was not so sure he would go so far as to call any policeman 'good', but he did not argue. 'Clacton's a bad 'un,' he said instead. 'You watch 'im, or 'e'll 'ave yer.'

'I know,' Monk agreed, but was startled that Scuff knew so much.

Scuff was not impressed. 'Do yer? Yer don't look ter me like yer know much at all. Yer in't got them thieves yet, 'ave yer!' That was a challenge, not a question. 'An' don' let 'em talk yer inter takin' on the Fat Man. Nobody never done that an' come out of it.' He looked anxious, his thin face pinched with anxiety.

Perhaps it was enlightened self-interest for all the hot pies, but Monk still felt a twist of pleasure inside him, and guilt. 'Actually I've been busy on something else,' he answered, to divert Scuff's attention. He and Orme had agreed on some preliminary plans, which Orme had been carrying out, but there was no point in frightening Scuff needlessly. 'Right now I'm busy trying to find out about a man who was killed just over a couple of months ago.'

'In't yer a bit late?' Scuff's young face puckered. Monk's incompetence puzzled and worried him. For some reason or other he seemed to feel responsible.

Monk was both touched and stung. He found himself defending his position, trying to regain respect. 'The police thought at the time that it was suicide,' he explained. 'Then his daughter

274

can I do to help? I have no idea where he went, except towards the main road. I imagine he would find a hansom and leave the area as fast as he could.'

'Oh, he did, ma'am. We traced him as far as Piccadilly, and the east after that,' Runcorn agreed. Not once did he glance at Monk. 'It's just that the cabby didn't look at him except for an instant, and he isn't all that good at description. If you could remember anything else at all about him it could help.'

She thought for several moments, withdrawing into herself. She gave a little shiver as if thinking not only of the cold of that night, but now also of what had taken place less than a hundred yards from where she had stood. Runcorn's admiration of her was clear in his eyes, but it was the vulnerability in her, the sadness that held him. Monk knew that because he had seen a flash of it before, and knew Runcorn better than he realised. There was a softness in Runcorn he had never before allowed, a capacity for pity he was only now daring to acknowledge.

Or was it Monk who had only just developed the generosity of spirit to see it?

Mrs Ewart was answering the question as carefully and with as much detail as she could. 'He had a long face,' she began. 'A narrow bridge to his nose but his eyes were not sma and they were heavy-lidded.' Suddenly opened her own eyes very wide, as if sta 'They were light! His skin was dark and hi which was above his collar, was black — it looked black in the streetlights. And h fell off the bridge, and that was my case. In looking back at that, I found out about the father, and it began to look as if it wasn't suicide after all.'

'Wotcher mean, fell off the bridge?' Scuff demanded. 'Nobody falls off bridges. Yer can't There's rails an' things. Somebody kill 'er too, or she jump?'

'I'm not sure about that either.' Monk smiled ruefully. 'And I saw it happen. But when two people are struggling a distance away, in the half-light just before the lamps go on, it's difficult to tell.'

'But 'er pa were killed by someone else?' Scuff persisted.

'Yes. The man was seen leaving. I know pretty well what he looks like, and that he went east beyond Piccadilly.'

Scuff let out a sigh of despair. 'That all yer got? I dunno wot ter do wi' yer!' He sniffed and wiped his nose on his sleeve.

Monk hid his smile with difficulty. Scuff had apparently adopted him, and felt every parent's exasperation with an impossible child. He found himself ridiculously caught in an emotion that all but choked him. 'Well, you might give me a little advice?' he suggested tactfully.

'Forget about it,' Scuff replied.

'You won't give me any advice?' Monk was surprised.

Scuff gave him a widening look. 'That's me advice! Yer in't gonna find 'im.'

'Maybe not, but I'm going to try,' Monk said firmly. 'He murdered a man and made it loc like suicide, so the man was buried outside Christian ground, and all his family believed he was a coward and a sinner. It nearly broke his youngest daughter's heart, so she spent all her time trying to prove that it wasn't so. And now it looks as if she might have been killed for it too. Only they buried her outside Christian ground as well, and marked her as a suicide.'

Scuff skipped a step or two to keep up with Monk. 'Yer daft, you are.' But there was admiration in his voice. 'Well, if you won't be told, I s'pose I'd better 'elp yer. Wot's 'e like, this man wot killed the girl's pa?'

Monk thought for a moment. What risk was there in telling Scuff? If he kept it vague, none at all. 'Thin, dark hair,' he replied.

Scuff looked at him, his eyes hurt, his mouth pinched. 'Yer don' trust me,' he accused.

Monk felt a twist of guilt knot inside him. How could he undo the insult, the rejection? 'I don't want you to get involved,' he admitted the truth. 'If he kills people for money, he won't think twice about getting rid of you if you get anywhere near him.'

'Me?' Scuff was indignant. 'I'm not 'alf as green as you are! I can look arter meself! Yer don't think I got no brains!'

'I think you've got plenty of brains — quite enough to get close to him, and get hurt!' Monk retorted. 'Leave it alone, Scuff! It's police business. And you're right,' he added. 'I'll probably never find him. But it's the man who paid him I want most.'

Scuff walked in silence for fifty yards or so.

They crossed the road and started along the next stretch.

'Will they bury that girl proper then?' he asked finally.

'I'll see that they do,' Monk answered, pleased that Scuff had seen the heart of the matter so quickly. 'I'm cold. Do you want a hot drink?'

'Don't mind if I do,' Scuff said, but grudgingly. He was still hurt. 'If this man weren't killed on the river, why in't the reg'lar rozzers doin' it?'

'They are, as well.' They turned the corner, away from the river and out of the worst of the wind. The pavements were slick with ice. A coal cart rattled sharply over the stones, the horse's breath steam in the air.

'S' pose yer don't trust them neither,' Scuff said dourly.

'It isn't a matter of trust,' Monk told him. 'We need all the help we can find. We're searching for one man in all London who makes a living killing people! I know what he looks like, but that's all. He shot one man, and caused the death of his daughter. An innocent man may go to prison for the murder, and the one who paid him is going to get away with it. And worse than that, we'll never prove the real reason for it, and there could be a cave-in in one of the new sewer tunnels that would kill scores of men! So no matter how difficult it is, I've got to try! So let's get a cup of hot tea and a hot pie each, and stop sulking!'

Scuff digested that in silence for a few minutes.

'Don't yer know nothin' 'cept 'e's thin an' got

black 'air?' he asked finally, giving Monk a sunny smile. 'Somebody saw 'im, so yer gotta know more'n that!'

'He had a narrow nose and quite big eyes,' Monk replied. 'Blue or grey. And his teeth were unusually pointed.'

Scuff shrugged. 'Oh well, mebbe you'll find suffink then. There's a man wi' real good pies round there, on the other side o' the road.'

'And tea?'

Scuff rolled his eyes in exasperation. 'O' course 'e's got tea! Pies in't no good wi'out tea!'

*　*　*

In the afternoon Monk went back to his river patrol duties, forcing the Havilland case and all its implications out of his mind. The thefts had to be dealt with. He owed that to Durban, but more than that, to Orme. There was also the question of Clacton. He was very well aware that he had dealt with him only temporarily. Clacton was watching, waiting his chance to catch him in another weakness or error. It was about more than money. His own promotion? To please someone else? Simply to gain another commander, one he could manipulate more easily?

The reason mattered little. It could not wait much longer. Orme, at least, was expecting him to act. Maybe they all were. Had Runcorn dreaded Monk the same way, as one of the burdens that comes with leadership, to be endured until it can be dealt with? He winced at the thought.

The river was cold, the incoming tide swift and choppy, and he was kept very fully occupied dealing with a warehouse theft. At half-past six it was solved and he stood alone on an old pier beyond King Edward's Stairs. It was totally dark in the shelter of a half-burned warehouse. Across the water the shore lights glittered as the wind blurred them. Lighter men were calling out to each other below him on the river, gusts of wind snatching their voices and distorting the words.

He heard the boat bump against the steps and someone's feet climbing up, then Orme's solid figure silhouetted against the faint light on the water.

Monk moved forward. 'Found the cargo,' he said quietly. 'Did you get the boat they used?'

'Yes, sir. Butterworth's gone to assist 'em now. I 'ear as the Mets took Sixsmith. That true? Must say, I believed it were Argyll. Not as clever as I thought I were.' His voice was rueful.

'So did I,' Monk agreed. 'I still do.' He told Orme briefly of his intention to find the assassin.

Orme was dubious. 'Yer'll be lucky ter see 'ide nor 'air of 'im, Mr Monk. But I'll 'elp you all I can. If anyone'd know 'im, it'd be river men, or folks that live in the tunnels, or Jacob's Island. 'E could be just a passing seaman, off to Burma or the fever jungles o' Panama, or the Cape o' Good 'Ope by now.'

'He wasn't a seaman,' Monk said with conviction. 'Pale face, thin, and he used a gun. In fact he used what appeared to be Havilland's own gun. Although there was a good deal of careful planning in this. So perhaps it was he

279

who bought the gun at the pawn shop, not Havilland at all. I think he kills for a living.'

'There's them as do,' Orme agreed.

The subject then turned to the careful laying of the trap that would not only catch the actual thieves on the passenger boats, but would lead, with proof, to the hand behind them. Monk and Orme sincerely hoped that that was the Fat Man.

'It'll be dangerous,' Orme warned. 'It could turn ugly.'

Monk smiled. 'Yes, I'm sure it could. There's been something ugly about it from the beginning.'

Monk expected Orme to respond, perhaps to deny it, but he remained silent. Why? Did he not understand what Monk was alluding to, or did he already know the answer? Why should he trust Monk, a newcomer to the River Police? He barely knew him. They had never faced a real danger together — nothing more than choppy weather, the odd barge out of control, night work when, on the river, a slip in the dark could be lethal. It was not enough to test a man's courage or loyalty to his fellows. Trust needed to be earned, and only a fool placed his life in another man's hands blindly.

Or was Orme protecting someone? Could he want Monk to fail, spectacularly, so he could take Monk's place? Orme deserved it. The men trusted him. Durban had. Which brought Monk back to the old question: why had Durban recommended Monk for the post and not Orme? It made no sense, and standing here in the dark on the windy embankment with the constant slap of the water against the stones, he felt as exposed as if he had been naked in the lights.

Still he asked the question. 'Who put out the word that we are corrupt? It came from someone.'

'I dunno, sir.' Orme's voice was low and hard. 'But certain as death, I mean to find out.'

They heard the boat bump against the steps. It was time to go on patrol. Neither said anything more. The plan would begin the following afternoon. There was much to go over and prepare before then.

* * *

In order to catch the Fat Man himself they needed the thieves to steal one article of such value that they could neither divide it as they would a haul of money, nor break it up as they would a piece of jewellery, selling the separate stones. It had to be something that was of worth only if it remained whole, yet too specialist and too valuable to sell themselves.

Monk and Orme had obtained Farnham's permission to borrow an exquisite carving of ivory and gold. Intact, it was worth a fortune; broken, only the weight of the gold, which made it surprisingly little value. Even at a glance, a pickpocket would know it was worth enough to keep him for a decade, if fenced successfully.

Farnham had insisted that Monk himself carry it.

'You can look the part,' he said with a curl of

his mouth as he passed over the figure, wrapped in a soft chamois leather cloth. He surveyed Monk's beautifully cut jacket and white shirt with its silk cravat, and then his trousers and polished boots. Such clothes were a legacy from Monk's earlier years before the accident, when most of his money went on his tailor. They were not the fashion of a season, as a woman's gown would have been, but timeless elegance. They spoke of old money, the kind of taste that is innate, not put on to impress others. Farnham might not have been able to describe it, but he knew what it meant. It was inappropriate in a subordinate, which was why Farnham's smile troubled Monk. He remembered how Runcorn had hated his attire, and it made him even more uneasy.

'Thank you, sir.' He took the carving and slipped it into the inside pocket of his coat. It made a slight bump, pulling it out of shape.

'Take care of it, Monk,' Farnham warned. 'The River Police will go out of business if you lose that! With the word going around now, no one will believe we didn't take it ourselves.'

Monk felt odd. Was he walking straight into a trap, knowing it and yet still stupid enough to step in? Or caught tightly enough to have no choice?

'Yes, sir.' His voice was rasping, as if the air off the river had caught in his throat already.

'Orme will give you a cutlass later,' Farnham added. 'Can't let you have a weapon yet. Even a knife a thief would feel and know there was something wrong. It's a shame. Leaves you a bit vulnerable, but can't be helped.' He was still smiling, thin-lipped, barely showing his teeth. 'Good luck.'

'Thank you.' Monk turned and left, going to the outer room where the other men were waiting. Two of them were dressed as passengers, in order to keep a first-hand watch on the thieves. The rest were to remain in their own police boats close at hand, so they could follow anyone easily if they were to escape by water.

Orme nodded and signalled the men to go. Monk noticed with a chill and an anxious dryness in his mouth that they all carried cutlasses in their belts. Three of them carried extra weapons as well, to arm those who were disguised, should the whole operation end in violence. Monk had no idea if he had ever fought hand to hand in his years before the accident, and certainly he had not since then. He was a detective, not a uniformed officer. It was too late now to wonder if he was up to it — strong enough — quick enough — even if he had any skill with a cutlass.

He followed the men out into the hard, cold wind. They were each prepared, knowing their duty, the main plan and the contingency. There was nothing more to say.

Outside on the quay, Orme took his armed men in three boats and they pulled out and upriver. Monk and the two others who were dressed as passengers took a hansom up to Westminster, where they boarded the next ferry down towards Greenwich.

The tide was slack, but the wind was raw. As

the ferry pulled out into the river, Monk was glad to go with the other passengers below deck into the cramped cabin where there was some shelter. There were at least fifty other people on board: men and women and several children. Everyone was wrapped up in winter coats, hats and scarves that offered a host of places easy enough to hide the proceeds from picked pockets. One obese gentleman wore a fur-collared coat open, which flapped as he walked. He could have hidden half a dozen pound bags of sugar without causing any further bulges on his person.

A thin woman with voluminous shawls scolded three children who trailed after her. She looked like an ordinary housewife, but Monk knew perfectly well that she could also be a passer of stolen goods, one to whom the pickpocket gave them until he was safely free enough of suspicion to take them back. She would get her cut, in time.

The plan was that if no one robbed him on the way down to Greenwich he was to meet with one of the other police who was dressed as a passenger and show him the carving, as if intending selling it to him. The policeman would pretend to decline and Monk would return to Westminster. He refused even to imagine the possibility of the thieves taking it and not being caught.

There were several stops along the way when anyone could get off. If the thieves were to be arrested too soon then the whole operation was abortive. The police would have the culprits

— the fingers of the crime — but not the brain or the heart.

A man bumped against Monk, apologised and moved on.

Monk's hands went to his pocket. The carving was still there.

It happened again, and again. He was so nervous his fingers were stiff and trembling.

Butterworth bumped into him and apologised, using the password to let him know that he had been robbed. Why was the carving not gone? Without that they would not need to find the Fat Man!

They were past the Surrey Docks and heading down the Limehouse Reach.

Ten minutes later Monk's pocket was empty, and he had not even felt it! Panic broke over him in a wave, the sweat hot and then cold on his skin. He had no idea who had taken the carving, not even whether it was man or woman. He spun around. Where was Butterworth?

'Thin man, moustache, sad face, like a rat,' Constable Jones said almost at his elbow. 'Over there, by the way up to the deck.'

Monk found himself gasping with relief, barely able to draw enough air into his lungs. Should he say he knew who had taken the statue? The lie died on his lips. Jones would see in his reaction that he had not. 'Thank you,' he said instead. 'He's the one we have to watch, never mind the others.'

Butterworth was almost six feet from the man with the moustache. He was pretending to look for something in his coat pocket, but his eyes were on the man. He had seen too. He and Jones were good, quicker than Monk.

The boat reached the Dog and Duck Stairs and the man with the carving got off. Monk, Jones and Butterworth got off behind him, as did half a dozen others.

The man walked down the quay back towards the Greenland Dock. It was dark, and there was a smell of rain in the wind. Here and there the streetlamps were lit. It was in some ways the most difficult time to keep anyone in sight. The shadows were deceptive; you thought you saw someone, and suddenly you didn't. There were pools of light, and long stretches of gloom. The sound and movement and shifting reflections of water were everywhere.

Monk, Jones and Butterworth moved separately, trying to give themselves three chances not to lose the thief. It would be better to arrest him and catch no one else than lose the carving. But then the whole exercise would have been a failure. One thief was hardly here or there. They would have betrayed their hand for nothing.

They were moving south again. Orme and his men should be keeping pace with them along the river.

There was another man in the shadows. Monk stopped abruptly, afraid of catching up and being seen. Then he realised he should not have stopped. It drew attention to him. It was years since he had done this sort of thing. He retraced his steps a couple of yards and bent down as if to pick up something he had dropped, then went forward again. The new man had caught up with the thief. His outline under the lamppost looked familiar. He was short and fat with a long overcoat and a brimless hat. He had been on that boat — another thief?

A third man had joined them by the time they turned right and reached another ancient set of steps down to the water. A boat was waiting for them and almost immediately the darkness swallowed them.

Monk stood alone, shifting from foot to foot, desperately searching the darkness for Orme. Where the devil was he? There were barges moving upstream, their riding lights glittering. An ice-cold wind was whining in the broken pier stakes.

There was a noise behind him. Monk spun round. A man stood ten feet away. He had not even heard him coming; the slurp of the water masked his footsteps. Monk had no weapon, and his back was to the river.

A boat scraped against the steps. He strode over and saw four men in it, randan, police formation. There was room for two more, which would be cramped although not dangerous. Orme was in the stern. Monk could not see his face, but he recognised the way he stood, outlined solid black against the shifting, dimly reflecting surface of the water.

Monk went down the steps as fast as he could, his feet slithering on the wet, slime-coated stone. Orme put out his hand and steadied him as he all but pitched forward on the last step. He landed clumsily in the boat and scrambled to take one of the seats. The next moment his hands closed over an oar and he made ready to throw his weight against it on the order.

Butterworth came down the steps, boarded and crouched in the stern. Once given the word, they pulled out into the stream and heaved hard to catch up with the thieves' boat.

No one spoke; each man was listening to the beat of the oar. In the stern, Orme was straining to see ahead and to steady them against the wash of barges going up- or down-stream, and to avoid any anchored boats waiting to unload on the wharfs at daylight.

Where were they going? Monk guessed Jacob's Island. He tried to distinguish through the gloom the chaotic shapes of the shore. There were cranes black against the skyline, and the masts of a few ships. There was a break in the roofs, as if the inlet to a dock, then more warehouses again, this time jagged, some open to the sky, walls askew as they sank into the mud. He was right — Jacob's Island.

Ten minutes later they were all on the soggy, rubble-strewn shore, creeping forward a few inches at a time, feet testing the ground for litter, traps where the planking had rotted and given way and broken timbers protruded through. Somewhere ahead of them the thieves were gathering. From the thefts they had counted ten.

Monk had a cutlass in his hand, given him by Orme. The weight of it was unfamiliar, but deeply reassuring. Please God he would know how to use it if he should have to.

They continued forward, eight River Police surrounding an unknown number of thieves, and

288

perhaps their receivers as well. They were inside the first buildings now, the remnants of abandoned warehouses, cellars already flooded. The sour stench of tidal mud and sewage, refuse, and dead rats was thick in the throat. Everything seemed to be moving, dripping, creaking, as if the whole edifice were slipping lower into the ooze, drowning inch by inch.

A rat scuttled by, its feet scraping on the boards, then it plopped into a puddle of water and the empty sounds of the night closed in again. There was no living slap of the tide here, only the groan of timber settling and breaking and sagging lower.

There were voices ahead, and lights. Monk, cutlass ready, stood half behind a doorway and watched. He could see the squat shapes of nine men now no more than humps, a deepening of the shadows, but the man with the ivory carving was there.

Monk froze, barely breathing. He did not catch the words they said, but flight actions were plain. They were dividing the spoils of the day. His stomach knotted at the sight of how much they had. It was far more than he had known about.

He waited. Orme was somewhere to the left of him, Butterworth to the right; Jones and the others had gone around behind the chairs to encircle them.

The thieves were arguing over how to sell the ivory carving. The argument seemed to go on interminably. There were nine of them, not ten. Monk must have miscounted earlier. He was cold to the bone, his feet numb, his teeth chattering. The odds were not good. He had only seven men. But the statue was what mattered; above all he must get that, that and the Fat Man.

The stench of the mud almost choked him.

Why didn't they agree to the obvious and take the carving to the Fat Man? He was the king of the opulent receivers. He would give them the best price for it because he would be able to find a buyer.

They weren't going to! They knew he would take half, so they were going to try to sell it themselves! Then all Monk would get would be the carving back, and a handful of petty thieves. It would stop the robberies perhaps for a week or two, but what was that worth? Instinctively he turned towards Orme and saw his face for an instant in the faintest light from the thieves' candles. The defeat in Orme's features twisted inside Monk as if he himself were responsible for the failure.

Another rat squeaked and ran, claws rattling on the wood. Then there was a different sound: softer, heavier. Monk's heart pounded in his chest and his mouth was dry. Orme turned the same instant as he did and saw the shadow of a man blend into the sagging walls and disappear.

Monk swivelled around the other way. To his right Butterworth was rigid, listening. He too had heard something and was straining his eyes, but not to where Monk had seen the man disappear. Butterworth was staring at least fifteen feet away.

Monk was freezing. His hand, clenched on the

hilt of the cutlass, was like ice, clumsy, all thumbs. His body was shaking.

He had been right the first time. There had been ten, but one of them had left, betraying his fellows. To whom?

The answer was already emerging into the pool of candlelight in what remained of the room. A grotesquely fat man stepped forward. His distended stomach was swathed in a satin waistcoat, his bloated face wreathed in smiles, his eyes like bullet holes in white plaster.

Silence gripped the thieves as if by the throat.

'Well!' said the Fat Man in a voice little more than a whisper. 'What a pretty piece of work.' Monk was not certain if he meant the betrayal or the ivory.

One man squeaked half a word, then stifled it instantly.

The Fat Man ignored him. 'Discipline, discipline . . . ' He shook his head and his massive jowls wobbled. 'Without order we perish. How many times have I told you that? If you had given that to me, openly and honestly as we agreed, I would have sold it and given you half.' His mouth hardened. He stood motionless. 'But as I have had to take the trouble of coming for it myself, and bringing my men with me, I shall have to keep all of it. Expenses, you see?'

No one moved.

'And discipline . . . always discipline. Can't have things getting out of control. No!' He barked the last word as one of the thieves made to stand up, his hand going to his waist for a weapon. 'Very foolish, Doyle. Very foolish indeed. Do you imagine I have come unarmed? Now you know me better than that! Or perhaps you don't, or you would not have tried such a stupid piece of duplicity.'

But the man was too angry to heed a warning. He drew a dagger out of his belt and lunged forward.

The Fat Man shouted, and the next moment the shadows came alive. There was a mêlée of heaving bodies, flying arms and legs, and the candlelight on the sudden, bright arcs of knives and cutlasses. It took less than a minute for Monk to realise that the Fat Man's followers were getting the better of it. There were more of them and they were better armed.

Orme was staring at Monk, waiting for the word.

For a sick, blinding instant Monk wanted to escape. How many men could he lose in a swordfight in the candlelight, with the thieves and the Fat Man's men against them?

What were the odds to do with anything? They were policemen. They wore the Queen's uniform. The Fat Man would take the carving and the police would have stood by like cowards and watched. Monk knew exactly how many men he would lose then — all of them.

'Forward!' he said, and charged, heading for the Fat Man in the lead.

The next moments were violent, painful and terrifying. Monk was in the thick of it and at first the cutlass felt strange in his hand. He was not sure whether to stab with it or hack. A thin man, scrawny but surprisingly powerful, swung at him with a cudgel and caught him a glancing blow on the arm. The pain of it jerked him into reality, and hot anger. He swung back with the cutlass and missed. A knife tore the flesh of his right shoulder and he felt the hot blood. This time his cutlass did not miss and the jar of its blade on bone rocked him.

But beyond the first taste of bile in his mouth, there was no time to think what he might have done. Orme was to his right, in trouble, and Clacton beyond was struggling. Jones came to his rescue. Where was the Fat Man?

Monk turned and slashed at Orme's attacker, catching only his sleeve. Then again and again the metallic clash of steel, the smells of sweat and blood fresh over the stink of slime.

Monk was hit from behind and fell forward, managing at the last moment to hold his blade clear. He rolled over and scrambled up again. He lashed back and this time struck flesh. There was a yell, and curses all around him. At least his own men were easier to recognise by the outline of their uniform tunics, although most of their hats had been lost in the battle.

Some memory within his own muscles brought back the skill to balance and lunge, to duck, keep upright, push forward and strike. His blood was hot and in some wild way he was almost enjoying it. He barely felt his own pain.

Then suddenly he was backed into a corner. There were two men in front of him, not one, and then a third. Fear was sick and real. He could not fight three men. How had he been so careless?

A blade arced up. He saw it gleam in the candlelight, and beyond it for an instant, Clacton's face a couple of yards away, smiling. He could see him, and Clacton was not going to help.

There was nowhere for Monk to run, no room to step left or right. He'd take on one of them at least, two if possible. He dared not raise his arm to slash. There was no space to swing. He checked and lunged forward, skewering the man to his left, expecting any second to feel the blade through his own chest and then darkness, oblivion.

He tried to yank his blade out but there was someone on top of it, heavy, lifeless, pinning his arm down. Then he saw Orme pulling his own blade free, and understood what had happened.

'Better be quick, sir,' Orme said urgently. 'We've done a good job. One of the Fat Man's men killed the thief with the carving and now the Fat Man's got it himself. We've got to get back to the boats.'

Monk responded without hesitation. The thieves could fight it out among themselves. He must get the Fat Man and the carving. They could still win, perhaps more swiftly and completely than in the original plan. He snatched up the thief's cutlass that moments ago would have meant his own death. Shuddering and stumbling, he went back through the wreckage of the building after Orme. He blundered into wreckage and tripped, falling headlong more than once, but when he emerged into the winter night, which was clear-mooned and stinging with frost, Orme was a couple of yards in front of him. Twenty feet beyond, the Fat Man floundered, coat waving like broken wings, his right fist held high with something clenched in it. It had to be the carving.

Orme was gaining on him. Monk forced himself to run faster. He almost caught up with them just as they reached the edge of the rotted pier jutting twenty feet out into the river. The boat was already waiting for the Fat Man, and Orme's men were beyond sight.

The Fat Man turned with a wave of triumph. 'Good night, gentlemen!' he said with glee, his voice rich and soft with laughter. 'Thank you for the ivory!' He pushed it into his pocket and swivelled. There was a crack as the last whole piece of timber snapped under his vast weight. For a hideous instant he did not understand what had happened. Then, as it caved in, he screamed and flailed his arms wildly. But there was nothing to grasp on to, only rotting, crumbling edges. The black water sucked and squelched below, swallowing him with one immense gulp. The moment after there was only the rhythmic slurp again as if he had never existed. His heavy boots and his immense body weight had dragged him down, and the mud beneath had held him, as if in cement.

Orme and Monk both stopped abruptly.

The Fat Man's boatman saw them and scrabbled for the oars, sending the craft back into the night. In the moon's glow, the water was silver-flecked and they were easily visible. One of the police boats appeared from round the stakes of the next pier and went after them. A second came for Monk and Orme, and then a third.

'He's got the ivory,' Monk said. It made the victory hollow. Farnham would consider it too high a price to pay for the evening's triumph, and he would not let Monk forget it.

'We'll get 'im up,' Orme assured him quietly.

'Up? How? We can't go down there. A diver would be lost in minutes. It's mud!'

'Grapples,' Orme answered. 'Get 'em this tide, we'll find 'im. 'E's got it in 'is pocket. It'll be safe enough.' He looked Monk up and down with concern. 'You got a nasty cut, sir. Best get it attended to. You know a doctor?'

Now that he thought about it, Monk was aware that his arm hurt with a steady, pounding ache and that his sleeve was soaked with blood. Damn! It was an extremely good coat. Or it had been.

'Yes,' he said absently. It would be the sensible thing to do. 'But what about the Fat Man? That ooze could pull him down pretty far.'

'Don't worry, sir. I'll get a crew with grapples straight away. I know what that carving's worth.' He gave a grin so wide his teeth gleamed in the moonlight. 'An' it'd be nice to pull the old bastard up an' show 'im off. Better'n just tellin' folk.'

'Be careful,' Monk warned. 'Sodden wet and covered in mud he'll weigh half a ton!'

'Oh, at least!' Orme started to laugh. It was a rich, happy sound, a little high, as if he was now realising how close they had all come to defeat, and he still did not know how badly any of the rest of his own men had been injured, or even killed.

Then Monk remembered Clacton. Did Orme know that he had deliberately held back? If he did, would he do anything about it? Would he expect Monk to? Even as the thought came to him, Monk half made up his mind to face Clacton, not as a betrayer but as a coward. It might be the better way.

He held out his left hand. 'A good night,' he said warmly.

'Yes, sir,' Orme agreed, taking it with his own left. 'Very good. Better'n I thought.'

'Thank you.' It was not a formality; he meant it.

Orme caught the inflexion. 'Yer welcome, sir. We done good. But yer'd best get that arm seen to. It's a nasty one.'

Monk obeyed and got into the waiting boat, a little awkwardly. His arm was stiffening already.

* ★ ★

It was nearly an hour later, on the north bank again, and close to midnight, when he finally sat on a wooden chair in the small back room of a young doctor known as Crow. Monk had met him through Scuff last year when Durban was alive and they were working on the Louvain case.

Crow shook his head. He had a high forehead and black hair, which he wore long and cut straight around. His smile was wide and bright, showing remarkably good teeth.

'So you got 'em,' he said, examining the gash in Monk's arm while Monk studiously looked away from it, concentrating his anger on the wreck of his coat.

'Yes,' Monk agreed, gritting his teeth. 'And the Fat Man.'

'You'll be clever if you get to gaol him,' Crow said, pulling a face.

'Very,' Monk agreed, wincing. 'He's dead.'

'Dead?' Without meaning to, Crow pulled on the thread with which he was stitching Monk's arm. 'Sorry,' he apologised. 'Really? Are you sure? The Fat Man?'

'Absolutely.' Monk clenched his teeth tighter. 'He fell through a rotted pier on Jacob's Island. Went straight down into the slime and never came back up.'

Crow sighed with profound satisfaction. 'How very fitting. I'll tell Scuff. He'll be glad at least you got that sorted. Hold still, this is going to hurt.'

Monk gasped and felt a wave of nausea engulf him for several moments as the pain blotted out everything else. Then there was a sharp, acrid sting in his nose that brought tears to his eyes. 'What the hell is that?' he demanded.

'Smelling salts,' Crow replied. 'You look a bit green.'

'Smelling salts?' Monk was incredulous.

Crow grinned, all teeth and good humour. 'That's right. Good stuff. So you got the Fat Man. That'll help your reputation no end. Nobody ever did that before.'

'Our reputation was rather in need of help,' Monk said, his eyes still stinging. 'Somebody's been spreading the word that we were not only incompetent but very probably corrupt as well. I'd dearly like to know who that was. I don't suppose you've any idea?' He looked at Crow as steadily as his groggy condition would permit.

Crow shrugged and turned his mouth down at the corners. 'You want the truth?'

'Of course I do!' Monk said tartly, but with a touch of fear. 'Who was it? I can't survive blind.'

'Actually it weren't so much the whole River Police as you personally,' Crow answered. 'Everybody that matters knows it was never Mr Durban. And Mr Orme's pretty good. He can't help being in the police.'

'Me?' Monk felt dizzy again and the wound in his arm throbbed violently. It was hard to believe it was only a cut — nothing to worry about, Crow had insisted. It would heal up nicely if he gave it a chance. 'You didn't say who it was!'

'You've got enemies, Mr Monk. You've upset somebody with a lot of power.'

'Obviously!' Monk snapped. He clenched his fist, then wished he hadn't.

Crow gave him a sudden, dazzling smile. 'But you've got friends as well. Mr Orme made sure you all stood together. Best you don't know any more.'

'Crow . . . ' Monk began.

Crow blinked and the smile remained. 'You look after Mr Orme; he's a good one. Loyal. Worth a lot, loyalty. I'll get a cab to take you home. You'll only fall on your face, and you don't want to have to explain that — you a hero an' all.'

Monk glared at him, but actually he was grateful — for the ministration, for the cab, but above all for knowing of Orme's loyalty. He made up his mind that from now on he would try harder to deserve it.

But who had spread the word about him, that he was corrupt personally? Argyll again?

9

It was well into February when Aston Sixsmith came to trial. He had been free on bail since shortly after his arrest, having been charged only with bribery.

'But you are going to be able to prove Argyll's complicity?' Monk said to Rathbone the evening before the trial began. Monk's wound was healing well and they were comfortable before a brisk fire in Rathbone's house. Rain was beating against the windows, and the gutters were awash. They still had not found the actual assassin, in spite of every effort, and River Police duties had consumed most of Monk's time since the death of the Fat Man. It had been a hideous job catching grapples into the corpse and hauling it up through the jagged hole in the pier. But the carving had been retrieved, to Monk's intense relief, and mixed emotions in Farnham. If it had been lost he would have blamed Monk, not himself.

As it was, Monk was now more firmly entrenched in his new position than was entirely comfortable for him, and Clacton was inexplicably subdued. He obviously loathed Monk, but something compelled him to treat his new commander with respect. Monk had yet to learn what this new element was.

'Argyll's guilty of murder,' Monk insisted to Rathbone. 'And more important than that, there is still the danger of the disaster in the tunnels that Havilland feared.'

'But you can't tell me what it is!' Rathbone pointed out. 'They are using the same engines as before, and nothing has happened.'

'I know,' Monk admitted. 'I've searched everything I can find, but no one will talk to me. All the navvies are afraid for their jobs. They'd rather face a possible cave-in in the future than certain starvation now.'

'I'll do what I can,' Rathbone promised. 'But I have no idea yet how to disentangle the guilty Argyll from the relatively innocent Sixsmith. Not to mention Argyll's wife, who is no doubt afraid to face the truth about him and fears public disgrace and the loss of her home. And the MP Applegate, who gave Argyll the contract, and the totally innocent navvies who operate the machines. And there's also Superintendent Runcorn, who conducted the original inquiry into Havilland's death, and will be blamed for having called it suicide and closed the case. Are you prepared for all of them to go down as well, tarred with the same brush? Guilty by association!'

'No,' Monk said flatly. 'No, I'm not.'

'Well, it might be a choice between having them all to be sure of getting the guilty one, or letting them all go, to be sure of saving the innocent,' Rathbone told him.

'If it comes to that, then I'll let them go,'

Monk said harshly. 'But not without damn well trying!'

Rathbone looked at him sadly. 'Accusation without proof will damn the innocent and let the guilty go free.'

Monk had no argument. What Rathbone said was true, and he understood it. 'We're too late to back out now.'

'I could drop the charge against Sixsmith?'

Driven by something more than anger at Argyll, or the need to win, Monk said, 'We have to do everything we can to find out if Havilland was afraid of a real disaster, or just of tunnelling in the dark. And if Mary learned it too, and was killed for it, then we can't walk away.' He knew as he said it that that was not entirely what was driving him. It was Mary Havilland's white face smeared with river water that haunted his mind. Even if all those other elements were solved, it would never be enough until her name was cleared and she and her father were buried as they would have wished. But Rathbone did not need to know that. It was a private wound, deep inside Monk, inextricably woven into his love for Hester.

Rathbone was looking at him. 'I've investigated Argyll's engines. They're pretty much the same as everyone else's. Better, because they've been modified with great skill and considerable invention, but no more dangerous.'

'There's something!' Monk insisted.

'Then bring it to me,' Rathbone said simply.

* * *

In the Old Bailey the next morning, after the appointing of the jury and the opening address, Oliver Rathbone began the case for the prosecution. His first witness was Runcorn.

Monk sat in the public gallery, with Hester beside him. They were neither of them witnesses so it was permissible for them to attend. He glanced at her grave face. It was pale, and he knew she was thinking of Mary Havilland. He imagined what she must be remembering of her own grief, and the sense of helplessness and guilt because she had not been there at the time of her father's death. There was always the belief, however foolish, that there was something one could have said or done that would have made a difference. He had not seen the anger in her, or heard her blame her brother, James, for not somehow preventing it. She had never lashed out at him, that Monk knew of. How did she keep at bay the bitterness and the sense of futility?

Then a sudden thought struck him. How incredibly stupid he was not to have seen it before! Was her need to throw herself into fighting pain, injustice, helplessness, her way of making the past bearable? Was her readiness to forgive born of her own understanding of what it was to fail? She worked with all her strength at Portpool Lane, not only to meet a fraction of the women's needs, but to answer her own as well. Anything short of her whole heart in the battle could never be enough for her. He was guarding her from the danger without, because he was afraid for himself, and what losing her would mean. He was thinking of his own sleepless nights, his imagination of her danger. All the time he was increasing the danger within.

Impulsively he reached across and put his hand over hers, holding her softly. After a moment her fingers responded. He knew what that moment meant. It was the acknowledgement of the loss of something inside her that he had taken away. He would have to put it back, as soon as he could, however afraid he was for her, or for himself without her.

Right now Runcorn was climbing the twisting steps to the high, exposed witness stand. He looked uncomfortable, in spite of the fact that he must have testified in court countless times over the years. He was neatly dressed, even excessively soberly, as if for church, his collar starched and too tight. He answered all Rathbone's questions precisely, adding nothing. His voice was uncharacteristically touched with grief, as if he too were thinking not of James Havilland but of Mary.

Rathbone thanked him and sat down.

Runcorn turned a bleak face towards Mr Dobie, counsel for defence, who rose to his feet, straightened his robes and walked forward into the well of the court. He looked up at the high witness stand with its steps, and squinted a little at Runcorn as if uncertain exactly what he saw. He was a young man with a soft face and a cloud of curly, dark hair.

'Superintendent Runcorn — that is your rank, isn't it?' he asked. His expression was bland, almost timid.

'Yes, sir,' Runcorn replied.

'Just so. That implies that you are considerably experienced in investigating violent deaths, accidental, suicidal and murder?'

'Yes, sir.'

'You are good at it?'

Runcorn was startled.

'I apologise.' Dobie shook his head. 'That was an unfair question. Modesty forbids that you reply honestly. I will accept that you are.' He glanced momentarily at Rathbone, as if half expecting an objection.

Rathbone would not object, and they both knew it. 'I have no quarrel with Mr Dobie's conclusion, my lord, even if it seems a little premature.'

The judge's face tightened in appreciation of his predicament.

In the dock, high above the proceedings and where those in the gallery had to crane their necks sideways to see him, Aston Sixsmith sat gripping the rails with his hands. His knuckles were white, and his eyes unmoving from Dobie's figure.

Dobie looked at Runcorn. 'May we assume that you took the death of James Havilland very seriously?'

'Of course.' Runcorn could see where this question was leading, but still he could not avoid the trap. He had long since learned not to add anything he did not need to.

'And you concluded that he had taken his own life?'

'Yes, sir, the first time.' Runcorn was forcing himself not to fidget. He stood as if frozen.

Dobie smiled. 'I will ask you in due course why you judged it necessary to consider it a second time. You did judge it necessary, didn't you? It was not some other sort of reason that drove you to go back again to a closed case? A favour owed, a sense of pity, for example?'

'No, sir.' But Runcorn's face betrayed that the answer was less than the whole truth.

Monk moved uncomfortably in his seat. He ached to be able to help Runcorn, but there was nothing at all he could do.

'What made you conclude that Havilland had killed himself? The first time, that is?' Dobie asked with gentle interest.

'The gun beside him, the fact that nothing was stolen and no sign of a break-in,' Runcorn said miserably.

'Was there anything of value a thief could have taken?'

'Yes, sir.'

'Did you find any evidence that Mr Havilland had been anxious or distressed recently?'

'No one expected him to take his own life,' Runcorn insisted.

'People seldom do.' Dobie gave a slight shrug. 'It is always difficult to imagine. Whose gun was it that he used — I'm sorry: that was used, Superintendent?'

Runcorn's face was tight, his jaw clenched. His large hands gripped the rail of the stand. 'His own.'

'And of course you verified that?'

'Yes.'

'Perhaps you would be good enough to tell the

court what on earth made you go back two months later and question your first decision? It seems eminently sensible, in fact the only decision you could have reached.'

Runcorn's face was deep red, but his gaze back at Dobie did not waver. 'His daughter also died in tragic and questionable circumstances,' he replied.

'Questionable?' Dobie's eyebrows rose and his tone was one of disbelief. 'I thought she also took her own life. Have I misunderstood? Is she not also buried in a suicide's grave?'

It was his first tactical error. Beside Monk, Hester closed her eyes and the delicate corners of her mouth tightened. She sat motionless, old memories raw inside her. In the rest of the gallery there was a slight sigh of breath. Monk turned to see the jurors' faces and found pity and distaste. They might not disagree, but they found the reference cruel.

Dobie had not realised it yet. He was waiting for Runcorn to answer.

Runcorn's face was bleak, his voice soft and startlingly full of emotion. 'It was the haste and possible injustice of that which made me look at Mr Havilland's death again,' he replied. 'I knew Mary Havilland because of her father's death. She was always certain he was murdered. I didn't believe her then, but it drew me to go back and look at his death again.'

There was a flush of anger on Dobie's lineless face. 'Are you being strictly honest with us, Superintendent? Was it not actually a visit from a certain Mr Monk which caused you to look at it

308

again? He is a friend of yours, is he not? And please do not be disingenuous.'

Runcorn was tight-lipped. 'Monk and I served together some years ago,' he answered. 'He's now with the River Police, and since he was investigating Mary Havilland's death and heard about her father, yes, of course he came to me to find out in more detail what happened.'

'And you told him what you had originally concluded, that Havilland shot himself?'

'I told him the details of our investigation. In light of the daughter's death as well, we looked into it again,' Runcorn said doggedly.

'In case you were mistaken, Superintendent?'

'I hope not. But if I am, I'm man enough to own it!'

A second tactical error. There was a rumble of applause in the gallery.

Hester smiled, her eyes bright with approval.

Dobie ridiculed Runcorn a little further, then realised he was doing his case more harm than good and let him go.

The police surgeon gave a very wide possibility for the time of Havilland's death in answer to Rathbone's questions. Dobie picked it out, but did not argue.

Rathbone called Cardman, who stood in the witness box ramrod stiff like a soldier facing a firing squad, his lips tight and his skin almost bloodless. Monk could only imagine how he must loathe this. In as few words as possible he answered Rathbone's questions about the letter that was delivered and given to Havilland. He described Havilland's response, dismissing the servants to retire and expressing the intention to stay up late and that he would secure the house for the night himself. He identified the hand-writing on the envelope as that of Havilland's elder daughter, Mrs Argyll. Rathbone thanked him.

Dobie rose to his feet, a slight smile on his face. 'This must be very unpleasant for you.'

Cardman did not answer.

'Did you see the contents of the envelope?'

Cardman was startled. 'No, sir, of course not!' The suggestion that he would read his master's mail was clearly repugnant to him.

'Did Mr Havilland tell you what was in it, perhaps?'

'No, sir.'

'So you have no idea as to its contents?'

'No, sir.'

'Do you know where this letter is now?'

'Mr Havilland destroyed it, I believe.'

'You believe?'

'That is what the maid said who took it to him!'

'Destroyed it? I see.' Dobie smiled. 'Perhaps that accounts for why Sir Oliver has not given us the privilege of reading it. Mr Cardman, have you any reason whatever to believe that this . . . letter . . . has anything whatever to do with Mr Havilland's death?'

Cardman took a deep breath and let it out soundlessly. 'No, sir.'

'Neither have I,' Dobie agreed. He gave a little shrug and turned out his hands, palms upward. 'Neither has anyone!'

The first witness of the afternoon was Melisande Ewart. Runcorn, having given his own evidence, was free to remain in the courtroom. He sat on the other side of the aisle in the gallery. Monk was acutely conscious of his stiff shoulders, clenched hands, eyes never moving from Melisande's face.

She stood in the witness box, calm but with two spots of colour high in her cheeks.

Rathbone was gentle with her, drawing from her bit by bit the account of Runcorn and Monk's visit to her and exactly what she had told them. Finally he had her describe the man who had emerged from the mews and bumped into her.

'Thank you, Mrs Ewart,' he concluded. 'Please remain where you are in case Mr Dobie wishes to speak to you.'

Monk looked again at the jury and saw sharp interest in their faces, and approval also. Melisande was a woman of gentleness and considerable beauty, and she had conducted herself with quiet grace. Dobie would be a fool to attack her. Nevertheless he did.

'You were returning from the theatre, you said, ma'am?' he began.

'Yes,' she agreed.

'At about midnight?'

'Yes.'

'A little late. Did you attend a party after the final curtain?'

'No. The traffic was very heavy.'

'It must have been! What play did you see?' Obviously he already knew the answer.

'*Hamlet*,' she answered.

'A great tragedy, perhaps the greatest, but full of violence and unnatural death,' he observed. 'Murder after murder. Including Hamlet's own father! As he finally succeeded in proving.'

'I am familiar with the plot,' she said a little coldly.

Runcorn's knuckles were white and his big hands clenched and unclenched slowly.

'And just as you arrived home,' Dobie went on, 'late and emotionally drained by one of the most powerful plays in the English language, you see a man emerge from the mews near your home.' He sounded reasonable, even soothing. 'It is dark, he almost bumps into you. He apologises for being clumsy, and a little drunk, and goes on his way. Have I summarised correctly, what actually happened, Mrs Ewart?'

She hesitated, her eyes going to Rathbone as if for help.

Runcorn half rose in his seat, and then subsided, his face tight with anger.

Hester grasped Monk's arm, her fingers digging into him.

'You are not incorrect, sir, so much as incomplete,' Melisande replied to Dobie. 'The man was a stranger in the area and he had no legitimate business in the mews. There was a large, dark stain on the shoulder of his jacket. I did not ask about it, but he saw that I had noticed it, and he told me that it was manure. He had tripped and fallen in the mews. But it was a lie. I was close enough to him to have smelled manure. It looked more like blood.'

312

'Even if it was blood, that does not mean he was guilty of murder,' Dobie argued.

Melisande's eyes widened. 'You mean he might have been in Mr Havilland's stable and fallen over his dead body innocently, without thinking he should mention it?'

Dobie's face flamed, and there was a titter of embarrassed laughter around the courtroom.

'Bravo,' Hester whispered to Monk.

Runcorn was smiling, his eyes bright, his cheeks hot.

Dobie returned to the attack, but he was losing and he knew it. Moments later he retreated. Rathbone thanked Melisande again, and then called the first of his nervous, uninteresting but very necessary witnesses who were going to prove the trail of the money Aston Sixsmith had paid to the assassin. They detailed the money's every move from Argyll's bank to its final destination. This line of enquiry was tedious, but necessary. It would continue for the rest of the day — and if Dobie wanted to contest any of it, it would go on probably longer than that.

When the court adjourned, there was no time for private conversation. Monk excused himself from Hester, and caught up with Rathbone in the corridor outside. 'I need to speak with Sixsmith,' he said urgently. 'Can you manage it? Persuade him to see me.'

'How?' Rathbone looked tired, in spite of the victory with Melisande Ewart, such as it was. 'I've already gone over every argument I can think of with Sixsmith. The man is desperate and numb with what has happened to him. He has worked for Argyll for years and feels totally betrayed.'

'So he should,' Monk answered, matching his stride with Rathbone's. 'And if we prove it was murder, but not that Argyll's the one who hired the assassin, then Sixsmith will pay for it on the end of a rope!'

'All right,' Rathbone said quickly. 'You don't need to labour the point. But don't give him false hope, Monk.' There was warning in his eyes, even fear.

'I don't intend to,' Monk promised, hoping he could keep his word. 'Exactly the opposite.'

It took Rathbone half an hour to arrange the meeting in a room off the corridor leading away from the court itself. Sixsmith looked somehow smaller than he had in the tunnel when Monk had seen him before. Dressed in an ordinary suit, he was broad-shouldered and solid, but not so tall. His hair was neatly barbered and his shirt white, his hands clean. His nails were unbroken — remarkably so, considering the surroundings in which he usually worked.

He sat in the chair opposite Monk, putting his hands on the table between them. His skin was pale and he had cut himself shaving. There was a tiny muscle that ticked in his temple on the left side. 'What is it?' he said bluntly. 'Haven't you done enough?'

There was no time for Monk to soften any of what he must say, however harsh it sounded. 'Sir Oliver Rathbone can tie up every detail of the money all the way from Argyll's bank to you passing it to the man who murdered Havilland.'

314

'If you think I'm going to plead guilty you are wasting your time,' Sixsmith said angrily. 'And more to the point, you're wasting mine as well. I never denied that I paid the money! I thought it was to bribe a bunch of ruffians to see off some of the toshers that were giving us a hard time and spreading rumours about uncharted underground rivers and scaring the hell out of some of the navvies.'

'Then say so!' Monk challenged him.

Sixsmith's heavy lip curled. 'Admit to bribing thugs to knock around a few men who are no more than a nuisance? They'll have me in gaol so fast I'll barely see the ground. Are you a fool?'

'No, but you are!' Monk responded. 'Rathbone will prove it anyway. If you want to come out of this alive, you'll admit to the attempt to bribe. It didn't work, so there was no crime actually committed — '

'There was murder!' Sixsmith said savagely, his face dark with emotion. 'If that's not a crime, what in God's name is?'

'Did you know it was going to be murder?'

'No, of course I didn't!' Sixsmith's voice was harsh, desperate. 'But I know beating the toshers was illegal. But what the hell do the men in Parliament know about the real world? Would they bend their backs to a day's labour hacking and piling earth and rocks, winching them up to the surface? Or living all the daylight hours in some stinking, dripping, rat-infested hole, burrowing like a damn rat yourself, so the sewers can run clean?' He took a deep breath, his chest heaving. 'We've got to get rid of the toshers who

315

are spreading fear just to keep their old beats in the sewers that are left. Do you know what a tosher's beat is worth?'

'Yes,' Monk said tartly. 'And I know they hate change. So tell the court that! Tell them that Argyll knew it too, and couldn't afford to let it go on.'

Sixsmith looked exhausted, as if he had been battling the same arguments in his head for weeks.

Monk felt an intense pity for him. 'I'm sorry,' he said gently. 'To be betrayed by someone you trusted is one of the worst pains a man can know. But you have no time now to dwell on it. You must save yourself by telling not just the truth, but everything.'

Sixsmith raised his head and gave him a smile that was more a baring of the teeth. 'Argyll will simply say that he gave me the money to buy off the toshers so they would leave the navvies alone, and I am the one who used it to have Havilland killed.'

'Why would you do that?'

Sixsmith hesitated a moment.

'Why?' Monk repeated. 'It's Argyll's company, not yours. Your reputation is excellent. If he went under, you could find a new position in days.'

'You know my reputation?' Sixsmith sounded surprised.

'Of course. Argyll couldn't afford to have Havilland sabotage his tunnel. He must have contacted the assassin, but got you to hand the money to him. Why would he do that, except to incriminate you if anyone ever discovered Havilland's death was murder. It was deliberate!'

316

Sixsmith blinked rapidly, his face a mask of pain, still fighting not to believe it.

'Were you the first to speak to the assassin?' Monk pressed. He hated forcing Sixsmith to see it, but his life could depend on it. 'Or did Argyll set up the meeting, give you the money and tell you to pass it over?'

'Of course he did,' Sixsmith said in a whisper.

'Do you know who the assassin was? Do you know where to find him now? Or anything about him at all?' Monk asked.

'No.' Sixsmith stared at him. 'No . . . I don't.'

'Who was it asked Mrs Argyll to write to her father and have him go out and wait in the stables at midnight?'

'You believe there really was a letter?' Sixsmith's eyes widened. 'Did anyone see it?'

'Yes, I believe there was,' Monk answered. 'She admitted it, but we can't force her to testify against her husband.'

Sixsmith dropped his head in his hands, as if someone had offered him hope, then dashed it from his lips.

'We can try to persuade her.' Monk wanted passionately to help him, give him the strength to go on. 'For your own sake,' he said urgently. 'Tell the truth about the money! Tell Dobie everything.'

'He can't help,' Sixsmith whispered. 'He thinks he can, but he's young and imagines he'll always win. He won't this time. Argyll's surrounded himself with too many people who are innocent. There's Jenny, poor Mary Havilland, the navvies who carried out his orders

317

to fight the toshers now and then. The poor devils don't have a choice! It's work or starve. And we have to meet the deadline in the contract or we won't get another.'

He looked at Monk as if trying to discern if he understood. 'And there's the MP, Morgan Applegate, who gave us the contracts for those sites. He could be implicated in bribes and profit. Argyll knows all that; he arranged it that way. I haven't a chance, Mr Monk. I'd best go down for bribing someone to murder a man, and not take all those others with me. I'll go anyway; he's seen to that.' He faced Monk with haunted eyes, still clinging to a hope beyond reason, but on the edge of losing it.

Monk did something he had sworn he would not do. 'Rathbone doesn't want to convict you,' he said quietly. 'It's Argyll he's after. He knows as well as you do that he's the man behind it. Tell the truth, fight for your life, and he'll help you.'

Sixsmith stared at him, aching to believe him. The struggle was naked in his eyes, in the bruised planes of his face and the twist of his mouth. At last, very slowly he nodded.

★   ★   ★

Hester had been to see Rose Applegate more than once since their mutual plan to do what they could to clear Mary Havilland's name from the stigma of suicide. Two days before the trial they had gone together to a charity afternoon reception organised to raise money for orphans and give them a decent education so that they might be of use both to themselves and to society. It was the sort of obviously worthy cause to which even a woman in mourning, such as Jenny Argyll, might still feel free to attend.

'Are you sure she will be there?' Hester had asked anxiously.

'Certainly she will,' Rose had assured her. 'Lady Dalrymple specifically invited the Argylls and she is at just the level of society one dare not disappoint. She is sufficiently *nouveau riche* to notice and take offence if one declined, unless you positively had a contagious disease. Anyway, Mrs Argyll has spent the entire winter season in mourning, so she is desperate to get out before she dies of boredom, and everyone who is anyone has forgotten who she is!'

So Hester and Rose had set out to join the worthy women who had attended the event, and had contrived to spend quite a good amount of time in Jenny Argyll's company. They had managed to fall with apparent ease into the subject of bereavement, and the whole ghastliness of the upcoming trial of Aston Sixsmith.

'She knows something,' Rose said to Hester when they met the following day, on the eve of the trial.

They were alone in Rose's withdrawing room, sitting beside the fire. Outside the February rain lashed the windows, streaming down the glass until it was impossible even to see the traffic passing in the street beyond.

'I am quite sure she will refuse to see us again unless she has absolutely no alternative,' Rose said miserably. 'And how would we possibly run into her? With Sixsmith on trial for arranging the murder of her father, and herself in mourning for both her father and her sister, she is hardly going to attend any public functions! Lady Dalrymple's ghastly affair for the betterment of orphans isn't going to happen again for years.'

'Isn't there any sort of function she might go to?' Hester asked. 'Even if just to show a certain bravado. There must be something suitably sombre, and — '

'Of course!' Rose said, her face alight with glee. 'The perfect thing! They are holding a memorial service for Sir Edwin Roscastle tomorrow.'

Hester was at a loss. 'Who was he? And would she go?'

Rose's expression was comical with distaste.

'A frightful old humbug, but very influential because he made such a parade of being good. Could flatter all the right people and it got him no end of appreciation,' she replied. 'Everybody likes to be seen praising the virtuous dead. Makes them feel good by association.' She sniffed. 'Morgan doesn't have anything to do with it because he couldn't stand him, and didn't pretend his feelings were otherwise. But I know Lord Montague, who is arranging it, and I can persuade him to ask Argyll for a donation, and to become a patron of the memorial fund. He'd never refuse that — it's far too useful in business.'

'Are you sure?'

'Of course I am! It's at eight o'clock tomorrow evening, and we can both go.'

Hester was alarmed. It was a superb idea, far too good to miss, but it was years since she had been to such a function and she most certainly had nothing suitable to wear. 'Rose, I . . . ' It was embarrassing to admit, and might even look as if she had lost her nerve and were making excuses.

Rose looked at her, then suddenly understood. 'Short notice to get a gown,' she said tactfully. 'Borrow one of mine. I'm taller than you are, but my maid can take it up this afternoon. We must make a plan of action.'

★   ★   ★

Thus it was that Hester accompanied Rose Applegate to the memorial service for the late Sir Edwin Roscastle. It was an extremely formal affair with a large number of people attending, including the cream of society. They arrived at the church and alighted from their carriages in magnificent blacks, purples, greys and lavender, according to the degree of mourning they wished to display, and the colour they believed most became them. Some were deeply mistaken as to the latter, as Rose observed to Hester in a whisper as she pointed out who they were.

'There she is!' Hester interrupted as she saw Jenny Argyll walking up the steps, clothed in sombre but highly fashionable black. She moved with a certain grace, and a complete disregard for the biting easterly wind, although she did take care to keep to the leeward of her husband.

Rose shivered convulsively. 'We can go in now. Why on earth do they always seem to hold these things at the bitterest time of the year? Why can't people die with some consideration, in the summer?'

'It will be warmer at the reception afterwards,' Hester replied. 'I hope to heaven the Argylls stay for it!'

'Of course they will!' Rose assured her. 'That is where one can curry favour, make useful acquaintances and generally show off. Which, of course, is what everyone is here for.'

'Isn't anyone here to remember Sir Edwin?'

Rose gave her a startled glance.

'Certainly not! He was awful! The sooner he can be totally forgotten, the better. Dying was the best thing he did, and he did that far too slowly,' Rose retorted.

Hester thought the judgement rather harsh, but she liked Rose too much to say so. And by the time they had sat through the eulogies and she heard what kind of people admired the deceased and why, she was inclined to take a similar view.

The reception afterwards was a different matter. Everyone else seemed to be just as physically cold and emotionally bored as she and Rose were. They walked rapidly up the hundred yards or so of dark and windy street to the hall where delicate hot pastries, sausages and pies awaited them, and wine of their choice. Hester accepted a mulled claret with gratitude. She was surprised when Rose took a lemonade instead, but she made no comment.

They began to move among the other guests, intent upon approaching Jenny Argyll as soon as it could be done without appearing too obvious, and of course when Argyll himself wasn't too close to her.

Rose was wearing lavender and dark grey. With her fair hair and pale skin she cut an extremely elegant figure, which nobody could help noticing. It was hardly the occasion for laughter, but she had a warm smile and there was a kind of inner enthusiasm about her that attracted people. Hester was privately amused to notice that it was appreciably more the men than the women who responded.

'I'm so pleased you came,' Rose said warmly to Jenny as an opening gambit. 'There are few things one can do while in mourning without someone making a cutting remark. One feels dreadfully isolated. At least I did! Perhaps I am imagining mistakenly?'

Jenny could hardly fail to reply without being discourteous — added to which, Rose was the wife of the Member of Parliament most important to her husband. She gathered her wits with an apparent effort. 'Not at all. You are most sympathetic,' she responded.

Hester remained standing back a few steps, as if Rose were alone. Jenny Argyll looked composed, but Hester could see that the veneer was thin. Her movements were stiff and her skin looked bruised around the eyes as if from too many nights awake, and too much tightly held-in emotion she dared not let go of, in case she never grasped stability again. Hester would have been sorry for her if she had not been convinced Jenny had placed her own safety and continued wellbeing ahead of that of her sister.

Then as she watched Jenny force herself to be civil to Rose Applegate, she was overwhelmed with pity for her. Jenny's eyes were guarded and filled with fear. Hester was ashamed that she had judged her so thoughtlessly. She could not know what other factors weighed in Jenny's mind, what debts or dependencies she had, what hostages to chance. Jenny had lost her father and her sister. What price had she already paid?

Rose was talking again. Hester knew what she would be saying, trying to trap Jenny into an admission that she had written the letter that lured her father to his death, and that Argyll had asked her to, or even forced her.

Suddenly Alan Argyll was at Hester's elbow, a plate of savoury pastries in his hand.

'Excuse me.' He brushed past her, his attention focused on his wife, his face tight and angry. It were almost as if he were frightened that she would in some way betray him. He spoke to Rose, but his words were lost to Hester in the general babble of conversation. He put his hand on Jenny's arm, protectively. She moved sideways, away from him. Was it because there was a large woman in black wishing to pass, or because his touch displeased her? Her head was high, her face half averted. The movement was discreet, a shrinking away more than an actual step.

Rose spoke again, her eyes wide and tense.

Hester moved closer. She wanted to catch the words, the inflexion of the voices. Was Jenny Argyll protecting her husband because she wanted to, or because she needed to? Had she any idea of what he had done? Was that why instinctively she found his touch repellent?

Rose turned and saw Hester and introduced them. She hesitated a moment over Hester's name, knowing that 'Monk' would produce powerful and conflicting emotions in both Jenny and Argyll.

'How do you do?' Hester said as calmly as she could, looking first at Jenny, then at her husband. He did not attract her, but nor did she find him ugly. She did not see the cruelty in him that she had expected. Even the power in him seemed blunted. Was he at last afraid, not of the police in the court, but of his wife's ability to testify against him? It was her father and her sister whose deaths he had caused. What monumental arrogance in him had ever made him imagine she would endure that and do nothing? But was she still so terrified that even now she would shield him?

Was evil really masked by so ordinary a face? Or was Hester simply blind to it?

Rose was making some trivial conversation. They were waiting for Hester to play her part.

'Yes, of course,' she said, hoping it was a reasonably appropriate response.

Argyll was looking at her, his eyes cold and guarded. She tried imagining a life tied irrevocably to a man of such chilling indifference: living in his house, sometimes in intimacy, obliged to him not only for your food and your clothes but for those of your children as well. Your name and your honour were bound with his, and perhaps in the end your conscience also. What a total and crushing imprisonment! She was ashamed of what she had to do to Jenny, but the alternative was intolerable. Whether or not one cared that Mary would lie in a suicide's grave, as would her father, no one at all could argue that Aston Sixsmith should hang for a crime he did not commit.

Jenny's voice strained, too sharp and too high. The conversation was all trivial: a remembrance of the dead man and the causes he had supported. A footman passed by with a tray of glasses filled with mulled wine or lemonade.

They were a little crowded. There was no room for the footman to pass between them. Argyll took the tray from him and offered it to Hester. Considering the potency of the mulled wine she had drunk on entering, she decided that lemonade might be wiser this time.

'Thank you,' she accepted.

Because of the way they were standing, Jenny next to her husband, it was natural to pass it to her next. She hesitated a moment over the lemonade, then chose the wine.

Rose took lemonade as before. She lifted her glass. 'To the brave men who pioneer social reform!' she said, and drank deeply.

The rest of them echoed the sentiment. More food was offered. This time it was sweet pastries filled with crushed dried fruit, or delicate custards with unusual flavours. It was exceptionally good.

A portly man with heavy side whiskers took Argyll's attention.

A three-piece musical ensemble began playing something sad and with no discernible tune.

Rose turned to Jenny. 'Isn't it awful?' she said confidentially, pulling her mouth down at the corners.

Jenny was startled. So far they had shared the artificial conversation of acquaintances who did not care for each other, but were civil in their mutual interest.

Suddenly Rose giggled. It was a rich, absurdly happy sound. 'Not the food! The music, if you can call it that? Why on earth can't we be honest? Nobody feels like playing a dirge because the old fool is dead. Most of them couldn't wait for him to go. Death is about the only thing that finally made him hold his tongue.'

Jenny pretended she was not taken aback. She took a deep breath and answered with a slightly shaky voice. 'That may be true, but we would be wiser not to say so, Mrs Applegate.'

Hester realised she had been holding her breath, almost till it hurt. What on earth was the matter with Rose? This was no part of their plan.

'To be wise all the time is the utmost foolishness!' Rose said rather loudly. 'We are so careful being wise we never commit any indiscretions, unless they are colossal and catastrophic!' She swung her arms wide to show how very huge the indiscretions were, nearly knocking Jenny's glass out of her hand. 'Look what you're doing!' she reproached her. 'Bad wine stains, you know.'

Jenny looked embarrassed. Several other

people turned to look at Rose, then away again quickly.

A waiter passed and Rose seized another glass from his tray. She drank it down in one long draught, then tossed the glass over her shoulder. It fell on the floor with a tinkle as it broke. She ignored it entirely and strode over towards the musicians. She made a magnificent figure, head high, skirts swaying, her handsome face coloured with life. She stood in front of the dais.

'For heaven's sake stop that awful wailing!' she commanded fiercely. 'You on the violin, you sound like a cat wailing for a fish-head. Unless you think the poor old sod went to dismal torment, which I admit is likely, try to sound as if you believed in the forgiveness of God, and some chance of heaven for him!'

The violinist clasped her hands to her bosom and let the violin slither down her dress and fall on to the floor.

Rose stooped and picked it up. She put it under her chin, seized the bow and began to play astonishingly well. She began with the same music they had been playing, but she altered the tempo to that of the music hall, and then slid into one of the concert songs, swift and bawdy.

The pianist gave a little squawk of horror and sat stark still with her mouth open. The cellist burst into tears.

'Oh, stop it!' Rose commanded her. 'Pull yourself together! And hold that thing properly!' She pointed to the cello. 'Like a lover, not as if it just made you an indecent proposal!'

The cellist flung the instrument on the ground

and fled, the bow trailing behind her.

Someone in the audience fainted, or pretended to. Another began to laugh hysterically. A man started to sing the words to the song. He had a rich baritone voice and — most unfortunately — knew all the words.

Hester stood frozen, aware of Jenny beside her and Alan Argyll a few feet away, paralysed.

Rose did not hesitate a stroke but kept on playing in perfect time, swaying and tapping her feet.

Suddenly the pianist abandoned all propriety and joined in. Her face was fixed in a terrified smile, showing all her teeth.

Alan Argyll jerked to life, moving to stand at Hester's elbow. 'For heaven's sake,' he hissed. 'Can't you do anything to stop her? This is appalling! Morgan Applegate will never live it down!'

Hester realised she was probably the only person who could do anything. She was Rose's friend, therefore it was an act of the utmost compassion and necessity that she intervene. She walked forward to the dais, picked up her borrowed and rather long skirts and stepped up. Rose was still playing very elegantly. She was on to a different song now, but no more appropriate.

'Rose!' Hester said quietly but with as much authority as she could manage. 'That's enough now. Let the violinist have her instrument back. It's time we went home.'

'Home, sweet home!' Rose said cheerfully, and loudly. 'That's a terrible song, Hester. Positively maudlin! We're celebrating Sir whatshisname's death. At least — I mean we're remembering his life with . . . with regrets . . . I shouldn't have said that!' She started to laugh. 'Far too close to the truth. Should never speak the truth at funerals. If a man was a crashing bore, like Lord Kinsdale, you say he was fearfully well bred.'

There was a gasp of horror from a maid, hovering with fascinated horror and clutching a tray of pastries. 'If a woman had a face like a burst boot, such as Lady Alcott,' Rose went on regardless, 'you say what a kind heart she had.' She laughed again, stepping back out of Hester's reach and speaking even more loudly. 'If he was a liar and a cheat, like Mr Worthington, you praise his wit. If he betrayed his wife with half the neighbourhood you talk all about his generosity. Everyone keeps a straight face, and weeps a lot into their handkerchiefs to hide their laughter.' She hiccuped but ignored it. 'You don't understand,' she went on, looking a little dizzily at Hester. 'You've spent too much time in the army.'

'Oh God!' someone groaned.

Someone else began to giggle and couldn't stop. It was wild, hilarious, hysterical laughter, soaring higher and higher.

Rose was hopelessly drunk. She must have had far more than Hester had seen or realised. Was this the terrible weakness that Morgan Applegate had been trying to guard her against? Had he the faintest idea what she was like? What she was saying so devastatingly loudly was awful! The worse for being perfectly true, and what everyone was secretly thinking.

Rose was about to start playing the violin again. The pianist was waiting in half agony, half ecstasy. It was probably a night she would remember for the rest of her life. She kept her eyes straight ahead and took a deep breath then plunged in with a resounding bass chord, and then a trill on the top notes.

Hester was desperate. It was all completely out of control, and part of her was on the edge of laughter. It was only the knowledge of ruin that stopped her joining in. She snatched the violin bow from Rose, gripping it around the middle in a fashion which probably did it little good. She flung it behind her, towards the back of the dais where at least no one would tread on it. The original violinist was still collapsed in a heap and someone was waving a fan at her, quite uselessly. The cellist had disappeared completely.

'You are going home because you are no longer welcome here,' Hester told Rose as sternly as she could. 'Put that violin down and take my arm! Do as you are told!'

'I thought we could play a game,' Rose protested. 'Charades, don't you think? Or perhaps not — we're playing it all the time, really — aren't we? Or Blind Man's Buff? We could all grope around, bumping into each other and grabbing hold of the prettiest, or the richest . . . no, that's being done too. All the time. What do you suggest?' She looked at Hester expectantly.

Hester could feel her face burning. 'Come home,' she said between her teeth, suddenly overtaken with fury at the senseless destruction of a reputation. 'Now!'

Rose was startled by the tone rather than the words. Reluctantly she obeyed.

Hester put an arm around her and grasped her wrist with her other hand. Awkwardly but efficiently she marched her to the edge of the dais. Rose, however, misjudged the step, tripped over her skirt and pitched forwards, only just saving herself from serious hurt by dragging Hester with her, and at the last moment by putting out her hands to break her fall.

Hester landed hard, knocking the breath out of her lungs. This saved her from using a word that had not passed her lips since the days in the army that Rose had referred to. Actually, struggling to disentangle herself from her skirts and stand up without treading on Rose and falling flat again, she clambered with great difficulty to her feet. 'Get up!' she commanded furiously.

Rose rolled over slowly and sat up, looking stunned, then she began to laugh again.

Hester leaned forward, caught Rose's hand and jerked hard. Rose slid forward, but remained on the floor.

It was Alan Argyll who came out of the crowd. Everyone else was milling around trying to pretend nothing had happened and either looking at the spectacle surreptitiously, or studiously avoiding looking at all.

'For God's sake get her out of here!' he snarled at Hester. 'Don't just stand there! Lift!' He bent and hauled Rose to her feet, balancing with some skill so she would not buckle at the knees. Then, as she began to subside again he picked her up, put her over his shoulder and marched her towards the door. Hester could do nothing but follow behind.

Outside it was not a difficult matter to send for Rose's coachman. Ten minutes later Argyll assisted her, with considerable strength, into the coach.

'I assume you will go with her?' he said, looking at Hester with disdain. 'You seem to have arrived with her. Somebody needs to explain this to her husband. She can't make a habit of it, or she'd be locked up.'

'I shall manage very well,' Hester assured him tartly. 'I think she has gone to sleep. Her servants will help as soon as we get that far. Thank you for your assistance. Good night.' She was angry, embarrassed and, now that it was over, a little frightened. What on earth was she going to say to Morgan Applegate? As Argyll had pointed out, his political career would never recover from this. It would be spoken of for years, even decades to come.

The ride was terrible, not for anything Rose did but for what Hester feared she would do. They sped through the lamp-lit streets in the rain, the cobbles glistening, the gutters spilling over, the constant sound of drumming on the roof, splashing beneath and the clatter of hoofs and hiss of wheels. They lurched from side to side because they were going too fast. The coachman was afraid Rose was ill and needed help as fast as he could get her home.

Hester was dreading what Applegate would say. No words had been exchanged, but she felt he had trusted her to care for Rose. From the first time they had met, Hester had seen a protectiveness in him, as if he were aware of a peculiar vulnerability in his wife, and one he could not share with others. Now it seemed that Hester had quite extraordinarily let them both down.

Except that she had had no idea how it had happened.

The carriage came to an abrupt halt but Rose did not seem to wake up. There was shouting outside and more lights, then the carriage door opened and a footman appeared. He leaned in without even glancing at Hester, lifted Rose up with intense care, then carried her across the mews and in through the back door of the house.

The coachman handed Hester out and accompanied her across the yard and through the scullery also. Her skirts were sodden around her ankles; her shoulders and hair were wet. Nothing had been further from her mind on leaving the memorial reception than sending someone to fetch her cloak — or to be more exact, Rose's cloak.

Inside the warmth of the kitchen she realised how very cold she was. Her body was shuddering, her feet numb. Her head was beginning to pound as if it were she who had drunk far too much.

The cook took pity on her and made her a hot cup of tea, but gave her nothing to go with it, no biscuit or slice of bread, as if Hester were to blame for Rose's condition.

It was half an hour before Morgan Applegate came to the kitchen door. He was in his shirtsleeves, his face flushed but white about the lips, his hair tangled.

'Mrs Monk,' he said with barely suppressed rage, 'will you be so good as to come with me.' It was a command rather than a question.

Hester rose and followed him. She was deeply sorry for his distress, but she had no intention of being spoken to like a naughty child.

He walked into the library where there was a brisk fire burning. He held the door for her, then slammed it shut. 'Explain yourself!' he said simply.

She looked at him with as much dignity as she could manage, being sodden wet, in borrowed clothes, and having endured one of the most embarrassing evenings of her life. She reminded herself that she had survived and been useful in fever hospitals and on battlefields. This was a very minor tragedy. She refused even to be formal.

'I believe Rose has had too much to drink, Mr Applegate. I saw her take only lemonade, and although she cannot have drunk more than one or two glasses of wine as well, she seems to be unusually susceptible to alcohol. Unless, of course, it was remarkably strong. I did not drink more than a glass myself so I do not know.'

He was breathing deeply, as if he could not find immediate words to retaliate.

'I am extremely sorry it happened,' Hester continued. 'I'm afraid you know only the

335

simplest part of it yet.' Better to get it over now rather than leave it for him to discover in the most acutely embarrassing way. 'There was a very dismal musical trio playing, and Rose took the violin from the fiddler and played it herself, extremely well. Unfortunately she changed the tune into a funny but rather vulgar song from the music halls. The whole scene is something you would probably prefer not to know about, but it was . . . memorable.'

'Oh God!' He went ash white. 'How?'

She hesitated.

'How?' he repeated.

'She was very forthright over what people say about each other, and what they really mean. With names. I'm sorry.' She meant it deeply.

He stared at her, the anger draining out of him. 'I should have told you. She . . . she used to . . . ' He spread his hands helplessly. 'She hasn't done for years! Why now?' His eyes pleaded with her for a reason for the devastation that had descended on him with no warning.

Then suddenly she knew the answer. It was as obvious as a slap across the face. 'Alan Argyll!' she said aloud. 'He must have put something in her drink! He knew we were there to try to persuade Jenny to testify! It was after that that Rose started to behave differently. Could he have known about her . . . weakness?' She would not insult either of them by mincing words. It was far too late now.

'If he had cared to find out,' Applegate admitted. He sat down slowly in the large leather seat just behind him, leaving her to do as she wished. He looked crumpled, like a rag doll someone had torn the stuffing from. 'Was it awful?' he asked, without raising his eyes.

To lie would only leave him more vulnerable. 'Yes,' she said simply. 'It was also very funny and perfectly true, and it is the truth of it I fear people will neither forget nor forgive.'

He sat silently.

The fire was beginning to warm her through. The hem of her gown almost to the hearth was steaming gently. She kneeled down in front of him. 'I'm sorry. We believed it was a good cause, and that we could win.'

'It is a good cause,' he said quietly. He seemed about to add something more, then changed his mind.

'Will she be all right?' Hester asked. 'Tomorrow? The next day?' Then she thought with a chill how clumsy that was. It would never be all right for Applegate himself. His position would become untenable. He would never be able to take Rose to any social event after this. Possibly he would find it unbearable to go himself.

He lifted his head suddenly. His eyes were blurred with fear and exhaustion, but there was a light of decision in them. 'I'll give up my seat in Parliament. We'll go back to the country. We have a house in Dorset. We can do a lot of good there, without ever coming to London again. It's quiet, beautiful, and we can be more than happy. We'll have each other, and that will be enough.'

Ridiculously, Hester felt her eyes fill with tears. He must love her so deeply and unquestioningly that all his happiness lay in being with her. His anger had been on her behalf, not against her. Perhaps it was even against himself, because he knew her weakness and had not protected her from it.

'I'm sorry,' Applegate apologised. 'Would you like something to eat? You must be frozen. It's . . . I shouldn't have blamed you. You couldn't guard against something you knew nothing of. Or would you rather simply go home?'

Hester made herself smile at him. 'I think actually I would like to go home and put on some dry clothes. It's a rotten night.'

'I'll have my coachman take you,' he answered.

★ ★ ★

Monk flung the front door open almost before the carriage had stopped. When Hester alighted he strode out into the street, disregarding the rain.

'Where have you been?' he demanded. 'You're soaked and you look terrible. You were supposed to — ' Then he saw the expression in her face and stopped. 'What is it?'

Hester thanked the coachman and went inside. She was shivering again, so sat down in the chair nearest the fire and huddled into herself. Now that she was no longer faced with Morgan Applegate's grief or Rose's urgent need, a profound sense of defeat settled over her. She wondered how she could ever have been so stupid as to think they could beat such vested interests. Her hubris had created her own downfall, and in her unthinking ignorance she had taken Rose with her.

'What happened?' Monk said again.

She described the evening as accurately as she could remember, although she left out a good deal of what Rose had said and summarised the rest. 'Argyll must have put alcohol in her drink,' she finished. 'I don't know how — I didn't see anything more than his hand over it for a moment. After tonight's performance she'll have to disappear, and neither she nor her husband will be able to give evidence of anything. And we won't force anything out of Jenny Argyll either. I won't have any way of getting back into Society with Rose. In fact — ' the heat rose up her face — 'in fact I may be remembered rather unkindly for my part in this. I'm sorry. I'm terribly sorry.'

He was startled. 'You're . . . why are you apologising? What else is there that you haven't told me, Hester?'

She stared at him.

'Nothing! But they knew who I was, that I'm your wife. Aren't policemen's wives supposed to behave rather better than that?'

He gazed at her, wide-eyed, then he started to laugh. It was a deep, full-throated howl of incredulous hilarity.

'It's not that funny!' she said indignantly.

But he laughed even more, and there was nothing she could do but lose her temper, or join him. She chose the latter. They stood together in front of the fire, the tears running down their cheeks.

'I think you had better forget politics,' he said

at last. 'You aren't any good at it.'

'I'm not usually as bad as this!' she defended herself, but without conviction. There was still defeat in her eyes.

'Yes, you are,' he replied, suddenly gentle again. 'I think you should go back to nursing. At that you are superb.'

'No one will have me,' she told him ruefully.

'Yes they will. In Portpool Lane every one of them loves you — even Squeaky Robinson, in his own way.'

There was disbelief in her face, hesitation, then hope. 'But you said — '

'I know. I was wrong.' He did not add anything because she threw her arms around his neck and clung on to him, kissing him long and hard.

10

In spite of her personal joy, Hester woke in the morning with the utmost remorse over Rose. She packed up Rose's borrowed clothes and returned them. Her army experiences had taught her something of the suffering incurred after overindulgence in alcohol, and she knew how to minister to those afflicted. She spent several hours doing what she could for Rose, to both her and her husband's intense gratitude, then she wished them every possible happiness, and took her leave.

She arrived at the Argyll house shortly after noon.

'Good morning, Mrs . . . Monk,' Jenny said with some uncertainty when Hester was shown into the withdrawing room and the door closed.

'Good morning, Mrs Argyll,' Hester replied with a slight smile. 'I thought that after last night's disaster you would naturally be concerned for Mrs Applegate. I know that you and she were friends.' Without realising it she had already put it in the past. 'And I owe you something of an apology. Had I been aware of her susceptibility I might have been able to prevent it. There are some people to whom even a drop of alcohol is a kind of poison.'

Jenny cleared her throat. She was obviously profoundly uncomfortable. She was wearing black again, of course, but relieved at the neck and wrists with lavender. The possibilities of life, passion and laughter were there in her face, but masked by discretion.

'I suppose it must be.' She sounded acutely uncertain, but she could hardly ask Hester to leave, unless she was prepared to be inexplicably rude. 'It is something of which I have no knowledge.'

'I hope you never have to,' Hester said warmly. 'I learned when I was caring for injured soldiers, and those facing death on the battlefield.' She saw Jenny's face pinch with momentary pity. 'When one is facing decisions that are almost unbearable,' Hester went on, as if now there were some kind of bond between them, 'some of us do not easily find the courage to do what is right, if it might cost us all we hold dear. I am sure you have the sensitivity to understand that, Mrs Argyll.'

'I . . . er . . . ' Jenny knew instinctively that the conversation was leading somewhere she did not wish to go. There was a purpose in Hester's bearing she did not mistake. This was no idle call.

Hester forced open the crack of opportunity. 'I am sure you are looking for the kindest way to enquire how poor Rose is this morning,' she lied. 'I have been to see her and she is in great discomfort, but it will pass. I don't believe any physical damage has been done to her, but the injury to her reputation will never heal.'

'I imagine not,' Jenny agreed. At last she was on more familiar ground. 'Society could hardly forget, or overlook, what she did. I . . . I hope you are not considering asking my help?' Jenny swallowed. 'I have no influence in such matters.'

'I wouldn't think of it!' Hester said quickly. 'I have no idea what anyone could do that would help, or the faintest reason why you should compromise your own standing by attempting it.'

Jenny relaxed visibly, something of the natural colour returning to her cheeks. She unbent far enough to invite Hester to sit down, and did so herself. 'I think her best course would be to retire from society,' she added.

'I agree entirely,' Hester concurred. 'I knew you would have the compassion and the delicacy to understand.'

Jenny looked pleased but confused.

'I am so sorry,' Hester added.

'Sorry?'

'Rose did not drink the alcohol intentionally,' Hester explained. 'Or even knowingly. It was given her by someone who wished to discredit her to a degree where she would not be able to appear in public in the foreseeable future.' She had already decided that to blame Argyll immediately would be very bad strategy. She must adopt a more circumspect line.

Jenny paled. 'Why on earth do you think that? Surely . . . surely if she has such a . . . weakness . . . ' She left the rest unsaid.

Hester frowned, as if concentrating. 'She must have been aware of her trouble,' she replied. 'It can hardly have happened in public recently, or we would all know of it, therefore it took her by surprise also. Someone else caused it. She drank only lemonade.'

Jenny stared at her. She took several long breaths, steadying herself. 'There is always the pastries,' she suggested, her voice a little husky. 'Some cooks mix the dried fruits with brandy? Or the creams with liqueur?'

Hester had not eaten them, but she should have thought of that. So should Rose! 'Would . . . would it be enough?' she said to fill the growing silence. She was playing a game, a battle of wits and she had no time to spin it out. The trial was drawing closer to its verdict every day. Rathbone's time was short, and once the defence started he might not be able to introduce new evidence. She hated having to be so brutal.

Jenny shook her head. 'I have no idea. It would seem so. What we saw was . . . irrefutable. I'm afraid the poor woman was very intoxicated indeed.' She thought for a moment. 'I'm so sorry.'

Hester's mind raced. She must be able to use Jenny's pity, turn it into a feeling of guilt. She had no doubt it was Alan Argyll who had killed Havilland, morally if not physically, and with great skill caused Sixsmith to be blamed.

'Of course,' she agreed aloud. 'Sometimes the results of our actions are not even remotely as we have imagined they would be.' She was moving towards the subject of Jenny's letter to her father, approaching it softly.

Jenny paled. Her hands moved on the black fabric of her skirt, not quite clenching, then deliberately falling loose again. There was effort in it, control. 'I am sure she can have no idea that a few pastries would do such a thing.'

'It was after her lemonade, before the pastry,' Hester corrected her, not certain if that were true.

'How could anyone . . . ?' Jenny started. Her face was very white.

Hester shrugged. 'A little bottle, such as one uses for medicines. A distraction of attention, not so very difficult.'

Jenny was forced to fill the silence. 'Who on earth would do that?'

'Someone who wished to discredit her,' Hester repeated. 'Rose had been looking into the matters your late father was investigating, just to make certain that there was no danger of serious accident, and — '

Jenny cut her off. 'My father was disturbed in his mind!' she said abruptly. 'There was no danger at all. The machines my husband's company uses are the best there are. It is skill which has improved them, which is why they are faster — not that they are taking less care.' The colour was high in her face, her eyes brilliant. 'This whole terrible charge has arisen only because of my father's — I don't like to use the word, but — hysteria.'

Hester could almost believe her, but for the man Melisande Ewart had seen leaving the mews. 'And that is why you wrote to your father asking him to meet your husband in the stables?' she said, allowing doubt into her voice. 'And poor Mr Sixsmith is facing a charge of murder?'

Jenny's voice was half strangled in her throat. 'It isn't murder! It's . . . it's just bribery. And even that is nonsense. My husband will see that he is cleared of that. Mr Dobie is a marvellous lawyer.' Her hands were now clenched hard in her lap, knuckles shining.

'Will he?' Hester asked. 'Do you believe that, Mrs Argyll? Why on earth would he? Who else could have hired the man who shot James Havilland — your father?'

A succession of wild emotions crossed Jenny's face: terror; confusion; hatred; panic to escape the net of horror that was closing around her, and forcing her to face the unbearable.

Hester leaned towards her a little, hating the fact that she had to be the one to do this. 'Someone hired that man to kill your father, and so, in a way, your sister too. Can you live with not telling the court that your husband made you write a letter asking your father to be in his stables that night? Can you go forward into the future looking at your husband across the table every dinner time, across the bed, knowing that both of you allowed Aston Sixsmith to hang, when you of all people could have proved his innocence?'

The tears were running down Jenny's face. 'You have no idea what you're asking!' she gasped. 'No idea!'

'Perhaps not,' Hester admitted. 'But you do. And if you are honest, you know what it will cost not only yourself, and your children, but Mr Sixsmith as well, if you do not. Do you wish to explain that to your children, or live with it yourself? Later, when they are older, will they believe it was for them you did this, and love you for it? Or will they believe it was for yourself, your own comfort and safety, and despise you instead?'

'You are ruthless!' Jenny choked on the words.

'I'm honest,' Hester replied. 'Sometimes they seem like the same thing. But I take no pleasure in it at all. You can still see at least that your father is buried with honour and his name cleared.'

Jenny sat motionless, her hands locked together. The lamplight, necessary even at midday, bleached her skin of all colour.

'The truth can be very sharp,' Hester added. 'But it makes a cleaner wound than lies. It will not fester.'

Jenny nodded very slowly. 'Please do not come back,' she whispered. 'I will do as you say, but I cannot bear to see you again. You have forced me to look at a horror I believed I could avoid. Allow me to do it alone.'

'Of course.' Hester rose to her feet and walked slowly to the door. She knew that the servants would let her out into the street where Morgan Applegate's carriage would be waiting to take her home.

★   ★   ★

That same morning Monk went across the river as the light was dawning grey and shadowed in the drifting rain. He went first to the police station simply to ascertain that no crisis had arisen demanding his attention, then he took a

347

hansom westwards to the Old Bailey to see Rathbone.

'Drunk!' Rathbone said incredulously. 'Rose Applegate?'

'And unforgivably frank,' Monk added.

Rathbone swore, which was an extremely rare occurrence. 'We are losing this case, Monk,' he said miserably. 'If I'm not extremely careful I shall end up convicting Sixsmith whether I wish to or not, and Argyll will walk away free. The thought makes me seethe, but even if I destroy half the decent men around him, the navvies, the foremen, the bankers as well as Sixsmith himself, I still can't be sure of getting him. If Rose Applegate could have persuaded the wife to testify to anything that would have made her father's murder more believable, we might have shaken him.'

He sighed and looked at Monk with a dread of failure burning deep inside him. It was in the nature of his profession to gamble on his own skill, and he could not always win. But when it was another man who was going to pay, it cut to the bone of his self-belief. It was a pain he was not used to, and his confusion was naked for a moment in his eyes.

Monk was familiar with self-doubt. It had made him stronger to bear the weight of ugliness within himself and endure it, even forgive it. He wished he could help Rathbone, and knew it could not be done. There are places each man walks alone, where even friendship cannot reach; all it can do is wait, and be there before and after.

'I'll go back to looking for the assassin,' he said, turning to go.

'If you don't find him in the next couple of days it won't matter,' Rathbone told him. 'I'd rather let Sixsmith go and drop the case altogether than convict an innocent man.' He smiled with a downward turn of his lips. 'My foray into prosecution is not conspicuously successful, is it?'

Monk could think of nothing to say that was not a lie. He gave a very slight smile, and went out, closing the door softly.

He was within half a mile of the Wapping station when Scuff appeared out of the gloom. The boy was soaking wet and looking inordinately pleased with himself. He ran a couple of steps to keep up with Monk. 'I done it!' he said without the usual preamble of greeting.

Monk looked at him. His small face was glowing with triumph under its outsize cap. Monk had still not managed to tell him it needed a lining. 'What did you do?' he asked.

Scuff's expression filled with disgust. 'I found where the killer lives, o' course! Isn't that wot we gotter do?'

Monk stopped, facing Scuff on the footpath. 'You found out where the man lives who shot Mr Havilland?' The thought was overwhelming. Then he was furious. 'I told you not even to think about it!' His voice cut across the air, harsh with fear. A man who would shoot Havilland in his own stables would not think twice about strangling an urchin like Scuff. 'Don't you ever listen?' he demanded. 'Or think?'

349

Scuff looked confused and deeply hurt. This was the last thing he expected. He had clutched his achievement to him all the way here, expecting Monk's praise and happiness, and now the prize was dashed out of his hand. He took a deep breath and looked at Monk, blinking to keep back the tears. 'Don't yer wanna know, then?'

Monk felt a guilt so deep that for a moment he could not find the words to express it even to himself, far less to try to mend anything in the child staring at him, waiting.

'Yes I do want it,' he said at last. He must not intrude in Scuff's precious dignity, he had little else. He must never allow him to know he had seen the tears. 'But I don't risk my men's lives, even for that. That's something you have to learn.'

'Oh.' Scuff swallowed. He thought about it for a moment or two while they both stood in the rain getting steadily wetter. 'Not nobody's?'

'Nobody's at all,' Monk assured him. 'Even those I don't like much, such as Clacton, never mind those I do.'

'Oh,' Scuff said again.

'So don't do it,' Monk added, 'or you'll be in trouble. I'll let you off this one time.'

Scuff grunted. 'So yer wanna know where 'e lives, then?'

'Yes, I do . . . please.'

''E lives down the Blind Man's Cuttin', wot leads inter the old sewer an' tunnel. There's lots o' folk live down there, but I can find 'im. I'll take yer. 'E's a bad 'un, mind. An' 'e knows them sewers like a tosher, especial the old ones down near the Fleet.'

'Thank you. I think we had better take some men with us. We'll go to the station and find them.' Monk started to walk.

Scuff remained where he was.

Monk stopped and turned, waiting.

'I in't goin' in there,' Scuff said stubbornly. 'It's all rozzers.'

'You're with me,' Monk said quietly. 'Nobody will hurt you.'

Scuff looked at him gravely, his eyes shadowed with doubt.

'Would you rather wait outside?' Monk asked. 'It's wet, and it's cold. It'll be warm in there, and we'll get a drink of hot tea. There might even be a piece of cake.'

'Cake?' Temptation ached in Scuff's eyes.

'And hot tea, for sure.'

'An' rozzers . . . '

'Yes. Do you want me to send them all out into the rain?'

Scuff smiled so widely it showed his lost teeth. 'Yeah!'

'Imagine it!' Monk replied. 'That's as good as you'll get. Come on!'

Hesitantly Scuff obeyed, walking beside Monk until they reached the steps, then hanging back. Monk held the door for him and waited while he took smaller and smaller steps, then stopped altogether just inside, staring around with enormous eyes.

Orme looked up from the table where he was writing a report. Clacton drew in his breath,

351

caught Monk's eyes, and changed his mind.

'Mr Scuff has information for us which may be of great value,' Monk told Orme. 'He will give it to us, of course, but it would be pleasanter over a cup of tea, and cake, if there is any left?'

Orme looked at Scuff and saw a sodden wet and shivering child. 'Clacton,' he said sharply, fishing in his pocket and pulling out a few pence. 'Go and get us all a nice piece of cake. I'll make the tea.'

Scuff took another step inside, then inched over towards the stove.

★   ★   ★

Two hours later Monk, Scuff, Orme, Kelly and Jones, the men armed with pistols, descended down the open workings and along the sodden bottom between the high walls of Blind Man's Cutting. As it closed overhead, they lit their lanterns.

Monk glanced at the sides of the tunnel. The old bricks were set in a close, carefully laid curve, now stained and seeping with steady drips and slow-crawling slime. The smell was thick in the nose and throat, and unmistakably human waste. The skitter of rats' feet interrupted the slurp of water down the channel in the centre. Otherwise there was no sound except their own feet slipping on the wet stone. No one spoke. Apart from the frail beams from their lanterns, the darkness was absolute. Monk felt panic rising inside him almost uncontrollably. They were buried alive as if the rest of the world had ceased to exist. He could see nothing but dark wavering shadows and yellow light on wet walls. The smell was suffocating.

Perhaps their journey was no more than a mile, but it seemed endless until they met a junction of waterways. Scuff hesitated only a moment before turning to the right. He led the way into a narrower tunnel where they were obliged to stoop in order not to strike the ceiling. The gangers cannot have been this way recently, because the piled-up sludge beneath their feet was deep and dangerous, catching at them, dragging, holding back and sucking down.

Monk had no idea where they were. They had turned often enough that he had lost all sense of direction. Sounds echoed and were lost, then there was nothing but the steady drip all around them — above, behind and ahead. It was like endless labyrinths through hell, filled with the odour of decay.

One of the men let out an involuntary cry as a huge rat fell off the wall and splashed into the water only a couple of feet from him.

Another half-mile and they emerged into a dry tunnel, where the ceiling was considerably higher. There they met a pair of toshers, who were roped together for safety. They had long poles in their hands for fishing out valuables, or gripping on to the sides when caught by a sudden current after a rainstorm. They were dressed in the usual toshers gear: high rubber boots, hats and harnesses.

It was Scuff who spoke to them, leaving the

River Police in shadows with their lanterns half concealed.

Then they moved on again, probing the darkness with their feeble lights. The thought made Monk's stomach churn and his throat tighten: what would happen if they dropped the lamps? They would never get out of here. One day, in a week, or a month, some tosher would find their bones, picked clean by rats.

The last ganger they had questioned, half a mile back, had said there were people using this old way to get from one part of the city to another. The man they were looking for, whose name no one spoke, was one of them. In the subterranean world there seemed little of either friendship or enmity, simply coexistence with rules of survival. Those who broke them died.

It seemed an age before Scuff finally led them up a ladder. Their feet clanged on the iron rungs. A few yards later they passed a sluice rushing so loudly they could not hear their own voices. Above, in a dry passage leading to a blind end, a group of men and women were sitting beside a fire, the smoke going up through a hole a little distance away and disappearing into utter darkness.

A short whispered conversation followed between Scuff and an old woman.

'Which way, ma?' Scuff asked her, touching his eye tooth to remind her who he was referring to.

She shivered and jerked her head to the left. A younger man argued with her, pointing to the right. Finally Orme agreed to follow the youth one way with Kelly and Jones and return if he found nothing. Monk took the other two men and went with Scuff the way the old woman had indicated.

Half an hour later, after more twists and climbs, Monk's party emerged into an open cutting, air fresh and cold on their faces.

'She lied,' Scuff said bitterly. 'Scared, I 'spect. Daft ol' — ' He stopped short of using the word he had been going to say. 'That way.' He pointed back where they had come from and at the next branch in the tunnel, divided again. Monk and Scuff went alone down more iron steps and deeper into the bowels of the earth.

Monk stopped, Scuff close beside him. Their lights showed only ten feet ahead, and then there was impenetrable darkness. Now there was no sound at all except the steady drip from the ceiling. Monk's anger had worn off now, leaving him cold. He could not blame the old woman. He was shivering and clenched with fear himself. Had he ever felt this gut-churning, physical terror before? He could not remember doing so. Surely one would never forget it? It was primeval, woven into one's existence. His skin crawled as if there were insects on it, and he heard every sound magnified. His imagination raced. The river could have been twenty feet away, or twenty miles. Was the assassin really somewhere ahead of them, perhaps even waiting. He heard nothing but water, dripping, running, splashing around their feet. This part of the old system was no longer used. The stream was shallow, fed by nothing but rain down through the gutters, but it still smelled of stale human waste. The gangers had not been here for a long time. The piled up silt of excrement was like stalagmites.

There was a sound ahead. Monk froze. It was not the scratch of rats' feet but the heavier noise of a boot on stone.

Monk covered his lantern.

'It's 'im!' Scuff whispered, reaching up and gripping Monk's hand.

The noise of footsteps came again, then a light reflected yellow on the ancient, slimy stone of the tunnel. A shadow grew larger, moving, swelling.

Scuff was holding Monk's hand so tightly his ragged nails bit into Monk's flesh and it was all Monk could do not to cry out. He pulled Scuff closer and half shielded him behind him. His heart was pounding in his chest, choking him. Had he been above ground when he was facing the man, however dark the night, he would have been calm apart from heightened senses. He was glad he had a gun, although this was like meeting the devil in his own territory, alien and dreadful, a more than human evil.

The sound of a boot scraping on stone suddenly vanished as the man coming towards them trod in a drift of silt. There was nothing but the swelling shadow and the dripping of water.

Scuff's breath hissed in through his teeth and he clung on to Monk.

The man appeared round the corner only twenty feet ahead of them. He had come another five or six feet before he realised that the shadows of Monk and Scuff by the wall were human and not detritus heaped against the stone. He froze, his lamp unwavering in his hand, the yellow glare of it lighting his face like a lined yellow mask. He was thin, his hair was unkempt and ragged to his shoulders. The black slashes of his brows cut across his face. He had a long, narrow-bridged nose, flared nostrils, lantern jaw and wide, thin-lipped mouth. Surprisingly there was intelligence in the eyes, even humour.

Very slowly he smiled and Monk saw the sharp, oversized eyeteeth, the left bigger than the right. Monk froze, the picture indelible in his mind.

Then the man turned and with astounding swiftness loped away.

Monk was galvanised into action. He tore the cover off the lantern and, still grasping Scuff by the hand, floundered through the silt and water and up into the drier stream bed after the man. Scuff was now easily keeping up with him, so he let go of his hand. The man ahead was forced to keep his lantern high as he splashed, slipping, his huge shadow on the walls and ceiling like the image of a wounded bird trying to fly, arms wide. The yellow light jerked over the black, shining ooze on the walls and the slick surface of the stream.

There was a turn, and then utter darkness. Scuff was so close to Monk he pressed against him.

Monk realised how wet he was. His legs were frozen but his body was sweating. He could feel the perspiration running down his back and his chest.

There was a noise ahead, a splash. He jerked round to face it. The right tunnel.

'Rats!' Scuff whispered hoarsely. ''E's jiggered up them rats. Cm' on!' And without waiting to make sure, he plunged through the water.

Monk drew in his breath to cry 'Stop!', then bit it back. Sound echoed down here. He had no idea how far ahead the assassin was, perhaps only a few yards. He ran, slipping and struggling after Scuff. The dim reflection on the water made Scuff's small figure oddly elongated as it moved with a jerky, swaying gait.

The light ahead was there again, bright and unguarded. Monk saw the assassin turned to face them, his arm lifted. There was a sharp crack, a spurt of flame. Scuff cried out and crumpled up, slithering into the water.

Monk lunged forward, pulling his gun out of his pocket. He fired it again and again even after the figure had disappeared and there was no light in the suffocating darkness except his own.

He put his gun away and held the lantern high, staring at the stream, looking for the small figure. Scuff would be already floating, pulled along by the current, scraped by the sludge and filth. He saw him — and lost him — and found him again. He bent over awkwardly — because there was nowhere to set the lantern — and picked up the limp body. Scuff's face was white and wet, reminding him, with a lurch of pain, of Mary Havilland, but Scuff was far smaller, pinched and thin, the skin almost blue around his eyes and mouth. Thank God, he was breathing, in spite of the blood that oozed through his clothes and stained them scarlet around his shoulder and chest.

The assassin must be somewhere ahead of them, but the thought of leaving Scuff and going after him never entered Monk's head. Clumsily, because of the lantern, and trying to carry Scuff gently with only one arm, he turned and began the long way back. He walked in the centre of the sewer floor where he could move the most easily. He had very little idea where he was, but the only thought in his mind was to find the way up towards help.

He did not know how badly Scuff was hurt, but he could not stop here to find out. There were rats everywhere and they would smell blood. Far worse than that, the assassin knew he had hit Scuff. The fact that Monk had not followed him would tell him that Scuff was not dead, and Monk was trying to get back up again, hampered by carrying a wounded child. As soon as he was certain of that, would he double back and try to finish Monk off? If the positions were reversed, Monk would!

He was lost. There was a fork again: three ways, two ahead, one behind him. Which way had he come? Think! Scuff's life depended on it! The water was flowing around his feet quite rapidly. It must have been raining all day. What happened if it got harder, heavier? Flash floods, of course! Deep water. Enough to pull him off his feet, maybe even drown him, and Scuff. Was it still raining? He could feel the panic rising inside him. Stop it! Stop behaving like a fool! Think!

Water flows downwards. When he came had he been going with the flow or against it? With it, of course. Down, all the time, down. So go back against it now. Against it must be upwards. It didn't matter any more where he emerged, as long as it was into the air and where he could get help. Any opening would do!

So go against the stream all the time, upwards!

He started forward again. Scuff was growing heavy on one arm, but he had to hold the lantern high in order to see. Its weight was pulling on the wound from the fight in Jacob's Island, which was not yet fully healed. One good thing: if he were simply going up, and not necessarily retracing the way he had come, then there was no trail for the assassin to follow. Why had the killer never gone back to Sixsmith for the second half of his payment, nor apparently to Argyll either? Perhaps he had never expected to collect the second half. He might have asked for what he meant to have in the first payment! Maybe he feared that Argyll meant to kill him, tidy up the ends. Was he right?

Rathbone would have to drop the prosecution or risk hanging Sixsmith, and Argyll would escape. Neither Mary nor her father would ever be vindicated.

But all that mattered now was getting Scuff up to the top before he died of shock and the cold. Monk wanted to look at the wound but there was nowhere to lay Scuff down, nowhere to hang the lantern so he could see. His legs were freezing and clumsy, his heart was pounding and the stench of sewerage all but made him gag, but he was moving as fast as he could, always uphill, against the flow of the water.

Once he passed a series of iron rungs in the wall which alone he would have climbed, but not with Scuff.

He rounded a corner. The light seemed clearer now. He must be nearing the surface!

Then he saw the figure ahead of him, a man, thin, with his arm raised. There was a shout, but in the tunnel it echoed. Against the roar of the water going over the weir he could not make out the words. It must be raining harder.

The shot still took him by surprise, ricocheting off the wall, sending brick chips and dust flying. He threw himself against the wall, sheltering Scuff as much as he could with his own body.

There was another shout, and another, but they sounded further away. He looked round and at first he thought there was no one there. Then he saw the lantern held high, and Orme's familiar figure behind it. Relief washed over him like a warm tide, almost robbing him of the little strength he had left.

'Orme!' he shouted. 'Here! Help me!'

'Mr Monk, sir! Are you all right?' Orme ran over, slipping in the water, his lantern swaying wildly, his face crumpled with concern.

'Scuff's shot,' Monk said simply. 'We've got to get him up.'

Orme was aghast. 'Now? Just now?'

'No! No . . . we caught up with the assassin and he shot at us.'

'Right, sir. I'll lead the way,' Orme said

steadily. 'Come with me.'

It seemed a long time before they finally emerged into the open cutting. By now Monk had abandoned his lantern, simply following Orme's light ahead. He wanted to hold Scuff gently, in both arms. The boy was beginning to stir and every now and then he let out a soft groan.

When they reached the end of the cutting and were on the level ground again they stopped. For the first time Monk saw Scuff's face in the daylight. He was ashen white and there were already hollows of shock around his eyes. Monk felt a tight pinching in his heart. He looked up at Orme.

'You better get 'im to a doctor, Mr Monk,' Orme said anxiously.

Scuff's eyes flickered open. 'I want Crow,' he said weakly. 'It 'urts summink awful! Am I gonna die?'

'No,' Monk promised. 'No, you're not. I'm going to take you to the hospital — '

Scuff's eyes grew wide and dark with terror. 'No! No 'ospitil! Don't take me there, please, Mr Monk, don't take me . . . ' he gasped. His face turned even whiter. He tried to reach out his hand as if to ward off something, but only his fingers moved. 'Please . . . '

'All right,' Monk said quickly. 'No hospital. I'll take you home. I'll look after you.'

'You've got to get 'im treated proper, Mr Monk,' Orme's voice was sharp with fear. 'Just carin' isn't gonna be enough. That bullet's gotter come out an' the 'ole stitched up . . . an' clean.'

'I know,' Monk answered more sharply than he meant to. 'Get a message to Crow and have him come to my house. My wife's a battlefield nurse.'

Orme saw the futility of arguing when time was so desperately precious. He ran out into the street and stopped the first hansom passing, ordering the startled passenger out to find another hansom. This was police business. The man saw the injured child and made no demur.

Orme left to look for Crow.

It was a nightmare journey. Monk sat cradling Scuff in his arms, talking to him all the time, about anything and nothing, wishing he knew how to help. The trip seemed to last for ever, and yet it was perhaps no more than half an hour before he climbed out, paid the driver and carried Scuff to the front door.

The house was dark, empty and cold. God! Had she gone back to Portpool Lane already? He could have wept with fear and the aching loneliness of knowing he was inadequate to do what was needed. Where was Hester? Why was she not here? What could he do without her? He felt panicky and sick. There was no time to wait!

He must keep Scuff warm! He was slipping away, bleeding too fast. His face was grey and there was barely a flutter of his eyelids.

Monk must warm up the room, riddle the stove, put on more fuel. He should boil water to make it clean. Where was Hester? Why was she not here? He had no idea how to get a bullet out! He could kill Scuff just by trying!

He moved quickly, ramming the fire with the

363

poker. He must be careful; if he put on too much coal he would put the fire out. Then it would take ages to light again. Quickly! Blow at it, make it draw! He filled the biggest pan with water, then changed his mind and put on a small one instead. It would be quicker.

Finally there was no excuse to wait any longer. He lifted Scuff from the chair where he had put him and laid him on the table under the light. He must take off his coat and remove the bit of scarf Orme had put in to pack the wound. It was soaked through with blood. His hands shook as he pulled it off and saw the scarlet hole in the white skin, still welling up scarlet inside. Scuff was unconscious and barely breathing. Perhaps it was too late already?

Please God! Please God!

He did not even hear the front door. It was not until Hester was standing beside him that he realised his face was wet with tears of relief. He did not ask if she could save Scuff because he could not bear the answer.

She said nothing except to give orders: 'Pass me the knife; clean this for me; cut up my petticoat, it's soft; put the vinegar on this — yes, it's clean. They used to use it in the navy, in ships of the line. Just do it!'

They worked together. She probed for the bullet, pulled it out, packed the wound, and finally drew the flesh closed, and stitched it over with a darning needle dipped in boiling water. She used the only silk thread she had, a dark blue from a dress she had been altering. He obeyed, his teeth clenched, his body now shuddering with cold and exhaustion, his heart pounding with fear.

Finally they were finished. Scuff was bandaged and dressed in one of Hester's nightgowns, which was the only thing that was anywhere near his size, and laid gently on her side of the bed.

Only then did Monk finally ask, 'Will he live?'

She did not lie to him. Her face was pinched with grief and tiredness, and her blue dress was indelibly stained with blood. 'I don't know. We'll just have to wait. I'll sit here with him, try to keep his temperature down. There's nothing else to do now except wait. Go and wash, and put dry clothes on.'

He had totally forgotten that he was still sodden wet himself, and the stench of the sewer probably filled the whole house. 'But . . . ' he started, then realised she was right. There was nothing further he could do to help Scuff, and catching pneumonia himself would help no one. He was shaking with cold, his teeth chattering. He would change and then make them both a cup of tea. His stomach was chilled, empty and sick, and his arm was throbbing.

He was in the kitchen with the teapot when Crow arrived, ashen-skinned, eyes hollow. 'How is he?' he asked, searching Monk's face. 'God, you look awful!' His voice shook. Perhaps he should have been more professional but his emotions were too raw to hide.

'I don't know,' Monk admitted. 'Hester took the bullet out and stitched the wound, but he's terribly weak. He's upstairs, in my bed. Can you — '

Crow had a Gladstone bag with him; he had not even put it down. He turned and went up the stairs two at a time. Monk followed him five minutes later with scalding hot tea.

Crow was standing beside the bed. Hester was still sitting on the chair, Scuff's white hand in hers. Crow turned. 'She did a good job,' he said simply. 'There's nothing more that I can do. It's a bad wound, but the bullet's out and it's clean. It's not bleeding much any more. I've got bandages here and spirit to clean with, and a drop of port wine to lift him when he wakes.' He did not say 'if', but they all knew he meant it.

'Just . . . wait?' Monk wanted to do more than that. There must be something.

'Tea,' Crow said with a bleak smile.

Monk poured it and they sat down to endure the long night.

Scuff tossed and turned. By midnight he was feverish. Monk fetched a bowl of cool water from the kitchen and Hester kept sponging him down. By half-past one Scuff was more settled, breathing shallowly but not thrashing around any more, and no longer covered with sweat.

Crow took off the bandage and repacked the wound. It looked clean, but it was still bleeding slowly. He tried to give Scuff a teaspoonful of wine, but the boy would not take it.

Monk dozed a little in the chair, then changed places with Hester by the bed, watching and waiting.

Outside the rain turned to sleet, then to snow.

At five o'clock Scuff opened his eyes, but he

was barely half awake. He did not speak, and it seemed as if he had little idea where he was. Hester lifted him very slightly and gave him a teaspoonful of wine. He choked on it, but she gave him some more, and the second time he smiled very faintly. Almost immediately he slipped back into unconsciousness, but his breathing was a little steadier.

Monk went down to build the stove up again and boil more water for tea.

A little after seven Scuff spoke.

'Mr Crow? That you?'

'Yes, it's me,' Crow said quickly.

'Yer came . . . '

'Of course I did. Did you think I wouldn't?'

'Nah . . . I knowed. I done it.' He smiled weakly. 'Told yer.'

'What did you do?' Crow asked him.

'I found the feller fer Mr Monk. I 'elped 'im.'

'Yes, I know,' Crow agreed. 'He told me.'

'Did 'e?' Scuff frowned. He gave a deep sigh and fell back to sleep again, smiling.

'Is he going to be all right?' Monk demanded, his voice hoarse.

'Looks better,' was all Crow would say.

At eight o'clock Crow left, needing to see his other patients. There was no more he could do for Scuff now, and his manner more than his words said that he trusted Hester's ability as much as his own. He promised to return in the evening.

Monk was weary. His bones were aching and his eyes were smarting each time he blinked, as if there were sand in them. Nevertheless he knew he must go and tell Rathbone that he had seen the assassin, exactly as Melisande Ewart had described him, and that he had shot Scuff, and escaped. His existence and his nature at least he could attest to.

Hester was exhausted too, but she dared not sleep in case Scuff suddenly grew worse and she was not there to do all she could. Even so, she was only half awake when he spoke to her.

''Oo are yer? Are yer Mr Monk's wife?' His voice was surprisingly clear.

She opened her eyes, blinking. 'Yes, I am. My name's Hester. How are you?'

He bit his lip. 'I 'urt. I got shot. Did Mr Monk tell yer?'

'Yes. I know you did. I took the bullet out of your shoulder. That's why it hurts so much. But it looks as if it's getting better. Would you like something to drink?'

His eyes widened. 'Yer looked? Didn't yer faint, nor nuffink?'

'No. I was a nurse in the army. I don't faint.'

He stared at her, then moved experimentally. Suddenly he saw the lace on his sleeve. 'Wo's that? Wot yer done wif me clothes?'

'It's one of my nightgowns,' she replied. 'Your own clothes were wet from the sewers, and pretty dirty.'

He blushed scarlet, still staring at her.

'I've tended to soldiers before,' she said matter-of-factly. 'It's all the same, in battle. Not that I gave them my own nightgowns, of course. But I didn't have anything else for you, and no time to go and get anything. You needed to be warm and clean.'

'Oh.' He looked away, confused.

'Would you like something to drink?' she offered again.

He turned back to her slowly. 'Wot yer got?'

'Tea with sugar and a little port wine,' she replied.

'I don' mind if I do,' he said a trifle warily. He was obviously still turning over in his mind the fact that he was wearing her nightgown and he had no idea where his own trousers were.

She went down to the kitchen and made tea, then brought it up and added a few spoonfuls of port. She helped him drink it without any further conversation. His colour was definitely better when he lay back.

'Yer looked arter soldiers?' he asked doubtfully.

'Yes.'

'Why d'yer do that? Didn't Mr Monk mind?'

'I didn't know him then.'

'In't yer got no ma and pa ter look arter yer?' He frowned. She did not fit his picture of an orphan.

'Yes, I had then. They didn't like it a lot,' she said frankly. 'But quite a few young ladies, even very respectable ones, went out to help Florence Nightingale.'

'Oh! You one of them?'

'Yes.'

'Were yer scared?'

'Sometimes. But when things are at their worst you don't think of yourself so much, more of the men who are wounded, and if you can help them.'

'Oh.' He thought for a moment. 'I don't need no 'elp. Least, not most o' the time. I 'elp Mr Monk. 'E don't know much about the river. Not that 'e in't clever, an' brave, like,' he added quickly. 'E's just . . . '

'Ignorant,' she supplied for him with a smile.

'Yeah . . . ' he agreed. 'If yer knowed that, why'd yer let 'im go?'

'Because if you love someone you can't stop them doing what they believe they have to.'

He looked at her more seriously, with the beginning of something that could even have been respect. 'Is that why yer pa let yer go inter the army?'

'Something like that.'

'Wot's it like?'

She told him, fairly factually, what the troop ship had been like crossing the Mediterranean, and her first sight of Scutari. She was describing the hospital when she realised he was asleep. His breathing was even and his brow was cool, his skin dry and quite a good colour.

She lay down on Monk's side of the bed, and in spite of her intention not to, almost immediately fell asleep too.

When she woke Scuff was awake, looking uncomfortable. He had been lying close to her, perhaps afraid to move in case he disturbed her. Yet he remained there now when he did not have to, his eyes wary, waiting for her to say something, perhaps make some kind of demand.

She knew better. He may have been frightened, lonely, hungry for affection, but if she

370

offered it too soon he would reject it instantly. He needed his independence to survive, and he knew it.

'Are you all right?' she asked quite casually. 'I fell asleep,' she added unnecessarily.

'It 'urts,' he said, then instantly was ashamed of himself. 'I'm better, ta. I can go 'ome soon.'

It was not the time to argue with him. He needed to feel some part of his fate was in his own hands. He was afraid of losing his freedom, of becoming dependent, coming to like warmth and soft beds, hot food, even belonging.

'Yes, of course,' she agreed. 'As soon as you are a little better. I am going to get something to eat. Would you like something too?'

He was silent, uncertain whether to accept or not. In his world food was life. One never took it or gave it lightly. All his surroundings were unfamiliar and he was conscious enough now to be fully aware of that.

She stood up, tidying back a few strands of hair and making a poor job of it. In spite of her determination not to care for the boy, she cared intensely. If he knew, he would resent it, and feel trapped. She must not allow it to show. She went to the door without looking back, then forgetting at the last moment, she turned. He was lying in her place, white-faced, his skin pinched around his mouth, shadowed around his eyes. He looked very small. It was Monk's opinion he cared about, not hers.

'I'll be back,' she said, feeling foolish, and went down the stairs.

She returned half an hour later having made

an egg custard, something at which she was not skilled. She had had to work hard to get it right. She had it now in two bowls on a tray. She set them down on the dresser and closed the door, then offered him one dish.

He stared at it, no idea what it was, and raised his eyes to hers, uncertain.

She put some on a spoon and held it to his lips.

He ate it, tasting it slowly, carefully. He might never admit it, but it was clear in his expression that he liked it very much.

Slowly she fed him the rest, then ate her own. She had a ridiculous feeling of success, as if she had won a great prize. She looked forward to making something else for him.

'Is that wot yer feed soldiers when they're 'urt?' he asked.

'If we have the supplies, yes,' she replied. 'Depends where we're fighting. It can be hard to get things over great distances.'

'Wot kind o' things? Yer gotter 'ave food. D'yer 'ave guns an' things too?'

'Yes, and ammunition, and medical supplies, and more boots and clothes. All kinds of things.' Then she elaborated on army life and he sat with his eyes never leaving hers. They were still talking when Monk came back in the late afternoon.

He came up to the room quietly. He looked exhausted, but the moment he saw Scuff sitting up against the pillow he smiled.

Hester rose, anxious for him now. It was already darkening outside and he was spattered with rain even after having taken his coat off downstairs.

372

'Are you hungry?' she asked gently, trying to read from his face what he needed most.

'Yes,' he answered, as if surprised by it. 'Rathbone thinks Sixsmith may be convicted.'

'I'm sorry,' she said sincerely.

'Navvies' evidence,' he explained. 'Perhaps we shouldn't have started this, but it's too late to undo it now.'

'What about tomorrow?'

'More navvies, clerks, people who probably had no idea of any of it,' he answered. 'Let's eat. I've done all I can. Are you hungry, Scuff?'

Scuff nodded. 'Yeah, I am,' he conceded.

11

By the time Monk returned home to Paradise
Street after the following day's court, it was dark
and raining again. The gutters were awash, water
slopping over on to the cobbles. The reflections
from the lamps danced on wet stone, and the
clatter of hoofs was broken by splashing. The
cold wind coming up from the river carried
wreaths of mist that stretched out, wrapped
around trees and even houses, then elongated
and disappeared again.

Inside, the house was warm. The kitchen
smelled of new bread, clean linen and something
savoury. Hester greeted him at the door.

'He's fine,' she said before he asked.

He smiled as the sweetness of it soaked into
him.

'He's been asleep on and off,' she went on.
'He looks a lot better.'

He held her close, kissing her mouth, then her
cheek and eyes and hair, allowing the rest of the
world to be closed out for a few precious
minutes. Then he went upstairs to change into
dry clothes, and to see Scuff.

'How are you?' he asked.

Scuff stirred and sat up very slowly, blinking a
little. He seemed uncertain how to answer.

'Are you worse?' Monk said anxiously.

Scuff grinned lop-sidedly. 'It 'urts like bleedin' 'eck,' he said frankly. 'But that egg stuff as she makes is real good. D' yer know some o' them places she's bin?' His eyes were huge with amazement and more admiration than he was probably aware of. 'I in't never 'eard o' some o' them!'

'Neither have I,' Monk conceded, coming in and sitting on the edge of the bed.

'She told me about wot she done in the army an' such.'

'Me too, now and then. She doesn't talk about it a lot.'

'Sad, eh? All them men 'urt bad.' Scuff frowned. 'Lot o' them died. She didn't say so, but I reckon as they did.'

'Yes, I reckon so too. Are you hungry?'

'Yeah. Are you?'

'Yes.'

Scuff tried to climb over to the edge of the bed, as if he would come downstairs to eat.

'No!' Monk said sharply. 'I'll bring it up to you!'

'Yer don't 'ave ter . . . ' Scuff began.

'I'd rather carry the supper up than have to carry you again,' Monk told him drily. 'Stay where you are!'

Scuff subsided and inched back to the centre again. He lay against the pillow, watching Monk.

'Please don't fall out,' Monk said more gently. 'You'll hurt yourself worse.'

Scuff said nothing, but he did not move again. They were all three of them in the bedroom,

375

halfway through eating, when the interruption came. Hester was cutting up vegetables for Scuff and letting him pick them up with a fork. He did it carefully, uncertain at first how to manage. Monk was eating steak and kidney pie with a vigorous appetite. Suddenly there was a loud knocking on the door, again and again, almost as if someone were trying to break in.

Monk put his plate on the tray, the last mouthful uneaten, and went downstairs to find out who it was.

Orme stood on the step in the rain, his hair plastered to his head, his face white. He did not wait for Monk to ask what the matter was, nor did he attempt to come in.

'There's bin a cave-in,' he said hoarsely. 'Down at the Argyll tunnel. The 'ole lot. It all came in and God knows 'ow many men's buried.'

It was what James Havilland had feared, and Monk would have given everything he owned not to have had him proved right. 'Do they know what caused it?' he asked, his voice shaking. Even his hand on the door felt cold and somehow disembodied.

'Not yet,' Orme said, ignoring the rain dripping down his face. 'Suddenly the 'ole side just slid in, wi' water be'ind it, like a river. An' then about fifty yards further up the line another lot went. I'm goin' back there, sir, to see if I can 'elp. Although God knows if anyone can.'

'Another slide? That means there are men trapped between the two? Is there any sewage down there?'

'Dunno, Mr Monk. Depends on what it were that slid. It's close to one o' the old sewers as is still used. Could be. I know wot you're thinking — gas . . . ' He did not finish.

'I'll come with you.' There could be no hesitation or question of what he must do. 'Come in out of the rain while I tell my wife.' He left the door open and went up the stairs two at a time.

Hester was standing in the bedroom doorway, Scuff sitting up on the bed behind her. Both of them had heard Orme's voice and caught the sound of fear in it.

'There's been a cave-in. I have to go,' he told her.

'Injuries? Can . . . ?' Then she stopped.

He gave her a quick smile. 'No. Your place is here with Scuff. Just because he looks all right doesn't mean he is. You know that better than I. I'll be back when I can.' He kissed her quickly, harder perhaps than he meant to, then turned and went back down the stair, took his coat from the hook in the hall, and followed Orme out into the street.

There was a hansom waiting. They climbed in and shouted to the driver to hurry back to the tunnel. He needed no urging.

They clattered through the streets. The long whip curled over the horse's back, and water sprayed from the wheels on either side. The journey there took nearly half an hour, even at this time of night when there was no traffic. As Orme scrambled out, Monk paid the driver — overgenerously — then followed Orme into the darkness and the rain. Ahead of them, a maze of lamps was moving jerkily as men stumbled over rubble and broken beams as carefully as they could to avoid falling.

Monk was aware of shouting, the sting of wind and rain and — somewhere he could not see it — the thrum of one of the big engines for lifting the rubble. Beyond the periphery of the disaster area there were carriages waiting, and ambulances.

'Bloody awful mess!' Crow emerged into a small pool of light. His black hair was sodden wet, his face ashen, eyes like holes in his head. If he had ever had a medical bag he had lost it. His hands were covered with blood. Judging by the gash on his left forearm, at least some of it was his own.

'How can I help?' Monk said simply. 'Can we get anyone out?'

'God knows,' Crow answered. 'But we've got to try. Be careful, the ground's giving way all over the place. Watch where you put your weight, and if it goes, yell! Even in this noise, someone may hear you. Throw yourself flat, that'll give you at least some chance of finding a beam or a piece of something to hang on to. Stand straight and you'll go down like an arrow.' As he spoke he was leading the way towards a group of lanterns about a hundred yards further on, which were swaying as the men carrying them picked their footing to go deeper into the cave-in area.

'What happened?' Monk asked, having to raise his voice now above the thud and grind of the machine digging and unloading the rubble.

'Must have dug too close to a small river,' Crow shouted back. 'London's riddled with them. All this burrowing and digging around, and some of them have moved course. Only takes a couple of feet, a change from clay to shale, or striking an old culvert, a cellar or something, and the whole thing can turn. Sometimes it just goes round it and back to the — Watch your feet!'

The last was a shout of warning as Monk's foot sank into a squelching hole. He pitched forward, only just catching Orme's arm in time to pull himself upright and haul his foot out. His leg was now coated in sludge up to his knee. Shock robbed him of breath and he found himself gasping even after he had regained his balance.

Crow slapped him on the shoulder. 'We'd better stay together,' he said loudly. 'Come on!'

Monk leaped up with him. 'Could anyone have known this was going to happen?' he demanded.

'Sixsmith?' Crow asked, keeping moving.

'Havilland, actually,' Monk replied.

Crow stopped abruptly. 'Murdered because of it?' There was surprise in his voice and, but for the wavering lights, his expression was invisible. 'I don't know. If he had sense enough to listen to some of the older toshers, maybe. Some of them knew things that aren't written down anywhere. Just lore passed from father to son.'

They were at the edge of the crater, which seemed a fathomless pit. Monk felt his stomach clench, and his body shook in spite of tensing every muscle to try to control himself.

A little man, broad-shouldered and short-legged, came towards them. He had a lantern built into his hat so both his hands were left free. There was too much noise of clattering earth and the thrum of the great machine for him to attempt to be heard. He waved his arms for them to follow, then turned and led the way down.

Monk lost all count of time, and finally of direction also, even of how deep he was and the distance he would have to go upward to find clean air or feel the wind on his face. Everything was wet. He could hear water seeping down the walls, dripping, sloshing under his feet, sometimes even the steady flow of a stream: a sort of thin, wet rattle all the time.

Someone had given him a short-handled shovel. He ignored his painful shoulder and worked with Crow to begin with, digging away fallen debris by the dim light of lanterns, trying to reach trapped or crushed men. Then Crow went up again with bodies, and Monk found himself beside a barrel-chested navvy and a tosher with a broken front tooth that made his breath whistle as he heaved and dug.

The light was sporadic. One moment the lantern would be steady, held high to see an arm or a leg, distinguish a human limb from the timbers or a head from the rounded stones of the rubble. At others it rested on the ground while they dug, pulling, hoping, and then realising there was nothing to find, and moving on, going deeper.

At one point they broke through into a

pre-existent tunnel and were able to go twenty yards before finding another slide and starting to dig again. It was under this one that they found two bodies. One man was still just alive, but even with all they could do to help, the man died as they were trying to move him. His injuries were too gross for him to have stood or walked again, and yet Monk felt a crushing sense of defeat. His mind told him the man was better dead than facing months of agony, and the despair of knowing he would remain a cripple, in shattering pain and utterly helpless. But still death was such a final defeat.

He returned slowly, his body aching, to the heap of waste. He held his lantern high to see if the other man could be brought up for identification and burial, or if even to try would jeopardise more lives. He picked his way carefully, even though he knew it by now, and bent, holding the light towards where he thought the head was. He pulled away pieces of brick and mortar until he had uncovered the body as far as the middle of the chest. It would probably not be too difficult or dangerous to get the rest of him free. The dead man was so plastered with clay and dust Monk could distinguish very little of his features beyond that he had long hair and a thin, angular face.

There was a rattle of pebbles behind him and the bow-legged tosher appeared at his elbow. Silently they worked together. It took some time but eventually they freed the body and half carried, half dragged it along the old sewer floor. They had to pass through one of the small streams dribbling out of the side wall. It was ice cold and erratic, but at least smelling of earth rather than sewage.

When they reached the top at last Monk held the light to look at the man. The question of who he might be froze on his lips. The stream they had passed through had cleaned off the mud, and he saw the face clearly. It had stared at him in the lantern light of another sewer only a day and a half before. The black hair and brows like a slash across his face, and the narrow-bridged nose were etched on his mind for ever. With a shaking hand he touched the lip and pushed it back. There were the extraordinary eyeteeth, one even more prominent than the other. What irony! His hiding place had been the cause of his death! The very stream he had killed to conceal had in turn killed him.

''Oo is 'e?' the tosher looked at Monk, frowning. 'I seen 'im somewhere afore, an' I can't 'member where it were.'

'He's a man who killed other people for money,' Monk replied. 'The police are looking for him. I need to find Sergeant Orme. Can you send someone to fetch him? It matters very much.'

The tosher shrugged. 'I'll put out the word,' he promised. 'Are you goin' ter leave 'im 'ere?'

'I'm going to stay with him, at least until the police can take him away,' Monk replied. Suddenly he was aware of the cold, of his feet numb and his body shaking. Would this be in time to make a difference to the trial? It would at least prove that Melisande Ewart had seen a real

382

person. Might that be enough to swing the jury? Or to frighten Argyll?

He waited, crouching in the dark beside the corpse, hearing shouts and seeing waving lanterns in the distance across the rubble. It had started to rain again. The light shone yellow on the faces of the rocks and black pools of water between. The giant machine reared up in the mist like some monstrous, half-human creature, still grinding and thumping as more debris was hauled up. Monk was not sure if it was his imagination, but it seemed to be settling deeper into the earth.

It was about half an hour when at last Orme appeared, waving a lantern, Crow on his heels.

'You got 'im?' Orme asked, bending to look at the dead body.

'Yes.' Monk had no doubt at all.

Crow stared at him. His face was lit on one side, and shadowed on the other, but his expression was a mask of anger and scalding contempt. 'Doesn't look so much dead, does he!' he said quietly. Then he bent down, frowning a little. Experimentally he touched one of the man's hands, then picked it up. His frown deepened and he looked up at Monk. 'You think he was killed in the fall?'

'Yes. His legs are crushed. He was probably trapped.' He was half ashamed as he said it. 'I should feel sorry for anyone caught like that, but all I feel for him is angry we can't make him tell us who paid him. I'd bring him into court, broken legs and broken back.'

'Scuff'll be all right,' Orme said quietly,

looking not at Monk but at Crow. 'Won't 'e?'

'Yes, I should think so,' Crow agreed. 'But look at his legs, Mr Monk.'

'What about them? They're both broken.'

'See any blood?'

'No. Probably washed off in the water we took him through. I dragged him; he's heavier than you think.'

Crow looked at the body again, more carefully. Orme and Monk watched, growing more curious and then unaccountably concerned.

'Why does it matter?' Monk said finally.

Crow stood up, his legs stiff, moving awkwardly. 'Because he was dead before the slide hit him,' he replied. 'Dead bodies don't bleed. The only blood staining anything is on his coat, from the bullet hole in his chest. The river didn't wash that out.'

Monk found himself shaking even more violently. 'You mean he's been murdered? Surely he'd never have shot himself?'

'Not in the back, anyway,' Crow replied. 'Went in under his left shoulder blade, came out the front. I reckon whoever employed him paid his last account.'

Monk swallowed. 'Are you absolutely sure?'

Crow pulled his mouth tight and rolled his eyes very slightly. 'Take a look at the bastard yourself, but of course I'm sure! I'm no police surgeon, and don't want to be, but I know a bullet hole when I see one! Heavy calibre, I'd say, but ask the experts.'

Monk straightened up. 'Thank you. Will you and Sergeant Orme take him to the morgue and call the police surgeon? I must tell the prosecutor in the Sixsmith case, and Superintendent Runcorn. A man's life may hang on this.' It was an order, at least as far as Orme was concerned, and a request to Crow.

Orme relaxed. 'Of course,' he said resignedly. 'Come on!'

★ ★ ★

Monk went back to Paradise Street to tell Hester what had happened. No message from anyone else, however sympathetically or precisely delivered, would satisfy her, or Monk's own need to see her and tell her himself. He was confused and exhausted by the emotional horror of seeing so many people in agony of body and terror of mind whom he could not help. He knew those who were dead had been crushed, buried and suffocated in the darkness, and often alone, feeling life slip away from them, unhelped, even unknown. Hester could not heal him of that horror, no one could, nor erase the memory. But she would understand. Just to see her would ease the knots locked hard inside him.

It was only now that he realised, with amazement, that he had not had time, or emotion to spare, to be afraid for himself! It was a sweet, hot kind of relief. He was not a coward, at least not physically.

Now he needed to see for himself that Scuff was still recovering. It was absurd that he should feel so intensely about it. He had no medical knowledge and would understand nothing that

Hester could not tell him in words. Something gripped him inside, compelling him to see Scuff's face himself.

The moment he opened the door he heard movement upstairs. Before he was halfway along the passage he saw the light go up on the landing and Hester's figure on the top step. Her hair was unpinned and tangled from sleep, but she was still dressed, although barefooted.

'William?' she said urgently, her voice sharp with anxiety. She did not ask specific questions, but they were all there implicitly. Their understanding of each other was founded on the battles and the victories of the past.

He wanted to know about Scuff.

She answered him before he asked. 'He's getting stronger all the time,' she said, coming silently down the stairs. 'A little feverish about midnight, but it passed. It's going to take a week before he can get up much, and far more than that before he can go back to his own life. But he will.' Her eyes searched his face. She did not ask if it had been terrible; she read the answer in his experiences that night: the pallor of his skin; the stiff way he moved; the fact that he did not even try to find words for it.

She knew more of battle and death than he did, of the nightmare of slaughter. What senseless immaturity had ever made him imagine he wanted a woman of childlike innocence who was obedient and uncritical? And he had imagined it; dreaming of sweetness that now would cloy, obedience that now would bore him, and leave him at heart utterly alone. He had thought of an ideal woman who would see him without his human failings, weaknesses and errors of judgment; but a woman that innocent — even with all the words at his command — he could never share the passion, the hunger or the pain of his life with. Conversation of the heart would be impossible.

When Hester reached the bottom of the stairs, he took her in his arms and held her close, hard, wordlessly. In his mind he blessed over and over again whatever benevolence had led him to choose a woman whose beauty was of the soul: brave and vulnerable, funny, angry and wise, and to whom he need explain nothing.

Monk had no time to sleep, only to wash and change clothes and eat some hot breakfast. Of course he also went up to look for a few moments at Scuff, who was scrubbed clean and sound asleep. The boy was still wearing Hester's nightgown with the lace edge next to his thin little neck, his left shoulder sitting crookedly over his bandages.

★ ★ ★

At half-past eight Monk was at Rathbone's office, explaining the night's events. A messenger was dispatched urgently to bring Runcorn to the Old Bailey, after he had contacted Melisande Ewart with a request that she also attend. Were she unwilling, a summons would have been necessary.

By ten o'clock the court was in session and Rathbone had asked permission to call Monk to

387

the witness stand. Monk was startled how stiff he was and how his legs ached as he climbed up. He had to grip the rail to steady himself. Even after food and clean clothes he was exhausted. His shoulder ached, and the violence of the night invaded his mind.

Rathbone looked up at him anxiously. The barrister was as elegant as always — immaculately dressed, his fair hair smooth — but his eyes were shadowed and his lips pale and pulled a little tight. Because Monk knew him so well, he could see the tension in him. He knew how close he was to being beaten.

In the front row of the gallery Margaret Ballinger sat white and unhappy. Her eyes seldom left him, even though most of the time it was only his back and profile that she could see.

'Mr Monk,' Rathbone began, 'will you please tell the Court where you were last night?'

Dobie, who apparently had not heard the news, immediately objected.

'Very well, may I rephrase the question?' Rathbone said tightly, his voice scraping in his throat. 'As some in the court may know, my lord, there was a catastrophic cave-in in the Argyll Company's sewer construction last night.' He stopped while the public gallery gasped and one or two people cried out. The jurors looked at each other in horror. It subsided only at the judge's demand for order.

'Were you called to the scene, Mr Monk?' Rathbone concluded.

'Yes.' Monk kept his answers as bare and as direct as possible. He glanced only once at

Sixsmith up in the dock, his powerful face forward, his body rigid with tension and totally unmoving.

'Who called you?' Rathbone asked Monk.

'Sergeant Orme of the Thames River Police.'

'Did he say why?'

'No. I believe he assumed that since I had been investigating the risk of just such a disaster, because of James Havilland's fears, and his subsequent death, that I would be involved. Also, of course, we were doing all we could to help, as were the Metropolitan Police, the fire services and various doctors, navvies, toshers and any able-bodied man in the area.'

'Your point is taken, Sir Oliver,' the judge assured him. He turned to Monk. 'I would like to know, Inspector, what you found. Was it of the nature that you had been led to fear?'

'Yes, my lord,' Monk replied. 'That, and greater.'

'Please be more specific.'

It was the line that Rathbone had intended to take, so Monk was happy to respond. 'James Havilland had intimated that he feared a disaster if there were not a great deal more time and care taken in the excavations. He did not record precisely what he feared — or if he did, I did not find it. There are risks of land movement: slippage, subsidence in any major work. He seemed to fear something further. What seems to have occurred last night was that the diggings went too close to an underground river and the river burst the walls, carrying an enormous weight of earth and rubble with it, and flooded the tunnels . . . '

There was too much noise of horror and distress from the gallery and jurors for Monk to continue, and even the judge looked stricken. Obviously the news had not yet reached the daily papers, and few had heard it even by word of mouth.

'Silence!' the judge ordered, but there was no anger in his voice. He was calling his Court to order, but without criticism. 'I assume, Mr Monk, that you are here, in spite of your appalling night, because there is some evidence Sir Oliver feels pertinent to the case, even at this late stage of events?'

'Yes, my lord.'

'Very well. Sir Oliver, please ask your question.'

'Thank you, my lord,' Rathbone acknowledged. 'Mr Monk, during the course of the night, did you bring to the surface any bodies of the dead, or the still living?'

'Yes.'

'Were any of the people that you knew?'

'Yes.'

'Who were they?'

'Two navvies that I had spoken with, a tosher — a man who retrieves objects of value from the sewers — and one other man whom I had met once before.' He stopped abruptly, memory of that crowding darkness momentarily choking his breath, then the pistol shot and Scuff falling. He was so tired that past and present collided with each other and the courtroom seemed to sway.

'Where did you meet him, Mr Monk?'

Monk realised that Rathbone had asked him

twice. He stiffened his back and shoulders. 'In the sewers,' he replied. 'When I was looking for the man Mrs Ewart saw coming out of the mews after James Havilland was shot.'

'You did not arrest him?' Rathbone sounded surprised.

'He shot the boy who was guiding me,' Monk replied. 'I had to get the lad to the surface.'

The judge leaned forward. 'Is the boy in satisfactory condition, Mr Monk?'

'Yes, my lord. We got him medical treatment, took the bullet out. He seems to be recovering. Thank you.'

'Good. Good.'

Dobie rose to his feet. 'My lord, all this is very moving, but it actually proves nothing at all. This unfortunate man, who appears to be without a name, is dead — conveniently for the prosecution — so he cannot testify to anything at all. He may be no more than some unfortunate indigent who thought to sleep quietly in the Havillands' stable. Apparently he met his own tragic death when the excavations collapsed and buried him alive. We have no right, and no evidence, to make a villain of him now that he cannot answer for himself.' He smiled, pleased with his point, and looked around the courtroom before he resumed his seat.

'Sir Oliver?' the judge raised his eyebrows.

Rathbone smiled. It was a thin, calm gesture that Monk had seen on his lips before, both when he was winning and moving in for the final thrust, and when he was losing and playing a last, desperate card.

'Mr Monk,' he said smoothly in the utter silence, 'are you certain that this is the same man who shot the boy guiding you in the sewers? Surely the sewers are extremely dark? Isn't one face, when you are startled and possibly afraid, pretty much like another?'

Monk gave him a small, bleak smile.

'He held a lantern high up, I imagine in order to see us better and take aim.' The moment was branded on his brain as if etched with a blade. He gripped the rail in front of him. 'He had straight black hair and brows, a narrow nose and highly unusual teeth. His eyeteeth were prominent and longer than the others, especially the left one. When a man is drawing a gun at you, it is a sight you do not forget.' He decided not to say any more. The tension was too stark for decoration with words to be appropriate. No one in the room moved except one woman to give a violent shudder.

'I see,' Rathbone acknowledged. 'And did this unfortunate creature, malevolent or not, meet his own death as a result of last night's disastrous cave-in?'

'No, he was shot in the back. He was already dead when the cave-in occurred.'

Dobie shot to his feet. 'Objection, my lord. How can Mr Monk possibly know that? Was he there? Did he see it?'

Rathbone merely turned very slowly from Dobie to look at Monk, his eyebrows raised.

In the dock Sixsmith craned forward.

'The man's legs were broken by the timber and rubble that fell on him,' Monk replied.

'There was no bleeding.'

In the gallery a woman gasped. The jurors stared at Monk, frowning. Dobie shook his head as if Rathbone had taken leave of his wits.

Rathbone waited.

'The living bleed, the dead do not,' Monk explained. 'When the heart stops there is no more flow of blood. His coat around the wound was caked with dry blood, but his legs were clean. Rigor mortis had already set in. The police surgeon will give you time of death, I imagine.'

Dobie flushed and said nothing.

'Thank you.' Rathbone nodded at Monk graciously. 'I have no further questions for you.'

Dobie declined to add anything and Monk was excused.

He left the witness box but remained in the court while Rathbone called the surgeon, who corroborated all that Monk had said.

Then Runcorn slipped into a seat on the row opposite Monk's in the gallery just as Melisande Ewart took the stand. She walked up the steps of the witness box and faced the room. She was very composed, but even those who had not seen her before might have detected the effort her composure cost her. Her body was very stiff, shoulders rigid. Her dark wine-coloured woollen jacket gave her skin a touch of colour, but around the eyes and mouth she was totally white.

Monk glanced at Runcorn and saw him leaning forward, his gaze intent upon Melisande, as if by strength of will he would support her. Monk wondered if she had the faintest idea how profound was his feeling, and how extraordinary for a man such as he was. If she did, would it please her, frighten her, or would she treat tenderly that enormous compliment, and read its vulnerability as well?

Rathbone moved into the centre of the floor.

The jury sat silent, like men carved of ivory.

'Mrs Ewart,' Rathbone began. 'I believe Superintendent Runcorn of the Metropolitan Police has just taken you to identify the body of the man Mr Monk brought up from the cave-in at the construction. Is that correct?'

'Yes.' Her voice was clear but very quiet.

There was a murmur of sympathy around the gallery. Some of the jurors nodded and their faces softened.

Monk looked up at Sixsmith. His heavy face was motionless, crowded with some emotion impossible to read.

'Have you ever seen him before?' Rathbone asked Melisande.

'Yes,' she answered with a catch in her voice. 'I saw him coming out of the mews which serves the home where I live at the moment, and also served that of Mr James Havilland.'

'When did you see this man?'

'On the night of Mr Havilland's death.'

'At any other times?'

'No. Never.'

'You have seen him just once before today, and yet you are certain it is the same man?'

'Yes.' Now she did not waver at all.

Rathbone could not afford to let it go so easily. 'How is it that you are so sure?' he persisted.

'Because of his face in general, but his teeth in particular,' she replied. She was now even paler and she held tightly on to the rail as if she needed its support. 'Superintendent Runcorn moved the man's lips so I could see his teeth. I am confident enough to swear under oath that it is the same man.'

Runcorn relaxed and eased his body back into the seat, letting out his breath in a long sigh.

'Thank you, Mrs Ewart,' Rathbone said graciously. 'I have nothing further to ask you. I appreciate your time, and your courage to face what must have been extremely unpleasant for you.'

Dobie stood up, looked at Melisande, then at the jury. Straightening his gown on his shoulders, he sat down again.

Rathbone then played a desperate card, but he had no choice. He must show purpose and connection. He called Jenny Argyll.

She was dressed in full mourning and looked as if she were ready to be pronounced dead herself. Her movements were awkward. She looked neither to right nor left, and it seemed as if she might falter and crumple to the ground before she made it all the way to the top of the steps. The usher watched her anxiously. Even Sixsmith leaned forward, his face suddenly alive with fear. The guards beside him pulled him back, but not before Jenny had looked up at him. Now her eyes were burning, and it seemed as if she might actually collapse.

Alan Argyll had yet to testify, so he was not in

the court. Had he any idea of the net closing around him?

Rathbone spoke to Jenny, coaxing from her the agonising testimony he had wanted so badly and had despaired of, only a few days earlier.

'You wrote the letter asking your father to go to his stable at midnight, in order to meet someone?' he said very clearly.

'Yes.' Her voice was barely audible.

'Who was he to meet?'

She was ashen. 'My husband.'

There was a gasp around the entire room.

'Why in the stable?' Rathbone was asking. 'It was a November night. Why not in the house where it was warm and dry, and refreshment could be offered?'

Jenny Argyll was ashen. She had to force her voice to be audible. 'To . . . to avoid my sister interrupting. It was to be a secret meeting.'

'Who asked you to write the letter, Mrs Argyll?'

She closed her eyes as if the terror and betrayal washed over her like the black water that had burst through the sides of the tunnel engulfing the navvies deep underground. 'My husband.'

In the dock something indefinable within Sixsmith eased, as if he smelled victory at last.

Rathbone allowed a moment's terrible silence, then he asked the last question. 'Did you know that your father was to be killed in that stable, Mrs Argyll?'

'No!' Now her voice was strong and shrill. 'He told me it was to be a meeting to try to persuade my father that he was wrong about the tunnels, and to stop the navvies and toshers — I think you call them — from making any more trouble!'

'As Mr Sixsmith has told us,' Rathbone could not resist making the point. 'Thank you, Mrs Argyll.'

Dobie looked confused. Suddenly, at the moment when he expected to be swept off his feet, the tide had turned and retreated before him with no apparent explanation.

He asked only one question. 'It was your husband who asked this letter of you, Mrs Argyll? Not Mr Sixsmith?'

'That is correct,' she whispered.

He thanked her and excused her.

Monk looked at the judge, who was leaning forward a little, his face furrowed with puzzlement. It seemed that the prosecution and the defence had changed places, arguing each other's cases. Possibly he had understood what was happening, and as long as the law was not flouted nor brought into disrespect, he would leave it to play itself out. He adjourned the court for luncheon.

★   ★   ★

In the afternoon Monk and Runcorn were both there. Dobie called Alan Argyll to the stand, as Rathbone had fervently hoped he would. He had done all he could to make it virtually impossible for him not to.

Argyll walked across the floor white-faced and composed. He glanced upward once towards the dock but it was impossible to tell if his eyes met those of Sixsmith or not. Sixsmith was leaning forward still. The colour had returned to his face, but in two hectic spots. Surely he must see freedom almost in his grasp.

But Argyll had not been in the court for his wife's testimony. He did not know his grip over her was broken. He waited for Rathbone as if he thought he was still certain of victory. Perhaps he did not even see the hostility in the jurors' faces, which was now quite open. He looked at Dobie without a tremor, and his voice was clear when he answered.

'No. I did not ask my wife to write such a letter.' He even managed to affect surprise.

Dobie looked disbelieving. 'There is no question that the letter existed, Mr Argyll, or that your wife wrote it. She has admitted as much to this court. If not at your request, at whose would she do such a thing?'

Argyll paled. Monk could see, from the angle of his head and his hands gripping the rail in front of him, that he was suddenly frightened. He started to look up at Sixsmith, then forced himself not to. Was he beginning at last to understand?

'I have no idea,' he said with difficulty.

Dobie grew sarcastic. 'One of your children, perhaps? Your sister-in-law? Or your brother?'

Argyll's face flamed and his hands clenched on the rail. He swayed as if he might fall over. 'My brother is dead, sir! Because Mary Havilland dragged him down with her! And you stand there and accuse him of . . . of what? How much courage does it take to accuse a murdered man? You disgrace the office you hold and are a blemish to your profession!'

Dobie blanched, clearly embarrassed and momentarily at a loss to defend himself.

The judge looked from one to the other of them, then up at Aston Sixsmith, whose face was now expressionless. Lastly he looked at Jenny Argyll, who was ashen. Her eyes were fixed on space but as if she were held against her will by some inner vision, unable to tear herself from it.

Rathbone said nothing.

The judge looked at Dobie again. 'Mr Dobie, do you wish to rephrase your question? It seems inadequate as it is.'

'I will move on, with your lordship's permission,' Dobie said, clearing his throat and looking again at Argyll. 'James Havilland was in the stables alone at midnight. For whom else would he keep such an extraordinary appointment?'

'I don't know!' Argyll protested.

'Have you ever seen this man they describe, whose teeth are apparently so uniquely recognisable,' Dobie pressed, 'and it is suggested actually murdered your father-in-law?'

Argyll hesitated.

In the courtroom hardly anyone moved. There was a faint cough in the gallery, a creak of whalebone stays, then silence.

Jenny Argyll looked up at Sixsmith. Their eyes met, lingered for a moment, then she turned away. What was it Monk saw in Sixsmith's face? Pity for what she was about to lose? Forgiveness that she had not had the courage to do it before? Or anger that she had let him suffer right to the brink, and spoken up only when she had been forced to? His look was steady, tumultuous, and unreadable.

Argyll swallowed. 'Yes. As Sixsmith says, I wanted to hire someone to prevent the unrest among navvies regarding safety, and stop the toshers whose territories were disappearing from becoming violent and disrupting the excavations.' He drew in his breath. 'We have to finish the new sewers as soon as possible. The threat of disease is appalling.'

There was a rustle of movement in the room.

Monk stared at the jury. There was unease among them, but no sympathy. Did they believe him?

'We are aware of this, Mr Argyll,' Dobie answered, beginning to regain his composure. 'It is not what you are doing that we question, only the methods you are willing to employ in order to accomplish them. You admit that you met this man, and that you gave Mr Sixsmith the money to pay him for his work?'

The answer seemed torn from Argyll. 'Yes! But to quell violence, not to kill Havilland!'

'But Havilland was a nuisance, wasn't he?' Dobie raised his voice, challenging him now. He took another couple of steps closer to the stand. 'He believed you were moving too quickly, didn't he, Mr Argyll? He feared you might disturb the land, cause a subsidence and possibly even break through into an old, uncharted underground river, didn't he?'

Argyll was now so white he looked as if he might collapse. 'I don't know what he thought!' he shouted back, his voice ragged.

'Don't you indeed?' Dobie said sarcastically. He turned away, then spun round and faced the witness stand again. 'But he was a nuisance, wasn't he? And even after he was dead, shot in his own stables at midnight and buried in a suicide's grave, his daughter Mary pressed his cause and took it up herself, didn't she?' He was pointing his finger now. 'And where is she? Also in a suicide's grave! Along with your ally and younger brother.' His smile was triumphant. 'Thank you, Mr Argyll. The court needs no more from you, at least not yet!' He waved his arm to invite Rathbone to question Argyll if he should wish to.

Rathbone declined. Victory was almost within his grasp.

The judge blinked and looked at him curiously, but he made no remark.

Dobie called Aston Sixsmith. Rathbone's ploy was hardly a gamble any more.

Sixsmith mounted the stand. The man exuded intelligence and animal power, exhausted as he was. There was a rustle of sympathy from the crowd now. Even the jurors smiled at him. He ignored them all, hoarding his emotion to himself, not yet able to betray his awareness of how close he had been to prison, or even the rope. He looked once at Jenny Argyll. For an instant there was a softening in his face, gone again almost before it was seen. A sense of decency? His gaze barely touched Alan Argyll.

401

His erstwhile employer was finished, worthless. From the gallery Monk watched him with an increasing sense of incredulity.

Rathbone had won. Monk looked across at Margaret Bellinger and saw her eagerness for the moment, her pride in Rathbone's extraordinary achievement for justice.

Dobie was talking to Sixsmith, ramming home the victory. 'Did you ever meet this extraordinary assassin before the night you paid him the money Mr Argyll gave you?' he asked.

'No, sir, I did not,' Sixsmith replied quietly.

'Or after that?'

'No, sir.'

'Have you any idea who shot him, or why?'

'I know no more than you do, sir.'

'Why did you give him the money? For what purpose? Was it to kill James Havilland because he was causing you trouble, and possibly expensive delays?'

'No, sir. Mr Argyll told me it was to hire men to keep the toshers and gangers from disrupting the work.'

'And what about Mr Havilland?'

'I understood that Mr Argyll was going to deal with that himself.'

'How?'

Sixsmith's gaze was intense. 'Show him that he was mistaken. Mr Havilland was his father-in-law, and I believed that relations were cordial between them.'

'Could this man, this assassin, have misunderstood you?'

Sixsmith stared at him. 'No, sir. I was quite specific.'

Dobie could not resist making the very most of it. He looked at the jury, then at the gallery. 'Describe the scene for us,' he said at last to Sixsmith. 'Let the court see exactly how it was.'

Sixsmith obeyed him, speaking slowly and carefully, like a man emerging from a nightmare into the daylight of sanity. He described the room in the public house, the noise, the smell of ale, the straw on the floor, the press of men.

'He came in at about ten o'clock, as near as I can tell,' he went on in response to Dobie's prompting. 'I knew him straight away. He was fairly tall, thin, especially his face. His hair was black and straight, rather long on to his collar. His nose was thin at the bridge. But most of all, he had these extraordinary teeth, which I saw when he smiled. He bought a tankard of ale and came straight over to me, as if he already knew who I was. Someone must have described me very well. The man didn't introduce himself but used Argyll's name so I would know who he was. We discussed the problem of the toshers in particular, and I told him a little more about it. I gave him the money. He accepted it, folded it away, and then stood up. I remember he emptied the tankard in one long draught, and then he left without once looking back.'

Dobie thanked him and invited Rathbone to contest the testament if he wished.

Rathbone conceded defeat with both dignity and grace. Not by so much as a glance did he betray that it was actually the most elegant and perhaps the most difficult victory of his career.

The jury returned a verdict of guilty of attempted bribery and the judge imposed a fine that was no more than a week's pay.

The court erupted in cheers, the gallery rising to its feet. The jury looked intensely satisfied, turning to shake each other's hands and pass words of congratulation.

Margaret abandoned decorum and met Rathbone halfway across the floor as he walked towards her. Her face was shining, but whatever she said to him was lost in the uproar.

Monk also was on his feet. He would speak a word or two to Runcorn, thank him for his courage and honour in being willing to re-examine a case. Then he would go home to tell Hester — and Scuff.

12

The trial had finished promptly, so Monk was home comparatively early. The weather was bright and clear, and the February evening stretched out with no clouds — only trails of chimney smoke across the waning sky. It was going to freeze, and as he alighted from the omnibus the stones beneath his feet were already filmed with ice. But the air tasted fresh and the sweetness of victory was in it. The sun was low, and its reflection on the pale stretches of the river hurt his eyes. The masts of the ships were a black fretwork like wrought iron against the rich colours of the horizon beyond the rooftops.

He turned and walked smartly up Union Road to Paradise Street and then up the short path to his front door. As soon as he was inside he called out Hester's name.

She must have heard the triumph in his voice. Her face eager, she appeared at the top of the stairs, from the bedroom where she had been sitting with Scuff.

'We won!' Monk said, starting up the steps two at a time. He caught hold of her and swung her around, kissing her lips, neck, cheek and lips again. 'We won it all! Sixsmith was convicted of no more than attempted bribery, and fined.

Everyone knew that Argyll was guilty, and he's probably been arrested already. I didn't wait to see. Rathbone was brilliant, superb. Margaret was so proud of him she absolutely glowed.'

The bedroom door was open and Scuff was sitting up staring at them. He still looked scrubbed and unnaturally pink. His hair was actually much fairer than Monk had supposed. He seemed to have forgotten about the lace on his nightgown, or even that it was actually Hester's. His shoulder must hurt him, but he was making little of that too. Now his eyes were bright with expectation, longing to be told all there was to hear.

Hester led Monk into the room and sat on the bed herself so he could recount the events to them both.

'Yer won!' Scuff said excitedly. 'They gonna get Argyll fer killin' poor 'Avilland, an' Miss Mary as well? Yer gonna bury 'em proper?'

'Yes,' Monk said simply.

Scuff's eyes were shining. He was sitting close to Hester, quite naturally. Both of them seemed to be unaware of it. ' 'Ow d'yer do it?' he said, hungry for any piece of information. He had sorely missed being there to see it himself.

'Would you like a cup of tea before we begin?' Hester asked.

Scuff looked at her with total incomprehension.

Monk rolled his eyes.

She smiled. 'Right! Then you get nothing until it's all told, every last word!'

He began with the day's proceedings,

recounting them as a story of adventure with all the details, looking at their faces, and enjoying himself. He described the courtroom, the judge, the jurors, the men and women in the gallery, and every witness. Scuff barely breathed; he could hardly bring himself even to blink.

Monk told them how he had climbed the steps to the witness box and stared at the court below him; how Sixsmith had craned forward in the dock, and Rathbone had asked the questions on which the verdict had turned.

'I described him exactly,' he said, remembering it with aching clarity. 'There wasn't a sound in the whole room . . .'

'Did they know 'e was the man wot killed Mr 'Avilland?' Scuff whispered. 'Did yer tell 'em wot the sewer were like?'

'Oh, yes. I told them how we met him the first time, and he turned round and shot you. That horrified them,' Monk answered honestly. 'I described the dark and the water and the rats.'

Scuff gave an involuntary little shiver. Without realising it, perhaps at the memory of the terror, he moved a fraction closer to Hester, so that he was actually touching her. She took no notice, except that there was a slight softening of her lips, as if she wanted to smile, but knew she should not let him see it.

'Did Jenny Argyll give evidence?' she asked.

'Yes.' Monk met her eyes for a moment of appreciation, and memory of what it had cost Rose Applegate. 'She told it all. Argyll denied it, of course, but no one believed him. If he'd looked at the jurors' faces he could have seen his own condemnation then.' He realised suddenly what a final thing he had said. They had accomplished it, the seemingly impossible. Sixsmith was free and the law knew that Alan Argyll was guilty.

'Funny,' Hester said aloud. 'We'll never know his name.'

'The man who actually shot James Havilland? No,' he agreed. 'But he was only a means to an end, and he's dead anyway. The thing that matters is that the man behind it will be punished justly, and perhaps there will even be more care taken in the routing of new tunnels, or at least in the speed with which they're done.'

'But Argyll will be charged?' Hester insisted. 'So Mary Havilland can be buried properly and . . . and her father too?'

'I'll make certain.' He meant it as a promise. Seeing the warmth in her eyes, he knew that she understood it as such.

'Did Sixsmith give evidence?' she cut across his thoughts. 'Explain it all. He seemed like a decent man, a bit rough, perhaps, but it's a rough profession. He . . . he felt things deeply . . . I thought.'

Monk smiled. 'Oh, yes. It's always a risk putting an accused man into the dock, but he was excellent. He described exactly what happened, how Argyll gave him the money and what he told him it was for, which was to bribe the toshers who were making trouble. It made sense and you could see that the jury believed it.'

He remembered Sixsmith's face in the witness box as he told it. 'He said he had not known what the man looked like, and he sat waiting for him. The man recognised him immediately and came over. He was fairly tall, lean, with long, black hair on to his collar, and . . . ' He stopped. The room swaying around him, his limbs suddenly far away and cold, as if they belonged to someone else. Sixsmith had described the assassin as he had been when he was killed! Not when Melisande Ewart had seen him on the night of Havilland's death, or two days before.

'What is it? William, what's wrong?' It was Hester's voice calling from a great distance, fuzzy at the edges. She sounded frightened. Scuff was pressed up next to her, his eyes wide, picking up her emotion.

When Monk spoke his mouth was dry. 'Sixsmith said his hair was long. He swore he saw him only once, two days before Havilland's death. It was shorter then, much shorter. Mrs Ewart said above his collar but it was on to his collar when I found him dead.'

Hester stared at him, horror slowly filling his eyes. 'You mean Sixsmith saw him . . . just before he was killed? Then . . . ' She stopped, unable to finish the thought.

'He killed him,' Monk said it for her. 'Argyll was telling the truth. He probably gave Sixsmith the money to bribe the toshers, exactly as he told us. It was Sixsmith who gave the order to kill Havilland, and possibly Mary as well.'

'But Argyll couldn't be innocent,' Hester argued. 'It was he who had Jenny write . . . ' She tailed off. 'Or perhaps it wasn't? Perhaps she lied, and it was Sixsmith who told her to. But why? She had everything to lose!'

Scuff was looking at her anxiously, his mouth twisted down at the corners. He might be only eight or nine, but he had lived on the streets. He had seen violence, beatings, revenge. 'She 'ate 'im that much?' he asked wonderingly. 'That's daft! Less 'e knocked 'er 'alf senseless.'

'So she would lie to incriminate her husband, and get Sixsmith free?' Hester said with awe and disgust. 'Argyll might be cold, and bore her to death, but could she really be in love with Sixsmith to that degree — knowing what he did? Oh, William! He murdered her father, and her sister! Has she lost her wits completely? Or . . . ' her voice dropped, ' . . . or is she now too afraid of him to do anything else?'

'I don't know,' he admitted. 'I . . . I don't know.' His mind raced to the memory of Jenny Argyll's eyes in court, the power in Sixsmith and the way she had looked at him. It had not felt like fear then, more like hunger.

Scuff looked from one to the other of them. 'Wot yer gonna do?' he asked. 'Yer gonna let 'im get away wi' it?' There was incredulity in his face. It was impossible to believe such a thing.

'You can't be tried twice for the same crime,' Monk explained bitterly. 'The jury found him not guilty.'

'But they in't right!' Scuff protested. ''E done it! 'E paid the man wot shot Mr 'Avilland! It wasn't Mr Argyll arter all! Yer can't let 'im get topped fer it! It in't right, even if 'e is a greedy sod.'

'But he wasn't tried for shooting the assassin,'

Hester pointed out eagerly. 'Nobody was.'

It was true. No one had specifically made any charge about the murder of the assassin; it had simply been implicit that it was Argyll, because he had the motive. But Sixsmith could be charged with that! Legally it was perfectly possible! In fact it was absolutely imperative that he must be! Only then would charges be dropped against Argyll.

Monk stood up slowly, oddly stiff. 'I must go and tell Rathbone.'

Hester stood also. 'Tonight?'

'Yes. I can't leave it. I'm sorry.'

She nodded slowly. She did not explain that she could not come, or that she wanted to.

Scuff understood. 'I'm all right!' he chipped in.

'I know,' Hester agreed quickly. 'But I'm not leaving you anyway, so don't bother arguing with me.'

'But — ' he started.

She froze him with a look, and he subsided, wide-eyed, his lips quivering between tears and a smile, refusing to let her see how much her care mattered to him.

Monk looked at them for a moment longer, then turned and left.

★ ★ ★

The hansom dropped him outside Rathbone's house. He told the driver to wait. Although the lights were on, it might only mean that the manservant was in, but at least he would probably know where Rathbone could be found.

As it was, Rathbone was at dinner, as Monk had expected, with Margaret Ballinger. Mr and Mrs Ballinger were present also, as chaperones at this delicate stage in their betrothal. Also they were delighted to be included in what was also the celebration of a victory. They did not in the least understand its nature, but they were aware of its importance.

'I'm sorry,' Monk apologised to the butler in the hall, 'but it is imperative that I speak to Sir Oliver immediately, and in private.'

'I'm afraid, sir, that Sir Oliver is dining,' the manservant apologised. 'The soup has just been served. I cannot interrupt them at present. May I offer you something in the morning room, perhaps? That is, if you would care to wait?'

'No, thank you,' Monk declined. 'Please tell Sir Oliver that I have discovered a fact of devastating importance regarding the case. The verdict cannot be allowed to stand as it is. His attention cannot wait.'

The manservant hesitated, looked more earnestly at Monk, then decided to obey.

Five minutes later Rathbone appeared, supremely elegantly dressed in evening clothes. 'What is it?' he asked as he closed the door on the glittering dining room behind him, shutting out the voices, the laughter and the chink of glasses. 'I am in the middle of dinner and have guests. You are welcome to join us if you wish. Heaven knows, you did more than anyone else to bring about our victory.'

Monk took a deep breath. 'It was not a victory,

Rathbone. Do you remember Sixsmith describing the assassin when he passed him the money?'

Rathbone frowned. 'Of course. What of it?'

'Do you remember Melisande Ewart's description of him when he came out of the mews after he had just shot Havilland, two days after that?'

'Yes. It was obviously the same man. There can't be two looking like that!' Rathbone's face was puzzled, and on the edge of losing patience.

'Hair,' Monk said simply. 'I saw him when he was dead, and his hair was long on to his collar. So did Sixsmith. That was what he was describing on the stand.'

Rathbone blushed. 'Are you saying that he didn't pay him the money? What . . . ?' His eyes widened. Suddenly, with a feeling like opening a door on to ice, he understood and the colour died from his face. 'Sixsmith shot him! God in heaven — he was guilty all the time! We got him off! I got him off!'

'For killing Havilland, but not for killing the assassin!' Monk said quietly.

Rathbone stared at him with dawning comprehension.

There was a knock on the door.

Rathbone turned round slowly. 'Come,' he answered.

Margaret came in. She glanced at Rathbone, then at Monk, the question in her eyes. She was dressed in extravagant oyster satin with pearls at her ears and throat, and had a warmth in her face that no artifice could lend.

Rathbone went to her immediately, touching her with intense gentleness.

413

'We were wrong,' he said simply. 'Monk has just pointed out that Sixsmith must have shot the assassin, and more essentially, that we have convicted the wrong man. To free him, we must at the very least prove Sixsmith's guilt of the assassin's death, and if possible convict him of it.'

Margaret turned to Monk to verify from his face if that could possibly be true. She needed only an instant to see that it was. 'Then we must do it,' she said quietly. 'But how? The trial is finished. Would taking his testimony to anyone be sufficient?'

'No,' Monk said with certainty. 'We must prove the whole line of connection, the fact that he knew the man all the way through.' He saw in her face that she did not understand. 'If we charged Sixsmith now,' he explained, 'on the strength of his description of the assassin, he could say he heard it from Argyll, or anyone else. He might slip away again.' He smiled bleakly. 'We must be right this time.'

'I see.' Her answer was simple. She was not a beautiful woman, her looks being rather more individual, but at this moment there was a true beauty in her face as she turned back to Rathbone. 'We'll celebrate when we have it right,' she said calmly. 'I shall explain to Mama and Papa, and we can finish dinner quite pleasantly, and then go home. Please do what is necessary. It cannot wait. Whatever time it takes, however difficult it is, it must be accomplished before Argyll is charged and tried. They would hang him for James Havilland's death. Perhaps

414

for Mary's as well, although I suppose that could have been Toby who was to blame. Do you suppose Toby did that for Sixsmith?'

Rathbone was thoughtful, but he did not take his eyes from her face. 'Possibly, but he might not have realised all the implications. Sixsmith could have asked him to speak to her, try to persuade her that her father's death was suicide after all, and that she was only making it worse by continuing to probe it. Almost certainly he would try to persuade her that there was no danger in the tunnels.'

'Was that what James Havilland was afraid of, uncharted underground rivers?' She turned to Monk.

'Yes, I think so. Toby seems to have spoken to toshers a lot too, but that could have been to try and stop them from interfering with the work. That's what I thought to begin with. I don't think we'll ever know if he meant to kill Mary. Probably not. Not unless there was far more between him and Sixsmith than we know.' He tried to visualise again what he had seen on the bridge. 'I think it was an accident. She was frightened of him. Perhaps she thought Alan Argyll was behind her father's death, and that Toby was going to kill her too. She tried to get away from him, and whether she meant to or not, she took him with her.' As he said it he was not sure if that was what he really believed. Could Sixsmith deliberately have corrupted Toby Argyll? He remembered Alan Argyll's grief when he had heard of his brother's death. Grief, or guilt?

'We won't know, will we?' Margaret said sadly.

'Probably not,' he admitted.

'And Mrs Argyll?' she persisted. 'She swore it was her husband who told her to write the letter.'

'I know,' Rathbone answered her. 'There are a lot of things we still have to learn, and to prove. But we can't afford to wait. I'm sorry.'

'I understand.' She gave him a smile that was intimate and a little sad, but only for the moment missed, no more. She excused herself and left.

Rathbone looked at Monk. For the first time since Rathbone had first realised he was in love with Hester, there was no envy in his eyes, only a deep happiness that even this verdict deception could not destroy.

Monk smiled back at him, surprised how pleased he was. 'I'm sorry,' he said again.

'Where are we going to start?' Rathbone asked him.

Monk looked up and down Rathbone's elegant figure. 'With rather older clothes, I think. We need to find and prove the connection between Sixsmith and the assassin.'

Rathbone's eyes widened. 'For God's sake, Monk! How? Sixsmith worked in the sewer excavations. He could have been anywhere when he was out on bail. It was only a bribery charge! And no one has the faintest idea where the assassin was. We don't even have a name for him!'

'You've summed it up perfectly,' Monk said with a further smile, which was wider, more like a baring of teeth. 'I plan on enlisting all the help

I can. I'll start with Runcorn, Orme and as many of my own men as I can spare, then the doctor, Crow. He'll be happy to help because the assassin shot Scuff. Then I'll get as many navvies as'll help — they might, because of the cave-in — and toshers, gangers, watermen, of any sort too. And I'll try to get Sutton, the rat-catcher. He knows the hidden rivers and wells that very few other people do, all the hiding places. People will speak to him who won't speak to us.'

There was horror, disgust, and self-mockery in Rathbone's face. 'And what is it you imagine I can do in this . . . this pursuit of the unspeakable?'

Monk grinned now. 'Oh, you are in command,' he assured him. 'You will tell us what is proof and what is not.'

Rathbone gave him a dark, twisted look, and excused himself to change his clothes.

* * *

They went first to Runcorn, as a matter of geographical simplicity. He was horrified, as they had known he would be. Even more than that, he was angry with himself for not having seen the difference in the two descriptions of the assassin.

'No one did,' Monk assured him honestly. 'It was only when I was telling Hester about it and repeating it myself that I realised. That one detail too much was his only slip.'

Runcorn's face was hard and bleak. 'I'll trace each step of that bastard's way,' he promised. 'If

417

I have to climb or crawl through every sewer in London and question the bloody rats!'

Rathbone's face pulled tight, his mouth in a downward turn at the thought, but he did not argue.

Next they found Orme, waking him up out of his bed with apology for the hour, when he can barely have gone to sleep after a hard day. He made no complaints, even by change of expression on his face. Monk hoped profoundly that it was not because he did not dare to. He had earned the right to require respect and consideration for his feelings, his wellbeing, and the fact that he might have other cares and occupations in life than serving the demands of the River Police in general, or Monk in particular.

'I can't do it without you,' Monk said frankly.

'That's all right, sir. 'Ow's the boy?' Orme replied, forcing himself to wake up by dashing cold water on his face. They were standing in the kitchen of his small home where Monk had never been before. He was uncomfortably aware that not only had he intruded, uninvited to the one place where Orme had privacy, mastery, but he had also brought others who were strangers in all but name.

'Recovering well,' he replied. 'Can I make you a cup of tea while you dress?'

Orme stared at him. 'I'll make it, sir. If you just like — '

'I'll do it,' Monk cut across him. 'I'm not asking for instructions, just permission.'

'Yes . . . sir. The tea's in the caddy up there,'

he pointed to an Indian-designed tin at the back of the tidy kitchen shelf. 'The kettle's beside the stove, and there's milk in the pantry cupboard. Water's already pumped for the morning. But — '

'Thank you,' Monk interrupted him again. 'Just dress. There's no need to shave. We're going down the sewers.'

Orme obeyed. Monk moved around the small, immaculately tidy kitchen while Runcorn riddled the last ash from the stove and piled it delicately with new coal to make it burn up again, warm the kitchen and boil the water in the kettle. Rathbone sat and watched, knowing his skills were required later.

Seven minutes later Orme was back down, dressed for going on to the river. Then over hot, strong tea, they discussed the exact tactics of how they would hunt down the evidence they needed to hang Aston Sixsmith.

'What do we need, sir?' Orme looked at Rathbone.

Rathbone had obviously been considering it. 'We have Sixsmith's own admission that he knew this assassin.' He frowned. 'I wish we could find a name for the man! But we only need to prove he paid him on Argyll's request. We need unarguable evidence that Sixsmith knew him before that, and can make a credible assumption that he also knew his occupation. It seems obvious enough that Sixsmith told Argyll of the trouble toshers and other men were causing, and that they needed to be bought off. You might see if that's actually true. How much trouble were the toshers? Because the money went to the assassin, and yet the work is still apparently going on.' He looked at them in turn.

'What about the cave-in?' Runcorn asked. 'Do we know exactly what caused that, and if it was foreseeable? Was it what James Havilland was afraid of? Has it anything to do with Sixsmith?'

'And did Sixsmith know?' Monk added. 'And what about Mary?'

'That's another thing,' Rathbone cut across him. 'What connection was there between Sixsmith and Toby Argyll? In short, Argyll may be technically innocent of having hired the assassin, but is he innocent of everything? Is this one man, or a conspiracy?'

Orme looked at Monk. 'Questions, sir. We gotta find people 'oo've seen Sixsmith and the man wi' the teeth, before 'Avilland were shot, and prove as they know each other. We gotta find navvies and toshers an' the like 'oo know if Sixsmith knew about the dangers o' movin' that machine too fast an' cuttin' wi'out askin' enough about streams an' wells an' the like.'

Rathbone's eyes widened. 'Exactly,' he agreed. 'Very well summed up, Mr Orme.' He gave a very slight smile. 'Perhaps you don't really need my presence?'

Monk gave him a wry look and then smiled back. 'We couldn't possibly manage without you, Rathbone,' he replied.

They spent some further time apportioning duties and planning where to meet and how often in order to compare notes and keep each other informed. They had an hour's sleep sitting

420

in the chairs in the kitchen, then another hot cup of tea and several slices of thick toast. By half-past four they were on their way towards the main road where they caught a hansom and started the journey to the tunnel.

They stopped to pick up Crow. He was a sleepy and startled recruit, but when he heard the truth of events, willing enough. He sent a messenger to find Sutton and tell him where they were going, and that it was extremely urgent and important that he join them. They did not wait for him, but had a rendezvous arranged.

The wind was gusting hard and carried the smell of rain as they made their way down the muddy slope to the bottom of the tunnel. The walls oozed water in the lantern light, and on the bottom it was running slowly in between the broken bricks and pebbles. The wooden planks were slimy underfoot. When Monk held his lantern up the beam shone on the mist of fine rain, lighting the wet walls, the planks holding them back, but barely reached the higher beams that forced them apart, crisscrossing upwards to an invisible sky. The air smelled of earth, water and old wood.

Monk wrinkled his nose, not knowing if he really smelled the sour odour of sewers or if it was just conjured by memory and imagination. He had to make a greater effort than he had expected in order to force himself to walk calmly under the brick facing of the tunnel and the vast weight of earth on top of him. Their feet echoed on the boards and the water sloshed around the wood and up over the soles of his boots. It was bitterly cold.

Monk heard Rathbone gasp behind him, and wondered if the darkness suffocated him as much, if it brought out the sweat on his skin and made him strain his eyes and ears for anything that would give him a sense of proportion, direction, any of the things we take for granted.

A thousand yards on they separated, in order to cover as much ground as possible. For safety's sake they went in pairs: Runcorn and Orme, Rathbone and Crow, with Monk to wait at the appointed place for Sutton.

'Don't go by yerself, sir!' Orme warned, his voice sharp with anxiety. 'One slip an' yer finished. 'It yer 'ead an' the rats'll get yer. It in't a nice way ter go.'

Monk saw Rathbone's sensitive mouth twist in revulsion, and he smiled. 'I won't, Sergeant, I promise you.'

Orme nodded and disappeared into the darkness behind Runcorn, their lights swallowed up in moments.

Rathbone took a deep breath and, body rigid, followed after Crow without once looking backwards. Perhaps he was afraid that if he did he would lose his nerve to proceed.

Sutton arrived twenty-five minutes later, accompanied as always by the little dog. 'It's a bad business, Mr Monk,' he said grimly. 'Where d' yer wanna start?'

The decision had already been made. 'The other four are looking to find out if Sixsmith was ever seen with the assassin, if so when, and by whom. I want to find out more about the dangers of cave-in that Havilland was so worried about, and how much Sixsmith actually knew of it.'

'Yer mean could 'e 'ave stopped it?' Sutton asked. He frowned. 'Don't make no sense, Mr Monk. Why couldn't 'e 'ave gone careful, if 'e'd really 'ave understood? Cave-in don't do 'im no good.'

'When I thought he was innocent,' Monk explained, beginning to walk deeper into the tunnel, 'I assumed Argyll was giving the orders and he had little choice. I took it for granted that whatever he feared he would have told Argyll, and been ignored. But maybe that's not true. Is he callous, a villain, or just incompetent?'

'Why'd 'e kill 'Avilland?' Sutton asked curiously, following on Monk's heels. 'It's gotta be ter keep 'im quiet about the dangers, 'asn't it?'

'Yes. But that doesn't mean he believed him. He might have thought Havilland was just scare-mongering.'

Sutton grunted. 'Mebbe.'

The first thing they did was to find navvies at the excavation face and question them. They moved with speed. After the ordeal of the trial they did not expect Sixsmith back at the site today, but it was not impossible that he would be there. He was a man accused wrongly, according to the law, and found innocent by his peers. If they seemed to others to be harassing him now, their position would be unpleasant to say the least. Possibly he could even claim they were exceeding their office. Monk's career could be jeopardised, and possibly Orme and Runcorn's as well. Rathbone's reputation would not profit from his expedition into the sewers to pursue a man he had prosecuted and failed to convict. He would appear to be losing with neither dignity nor honour.

The navvies told them nothing, and after an hour or so Monk realised he was wasting his time. Instead he took Sutton's advice and sought out a couple of toshers. They were father and son, amazingly alike: both blunt-faced with cheerful and sarcastic disposition.

'Sixsmith?' the father said with a twist of his mouth. 'Strong feller, not scared o' nobody. Yeah. I knowed 'im. Why?'

Monk allowed Sutton to ask the question. They had already planned what to say. ''E din't kill 'Avilland after all,' Sutton replied casually. ''E really thought as the money were ter pay off toshers wot was makin' trouble.'

'An' I'm the Queen o' the fairies!' the father said witheringly.

'Yer sayin' as yer never took no money?' Sutton asked, his voice almost expressionless.

'Weren't nothin' ter take!'

'Sixsmith's a bleedin' liar!' the son added angrily. 'We weren't makin' no trouble, an' wot's more, Mr Sutton, just 'cos yer catches rats fer the gentry, don't give yer no right ter say as we were. Yer know that, yer scurvy bastard!'

'I know yer din't used ter,' Sutton agreed. ''Ow about others? Wot about Big Jem, or Lanky, or any o' them?'

'We in't stupid,' the father retorted. 'Gettin'

424

meself in gaol won't 'elp no one.'

'Did Mr Sixsmith know that?' Monk asked, speaking for the first time.

'Course 'e did!' the father looked at him, his face screwed up in disgust like a gargoyle in the lantern light. 'E's a fly sod, an' all.'

'Not fly enough to avoid a cave-in,' Monk observed.

'Course 'e were!' the father said intently. ''E knew as much about streams and wells and clay stretches as any o' us. 'E just don't give a toss.'

They asked other toshers, gangers and came back to navvies again, but nothing they could elicit contradicted the belief that there was no more trouble than usual, just the odd quarrel or fight. There had been no deliberate sabotage and the accidents were rather fewer than average for the heavy and dangerous work in progress.

The thing that struck Monk most forcibly, and that he told the others when they went up in the middle of the day, was that in everyone's opinion Sixsmith was an extremely clever and able man who was very well aware of all the risks and advantages of everything he did.

'So he knew about the streams and wells?' Rathbone said grimly. He looked strained. His nostrils flared with the stench he had been unable to avoid. His clothes were spattered with mud and clay and his boots sodden. Even the bottoms of his trousers were wet.

'Yes,' Monk agreed, knowing what the inevitable conclusion must be. 'It seems he did not care about the cave-in.'

'Or even that he wanted it!' Rathbone added.

425

'But why? What is it that we don't know, Monk? What's missing to make sense of this?' He turned to Runcorn and Orme.

''E knew the assassin,' Orme said, his face tight. ''Aven't got a witness as yer could bring inter court yet, but they're there all right. 'E knew 'is way around, did Sixsmith.'

'Don't put him in the past.' Runcorn looked at them each in turn. 'He's still very much here! We've got to hurry, before he covers his tracks — or us!'

Monk found himself shivering. Rathbone's face was bleak and angry. No one argued. Briefly they conferred on the next step, then set out again, cold, tired and determined.

⋆ ⋆ ⋆

Hester slept poorly after Monk had gone. The shock of defeat, just as they were savouring what she imagined to be one of their sweetest victories, had left her momentarily numb. She cleared away the supper dishes and tidied the house automatically, then went upstairs to see if there was anything more she could do for Scuff. She might have stayed up were it not for him, but she knew he could not rest were she not to do so as well.

She was lying awake at about five o'clock, wondering how they could have been so bitterly wrong, when Scuff spoke to her in a whisper.

'Yer in't asleep, are yer.' It was not a question. He must have known from her breathing.

'No,' she replied. 'But why aren't you?'

' 'Cos I can't.' He inched a fraction closer to her. 'Is Mr Monk gonna put it right?'

Should she lie to comfort him? If he found out it would break the frail trust he was building. She might never mend the damage. Wasn't truth better than the loneliness of that, no matter how harsh? That's what she would do if he were a man. But was a child different? How much should she protect him, and from what?

'Is 'e?' Scuff repeated.

He was not touching her and yet she knew his body was stiff.

'He'll try,' she answered. 'Nobody wins all the time. This could be a mistake we can't mend. I don't know.'

He let out his breath in a sigh and relaxed, inching another tiny fraction closer to her.

'Mr 'Avilland were right about their machines, weren't 'e?'

'I'm afraid he was,' she agreed. 'At least partly. He was also right about going ahead too quickly without making sure where all the streams were.'

'Mr Sixsmith were the boss down there. Yer'd think as 'e'd 'a told 'im, wouldn't yer?' he whispered.

'He must have,' she agreed. 'And he will have told Mr Argyll.'

As she said it she realised with a chill, in spite of the blankets over her, that that was not necessarily true. But it made no sense.

'Wot's the matter?' Scuff demanded.

'At least, I suppose he'll have told Mr Argyll,' she answered.

He put his hand on her shoulder, so lightly she

427

barely felt it, only its warmth. 'There's summink as don't make no sense, in't there? Is Mr Monk gonna be all right? I should 'a bin there to look arter 'im. I think mebbe that Sixsmith's real bad.'

'But what does Sixsmith want?' she said as much to herself as to him. 'Money? Power? Love? Escape from something?' She turned a little towards him. 'Do you suppose it was because of Mrs Argyll? She's in love with him, I think. And her husband is a cold man. She must feel terribly alone.'

'Weren't Mr 'Avilland 'er pa too?' he asked.

'Yes. I don't believe she knew the assassin was going to kill her father. And afterwards she thought it was her husband who had done it. Maybe she still doesn't know it was Sixsmith, and we can't prove it!'

'But 'e knows,' Scuff pointed out. 'So 'e din't do it for 'er! Yer din't kill someone's pa, if yer love 'em.'

'No.' She stared up at the ceiling, the faintest of lights coming through the curtains from the streetlamps outside. 'Maybe he doesn't love her so much as just want her. It isn't the same.'

'Mebbe 'e just 'ates Mr Argyll,' Scuff said thoughtfully. 'Yer gotta 'member 'e made it look like it were Mr Argyll wot paid the assassin. An' it were Mr Argyll's company wot caused the cave-in, and Mr Argyll wot's goin' ter prisin, or mebbe the rope, eh?'

'That's an awful lot of hate,' she said quietly, shivering again in spite of herself. 'Why would anyone hate that much?'

'I dunno,' he answered. 'Must 'a bin summink bad.'

'It must have been,' she agreed, but her mind was beginning to wonder what Jenny had felt. Did she believe that when her husband was imprisoned, or even hanged, she would be rescued from her boredom and emotional desert by Sixsmith? Was she so in love with him that she had thought no further than that?

What would happen when Argyll was shown to be innocent and Sixsmith guilty? She had lied about who told her to write the letter; that was what had turned the tide against Argyll. Sixsmith knew that! What sort of future awaited her then? Had she used Sixsmith to get rid of Argyll, so that her children would inherit the company, since Toby was also dead? And they would get whatever James Havilland had possessed also, since Mary was gone as well? Did she imagine that that would hold Sixsmith to her, and was that what she wanted? Surely if she had any sense she would fear for her own life?

Or did she believe he loved her, truly loved?

'Yer've thought of summink, 'aven't yer?' Scuff whispered beside her.

'Yes,' she answered honestly. 'I need to go and see Mrs Argyll. She lied in court, and she needs to know what that could cost her. I'll send a letter first thing to ask Margaret Ballinger to come to sit with you until I get back.'

'I don't need no one,' he said instantly. 'I'm almost better.'

'No you aren't,' she retorted. 'And whether you need anyone or not, I need there to be

429

someone here, so I can stop worrying about you and keep my mind on what I'm doing. Don't argue with me! I've made up my mind. And you'll like Margaret, I expect.'

'Mr Monk said as yer as stubborn as an army mule.'

'Did he indeed! Well, Mr Monk wouldn't know an army mule if it kicked him!'

Scuff giggled. Obviously the idea entertained him.

'But I would!' she added, before he got any ideas of insubordination.

'Yer'd kick it back,' he said with immense satisfaction, and moved the last couple of inches until he was next to her. She put an arm around him, very lightly. In five minutes he was asleep.

⋆ ⋆ ⋆

In the morning Hester sent one of the local boys to take a message to Margaret, wait for her answer, and return with it. She gave him fare for a hansom both ways, and something for himself. It was extravagant, but she judged it necessary, not only for her own peace of mind, but for Monk's also. She did not misread the affection for Scuff in his face, no matter how carefully he tried to mask it.

She arrived at the Argyll house a little after ten o'clock. It was strange to realise that the rest of the world still believed Argyll guilty and Sixsmith innocent. For a moment terror overtook her as she walked across the pavement to the steps up to the front door. What if Sixsmith were there already? If he and Jenny were lovers, they might have celebrated their victory together!

No! No, that would be foolish, even if Argyll had already been arrested. It might arouse suspicions. In order to preserve any dignity or belief in her, Jenny would have to play the shocked and grieving wife rescued in time by the innocent man. They would be two victims together of Argyll's wickedness.

Hester straightened her shoulders and mounted the steps to the front door, head high.

The bell was answered by a red-eyed parlour maid and Hester told her that she was here to see Mrs Argyll on a matter of great importance and urgency. Hester guessed from the girl's appearance that Argyll had already been arrested, and relief washed through her.

'I'm sorry, madam, but Mrs Argyll is unwell,' the maid began. 'She isn't receiving today.'

'I was in court yesterday,' Hester lied to give herself some authority in the maid's eyes. 'What I have to say will prove Mr Argyll's innocence.' She did not add that it would also prove Mrs Argyll's guilt.

The parlour maid's eyes opened wide, then she stepped back and invited Hester in. She was flustered, happy and still frightened. She left Hester in the withdrawing room, the only place even remotely warm from the embers of last night's fire. Such domestic duties had been utterly lost today.

Ten minutes later Jenny Argyll came in. Today her black gown was very well cut and flattered her slenderness. Her hair was styled less severely than earlier, but her face was almost bloodlessly pale and there were bruised shadows around her eyes. She looked feminine and vulnerable. Hester's last doubts were swept away that Jenny was in love with Sixsmith. She could have helped her acts, but her emotions were beyond her mastery. Of his she was far less certain.

'Good morning, Mrs Monk,' Jenny said with faint surprise. Her voice trembled a little. Was it tension, exhaustion or fear? 'My maid tells me you know something of urgent importance about my husband's arrest. Is that true?'

Hester had to force herself to remember Rose Applegate's humiliation in order to say what she must. She was certain now that it had been Jenny who had poisoned her food or drink with alcohol, not Argyll. It was she who had the motive, and surely it could only have been she who had known of her weakness? Had Rose's resolve slipped before, or had she confided in someone in a moment of weakness, perhaps as her reason for not joining them in wine, or a champagne toast at some event? One might require such an excuse to avoid giving offence, for example at a wedding.

Jenny was waiting.

'Yes, it is true,' Hester replied. 'I went into court at the beginning of the trial believing, as did my husband, that Mr Sixsmith was innocent of everything except the very understandable offence of trying to bribe certain troublemakers to stop sabotaging the construction. The only reason he was charged at all was in order to bring the whole subject of James Havilland's

432

death to court, and during the proceedings to prove that it was actually your husband who was guilty.'

'Then he succeeded,' Jenny said with almost no expression. 'Why have you bothered to come and tell me this? Do you imagine I care? What possible difference do your reasons or your beliefs make to me?'

Hester looked at her. Was any of that hurt or outrage real? Or was she showing that emotion to mask the sense of victory she must feel now the prize was almost in her hands?

'None at all,' Hester admitted calmly. 'It is the fact that we were mistaken that is of importance. Your husband was not guilty, and I am almost certain that we can prove that.'

Jenny stood motionless, her eyes wide, unfocused. For a moment Hester was afraid she might faint. 'Not . . . guilty?' she said hoarsely. 'How can that be? He has been arrested!' That was a denial, almost a defiance.

Hester hoped, please God, Sixsmith was not in the house. Was she taking a stupid risk? It was too late to retreat now.

'But you don't believe him guilty, surely?'

'How . . . how can I not?'

'Because you know without any doubt who it was that asked you to write the letter to your father, and since it was Sixsmith who paid to have him killed, it is impossible to believe that it was not also Sixsmith who arranged to have him be in the stables,' Hester replied.

Jenny drew in her breath, raising her hands as if to push Hester away physically. 'Oh, no! I — '

'Are in love with him,' Hester continued. 'Yes, I know. So much is apparent. But however infatuated you are, it does not excuse the death of your father and your sister, and the shame of suicides' graves.' The anger and all her own old pain poured into her voice until it shook also. She had to gulp for breath and try to steady herself. 'You may not have known at first, but don't tell me you don't know now!'

'I don't!' Jenny denied furiously. 'You're lying. My husband is guilty! The court knows that! Aston was acquitted! You have no right to come here saying such terrible things!' There were two high spots of colour in her face now.

'Terrible?' Hester challenged her. 'It is terrible that Sixsmith could be guilty of killing your father, but not that your husband is? I think that judgement betrays your loyalties rather clearly, Mrs Argyll!'

'You accuse me!' Jenny shot back.

'Of course I do. It was you who swore on oath that it was your husband who made you write the letter that lured your father to his death. You could not mistake such a thing. It had to be a deliberate betrayal of both your husband and your father! What does Sixsmith offer you that is worth that?'

Jenny gasped. 'Get out of my house . . . you . . . ' She could not find words, defiances, anything to protect herself.

'Is he such a lover?' Hester went on, allowing her own past helplessness to drive her anger.

'How dare you?' Jenny shouted. 'You ignorant, complacent, stupid woman, with your good works and your petty little ideas! What on earth do you know of passion?'

'I know love and hate, and the price you pay for each,' Hester replied. 'I know death, and I've seen better men than you've ever known give their lives for what they believed in. I've seen war and murder and grief. I've made more terrible mistakes, and I've loved till I thought I'd die of it. I've let people down because I've been weak or short-sighted, but I've never deliberately betrayed anyone. You betrayed your father, your sister, your husband, and Rose Applegate as well. Was that really worth it just to lie with Aston Sixsmith?'

Jenny swung her arm round and slapped Hester across the face as hard as she could, sending her staggering backwards until she fell on to the armchair several steps behind her.

Hester climbed to her feet slowly, hand to her burning cheek. 'I see that it wasn't,' she observed.

Jenny took a step towards her, face scarlet, eyes bright with rage.

Hester was prepared this time, her own hand ready, fist closed. 'Sixsmith murdered the assassin,' she said. 'Shot him and left him to be crushed and buried under the cave-in. And don't bother to argue that. It was what gave him away. He described the man as he was when he was killed, not when Sixsmith said he paid him. It was his only mistake, but it was enough. It'll save your husband from the rope. Or is that not what you want to hear?' That was an accusation with the bitterest contempt.

435

'I don't want any of it!' Jenny said desperately. 'And you're lying. It can't be true!'

Hester did not bother to argue. 'He murdered your father and your sister, and he's going to murder your husband. Is that the sort of man you trust to look after you, not to mention your children? If you've got any wits left at all, you'll save yourself while you can. Your husband's going to be freed, whatever you do, and Sixsmith will hang.'

Jenny looked at her with loathing. 'And what does it profit you, Mrs Monk? Why do you care if I survive or not? I think you're lying, and you need me to betray Aston, or he'll still beat you, and Alan.'

Hester forced herself to smile but she knew it was a cold, uncertain gesture. 'Are you prepared to wager your life on no one finding evidence, now that they know where to look? More than that, are you sure your own future is safe with a man who will kill when it suits him, betray the man who employed him and trusted him by taking his wife and setting him up to hang for a murder he didn't commit? Look who is dead! Are you sure you are not the next, when your usefulness to him is over, or he finds a younger, prettier woman who isn't weighed down with another man's children? Or could it be that your children are heirs to the whole Argyll inheritance? Could that be your value to him? And if you marry him, whose will it be then? Toby's dead too! And Mary.'

Jenny's face was ashen, almost grey. Hester imagined the memories that might be racing through her mind, moments of intimacy, of passion. Perhaps instead she was experiencing that sudden, terrible loneliness that drowns you when you realise the gulf between you and the person you love, and that you cannot cross it, you only think you can, to deceive yourself into a moment's comfort. Hester would have pitied her, had not so many others paid the price.

'Go to the police and confess perjury,' she said more gently, 'while you still have time. Make up some story that you were deceived and now you realise the truth. You might at least survive. You have a choice, today anyway. Live with Argyll, who may be a bore and a bully — or hang with Sixsmith, who is far worse.' She gave a very slight shrug. 'There's no profit in it for me, Mrs Argyll, but there is for your children. I suppose I care about that.' And she turned on her heel and walked out. She would go back home and have lunch with Scuff, and perhaps tell him what she had done. She would write a letter to Rose Applegate and tell her too, when it was all over.

*   *   *

Monk and all the others shared a brief lunch with some navvies. This time, having the benefit of far more knowledge, they questioned them not about Argyll but about Sixsmith. They were deep underground, sitting on stones in the rubble away from the pounding of the engine. It was an old tunnel where debris had been dumped rather than carry it all the way to the surface. The constant dripping of water filled the air with damp and the smell of sewage. The scrabble of rats' feet was closer than the clang and thump of the machine. The voices round them echoed until it was hard to tell from which direction they came. Darkness hemmed them in on all sides, crowding the frail heart of the lantern-light. They could have been twenty feet below the surface of the earth, or hundreds. Monk tried to drive the thought from his mind and keep his stomach from knotting.

Rathbone drank some water but was reluctant to eat the coarse bread. He did manage to keep the look of distaste out of his expression.

'So Miss Havilland asked Mr Sixsmith's help?' he said again.

'Yeah,' the navvy he was questioning agreed. He was a big, bull-chested man with fair hair receding at the front and an agreeable heavily weathered face. 'Course, 'e did. Went out o' 'is way ter give 'er wot she asked fer. Did fer 'er pa too.'

'Same information?' Rathbone asked.

'I s'pose.' The navvy crumpled up his face in thought. ''E 'elped a lot o' them. Never 'id nuffink. 'E must 'a told Miss 'Avilland wot she asked 'im fer, 'cos it were arter she spoke wiv 'im that she came ter know as 'er pa were murdered. Or leastways ter think as 'e were.'

Rathbone glanced at Monk, then looked back at the navvy. 'I think I might begin to understand this, Mr . . . ?'

'Finger,' the navvy supplied. ''Cos I lost me finger, see?' He held up his left hand, the middle finger missing from the knuckle.

438

'Thank you,' Rathbone acknowledged. 'Mr Finger, did Mr Toby Argyll work with Mr Sixsmith also?'

The navvy grinned, showing several gaps among his teeth. 'Jus' Finger. Yeah, course 'e did. Mr Toby were keen ter learn all 'e could about the machine, an' no one knowed as much as Mr Sixsmith. Mr Toby were down 'ere 'alf the time.'

'Right up until Miss Havilland was killed on the river?' Rathbone pressed.

'Yeah, even the day before, as I 'member.'

Monk suddenly understood what Rathbone was thinking, and perhaps a step beyond it as well. 'Finger,' he said quickly, 'why did Toby ask Sixsmith about the machine, rather than ask his brother, Alan Argyll?'

'Perhaps his brother wouldn't tell him?' Rathbone suggested, and looked questioningly at Finger.

'Nobody knows them machines like Mr Sixsmith does,' Finger replied with certainty.

'But Mr Alan was the one who invented the modifications that made the Argyll Company's machine better than anyone else's,' Monk pointed out, cutting across Rathbone.

''E owned it,' Finger said. 'It were Mr Sixsmith wot thought it up. 'E knew it better'n Mr Argyll, that I'd swear on me ma's grave, God rest 'er.'

'Ah!' Monk sat back, looking across at Rathbone. 'So Mr Sixsmith had the brains, but Mr Argyll took the credit, and the money. I imagine Mr Sixsmith was more than a little unhappy about that.'

They thanked Finger, who told them the direction to go to find a ganger who could help them further.

They had gone only another mile when there was a tremor in the ground, so faint as to be almost indiscernible. Then, the moment after, the rhythm of the machine altered slightly.

A wave of horror passed over Monk, bringing the sweat out on his skin, then crowding, desperate fear.

Rathbone froze.

'Can you smell something?' Sutton whispered.

'Smell something?' Rathbone said hoarsely. 'The stench of the sewers, for heaven's sake. How could anyone not smell it?'

Sutton stood still. In the wavering lamplight it was impossible to tell whether his face was paler or not, but there was a tension in him that was unmistakable.

Then it came again, a louder rumble this time.

'We gotta get out of 'ere!' Sutton's voice was sharp. 'There's more comin' down somewhere. C'mon!' He started forward. Snoot was at his feet, hackles bristling.

They crowded behind him, lanterns high. Monk saw the yellow light on the walls. Was it his imagination that they were bulging as if any moment they would rupture and the water burst through, drowning them all? He was gasping for breath now, his body trembling. Was he a physical coward after all? It was a new and shattering thought.

Was it pain he was afraid of, or death; the end of opportunity to try again, to do better; some kind of judgement when it was too late to understand or be sorry; or oblivion, simply ceasing to exist?

No, he knew he was afraid of the ultimate failure of being a coward. And that was something he could control. It might cost him everything he had, but it was still within his power to do it. It was within him, not beyond. He felt his heart steady.

He was treading Sutton's heels, and Rathbone on his, then Crow, Orme and Runcorn. They moved as quickly as they could, heads bent to avoid the low roof, feet slipping on rubble.

The smell seemed stronger. Monk felt it thick and pungent in his nose. It was not just sewage, it was gas. He strained his ears, but he heard no more rumbling, only the slosh of their feet in deeper water, and the increased skittering and squealing of rats, as if they too were panicking. It made the small hairs stand up on his skin, but he knew it was infinitely better than silence. If the rats were alive, then the air was breathable.

There was another fear that he would not express, but it kept beating in his brain — Sixsmith was free. No one else knew he was guilty except Hester and Scuff. All those who could prove it were here in this wormhole in the earth, about to be trapped, buried — by Sixsmith?

Sutton was still leading the way, but the water was flowing against them. He bent and picked up Snoot. It was too deep for the little dog to stand in, and he kept having to lift his head up.

No one remarked on the obvious. Monk turned and looked behind him once and saw their smudged faces, eyes reflecting fear. Rathbone pulled his mouth down at the corners, but he said nothing.

'Keep close,' Monk warned. 'Better put your hand on the man in front of you. Lose touch, and we'll all stop. That's an order!'

They pressed on. The smell was definitely stronger. There was another violent tremor. Sutton stopped and they looked at each other. No one spoke.

They began walking again and came to a fork. Sutton took the right turning and no one questioned him. Ten minutes later the water was shallower, and a few moments after that they came to a blank wall where the rock had fallen in. It was totally blocked. Not a breath of air came from the other side.

'Sorry,' Sutton said gently.

They each dismissed it and told him not to worry. They had barely finished speaking when there was a hollow roar beyond the fall, as if a train had gone by, and then utter, suffocating silence.

Sutton's lantern slipped out of his hand and crashed into the water, wavering under the thick, filthy stream for a moment or two, then going out.

'What was that?' Runcorn said hoarsely. 'Water?'

'No.' Sutton held more tightly on to Snoot.

'What?' Rathbone demanded.

'Fire,' Sutton croaked.

'God Almighty!' Rathbone leaned against the wall. In the yellow glare his face was grey.

'Reckon as Mr Sixsmith knows we're on to 'im,' Orme observed. 'Pity we didn't get 'im. 'E's a real bad one.'

'That hardly begins to describe him,' Crow said bitterly. 'We'll go back.'

No one answered him; none of them wanted to argue the realities. They turned and started to retrace their steps until they were at the fork again.

'Other way?' Runcorn asked Sutton.

Sutton shook his head. 'That's the way o' the fire. We need ter go back the way we come.'

'Water's deeper,' Crow pointed out.

'I know.' Sutton started forward without adding anything. They went after him, each apparently lost in his own thoughts.

Monk tried hard not to let his mind go to Hester and Scuff. It would take from him the anger and the strength to go on through the icy, stinking water up to his knees, and the filth that was in it. He knocked against the bodies of dead rats. Ahead of him Sutton was still carrying the little dog. Had he any idea at all where they were, or what was ahead or behind them, except rock-falls and fire?

They turned more corners and passed a weir. The water thundered over the drop so violently they could not hear each other, even if they shouted.

Sutton waved to the left, pointing to another passage.

'That's . . . ' Runcorn cupped his hands

around his mouth and yelled, but his words were lost.

Orme looked at Monk.

Crow shrugged and followed after Sutton.

Monk and Rathbone had no better knowledge of the tunnels. All six of them and Snoot crossed over, gripping on to each other through the fast-flowing stream, only just keeping their balance.

The tunnel curved around and started to go upwards. Then, just as Monk was thinking he could smell fresh air, it came to an abrupt end. There was water flowing from the left, a thin, steady spout out of the raw earth already carrying soil with it, and growing stronger even as they watched.

'It's going to burst through!' Rathbone said, his voice high, beyond his control. 'We'll be drowned!' He swivelled round to look for escape. The tunnel behind him sloped downward, the way the water would flow.

Monk saw it and understood. There was no escape. Oddly now, with disaster so close, his fear was under control.

Snoot began to bark, writhing to get from Sutton's grasp.

''E can smell rabbits,' Sutton said quietly. 'We ain't got no other way. If we break this the stream'll come, but it isn't big. I reckon as we 'it wot they used to call the Lark, afore it went under. It in't very deep. We'll get proper wet and cold, but keep goin' an' we'll come out.' And without waiting for approval he attacked the soil and started shovelling it with his hands.

Monk looked at Rathbone, then at the others. Snoot was already digging just as fiercely as his master. Monk stepped forward and joined them, then so did the others.

The stream broke through in a rush, almost knocking them off their feet. Sutton fell against Runcorn, and Crow bent to help them back to their feet, sodden wet. The lanterns were all shattered and they were plunged into obliterating darkness. There was no sense of direction except that of the icy water.

'C'mon!' Sutton shouted.

There was nothing to do for survival except to follow him into the stream. They crawled against the water, trying to breathe, to keep hold of anything, to move forward, upward, clinging, gasping, cold to the bone.

Monk had no idea how long it went on, how many times he thought his lungs would burst. Then suddenly there was light, real grey daylight, and air. He fell out after Sutton into the shingle bed and stumbled up the sides of the stone culvert. He turned immediately to see who was behind him. One by one the others dragged themselves out, filthy, sodden and shuddering with cold. He swung around to thank Sutton, and saw with a wave of boundless relief that he had Snoot in his arms. 'Is he all right?' he demanded.

Sutton nodded. 'Thought 'e weren't,' he said shakily. 'But 'e's breathin'.'

'Thank you, sir,' Rathbone held out his hand to Sutton. 'You have saved our lives. Now we must go and deal with Mr Sixsmith. I suggest you get your dog warm.' He fished in his pocket and brought out a gold sovereign. 'Be so good as to give him a teaspoon of brandy with my compliments.'

Monk felt the emotion well up inside him too intensely for him to speak. He met Sutton's eyes, looked again to make sure that Snoot was indeed breathing, then clasped Rathbone's arm very briefly. Then they followed Crow, who seemed to know which way to go.

The five of them were perished with cold and smeared with clay and remnants of sewage when they reached the head of the tunnel again. They found Finger and almost twenty other navvies near the great machine.

Finger saw Monk. 'We got another cave-in, bad one,' he said grimly. 'Blimey! Yer all right? Yer look like bloody 'ell!'

'Very well observed,' Monk replied. 'Too accurate to be accounted abusive language. Where is Sixsmith?'

'Down there,' Finger pointed at the entrance.

Monk looked at it and a wave of nausea enveloped him. He could not go in that again. He simply physically could not. His legs were shaking, his stomach sick.

It was Runcorn who walked forward, his face set like stone. 'I'll get that bastard up here,' he said grimly. 'Or I'll bring the whole bloody lot in on both of us.'

'What! Runcorn!' Monk shouted after him. He swore violently. He could not let Runcorn go in there. He had no choice. He charged back into the semi-darkness a pace behind him, still shouting at Runcorn.

Fifty yards in, the tunnel was still dimly lit from lanterns on the wall. A hundred yards and the glow came from ahead of them, and Runcorn stopped abruptly.

Monk caught up with him. 'Fire,' he said, his voice catching. 'I can feel the heat of it. Where's Sixsmith?'

Monk pressed forward again, more slowly now. He had covered another twenty yards round a curve when he saw the broad-chested figure ahead of him. It was unmistakably Sixsmith from the way he walked. He was coming towards them. He must have recognised Monk at that same moment. He stopped and stood with his arms loosely by his sides. If he was surprised to see Monk alone there was nothing in his voice to betray it.

'You'd better let me past. There's fire behind me, and I'm the only one who can put it out! If I don't, it could come up into the streets and burn the whole of London.'

'Did you mean to kill Toby Argyll?' Monk asked without moving.

'Eventually,' Sixsmith replied. 'But Mary taking him over with her was a piece of luck. I had intended to have him blamed for her death, but the way it worked out was better. Don't waste time, Monk. The fire'll break through soon. That whole tunnel behind me is ablaze. There's enough air in here to feed it.'

'Why did you do it? For the Argyll Company?'

'Don't be so damn stupid! For revenge. Alan Argyll took my invention, the money, and far

447

more than that, he took the praise for it! I don't give a damn if this whole thing blows up, Monk, but you do! You won't let the city burn, so get out of my way! I can put it out! Those fools up there don't know what to do.'

Behind Monk, Runcorn was moving. Monk swung round to see what it was, and at that instant Runcorn threw the rock. It caught Sixsmith just as he raised his hand with the gun in it. He fell backwards as the shot exploded and the bullet hit the rocks.

'Run!' Runcorn yelled, grabbing Monk by the waist and almost pulling him off his feet.

Side by side they hurtled towards the entrance again, feet flying, shoulders banging into the walls. Monk fell once. Runcorn stopped and hauled him to his feet, almost yanking his arm out of its socket, almost tearing his wound open. But they reached the entrance just as Finger fired the great lifting machine into life, under Orme's orders. The earth began to shudder and stones were dislodged. Boulders quaked and the whole machine slid forward. The giant stakes that held it were gone and it slithered and pounded, belching steam.

Finger jumped down and ran away from it as it lurched forward. The boulders crashed over and down, then gradually the entire wall and all its retaining boards and planks buckled and slid. Cross beams exploded like matchsticks. With a great eruption, the earth collapsed with a roar and crashed over the entrance and buried it as if it had never existed.

Pebbles rattled and dropped; steam exploded

from somewhere in a white column. Then there was silence.

Monk wiped his hand across his face and found he was shaking.

'Better Sixsmith be buried,' Rathbone said, his voice with only a shred of its old humour. 'I'm not sure I could have convicted him anyway.' He smiled ruefully. 'Don't bring me another case for a while, Monk. You've ruined my clothes.'

They stood in a row, five of them, filthy, freezing and strangely victorious.

'Thank you, gentlemen,' Monk said, and he had never meant anything more in his life.

We do hope that you have enjoyed reading
this large print book.

Did you know that all of our titles
are available for purchase?

We publish a wide range of high quality
large print books including:
**Romances, Mysteries, Classics
General Fiction
Non Fiction and Westerns**

Special interest titles available in
large print are:
**The Little Oxford Dictionary
Music Book
Song Book
Hymn Book
Service Book**

Also available from us courtesy of Oxford
University Press:
**Young Readers' Dictionary
(large print edition)
Young Readers' Thesaurus
(large print edition)**

For further information or a free
brochure, please contact us at:
**Ulverscroft Large Print Books Ltd.,
The Green, Bradgate Road, Anstey,
Leicester, LE7 7FU, England.
Tel:** (00 44) **0116 236 4325
Fax:** (00 44) **0116 234 0205**

Other titles published by
The House of Ulverscroft:

A CHRISTMAS GUEST

Anne Perry

Mariah Ellison is furious to learn that she won't spend Christmas at home with her married granddaughter. Instead, Grandmama is being packed off in the carriage to stay with her ex-daughter-in-law at her house on Romney Marsh. Mariah has never got on with Caroline and disapproves of her new husband Joshua, who is an actor and scarcely respectable. There will be nothing to do; it's going to be the worst Christmas of Grandmama's life. As if that weren't enough, another visitor is foisted on the household. Then something shocking happens. Has a crime been committed? Grandmama is surprised to find herself turning detective — another profession she deplores — and proving extremely good at it.

ANGELS IN THE GLOOM

Anne Perry

March 1916: Joseph Reavley, stumbling across the wastes of no-man's-land to rescue a comrade, is badly wounded and sent home on sick leave. He is cared for by his sister Hannah, who is anxious about her husband, Archie, away at sea. Hannah and Joseph are delighted when Shanley Corcoran, an old friend, comes to visit. Corcoran confides in Joseph that he's close to completing an invention that will paralyse the German U-boats. But soon afterwards, a scientist is found murdered, and it's evident that secrets have been betrayed to the enemy. Joseph's brother Matthew, of the S.I.S., comes to investigate, and together the men embark on a search that will solve the crime and lead them to the spy.

LONG SPOON LANE

Anne Perry

Early one summer morning, two bombs explode in an East London street, shattering most of the houses. Forewarned of an attack by anarchists, Thomas Pitt of the Special Branch arrives in time to chase the bombers to a run-down tenement in Long Spoon Lane. There, two men are arrested and one shot dead — but who and where is the killer? As Pitt starts to investigate the crime, he uncovers truths more disturbing than the acts of a few misguided idealists. There's a web of corruption within the police force, and all the clues point to Inspector Wetron of Bow Street as its mastermind. Worse, as head of the sinister, invisible Inner Circle, Wetron has powerful allies in every sphere, and it's almost impossible to pin his guilt to him.

A CHRISTMAS VISITOR

Anne Perry

It is mid-December and Henry Rathbone travels to the Dreghorn family manor house near Ullswater to comfort the family following the death of his friend, the master of the house. It seems that Judah Dreghorn slipped while crossing a stream on the estate in the middle of the night, and drowned. When Henry arrives, he finds that Ashton Gower, recently released from jail, is slandering Judah's name, claiming that his family rightfully owns the estate and that the forged deeds for which he was imprisoned were in fact genuine. To Henry and the two remaining Dreghorn brothers, also returning to the Lakes for Christmas, Judah's mysterious death and Gower's outrageous claims seem inextricably linked . . .

SHOULDER THE SKY

Anne Perry

In April 1915 Joseph Reavley is serving as chaplain on the Front Line at Ypres. To Joseph's sector comes an ambitious and insensitive young war correspondent, determined to evade Government censorship and expose the horrors of trench life as he sees it. His great story will be the terible deaths of soldiers in the first gas attack. But before he can dispatch his piece, he is found dead in no-man's land and Joseph is forced to accept that it can only have been a British soldier who killed him. Still seeking the man behind his parents' murder, and to protect his sister Judith, also at the Front, from the pain of an impossible romance, Joseph must find the truth.

THE SHIFTING TIDE

Anne Perry

When the *Maude Idris* docks at the Pool of London, laden with ebony, spices and tusks of ivory, Clement Louvain leaves four armed seamen on board to guard the precious cargo. But in the morning the ivory is gone and one of the seamen is dead. Hindered by his ignorance of the river and its customs, but badly requiring the huge fees that Louvain is prepared to pay, William Monk begins his investigation into the theft and murder. Meanwhile, Hester's work at the refuge for sick prostitutes is encountering acute financial difficulties. When a man arrives promising to pay a huge sum for the care of one particular woman, Hester is astonished. He is none other than Clement Louvain . . .